VOLUME
FIVE

IMAGE COMICS, INC.

Robert Kirkman
CHIEF OPERATING OFFICER

Erik Larsen
CHIEF FINANCIAL OFFICER

Todd McFarlane
PRESIDENT

Marc Silvestri
CHIEF EXECUTIVE OFFICER

Jim Valentino
VICE-PRESIDENT

Eric Stephenson
PUBLISHER

Corey Murphy
DIRECTOR OF SALES

Jeremy Sullivan
DIRECTOR OF DIGITAL SALES

Kat Salazar
DIRECTOR OF PR & MARKETING

Emily Miller
DIRECTOR OF OPERATIONS

Branwyn Bigglestone
SENIOR ACCOUNTS MANAGER

Sarah Mello
ACCOUNTS MANAGER

Drew Gill
ART DIRECTOR

Jonathan Chan
PRODUCTION MANAGER

Meredith Wallace
PRINT MANAGER

Randy Okamura
MARKETING PRODUCTION DESIGNER

David Brothers
CONTENT MANAGER

Addison Duke
PRODUCTION ARTIST

Vincent Kukua
PRODUCTION ARTIST

Sasha Head
PRODUCTION ARTIST

Tricia Ramos
PRODUCTION ARTIST

Emilio Bautista
SALES ASSISTANT

Jessica Ambriz
ADMINISTRATIVE ASSISTANT

www.imagecomics.com

ISBN 978-1-63215-438-5

SAGA, VOLUME FIVE. First printing. September 2015. Published by Image Comics, Inc. Office of publication: 2001 Center Street, Sixth Floor, Berkeley, CA 94704. Copyright © 2015 Brian K. Vaughan & Fiona Staples. Originally published in single magazine form as SAGA #25–30. All rights reserved. SAGA, its logos, and all character likenesses herein are trademarks of Brian K. Vaughan & Fiona Staples unless expressly indicated. Image Comics® and its logos are registered copyrights of Image Comics, Inc. All rights reserved. No part of this publication may be reproduced or transmitted, in any form or by any means (except for short excerpts for review purposes) without the express written permission of Brian K. Vaughan & Fiona Staples or Image Comics, Inc. All names, characters, events, and locales in this publication are entirely fictional. Any resemblance to actual persons (living or dead) or events or places, without satiric intent, is coincidental. Printed in the USA. For information regarding the CPSIA on this printed material call: 203-595-3636 and provide reference # RICH–619847.

FOR EIGN LICENSING INQUIRIES WRITE TO: foreignlicensing@imagecomics.com

FIONA STAPLES
ARTIST

BRIAN K. VAUGHAN
WRITER

FONOGRAFIKS
LETTERING + DESIGN

ERIC STEPHENSON
COORDINATOR

CHAPTER
TWENTY-FIVE

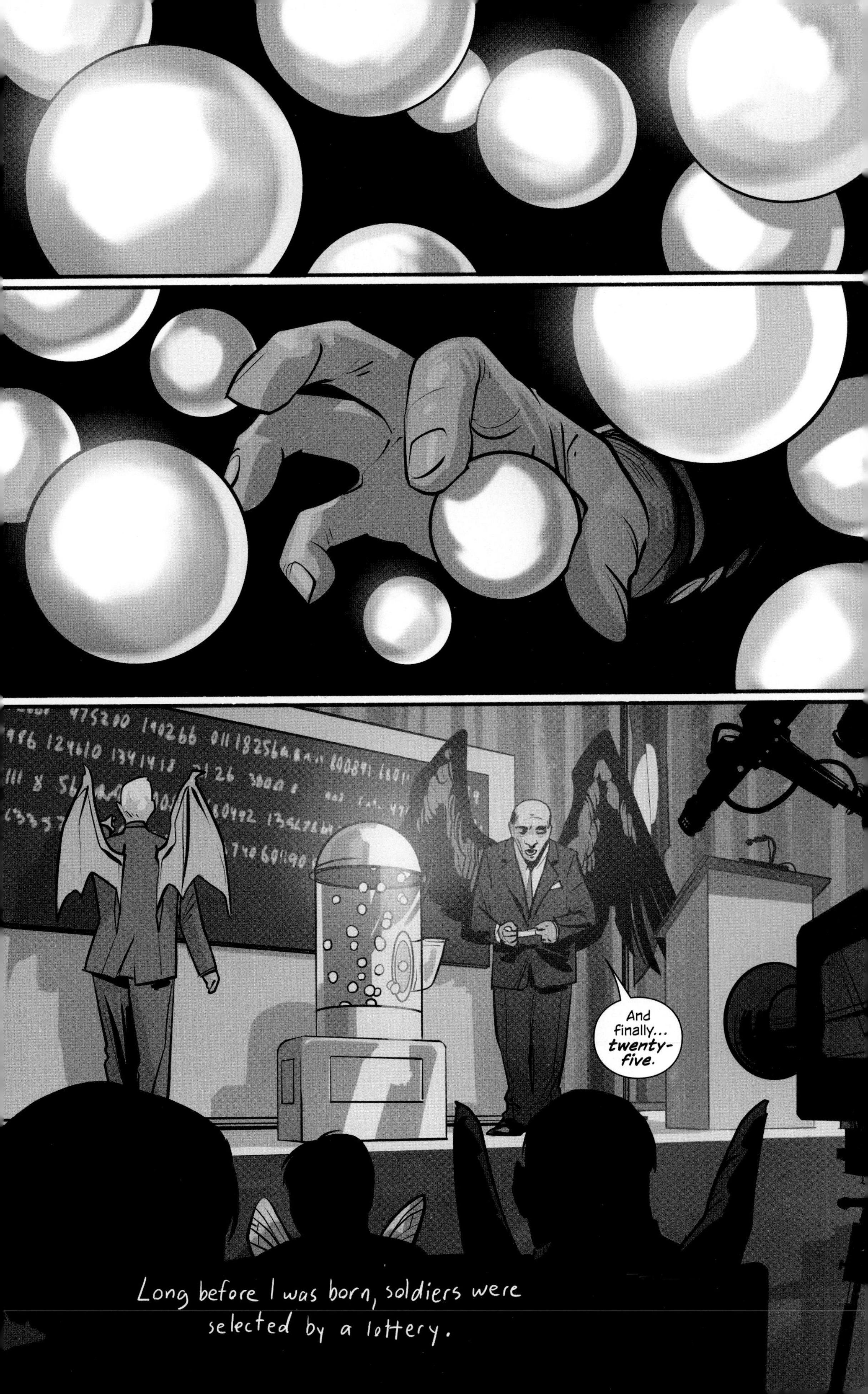
And finally... twenty-five.
Long before I was born, soldiers were selected by a lottery.

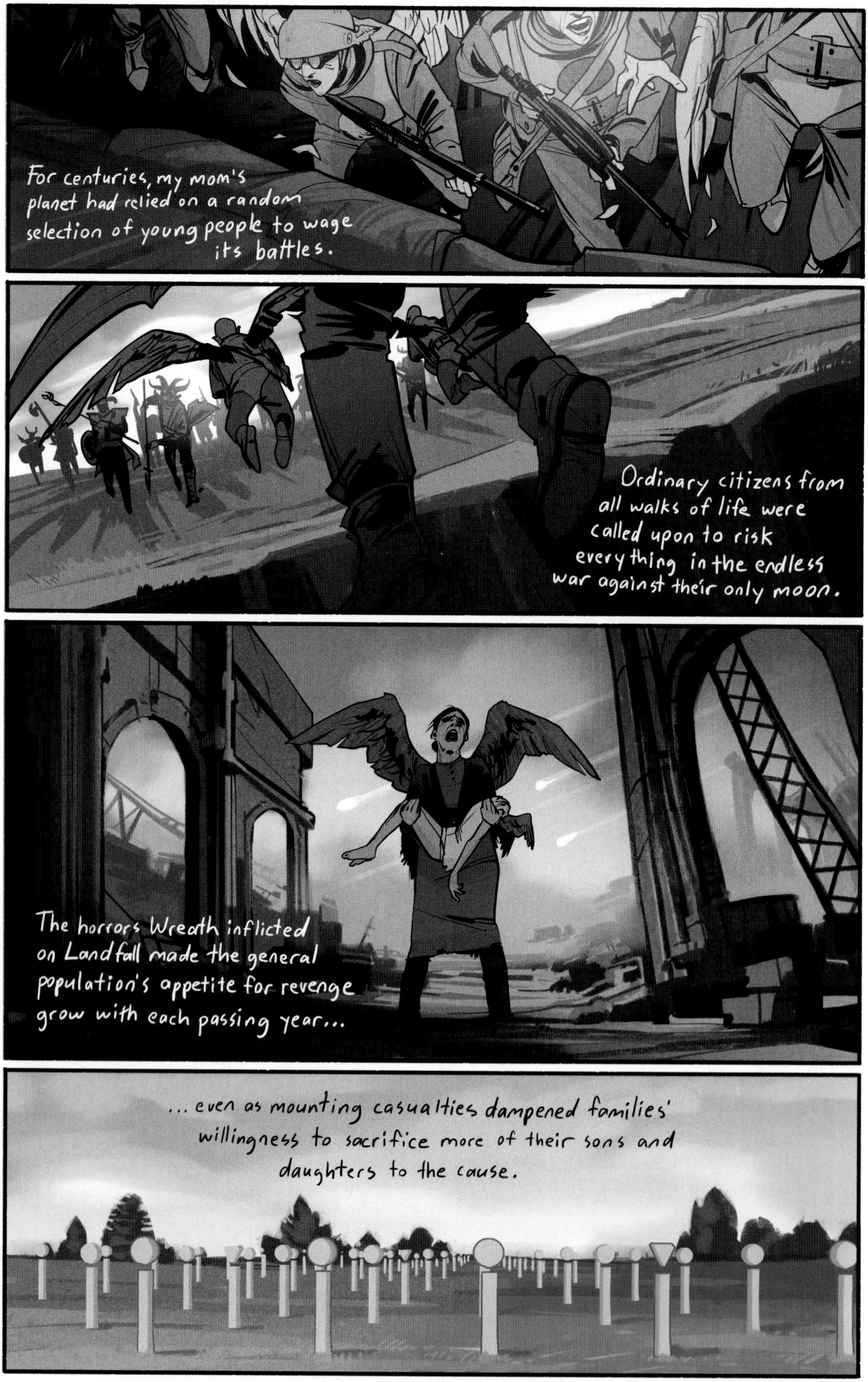
For centuries, my mom's planet had relied on a random selection of young people to wage its battles.
Ordinary citizens from all walks of life were called upon to risk everything in the endless war against their only moon.
The horrors Wreath inflicted on Landfall made the general population's appetite for revenge grow with each passing year...
...even as mounting casualties dampened families' willingness to sacrifice more of their sons and daughters to the cause.

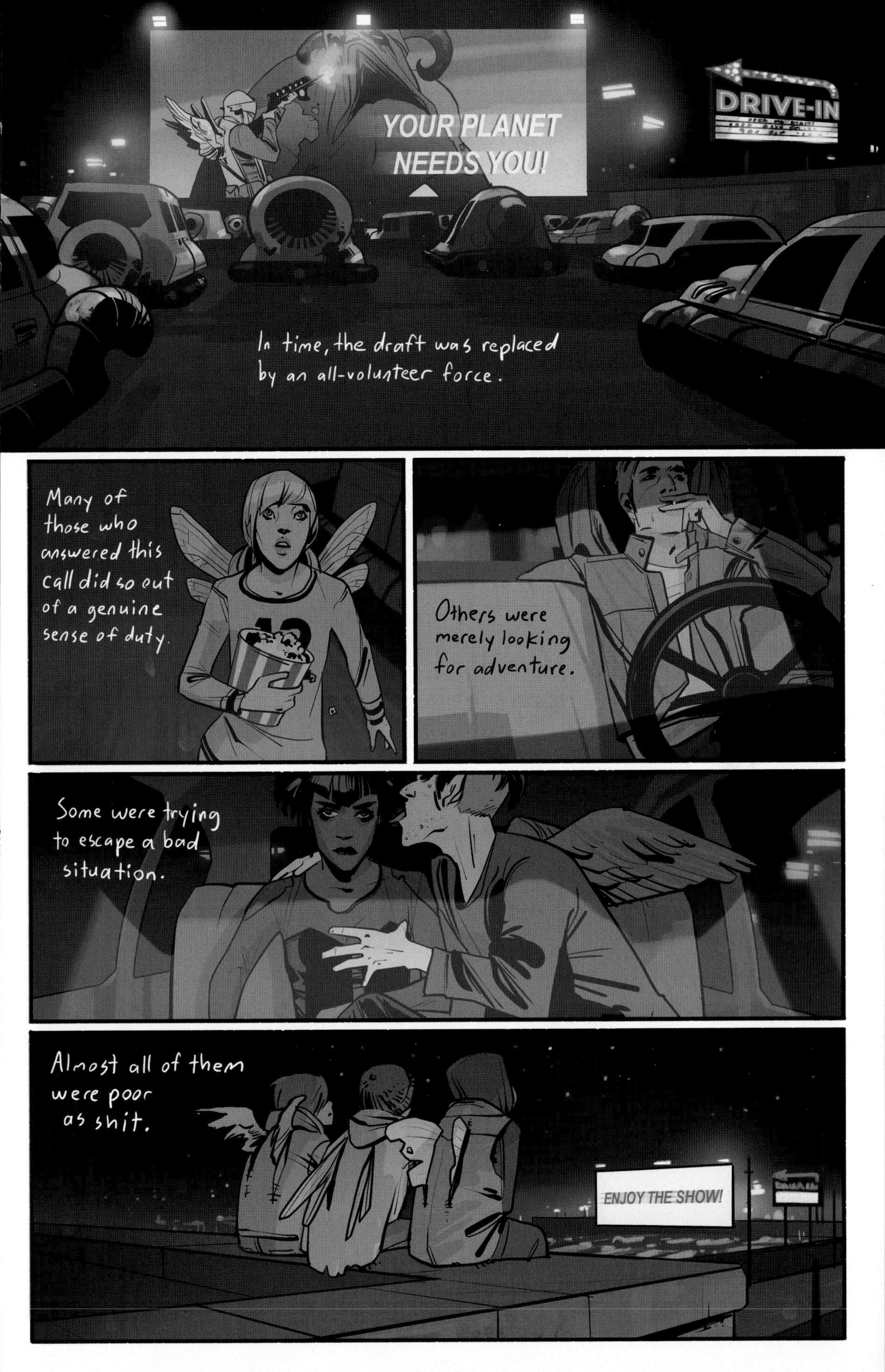
YOUR PLANET NEEDS YOU!
DRIVE-IN
In time, the draft was replaced by an all-volunteer force.
Many of those who answered this call did so out of a genuine sense of duty.
Others were merely looking for adventure.
Some were trying to escape a bad situation.
Almost all of them were poor as shit.
ENJOY THE SHOW!

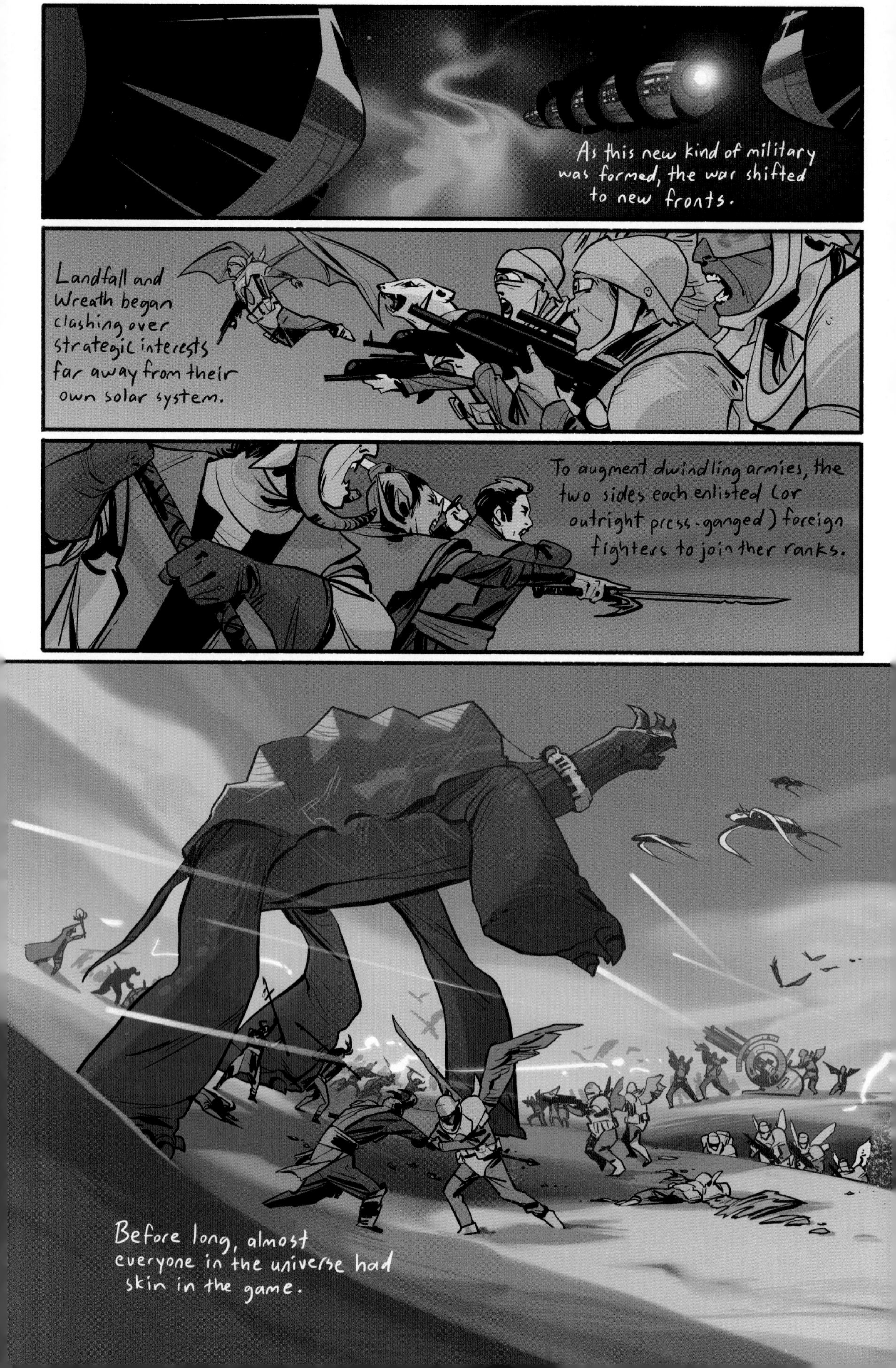
As this new kind of military was formed, the war shifted to new fronts.
Landfall and Wreath began clashing over strategic interests far away from their own solar system.
To augment dwindling armies, the two sides each enlisted (or outright press-ganged) foreign fighters to join ther ranks.
Before long, almost everyone in the universe had skin in the game.

But as the conflict moved further into the cosmos, an unfamiliar quiet fell over the two worlds that had given birth to this bloodshed.

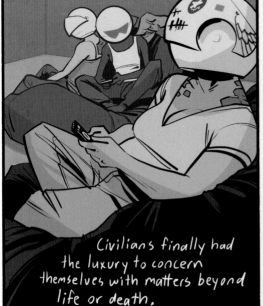

Civilians finally had the luxury to concern themselves with matters beyond life or death.

Everyone still supported the troops, of course, but in a more... abstract way than times past.

For most folks back on Landfall, war was something that would never directly impact their lives.

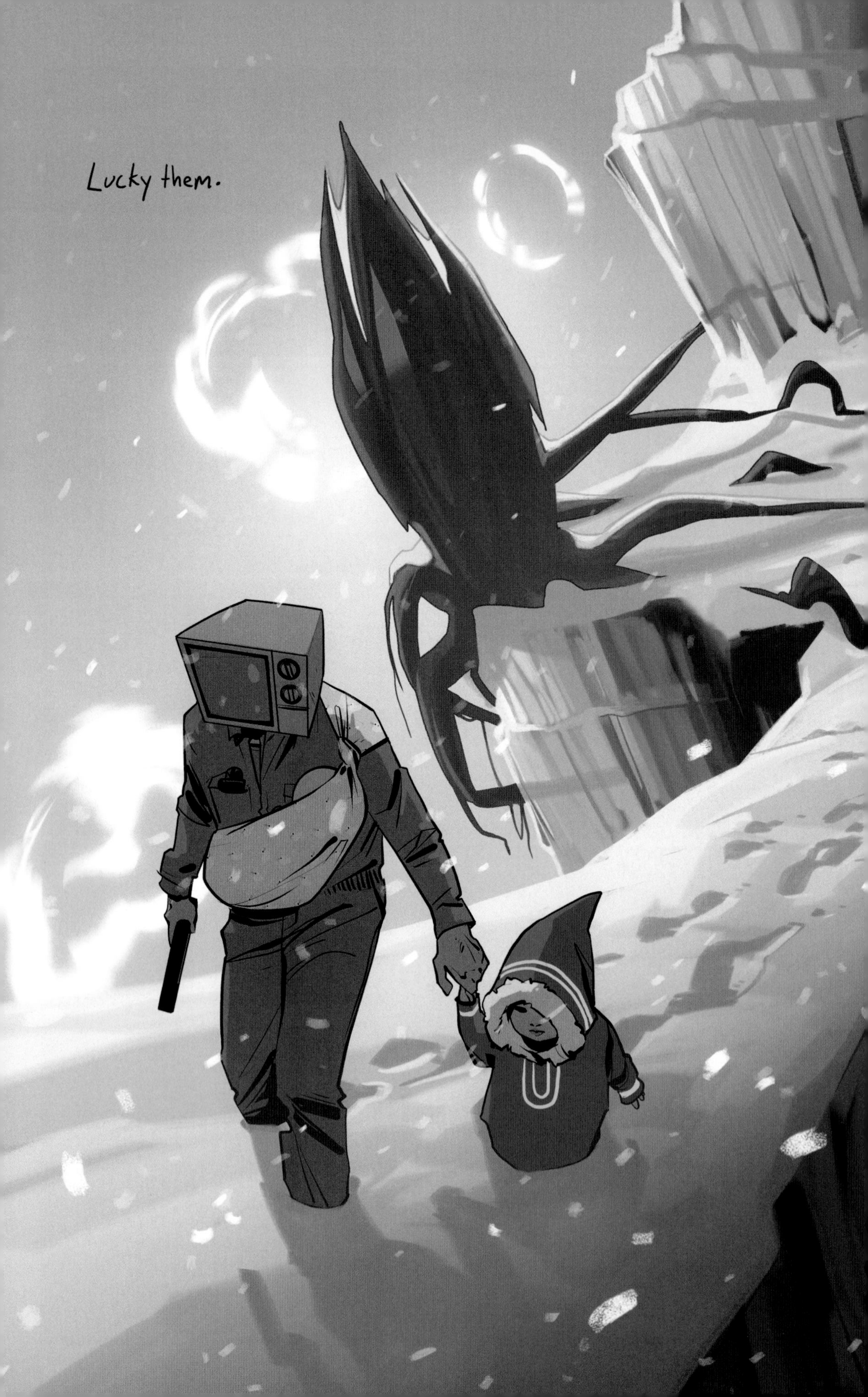
Lucky them.

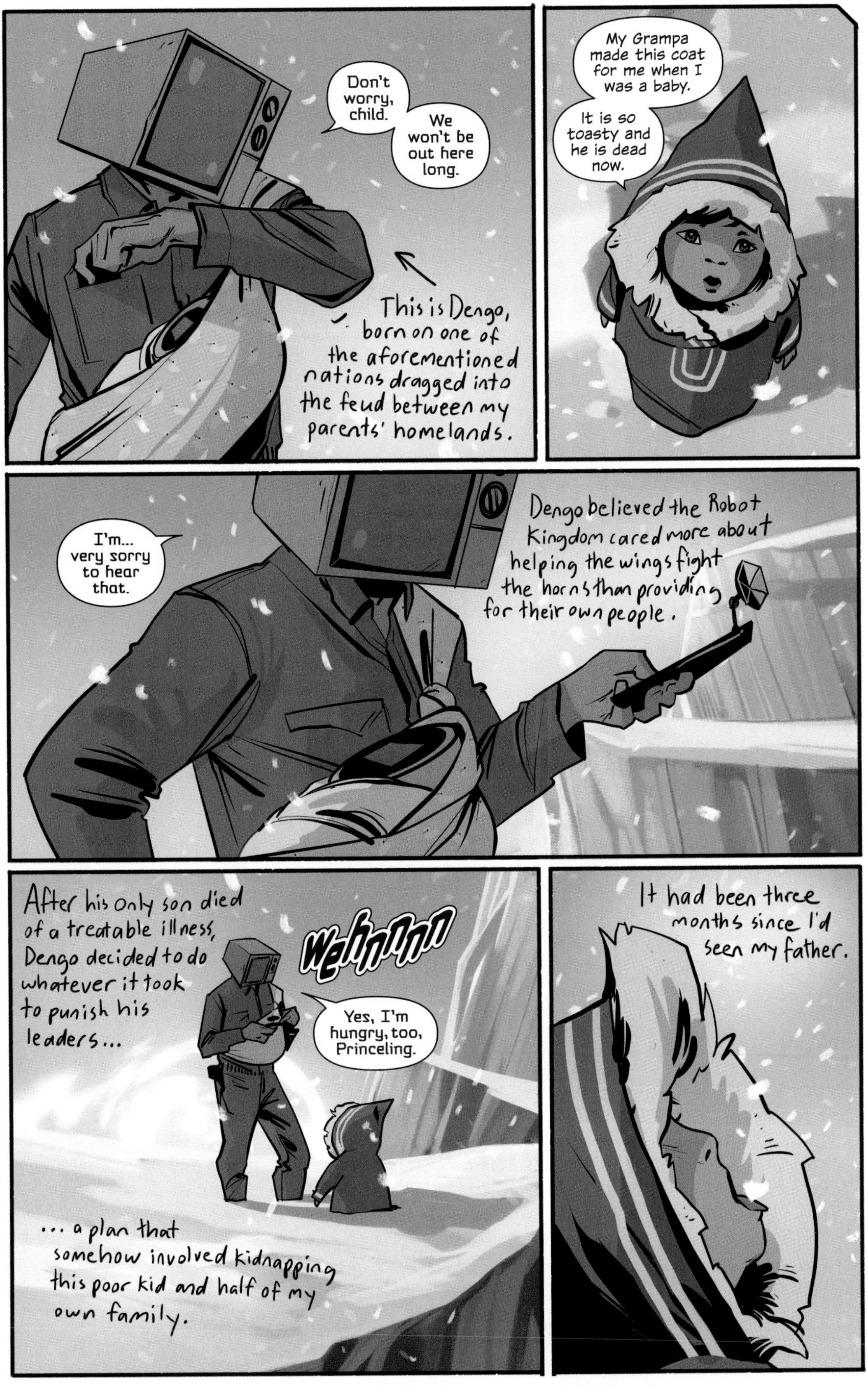
Don't worry, child.
We won't be out here long.
This is Dengo, born on one of the aforementioned nations dragged into the feud between my parents' homelands.
My Grampa made this coat for me when I was a baby.
It is so toasty and he is dead now.
I'm... very sorry to hear that.
Dengo believed the Robot Kingdom cared more about helping the wings fight the horns than providing for their own people.
After his only son died of a treatable illness, Dengo decided to do whatever it took to punish his leaders...
Wehhnnnn
Yes, I'm hungry, too, Princeling.
... a plan that somehow involved kidnapping this poor kid and half of my own family.
It had been three months since I'd seen my father.

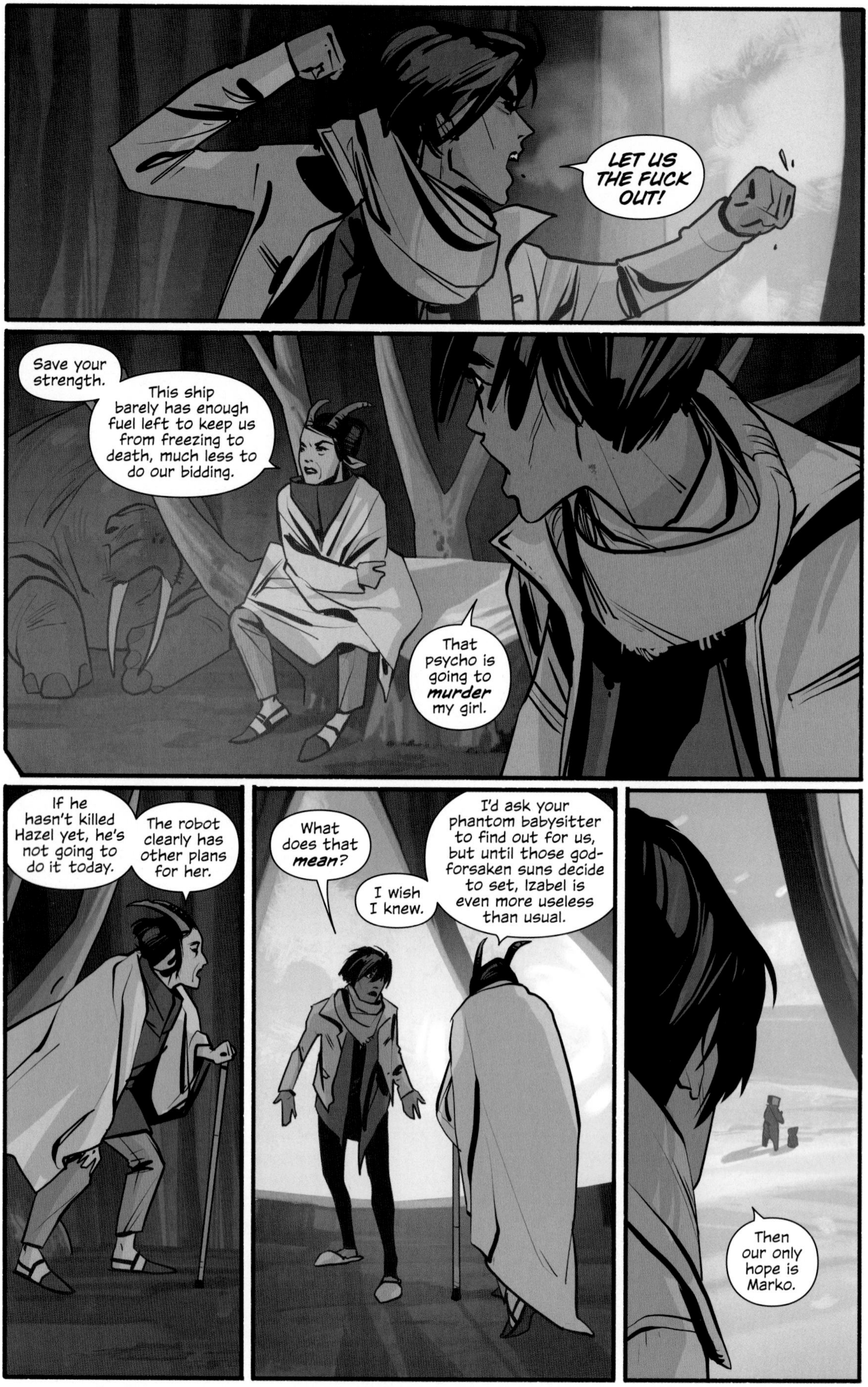
LET US THE FUCK OUT!
Save your strength.
This ship barely has enough fuel left to keep us from freezing to death, much less to do our bidding.
That psycho is going to murder my girl.
If he hasn't killed Hazel yet, he's not going to do it today.
The robot clearly has other plans for her.
What does that mean?
I wish I knew.
I'd ask your phantom babysitter to find out for us, but until those god-forsaken suns decide to set, Izabel is even more useless than usual.
Then our only hope is Marko.

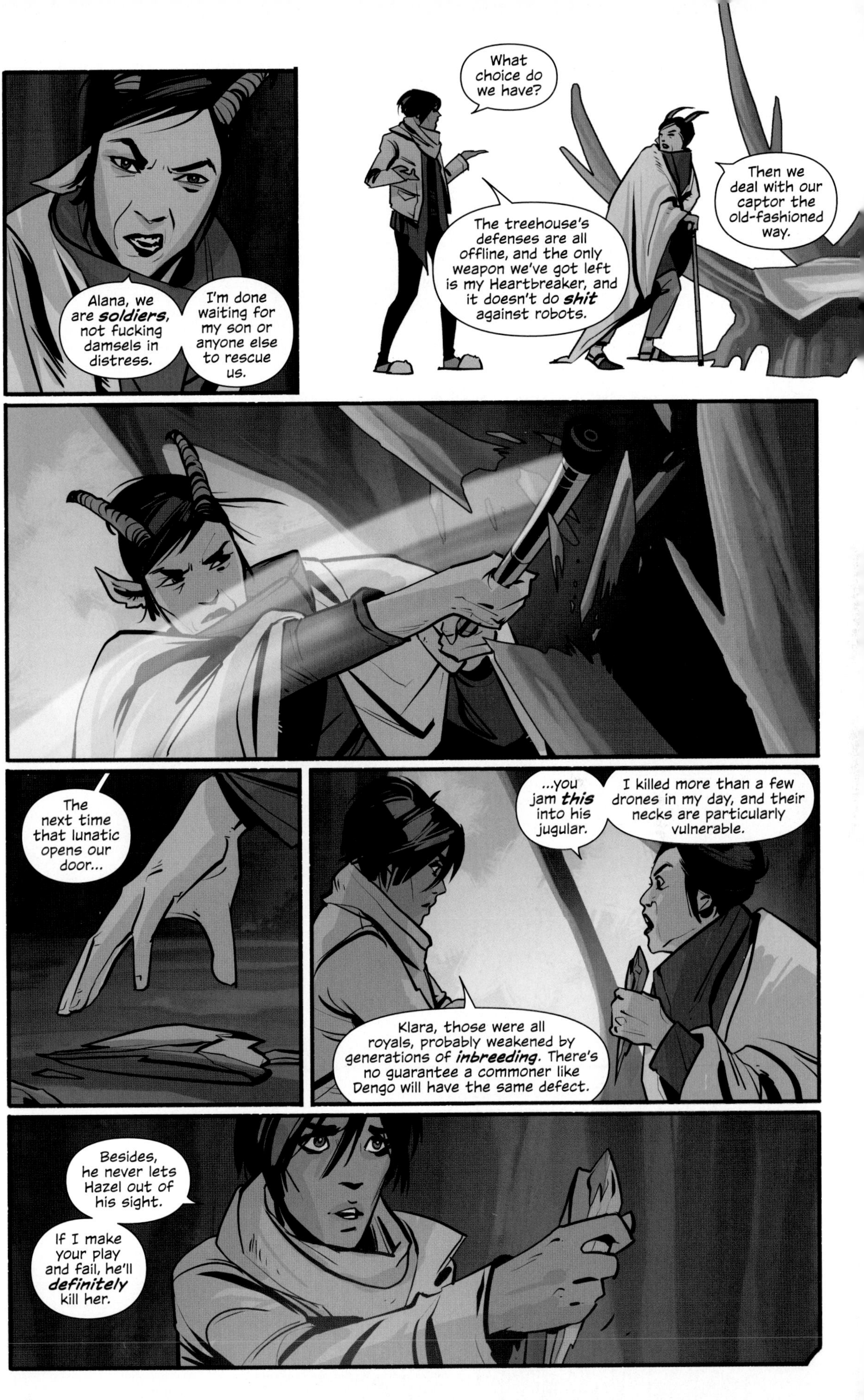
Alana, we are **soldiers**, not fucking damsels in distress.
I'm done waiting for my son or anyone else to rescue us.
What choice do we have?
The treehouse's defenses are all offline, and the only weapon we've got left is my Heartbreaker, and it doesn't do **shit** against robots.
Then we deal with our captor the old-fashioned way.
The next time that lunatic opens our door...
...you jam **this** into his jugular.
I killed more than a few drones in my day, and their necks are particularly vulnerable.
Klara, those were all royals, probably weakened by generations of **inbreeding**. There's no guarantee a commoner like Dengo will have the same defect.
Besides, he never lets Hazel out of his sight.
If I make your play and fail, he'll **definitely** kill her.

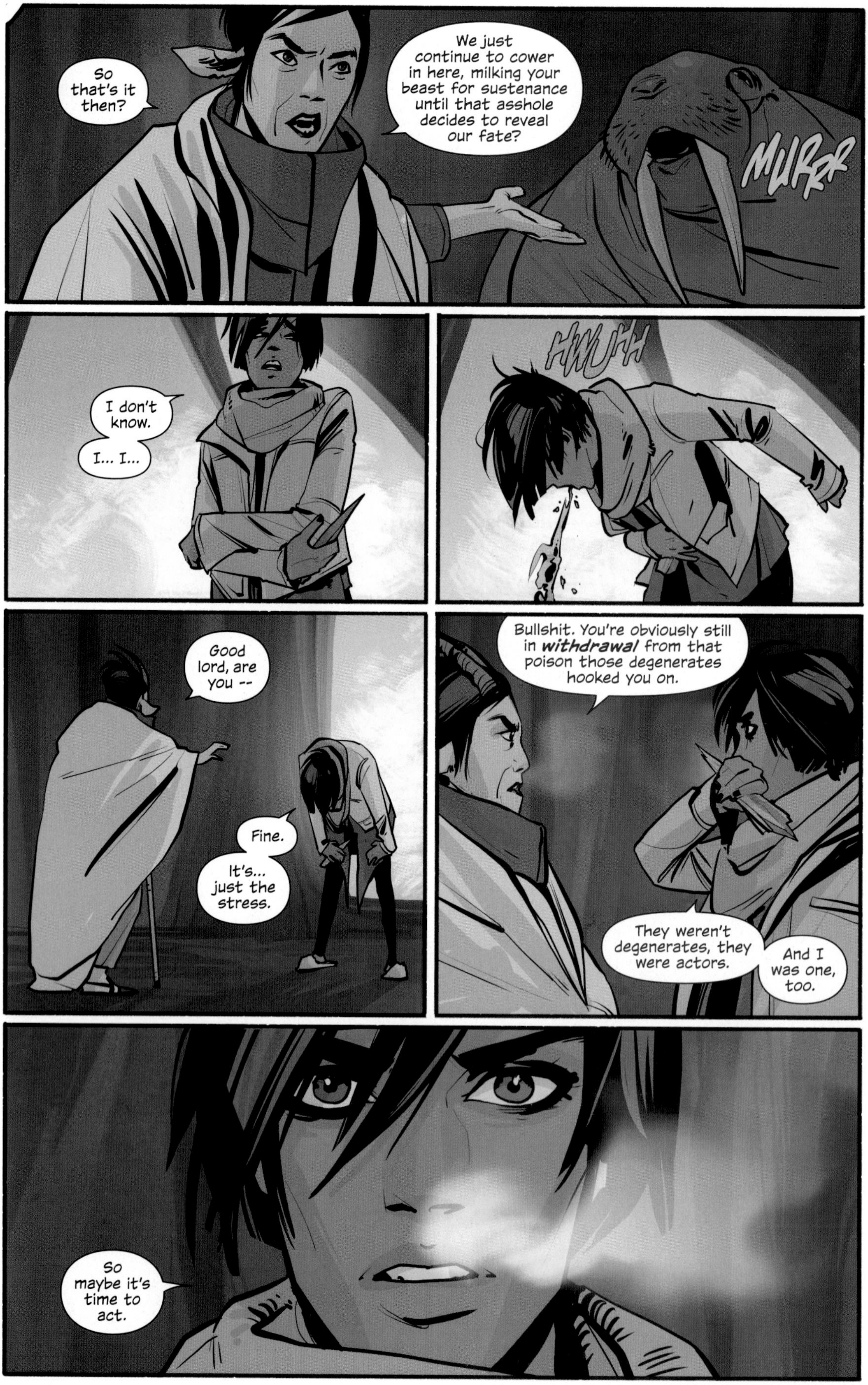
So that's it then?
We just continue to cower in here, milking your beast for sustenance until that asshole decides to reveal our fate?
MURRR
I don't know.
I... I...
HWUHH
Good lord, are you --
Fine.
It's... just the stress.
Bullshit. You're obviously still in *withdrawal* from that poison those degenerates hooked you on.
They weren't degenerates, they were actors.
And I was one, too.
So maybe it's time to act.

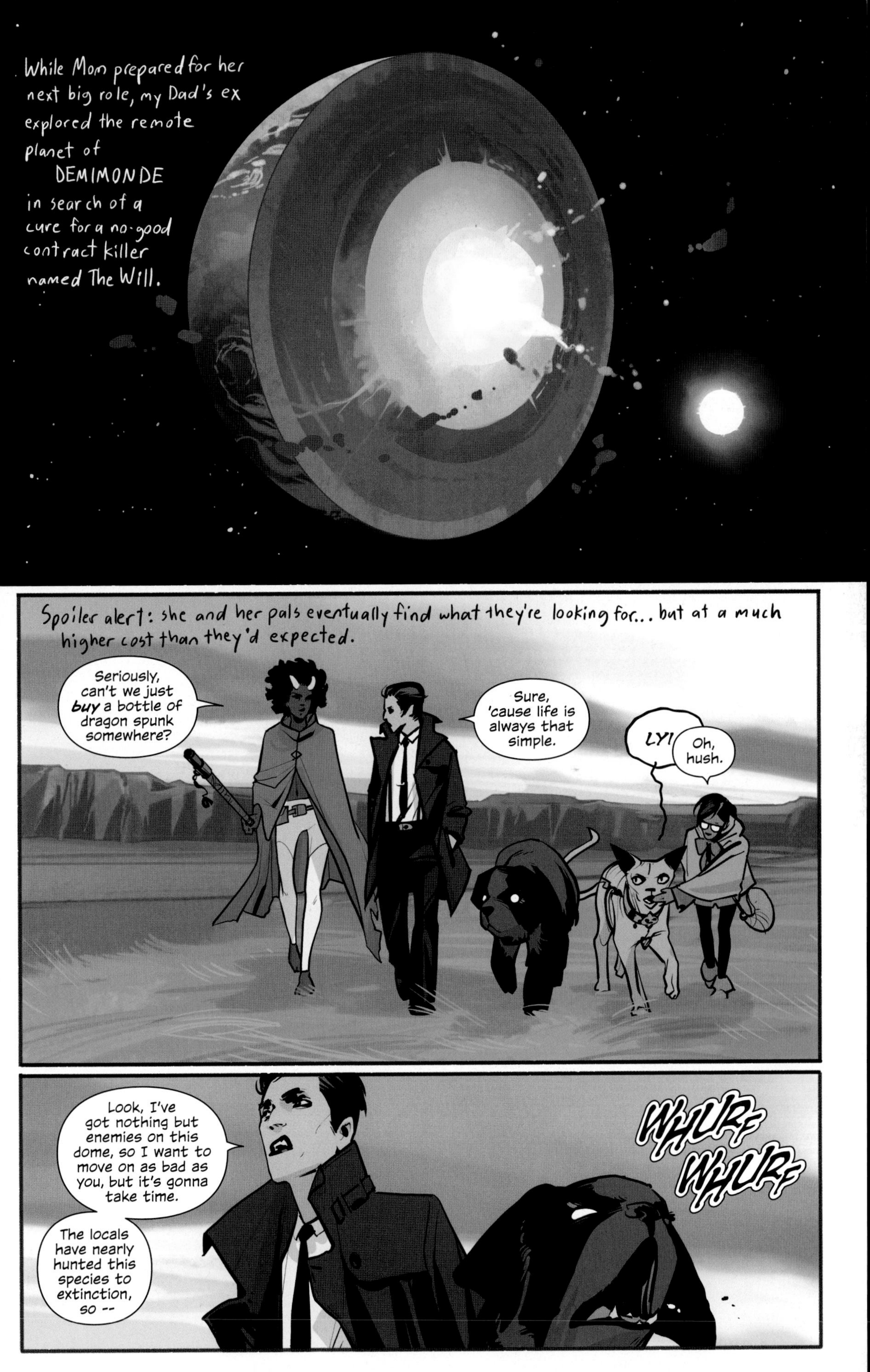

While Mom prepared for her next big role, my Dad's ex explored the remote planet of DEMIMONDE in search of a cure for a no-good contract killer named The Will.
Spoiler alert: she and her pals eventually find what they're looking for... but at a much higher cost than they'd expected.
Seriously, can't we just *buy* a bottle of dragon spunk somewhere?
Sure, 'cause life is always that simple.
LY!
Oh, hush.
Look, I've got nothing but enemies on this dome, so I want to move on as bad as you, but it's gonna take time.
The locals have nearly hunted this species to extinction, so --
WHURF
WHURF

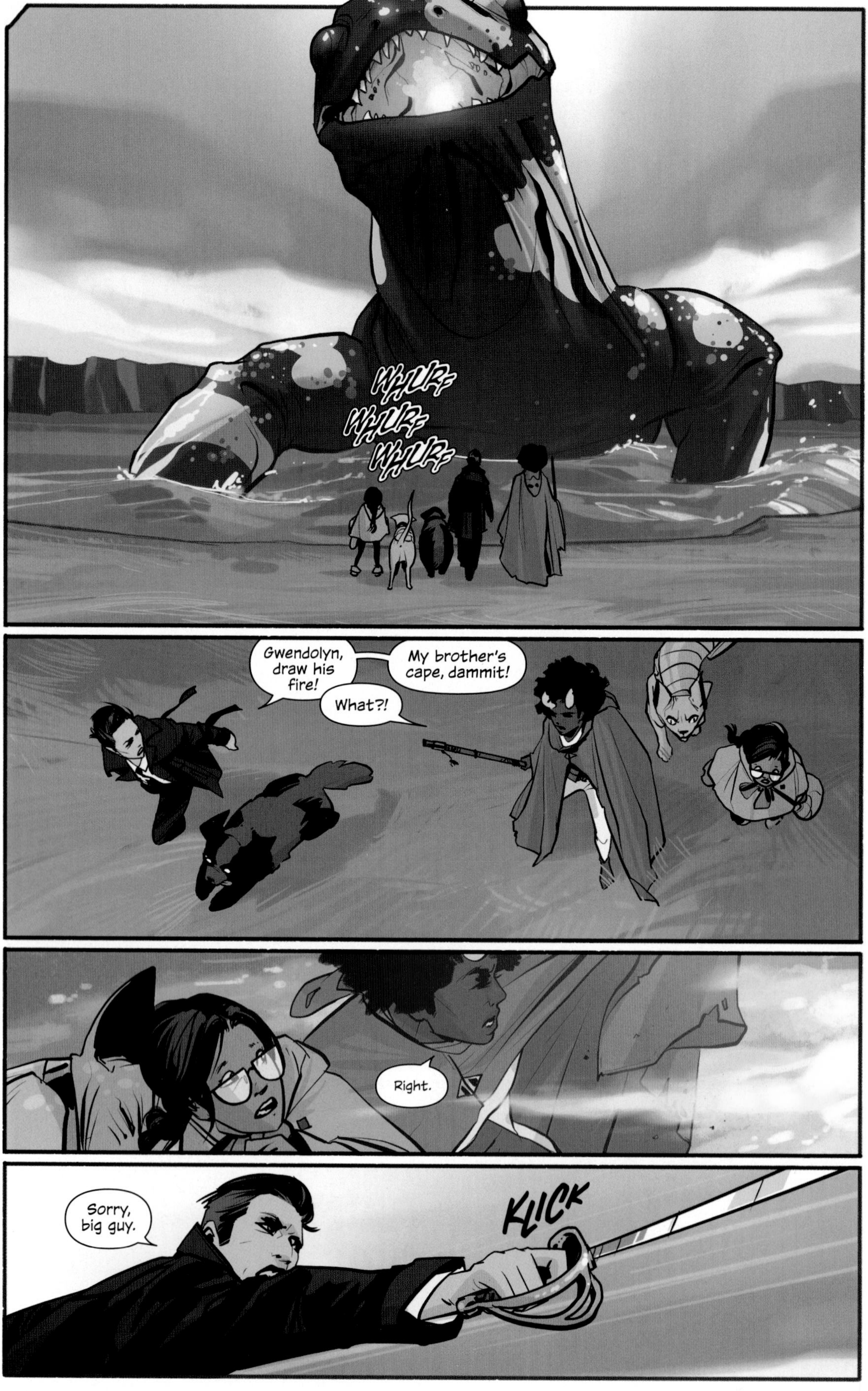
WHURF
WHURF
WHURF
Gwendolyn, draw his fire!
My brother's cape, dammit!
What?!
Right.
Sorry, big guy.
KLICK

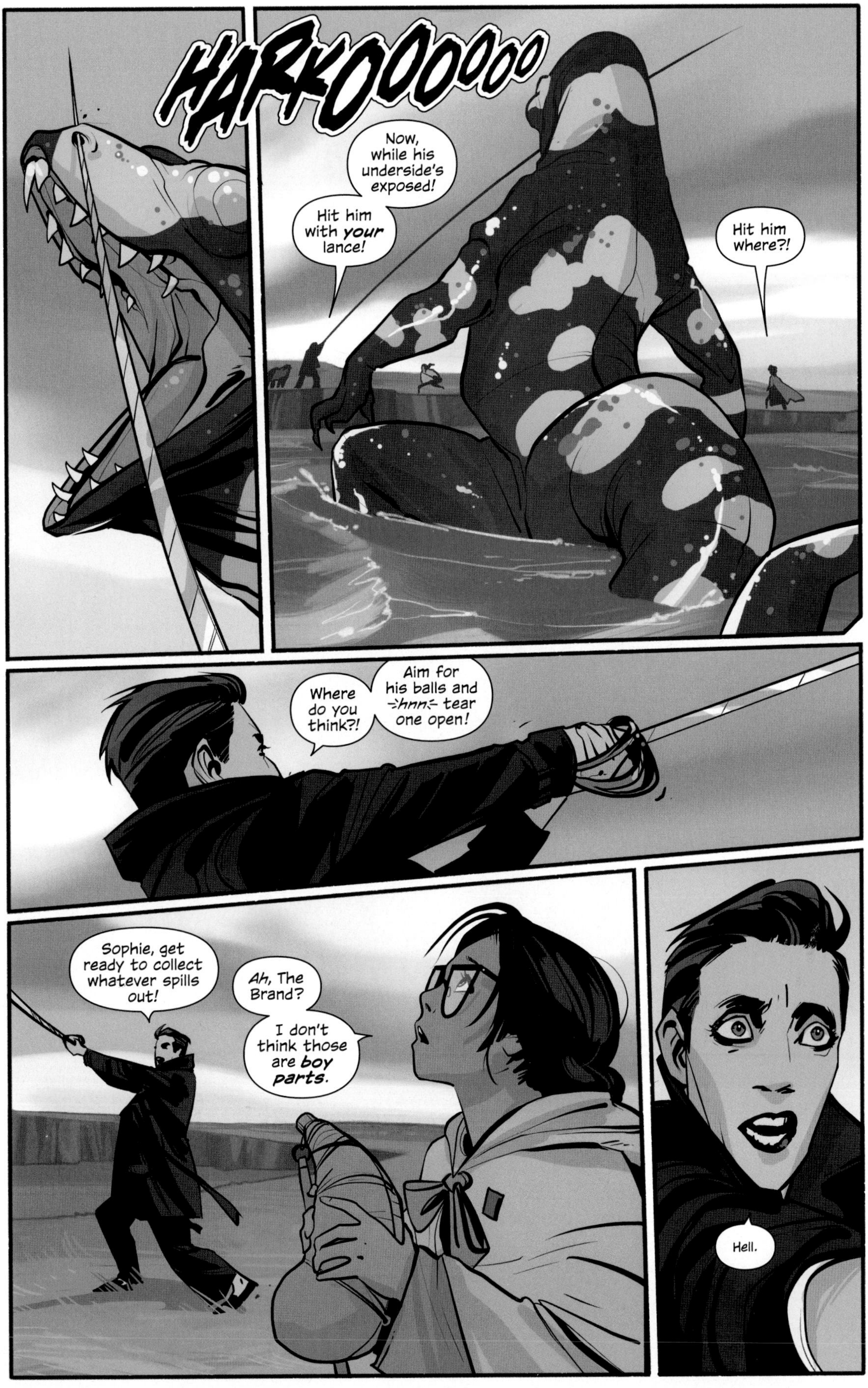
HARKOOOOOO
Now, while his underside's exposed!
Hit him with *your* lance!
Hit him where?!
Where do you think?!
Aim for his balls and -hnn- tear one open!
Sophie, get ready to collect whatever spills out!
Ah, The Brand?
I don't think those are ***boy parts***.
Hell.

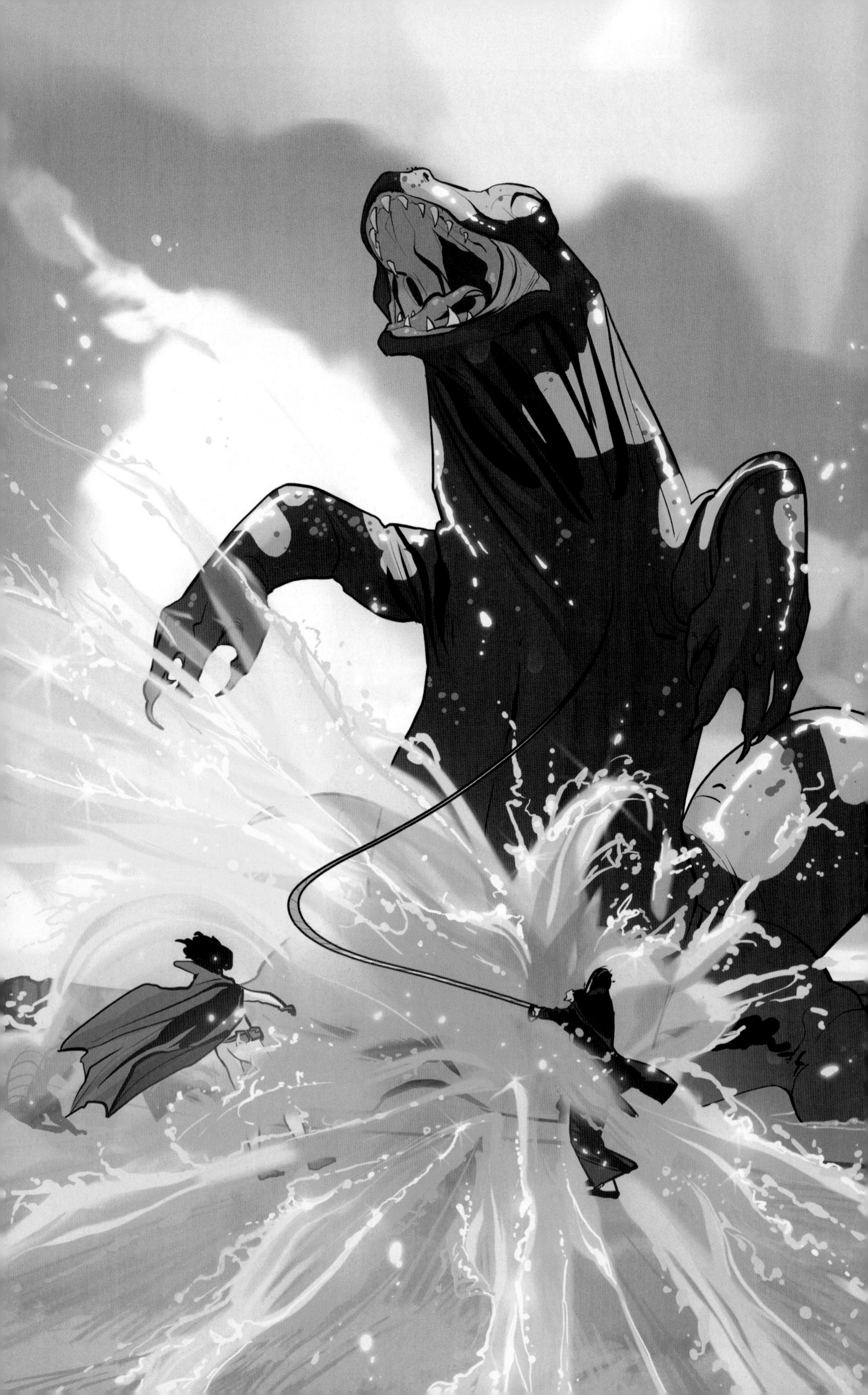

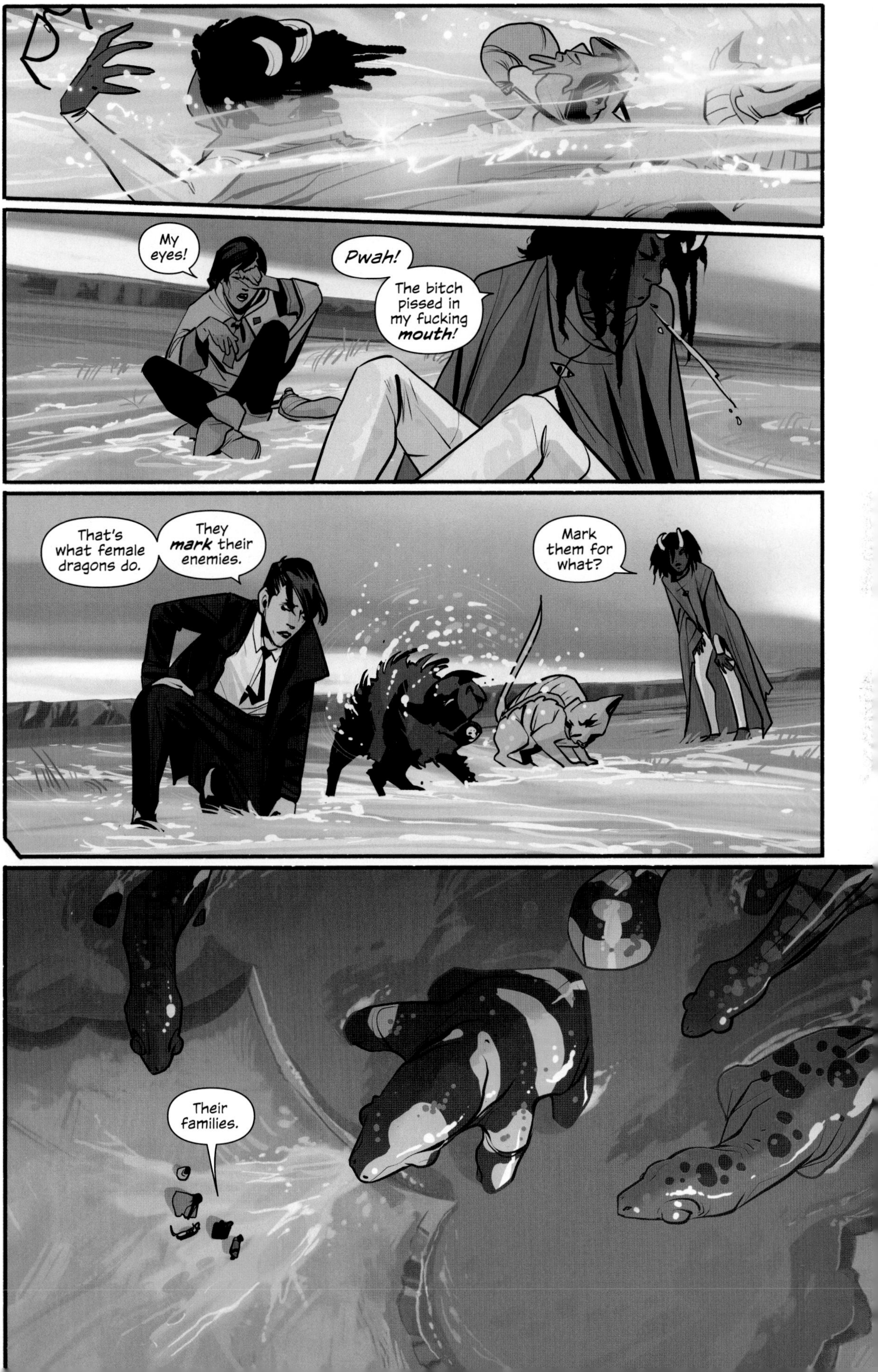
My eyes!
Pwah!
The bitch pissed in my fucking *mouth*!
That's what female dragons do.
They *mark* their enemies.
Mark them for what?
Their families.

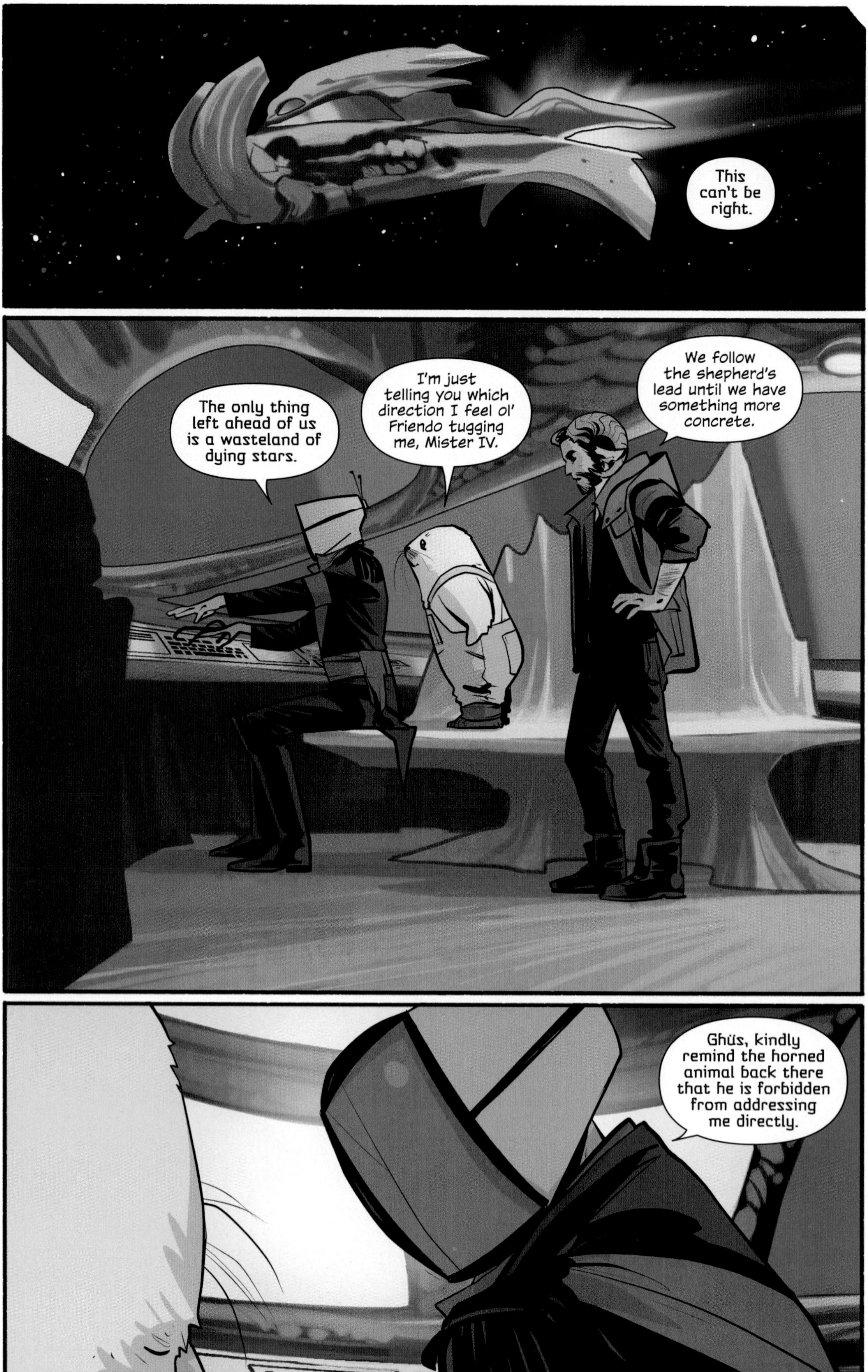
This can't be right.
The only thing left ahead of us is a wasteland of dying stars.
I'm just telling you which direction I feel ol' Friendo tugging me, Mister IV.
We follow the shepherd's lead until we have something more concrete.
Ghüs, kindly remind the horned animal back there that he is forbidden from addressing me directly.

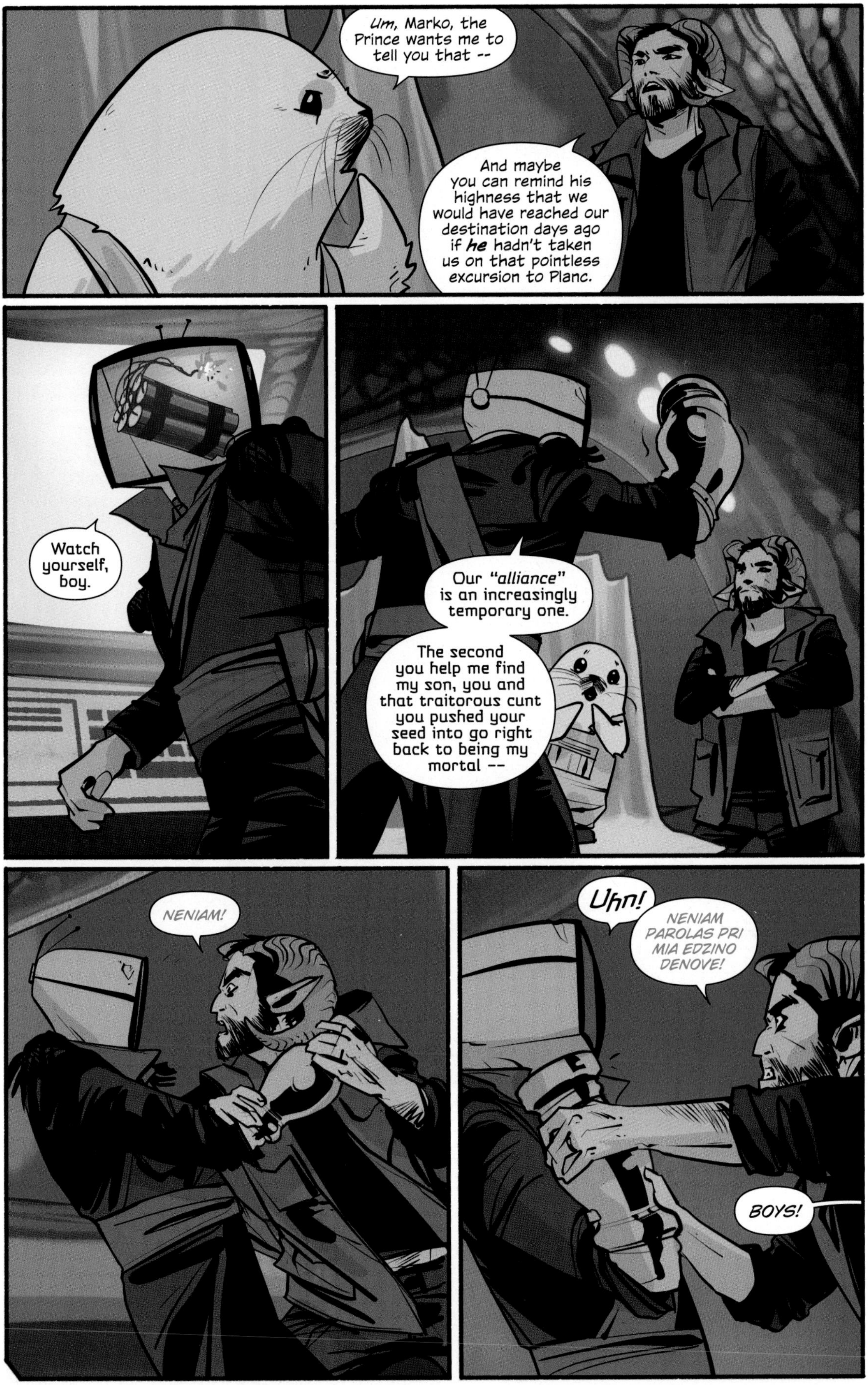
Um, Marko, the Prince wants me to tell you that --
And maybe you can remind his highness that we would have reached our destination days ago if he hadn't taken us on that pointless excursion to Planc.
Watch yourself, boy.
Our "alliance" is an increasingly temporary one.
The second you help me find my son, you and that traitorous cunt you pushed your seed into go right back to being my mortal --
NENIAM!
Uhn!
NENIAM PAROLAS PRI MIA EDZINO DENOVE!
BOYS!

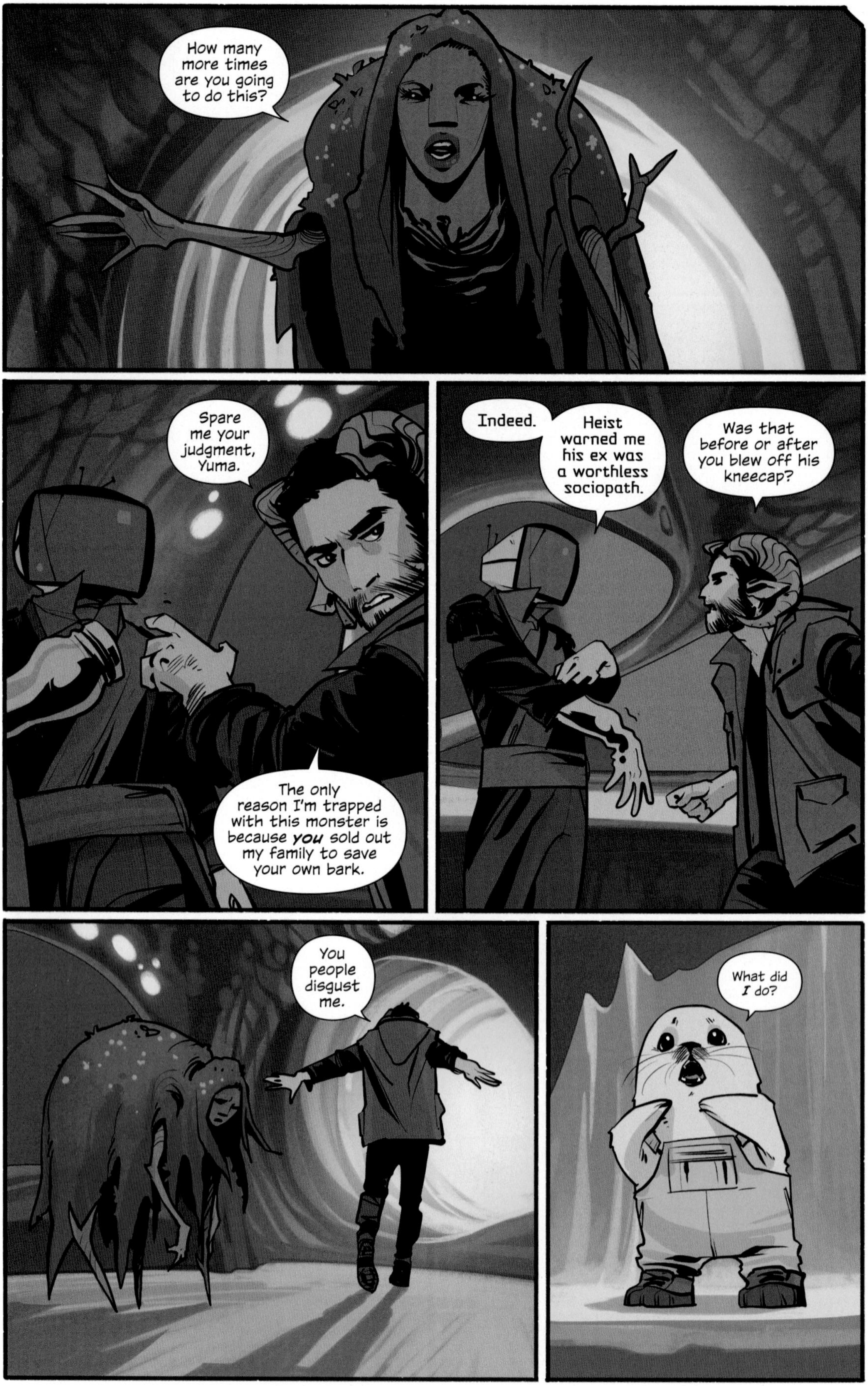
How many more times are you going to do this?
Spare me your judgment, Yuma.
The only reason I'm trapped with this monster is because *you* sold out my family to save your own bark.
Indeed.
Heist warned me his ex was a worthless sociopath.
Was that before or after you blew off his kneecap?
You people disgust me.
What did *I* do?

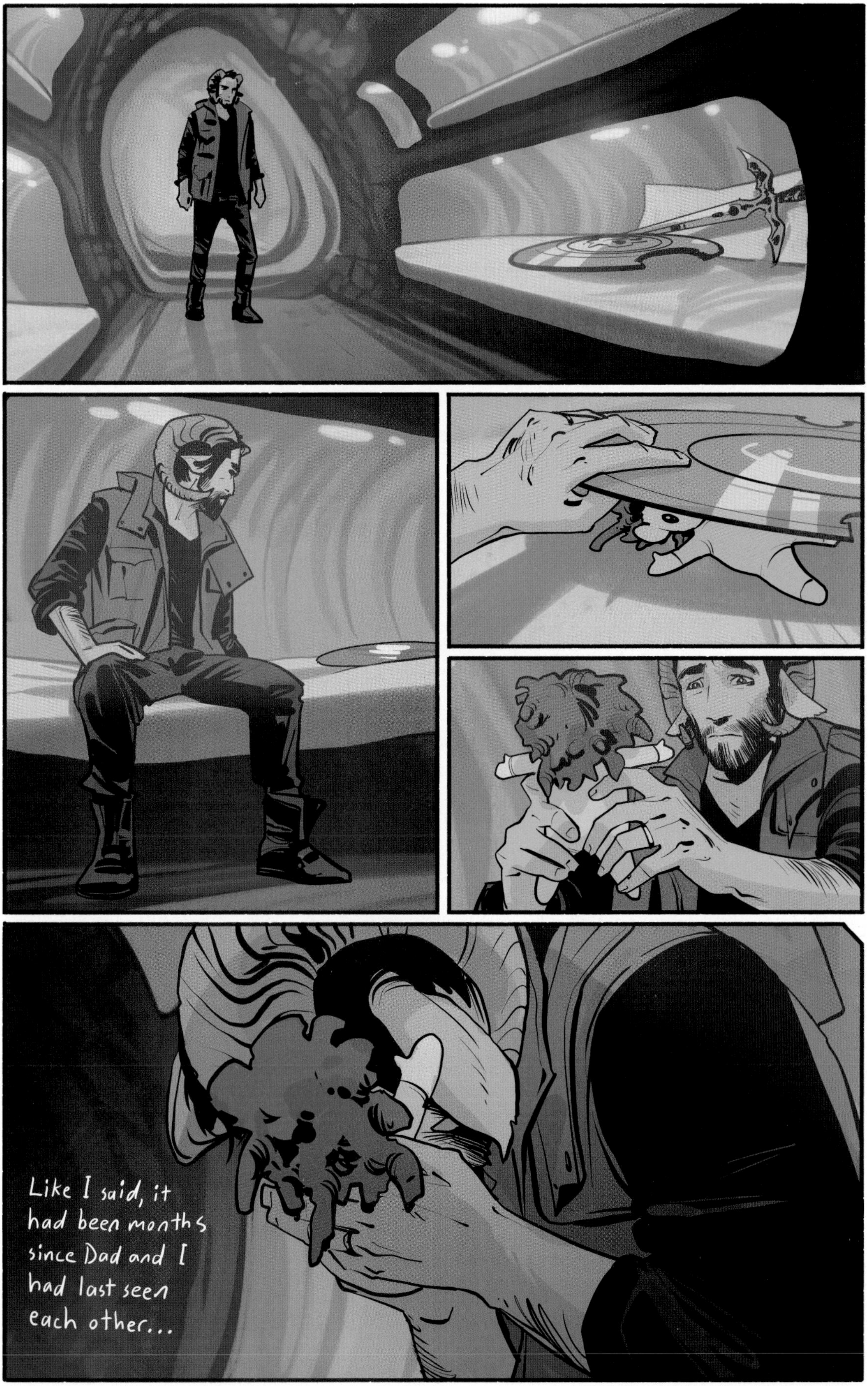
Like I said, it had been months since Dad and I had last seen each other...

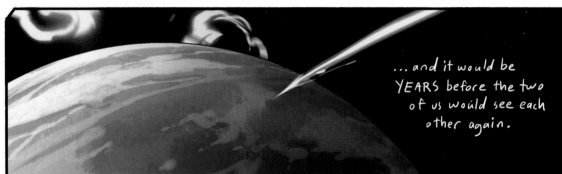

...and it would be YEARS before the two of us would see each other again.

What **is** that?

Looks like the hoof of an old **Astronomical**.

But Landfall decommissioned those things years ago.

NOK NOK

If Dengo really summoned the wings... they'll slaughter Hazel the moment they see the nubs on her head.

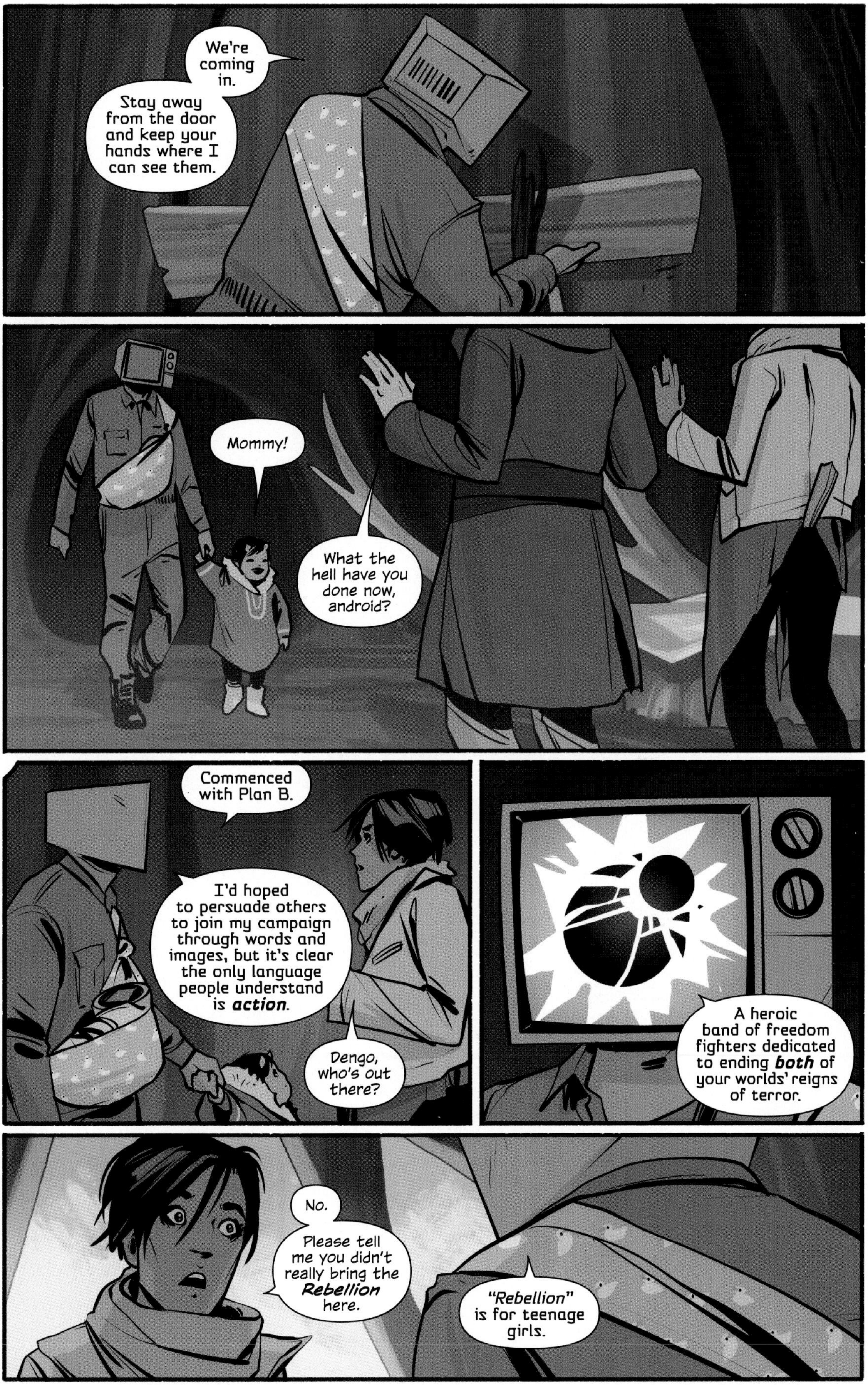

We're coming in.
Stay away from the door and keep your hands where I can see them.
Mommy!
What the hell have you done now, android?
Commenced with Plan B.
I'd hoped to persuade others to join my campaign through words and images, but it's clear the only language people understand is ***action***.
Dengo, who's out there?
A heroic band of freedom fighters dedicated to ending ***both*** of your worlds' reigns of terror.
No.
Please tell me you didn't really bring the ***Rebellion*** here.
"Rebellion" is for teenage girls.

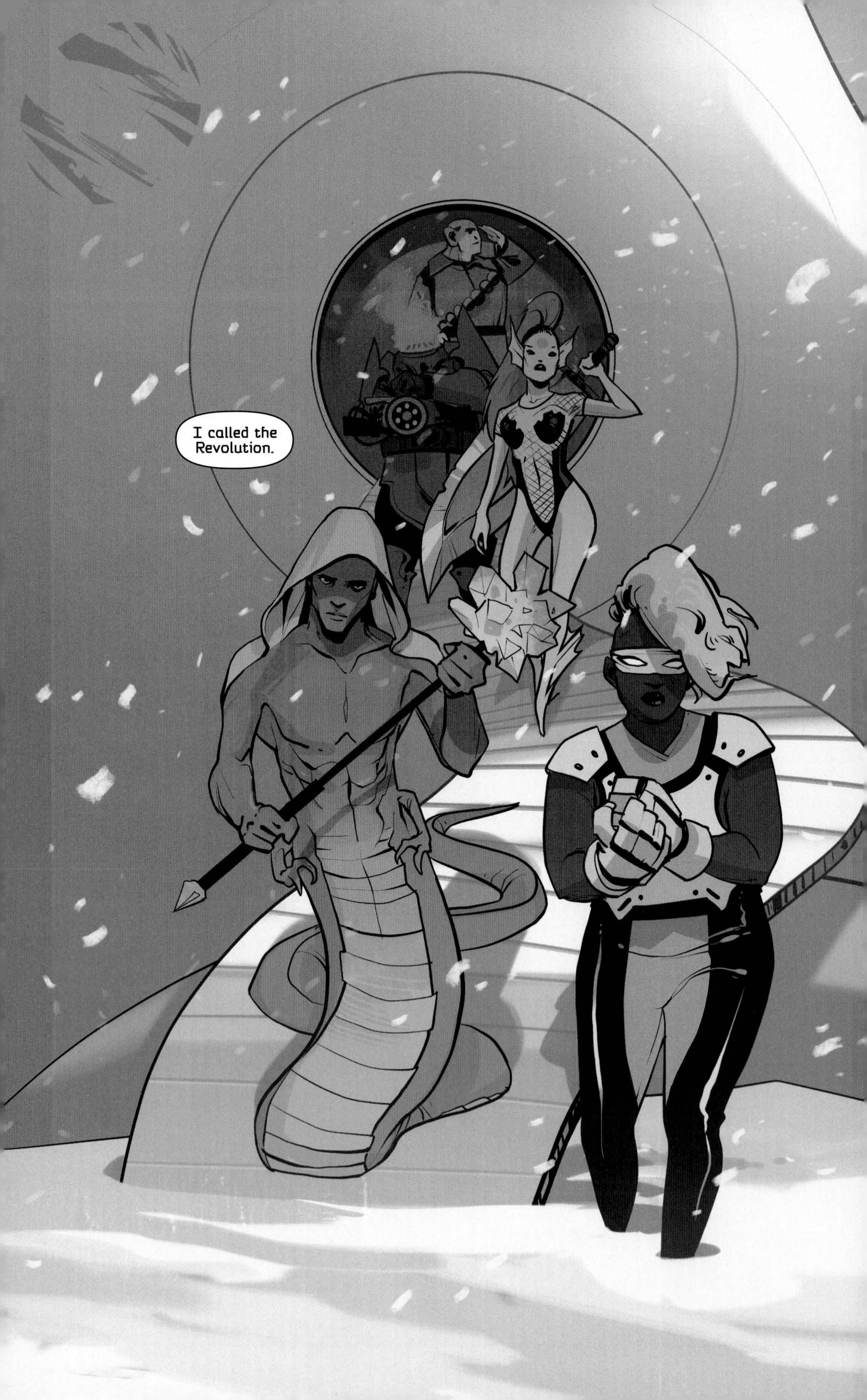
I called the Revolution.

end chapter twenty-five

CHAPTER
TWENTY-SIX

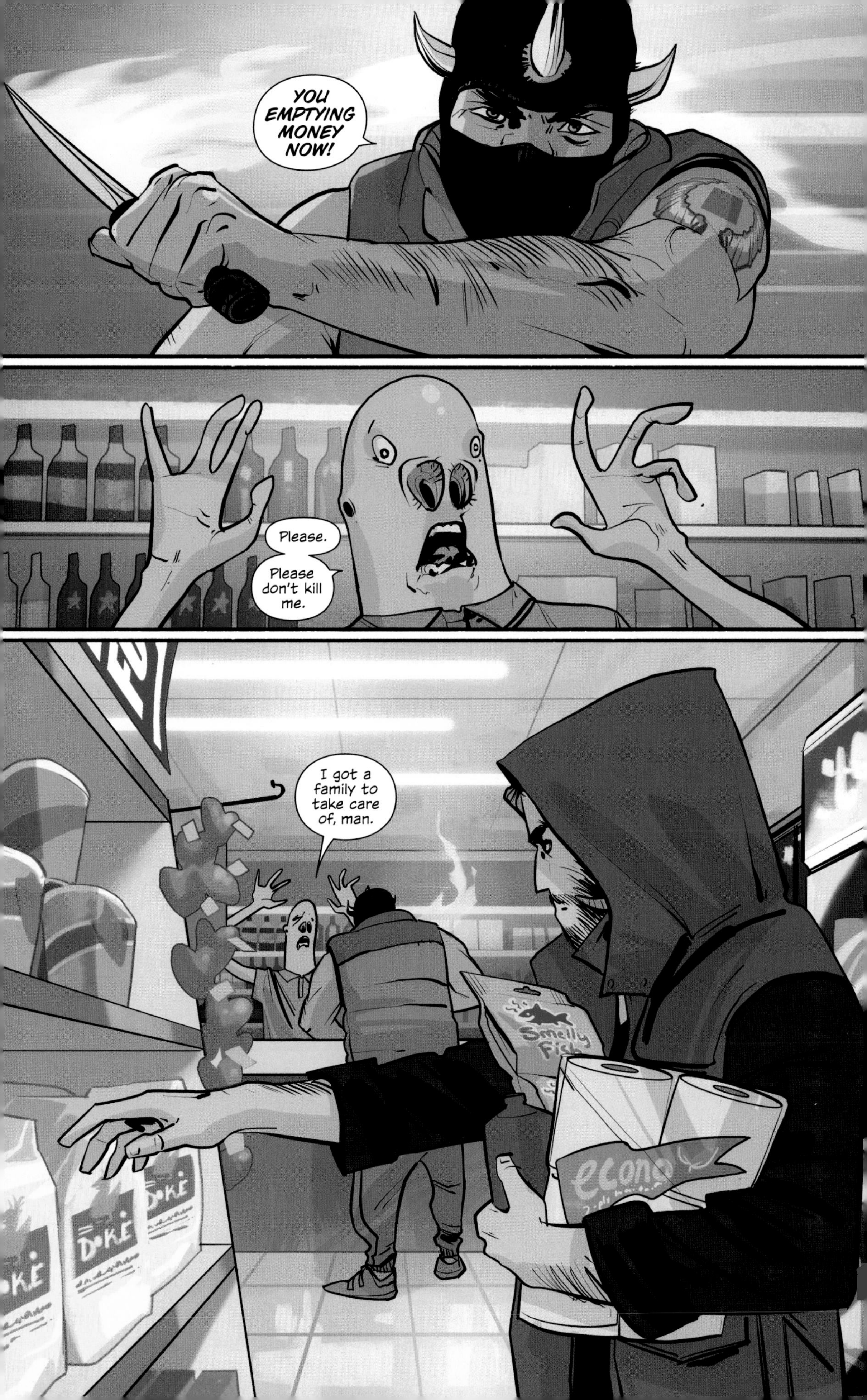
YOU EMPTYING MONEY NOW!
Please.
Please don't kill me.
I got a family to take care of, man.
Smelly Fish
econo

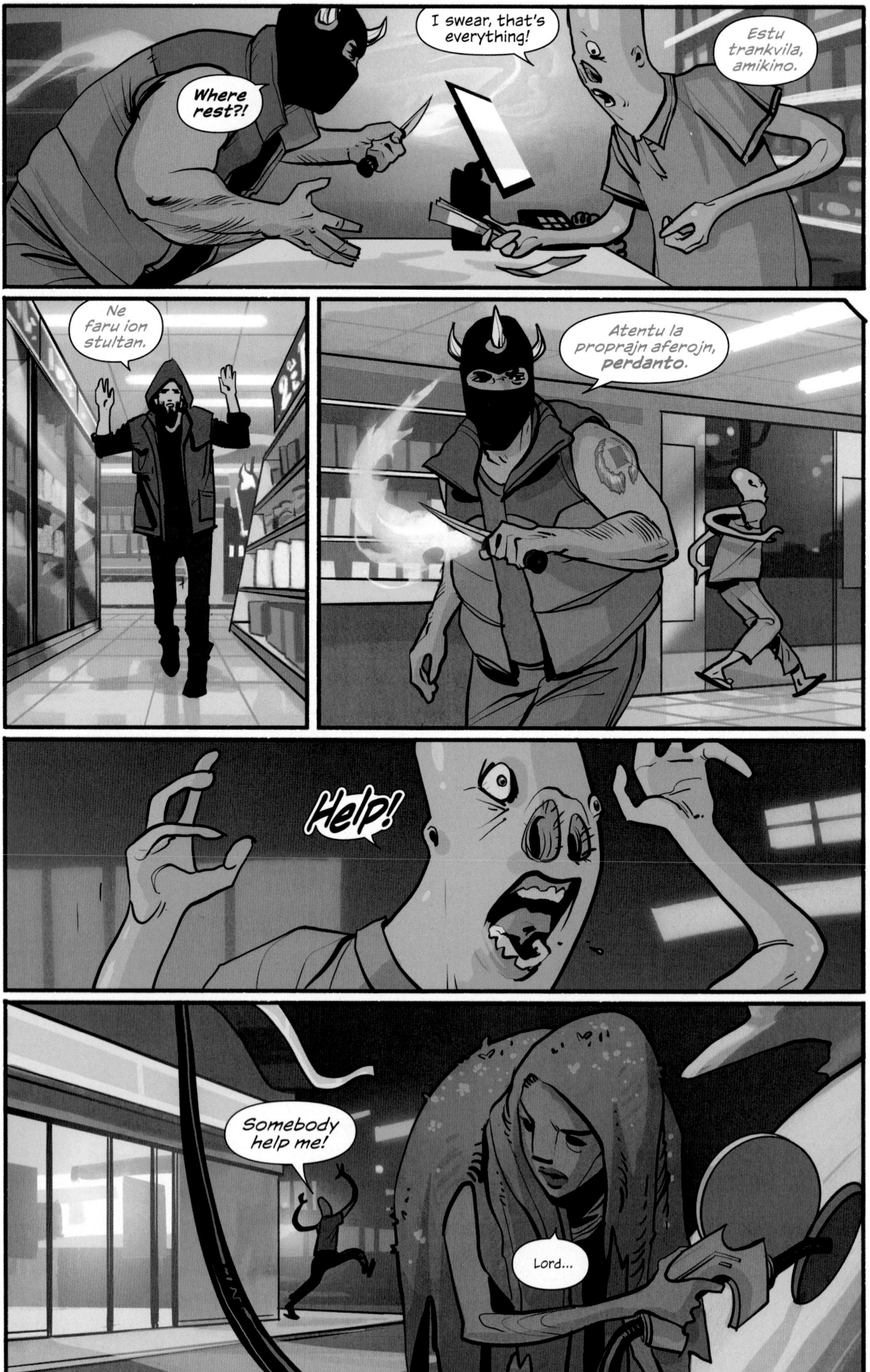
I swear, that's everything!
Where rest?!
Estu trankvila, amikino.
Ne faru ion stultan.
Atentu la proprajn aferojn, perdanto.
Help!
Somebody help me!
Lord...

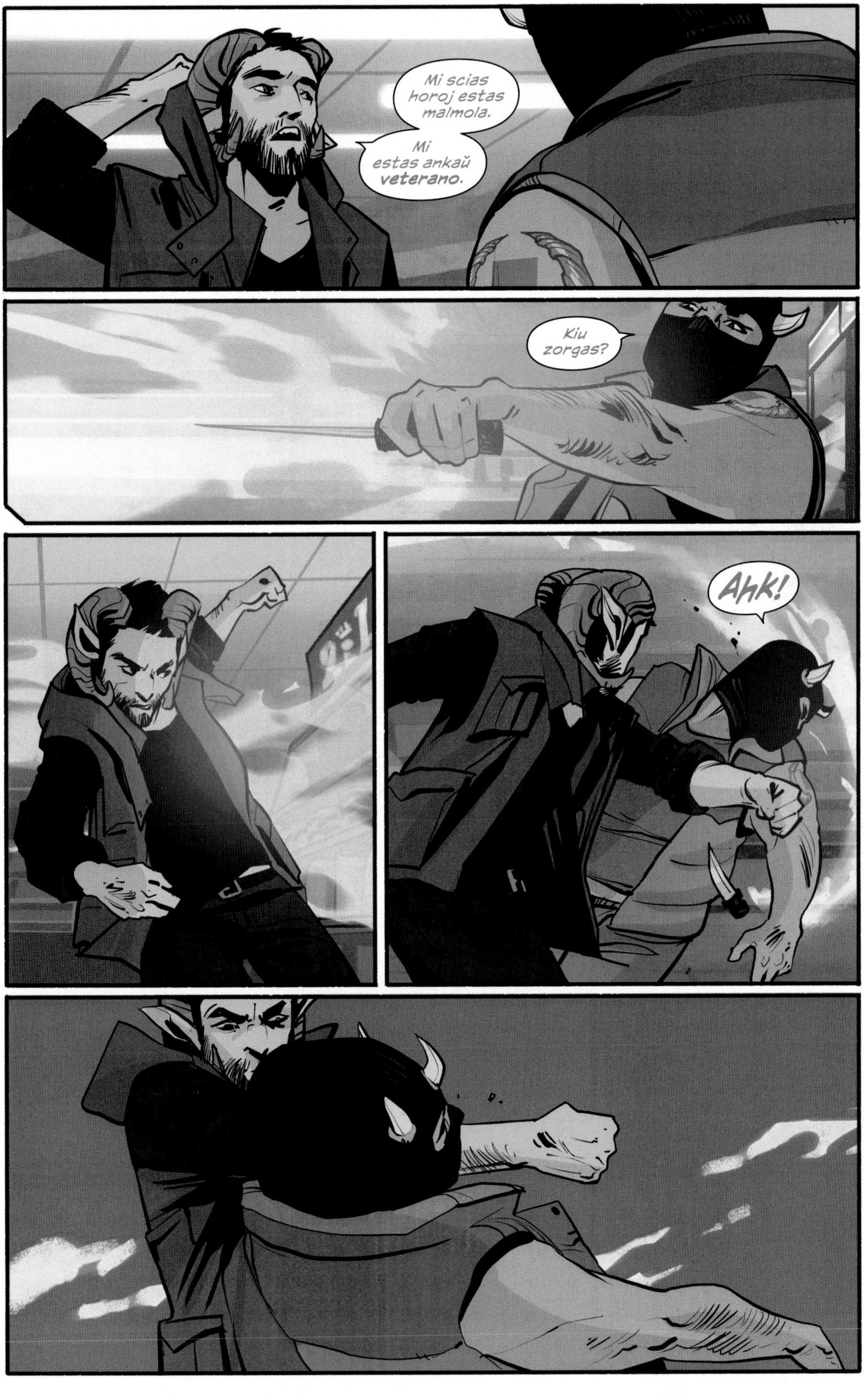
Mi scias horoj estas malmola.
Mi estas ankaŭ veterano.
Kiu zorgas?
Ahk!

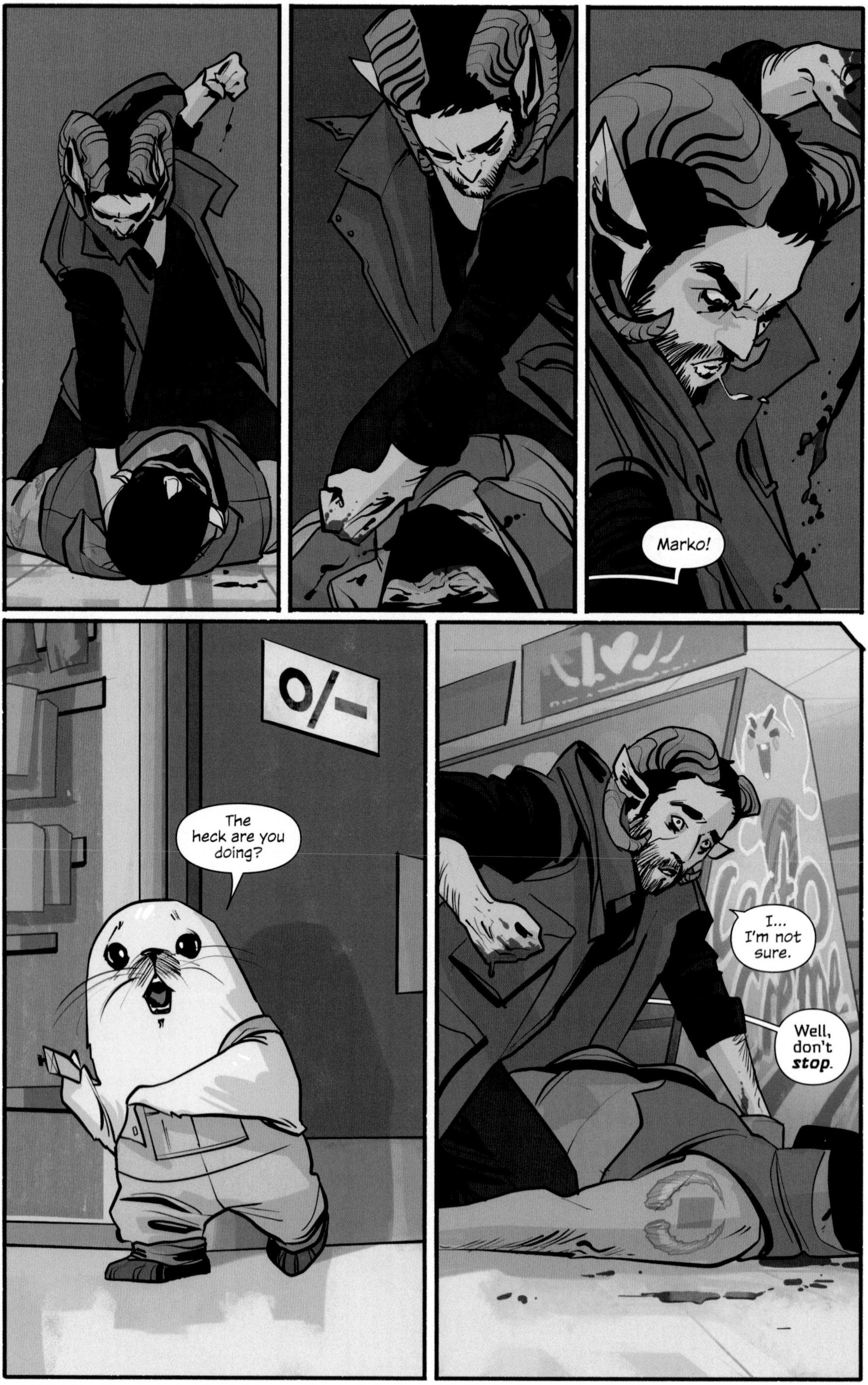
Marko!
The heck are you doing?
I... I'm not sure.
Well, don't **stop**.

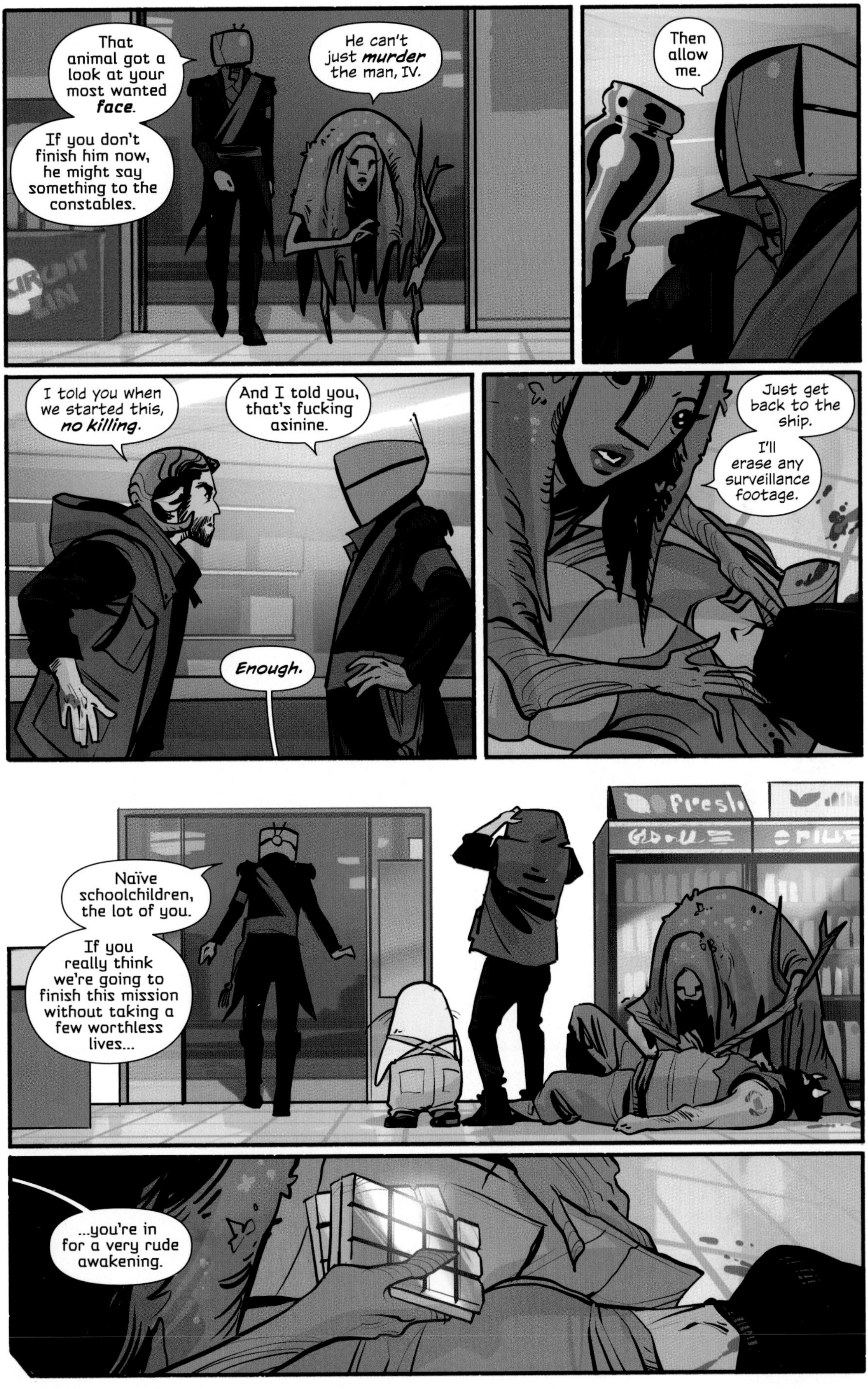
That animal got a look at your most wanted *face*.
If you don't finish him now, he might say something to the constables.
He can't just *murder* the man, IV.
Then allow me.
I told you when we started this, *no killing*.
And I told you, that's fucking asinine.
Enough.
Just get back to the ship.
I'll erase any surveillance footage.
Naïve schoolchildren, the lot of you.
If you really think we're going to finish this mission without taking a few worthless lives...
...you're in for a very rude awakening.

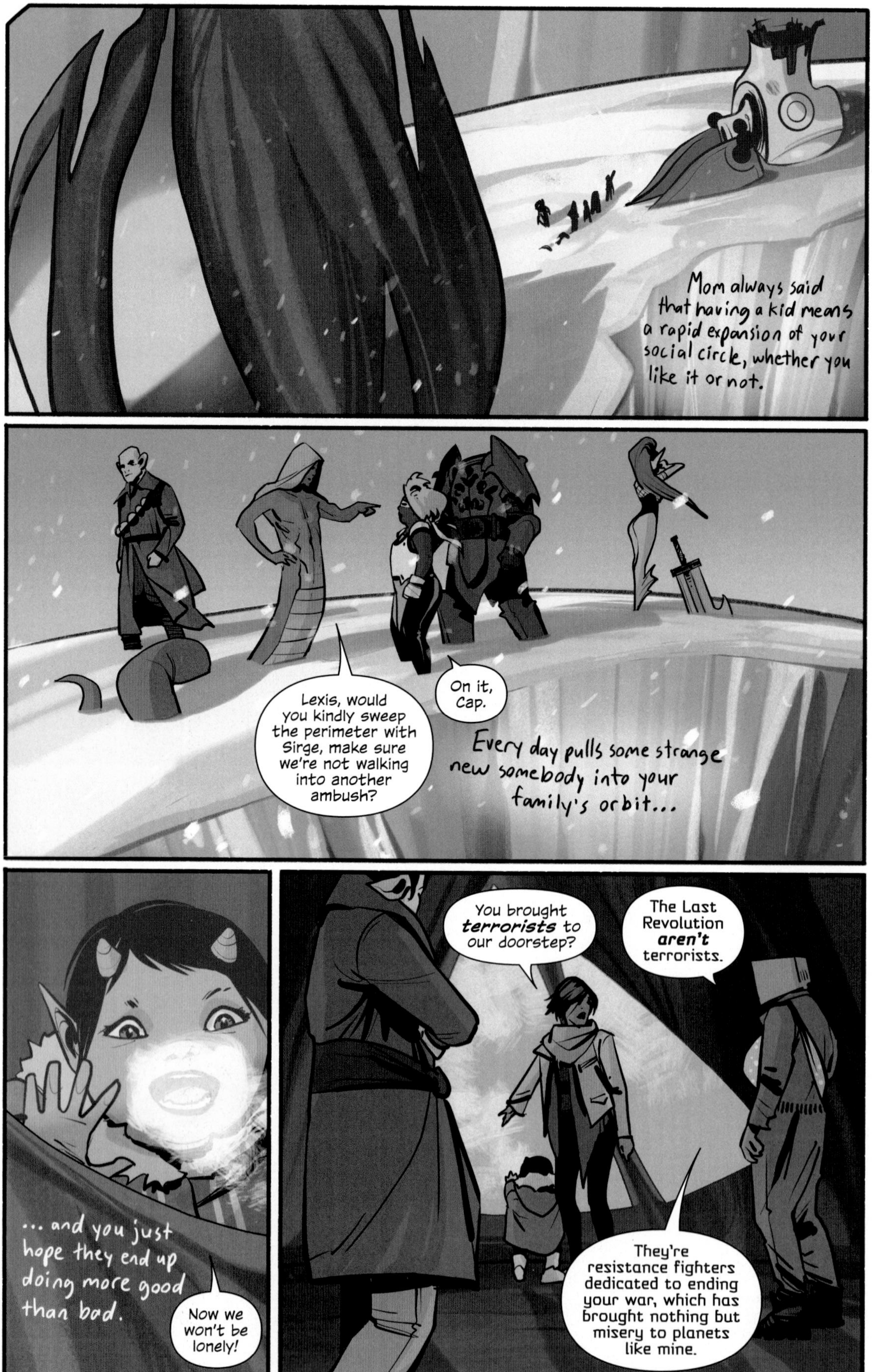
Mom always said that having a kid means a rapid expansion of your social circle, whether you like it or not.
Lexis, would you kindly sweep the perimeter with Sirge, make sure we're not walking into another ambush?
On it, Cap.
Every day pulls some strange new somebody into your family's orbit...
... and you just hope they end up doing more good than bad.
Now we won't be lonely!
You brought **terrorists** to our doorstep?
The Last Revolution **aren't** terrorists.
They're resistance fighters dedicated to ending your war, which has brought nothing but misery to planets like mine.

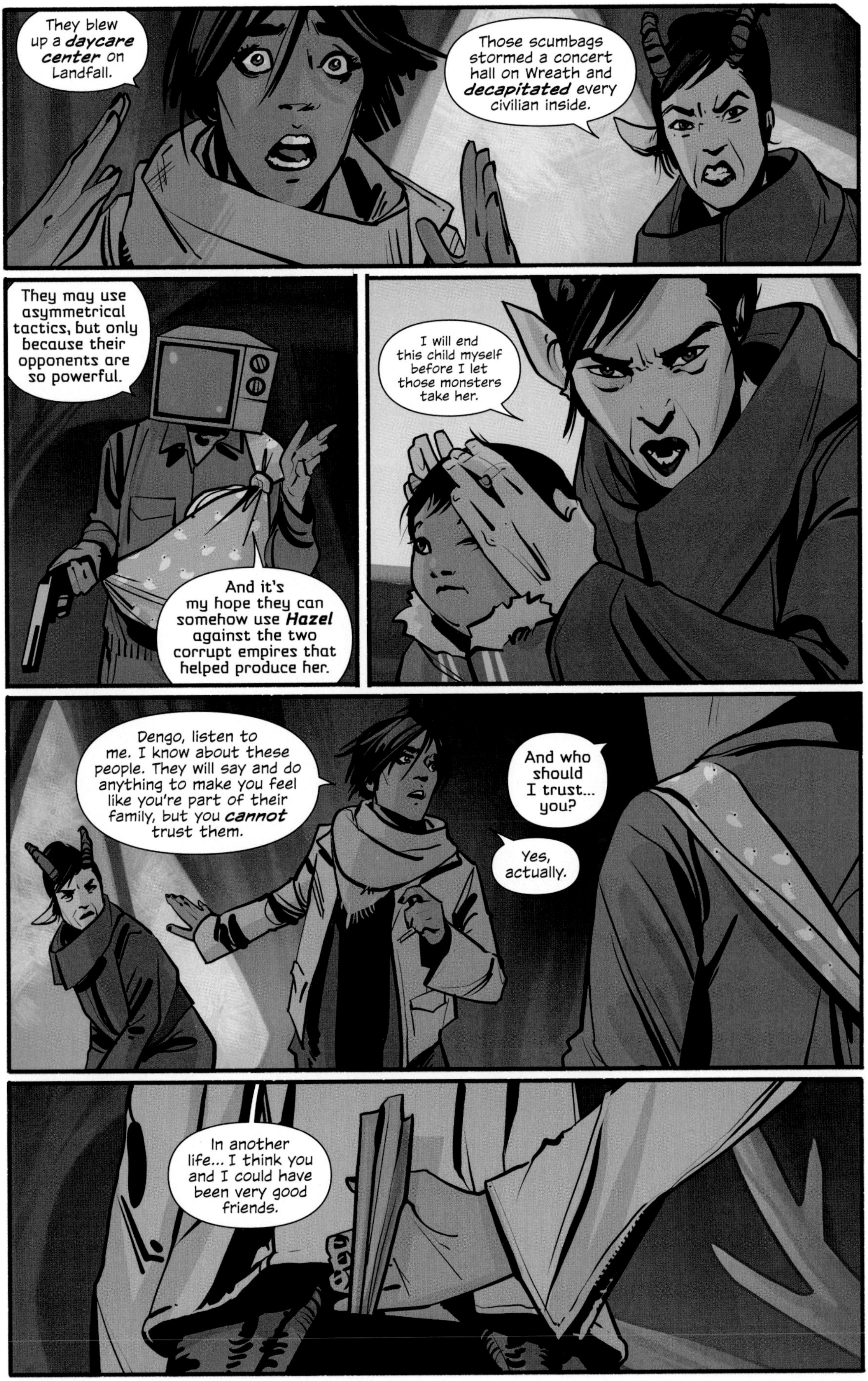
They blew up a *daycare center* on Landfall.
Those scumbags stormed a concert hall on Wreath and *decapitated* every civilian inside.
They may use asymmetrical tactics, but only because their opponents are so powerful.
And it's my hope they can somehow use *Hazel* against the two corrupt empires that helped produce her.
I will end this child myself before I let those monsters take her.
Dengo, listen to me. I know about these people. They will say and do anything to make you feel like you're part of their family, but you *cannot* trust them.
And who should I trust... you?
Yes, actually.
In another life... I think you and I could have been very good friends.

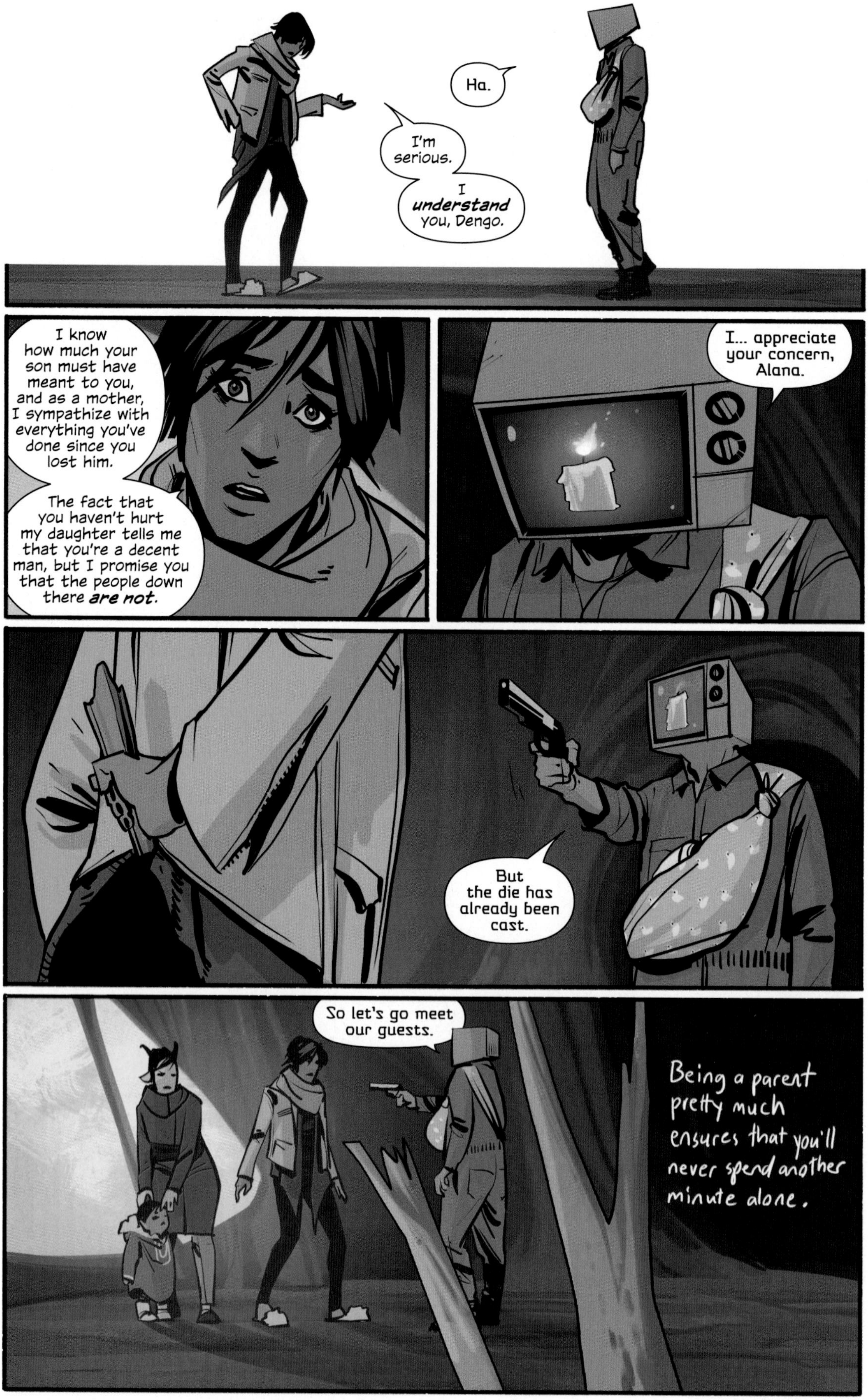
Ha.
I'm serious.
I understand you, Dengo.
I know how much your son must have meant to you, and as a mother, I sympathize with everything you've done since you lost him.
The fact that you haven't hurt my daughter tells me that you're a decent man, but I promise you that the people down there are not.
I... appreciate your concern, Alana.
But the die has already been cast.
So let's go meet our guests.
Being a parent pretty much ensures that you'll never spend another minute alone.

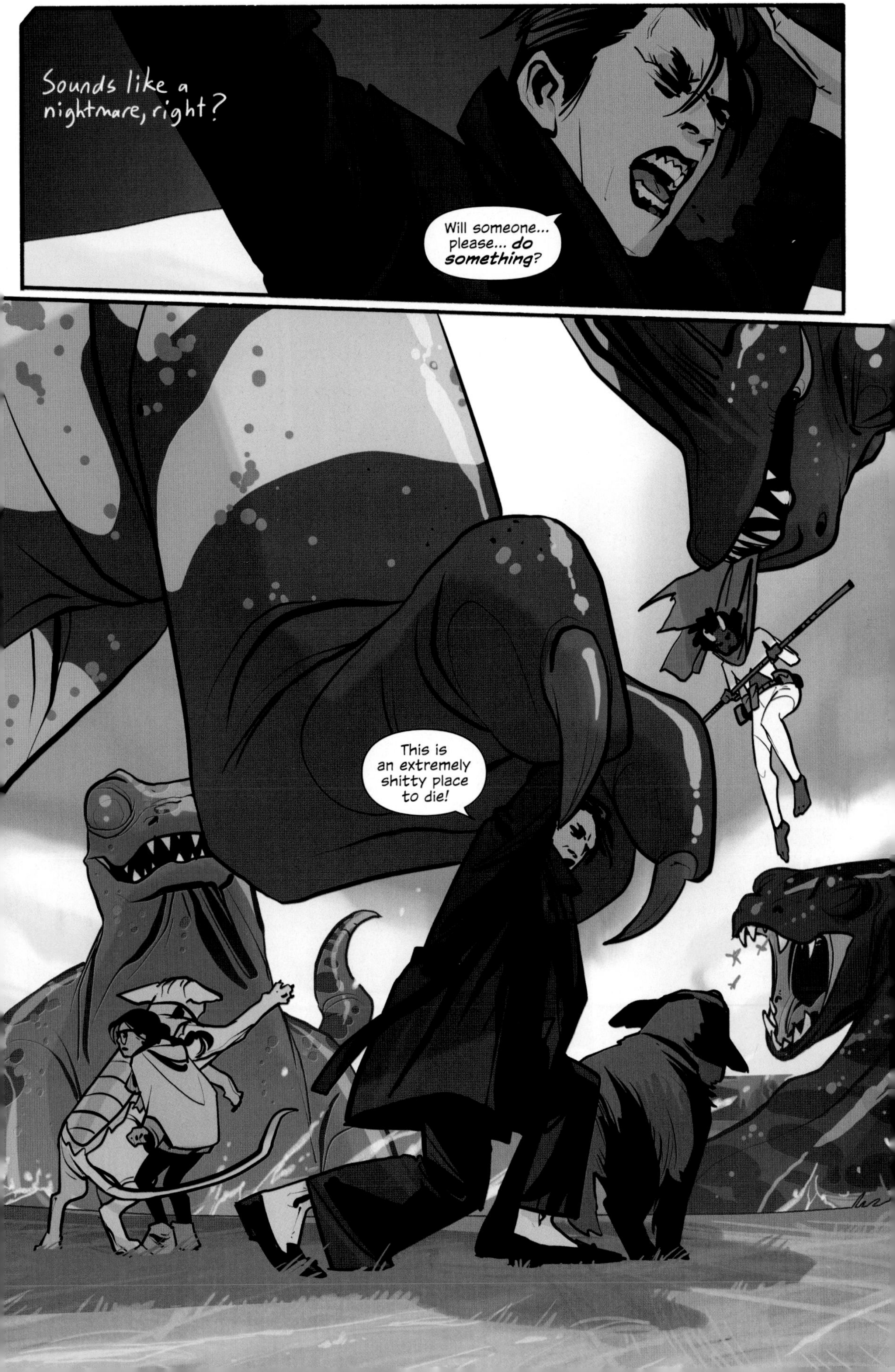
Sounds like a nightmare, right?
Will someone... please... do *something*?
This is an extremely shitty place to die!

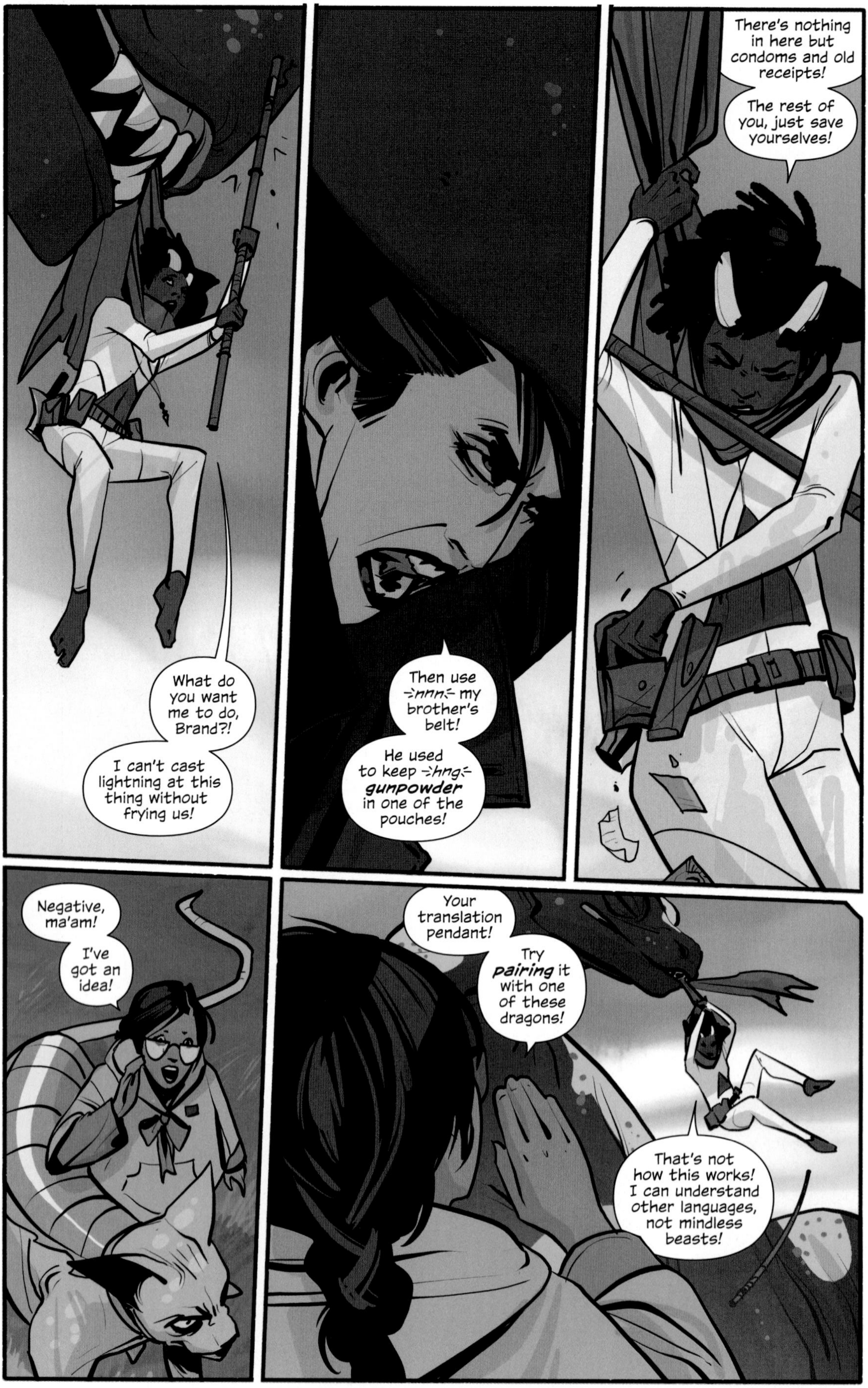

What do you want me to do, Brand?!
I can't cast lightning at this thing without frying us!
Then use -nnn- my brother's belt!
He used to keep -hng- *gunpowder* in one of the pouches!
There's nothing in here but condoms and old receipts!
The rest of you, just save yourselves!
Negative, ma'am!
I've got an idea!
Your translation pendant!
Try *pairing* it with one of these dragons!
That's not how this works! I can understand other languages, not mindless beasts!

I don't think they're mindless, Miss Gwendolyn!

They've got brains the size of bathtubs!

That doesn't mean they can *speak!*

Says the lady with the talking cat?

Just fucking try it!

Absurd.

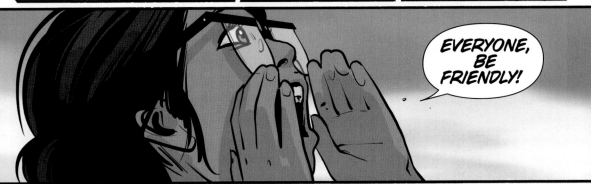

EVERYONE, BE FRIENDLY!

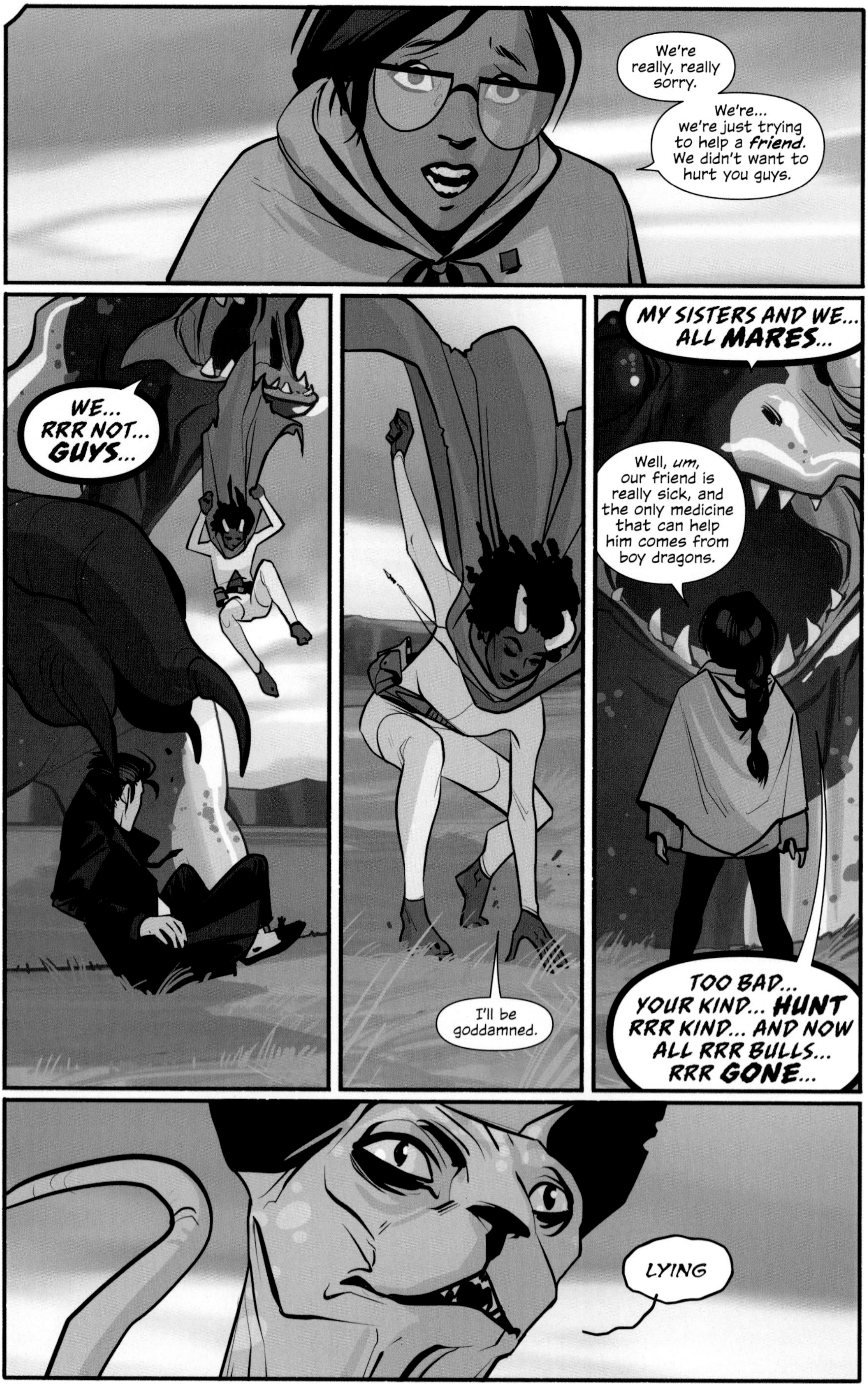
We're really, really sorry.
We're... we're just trying to help a *friend*. We didn't want to hurt you guys.
WE... RRR NOT... GUYS...
I'll be goddamned.
MY SISTERS AND WE... ALL MARES...
Well, *um*, our friend is really sick, and the only medicine that can help him comes from boy dragons.
TOO BAD... YOUR KIND... HUNT RRR KIND... AND NOW ALL RRR BULLS... RRR GONE...
LYING

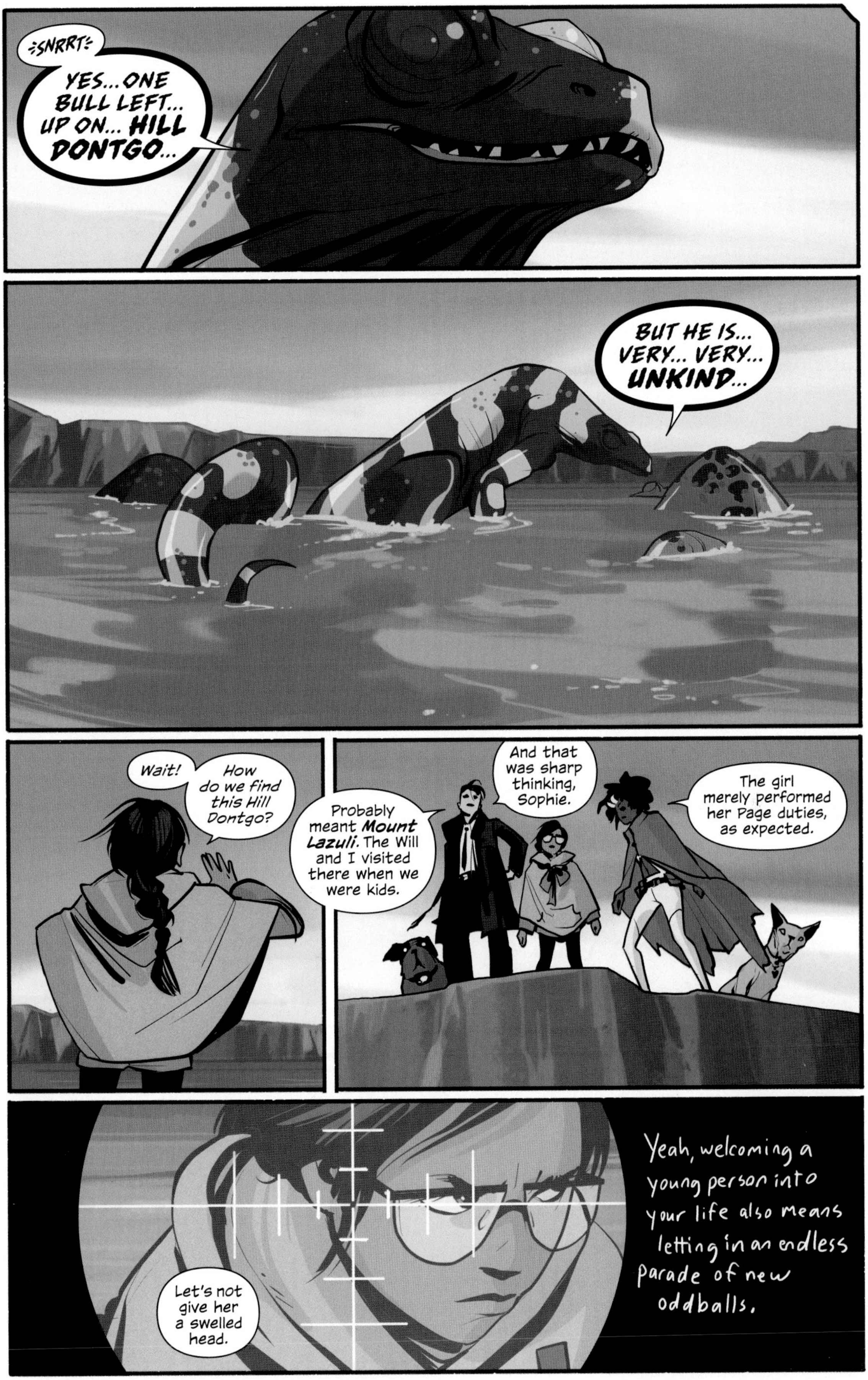

SNRRT
YES... ONE BULL LEFT... UP ON... HILL DONTGO...
BUT HE IS... VERY... VERY... UNKIND...
Wait!
How do we find this Hill Dontgo?
Probably meant Mount Lazuli. The Will and I visited there when we were kids.
And that was sharp thinking, Sophie.
The girl merely performed her Page duties, as expected.
Let's not give her a swelled head.
Yeah, welcoming a young person into your life also means letting in an endless parade of new oddballs.

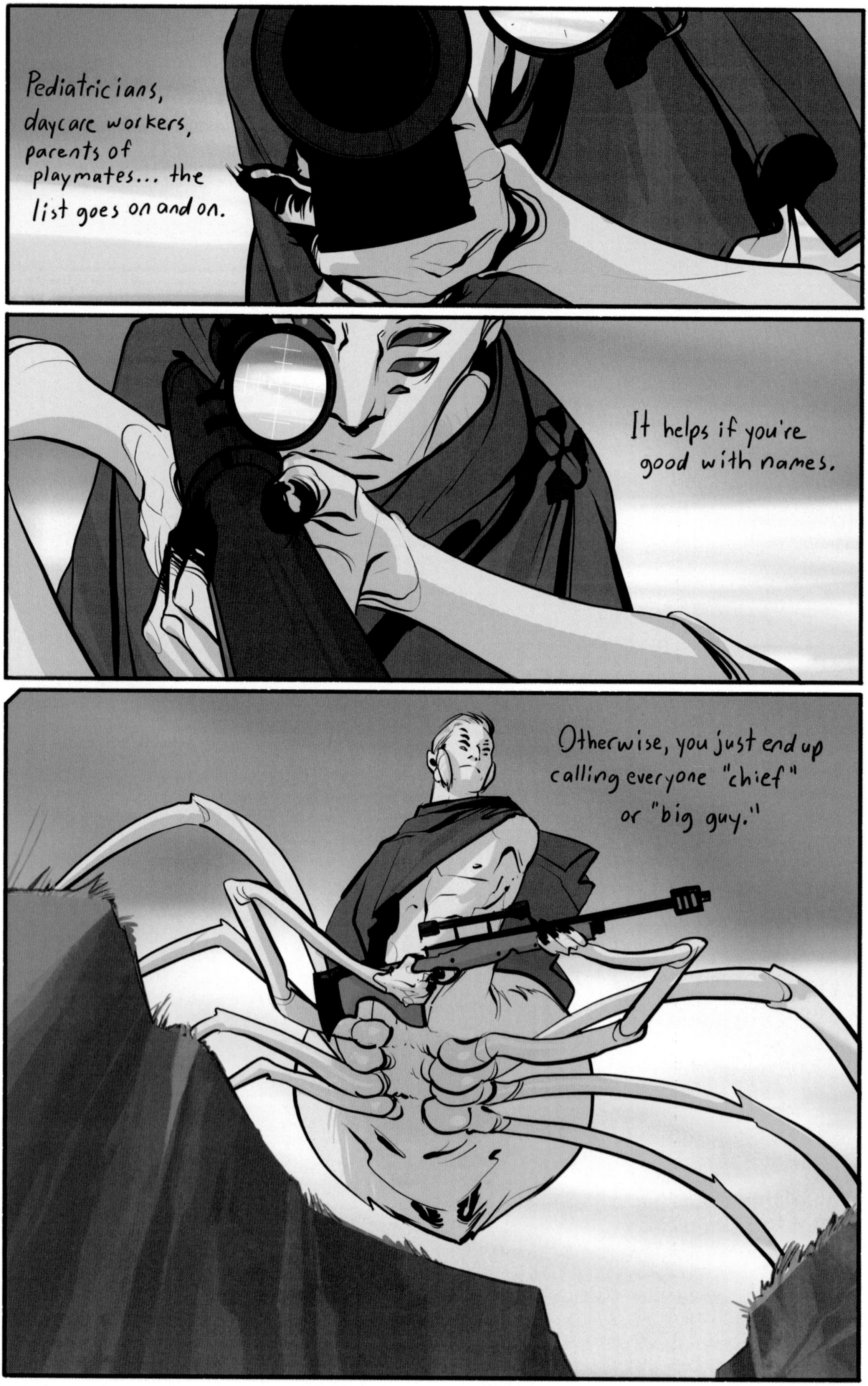
Pediatricians, daycare workers, parents of playmates... the list goes on and on.
It helps if you're good with names.
Otherwise, you just end up calling everyone "chief" or "big guy."

Cheer up, Beard of Sorrow.

We're going to get your family back.

All I care about is getting them to safety. I don't expect my wife and child to ever take *me* back.

What are you talking about?

I'm sick, Yuma. No matter how hard I try to quit, I'm obviously *addicted* to the very thing I've taken an oath against.

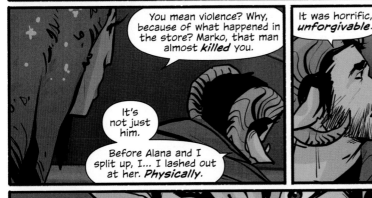

You mean violence? Why, because of what happened in the store? Marko, that man almost *killed* you.

It's not just him.

Before Alana and I split up, I... I lashed out at her. *Physically*.

It was horrific, *unforgivable*.

If I can't be trusted around the love of my life, why should I be allowed near Hazel again?

Whatever is inside of me is --

-- like the ink from some ancient sea creature. It's so perfectly black out there you can almost taste it.

Are you *high*?

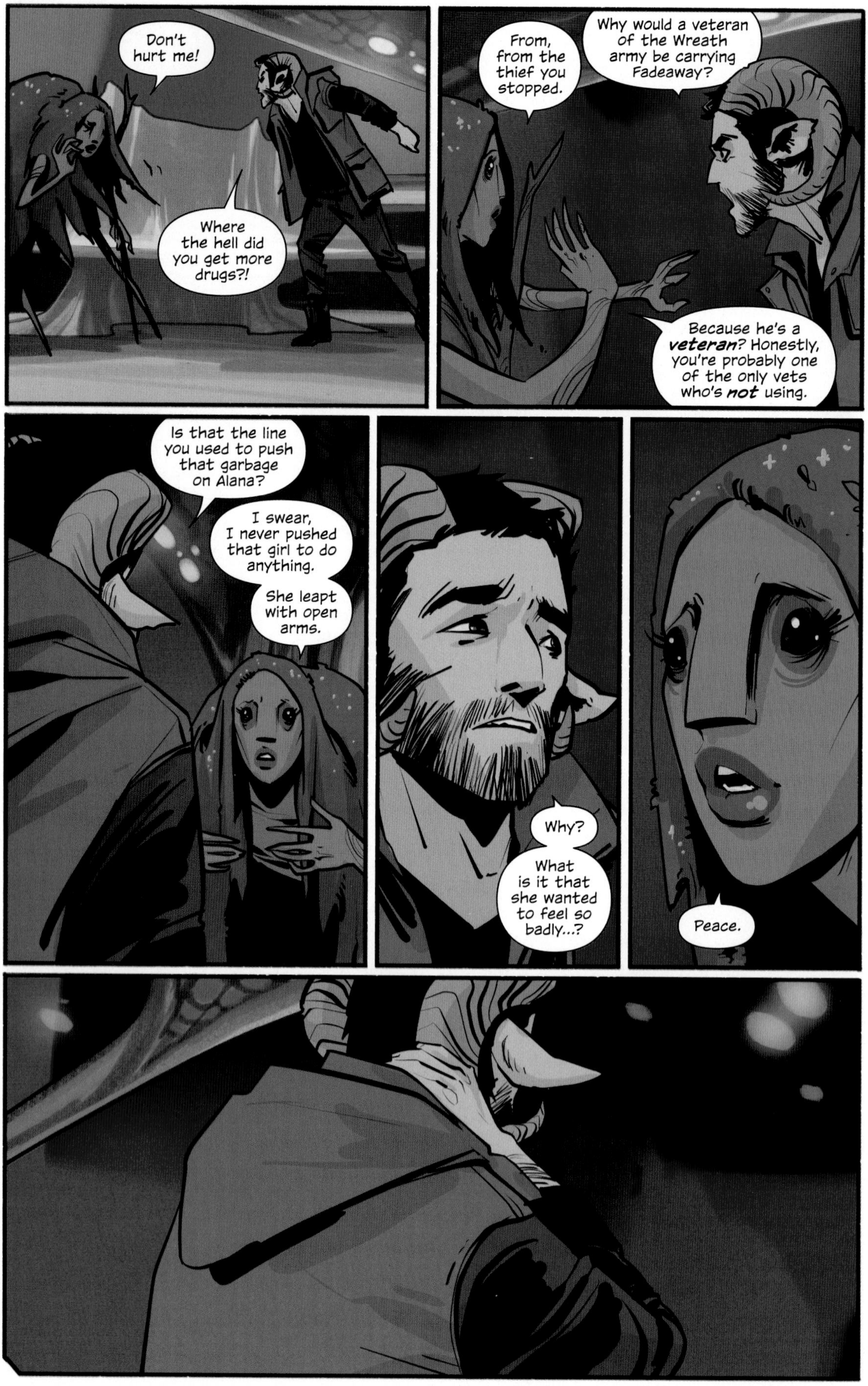
Don't hurt me!
Where the hell did you get more drugs?!
From, from the thief you stopped.
Why would a veteran of the Wreath army be carrying Fadeaway?
Because he's a **veteran**? Honestly, you're probably one of the only vets who's **not** using.
Is that the line you used to push that garbage on Alana?
I swear, I never pushed that girl to do anything.
She leapt with open arms.
Why?
What is it that she wanted to feel so badly...?
Peace.

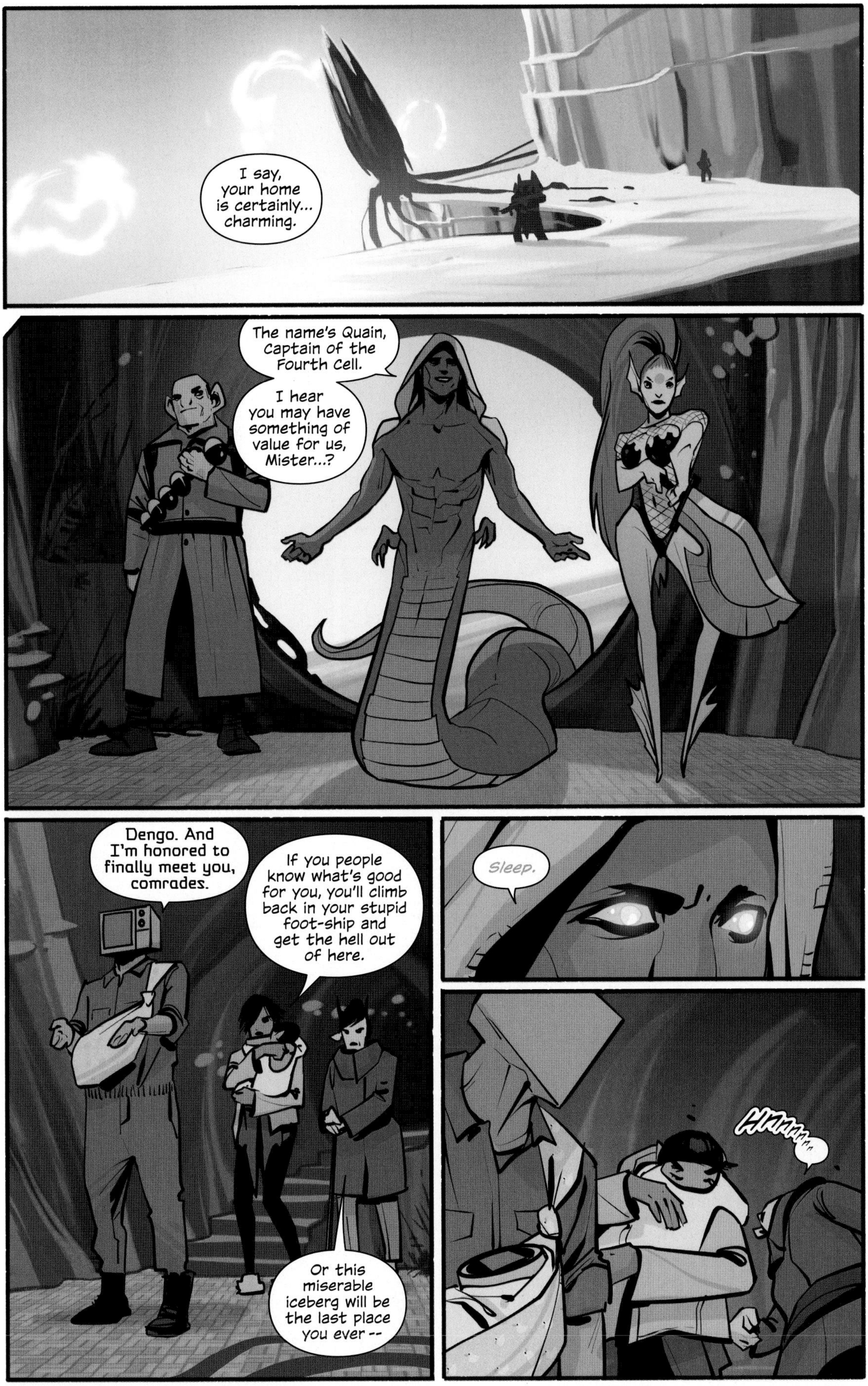
I say, your home is certainly... charming.
The name's Quain, Captain of the Fourth Cell.
I hear you may have something of value for us, Mister...?
Dengo. And I'm honored to finally meet you, comrades.
If you people know what's good for you, you'll climb back in your stupid foot-ship and get the hell out of here.
Or this miserable iceberg will be the last place you ever --
Sleep.
HMMMMm

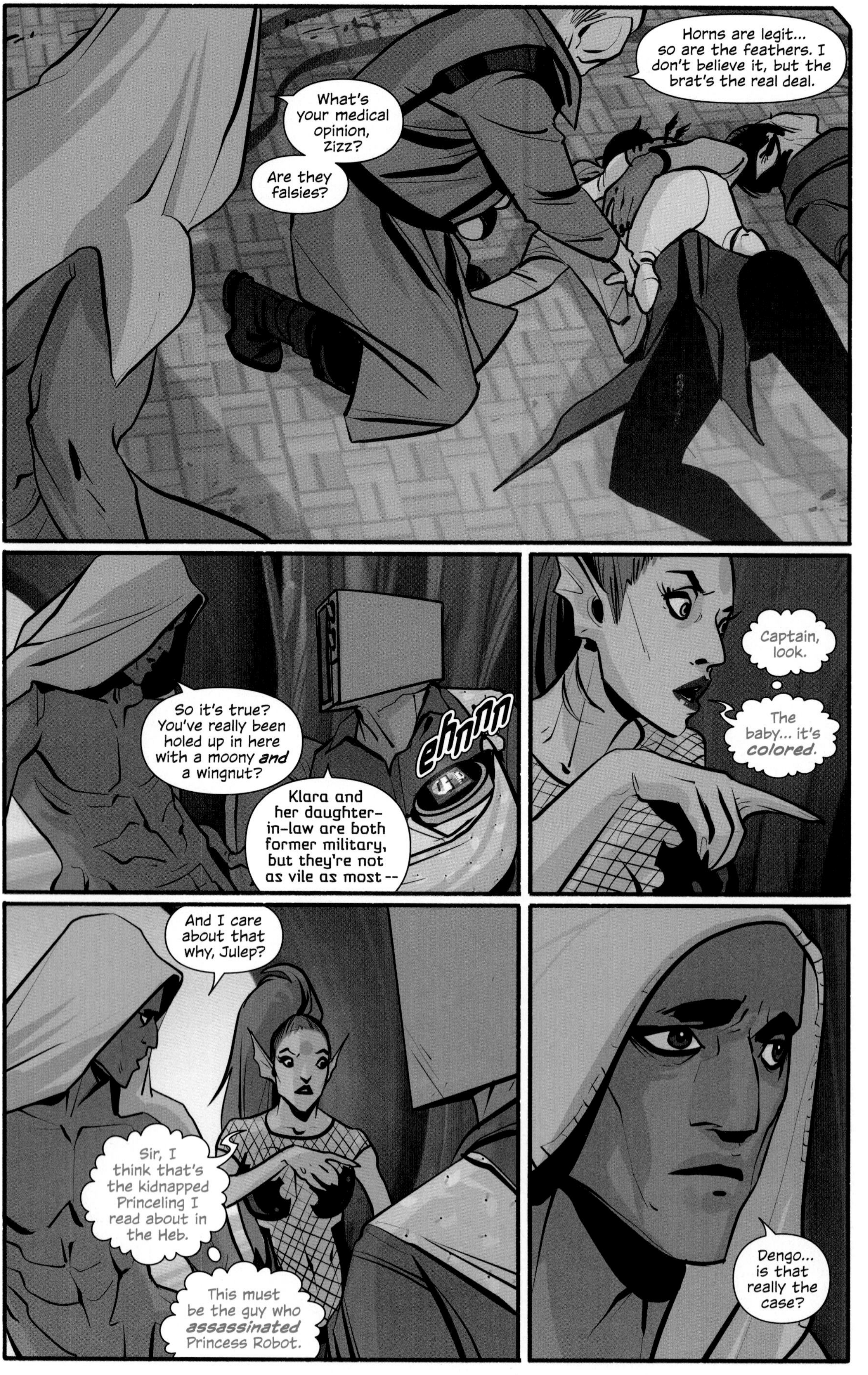
Horns are legit... so are the feathers. I don't believe it, but the brat's the real deal.
What's your medical opinion, Zizz?
Are they falsies?
So it's true? You've really been holed up in here with a moony *and* a wingnut?
ehnnn
Klara and her daughter-in-law are both former military, but they're not as vile as most --
Captain, look.
The baby... it's *colored*.
And I care about that why, Julep?
Sir, I think that's the kidnapped Princeling I read about in the Heb.
This must be the guy who *assassinated* Princess Robot.
Dengo... is that really the case?

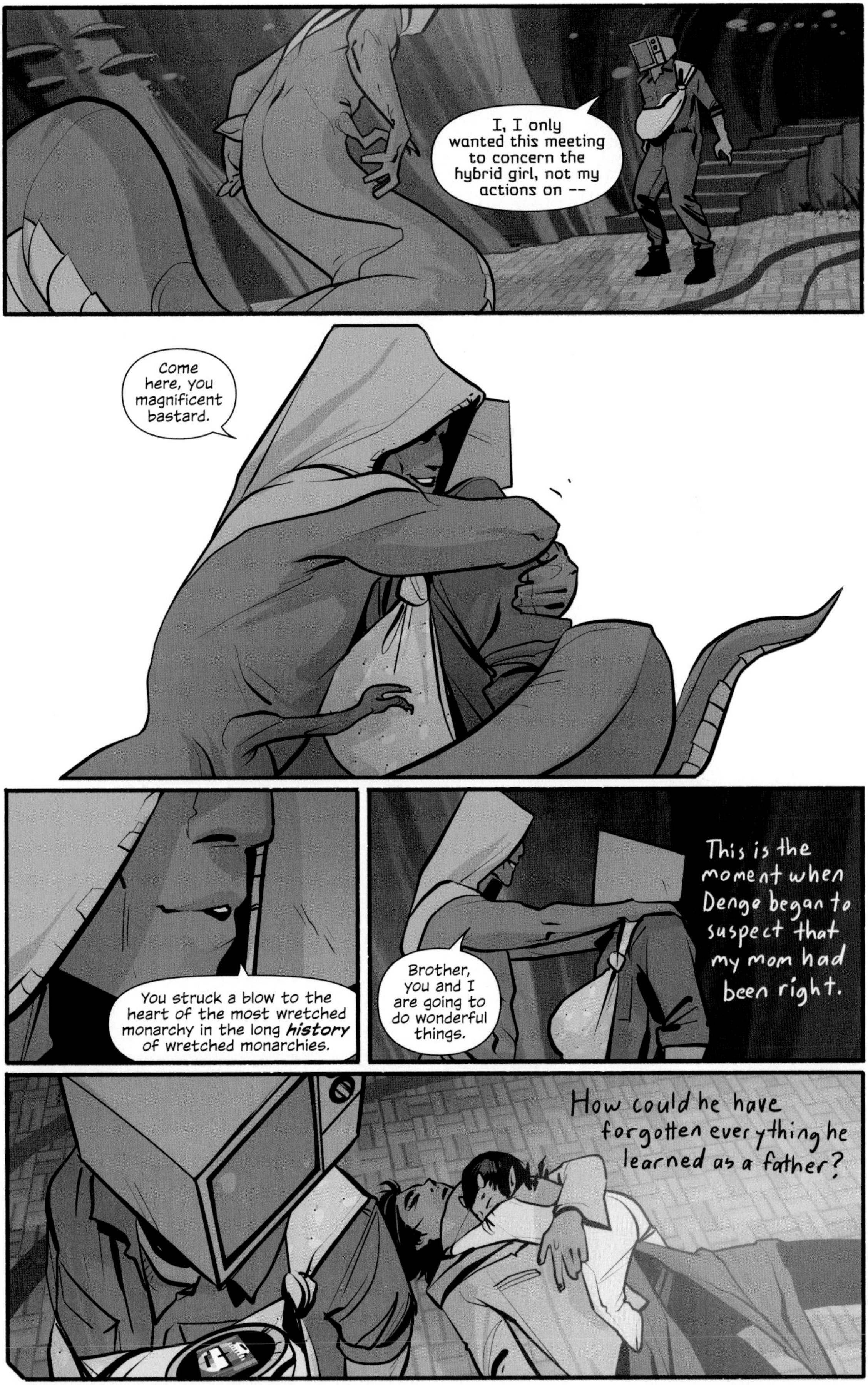

I, I only wanted this meeting to concern the hybrid girl, not my actions on --
Come here, you magnificent bastard.
You struck a blow to the heart of the most wretched monarchy in the long *history* of wretched monarchies.
Brother, you and I are going to do wonderful things.
This is the moment when Denge began to suspect that my mom had been right.
How could he have forgotten everything he learned as a father?

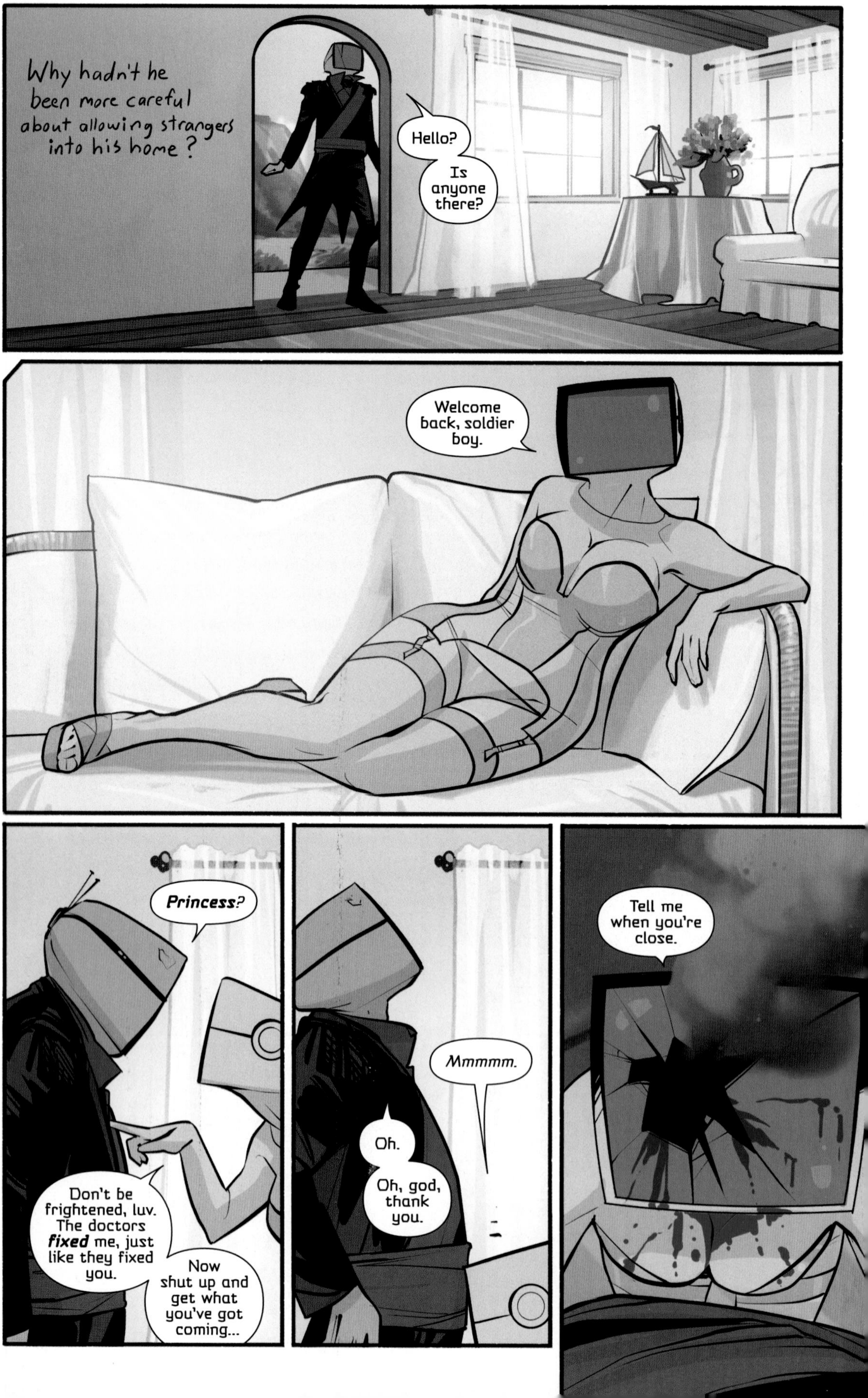
Why hadn't he been more careful about allowing strangers into his home?
Hello?
Is anyone there?
Welcome back, soldier boy.
Princess?
Don't be frightened, luv. The doctors ***fixed*** me, just like they fixed you.
Now shut up and get what you've got coming...
Mmmmm.
Oh.
Oh, god, thank you.
Tell me when you're close.

guh

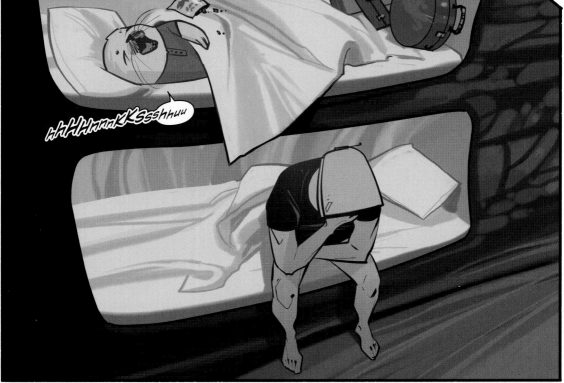

hhHHnnnKKSsshhuu

...bugger.

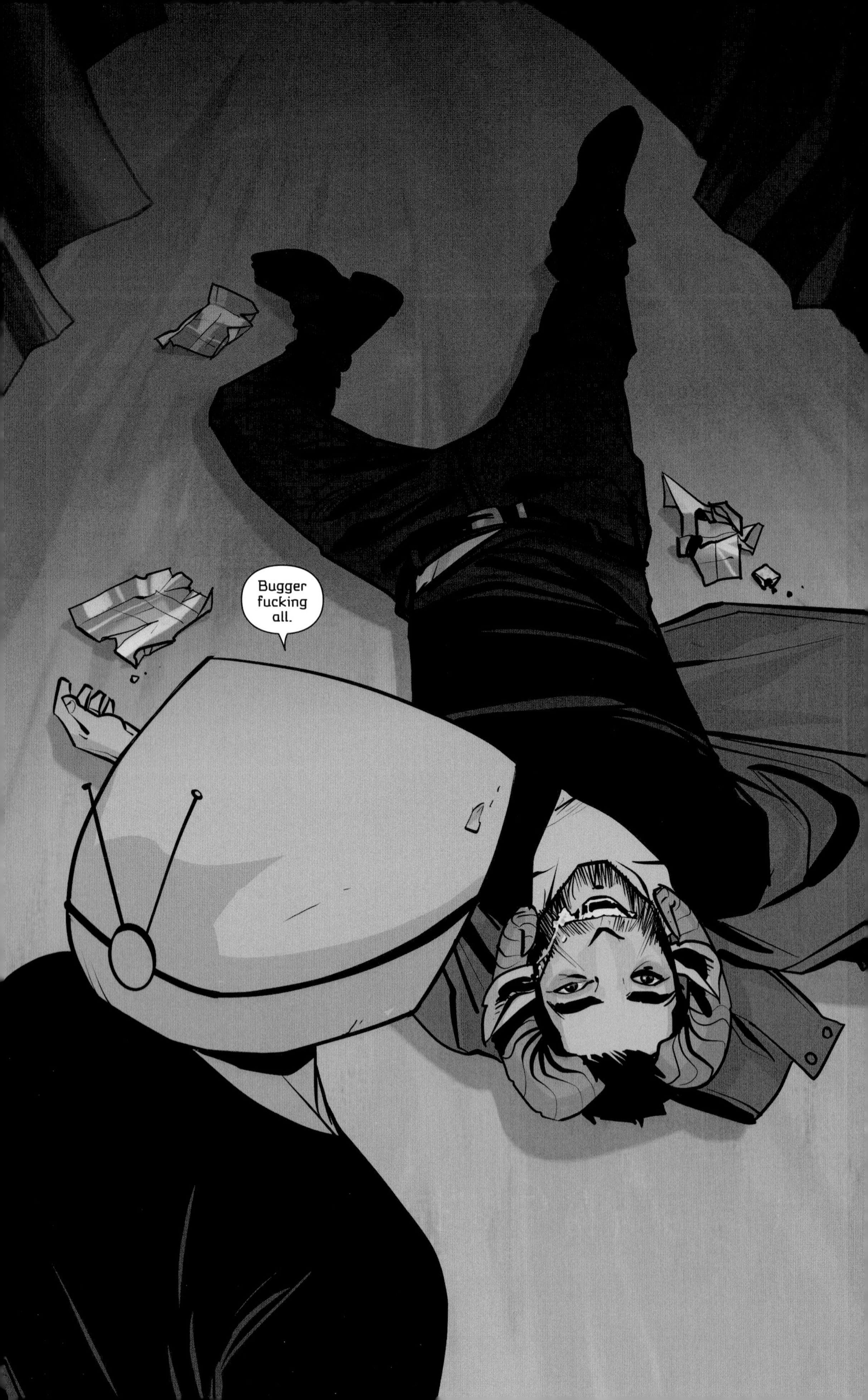
Bugger fucking all.

end chapter twenty-six

CHAPTER
TWENTY-SEVEN

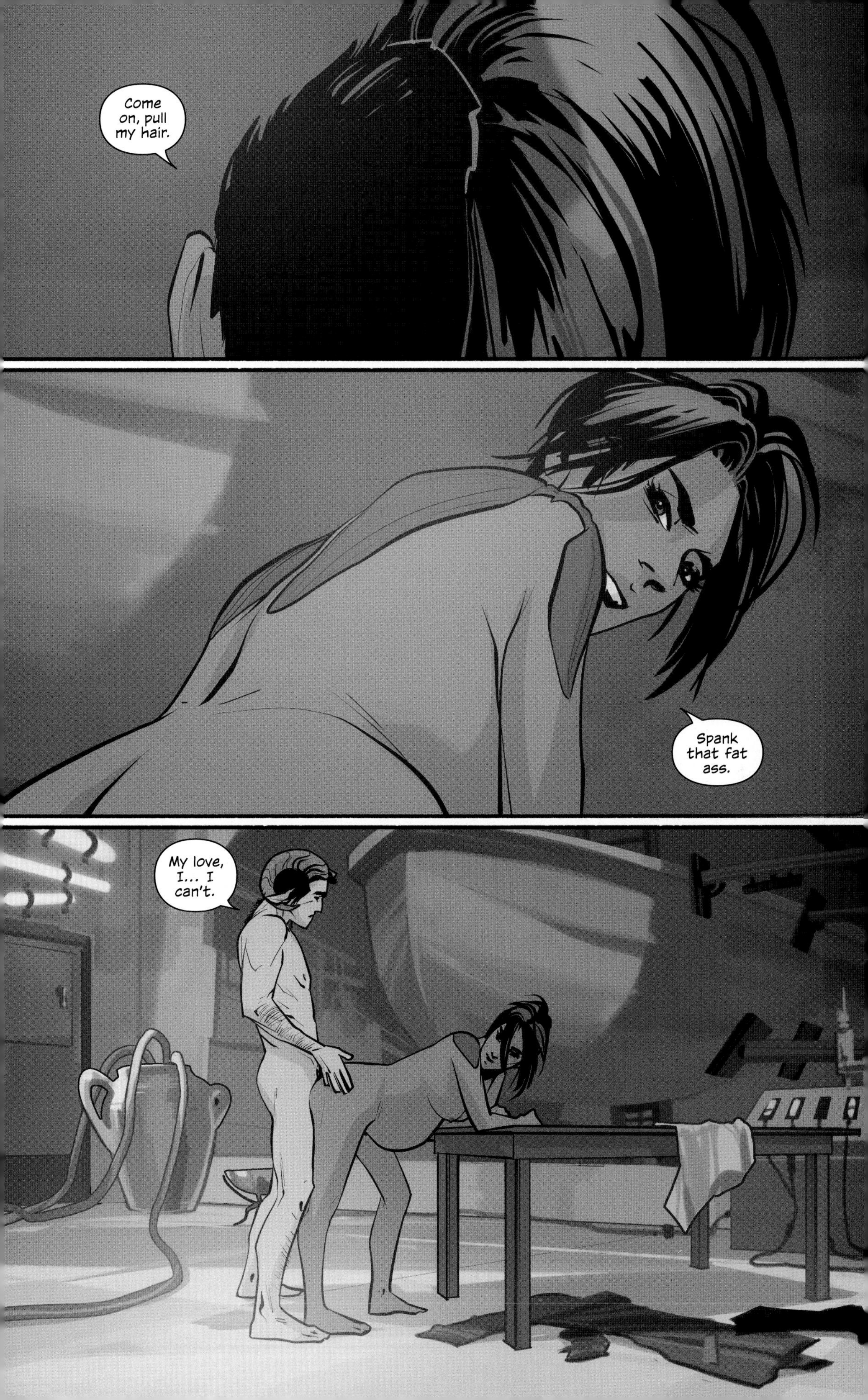
Come on, pull my hair.
Spank that fat ass.
My love, I... I can't.

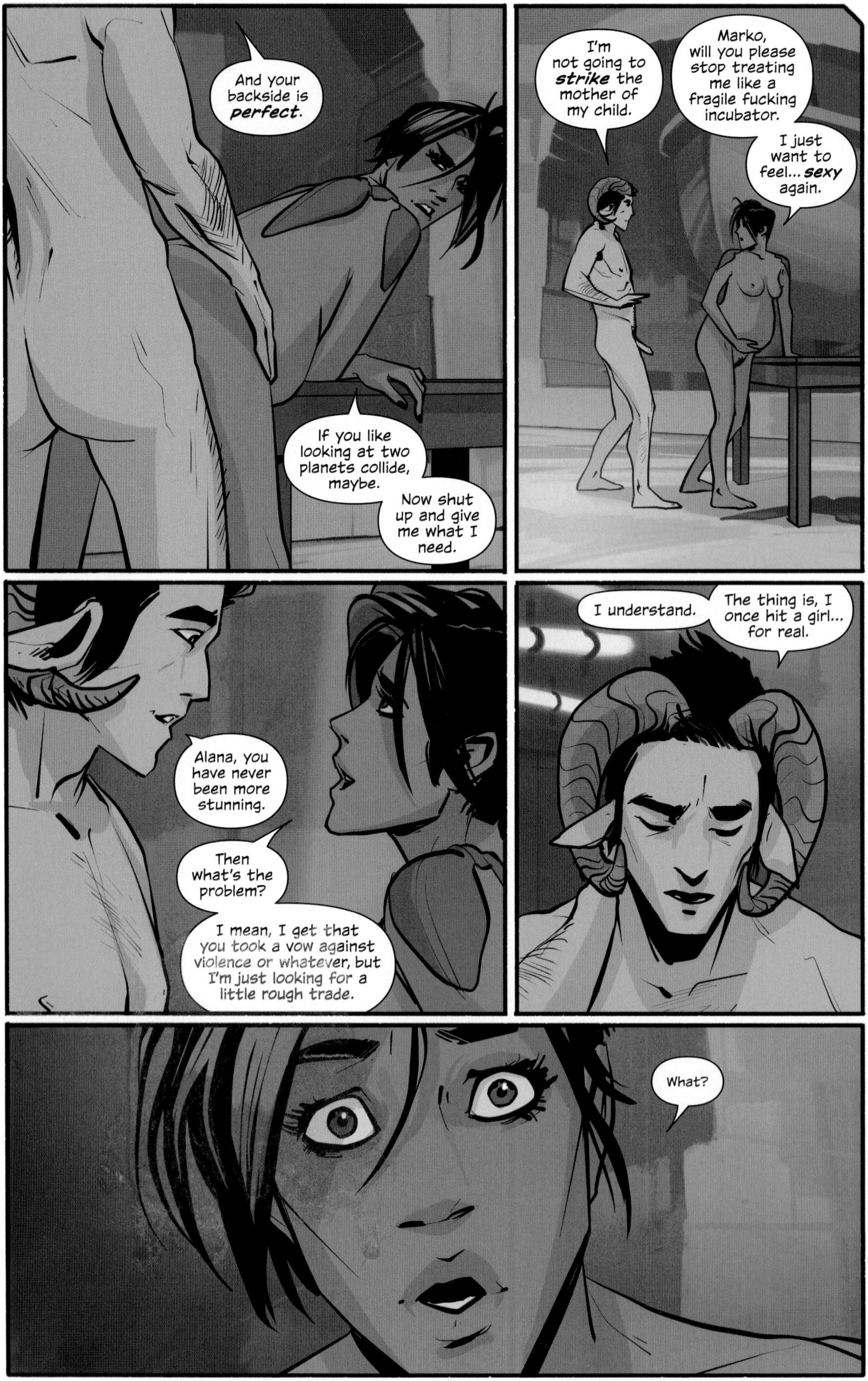
And your backside is *perfect*.
If you like looking at two planets collide, maybe.
Now shut up and give me what I need.
I'm not going to *strike* the mother of my child.
Marko, will you please stop treating me like a fragile fucking incubator.
I just want to feel... *sexy* again.
Alana, you have never been more stunning.
Then what's the problem?
I mean, I get that you took a vow against violence or whatever, but I'm just looking for a little rough trade.
I understand.
The thing is, I once hit a girl... for real.
What?

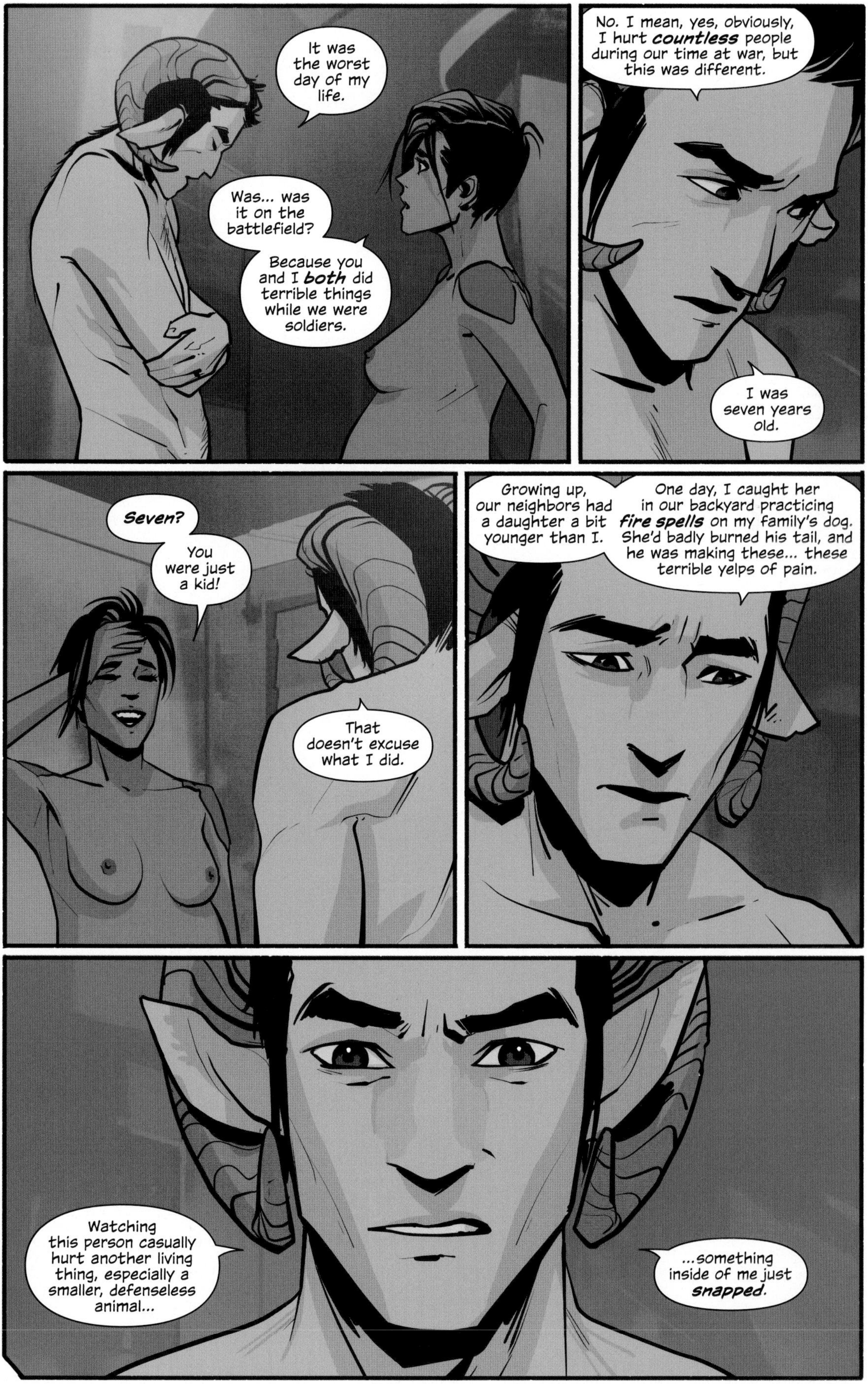
It was the worst day of my life.
Was... was it on the battlefield?
Because you and I both did terrible things while we were soldiers.
No. I mean, yes, obviously, I hurt countless people during our time at war, but this was different.
I was seven years old.
Seven?
You were just a kid!
That doesn't excuse what I did.
Growing up, our neighbors had a daughter a bit younger than I.
One day, I caught her in our backyard practicing fire spells on my family's dog. She'd badly burned his tail, and he was making these... these terrible yelps of pain.
Watching this person casually hurt another living thing, especially a smaller, defenseless animal...
...something inside of me just snapped.

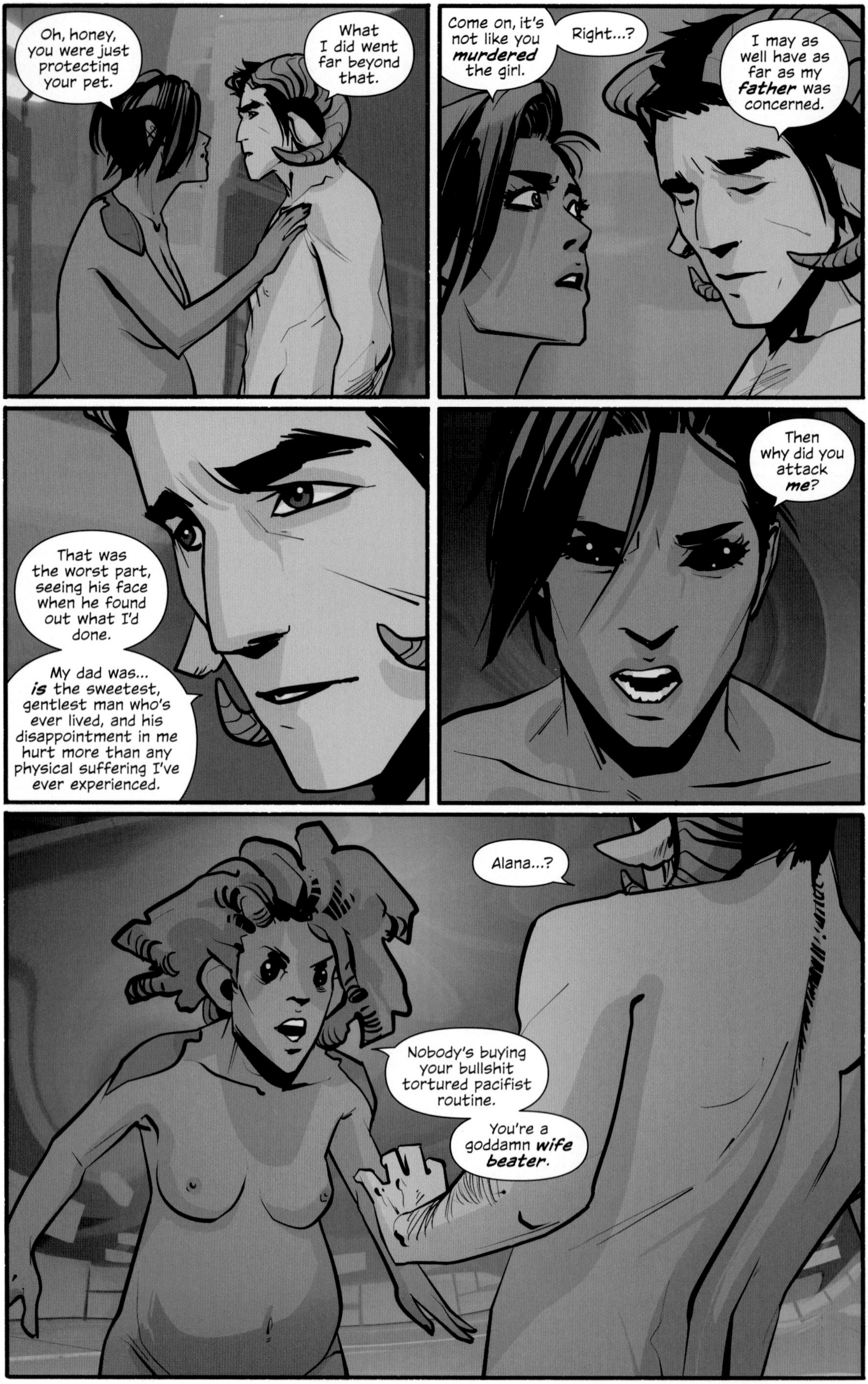
Oh, honey, you were just protecting your pet.
What I did went far beyond that.
Come on, it's not like you *murdered* the girl.
Right...?
I may as well have as far as my *father* was concerned.
That was the worst part, seeing his face when he found out what I'd done.
My dad was... *is* the sweetest, gentlest man who's ever lived, and his disappointment in me hurt more than any physical suffering I've ever experienced.
Then why did you attack *me*?
Alana...?
Nobody's buying your bullshit tortured pacifist routine.
You're a goddamn *wife beater*.

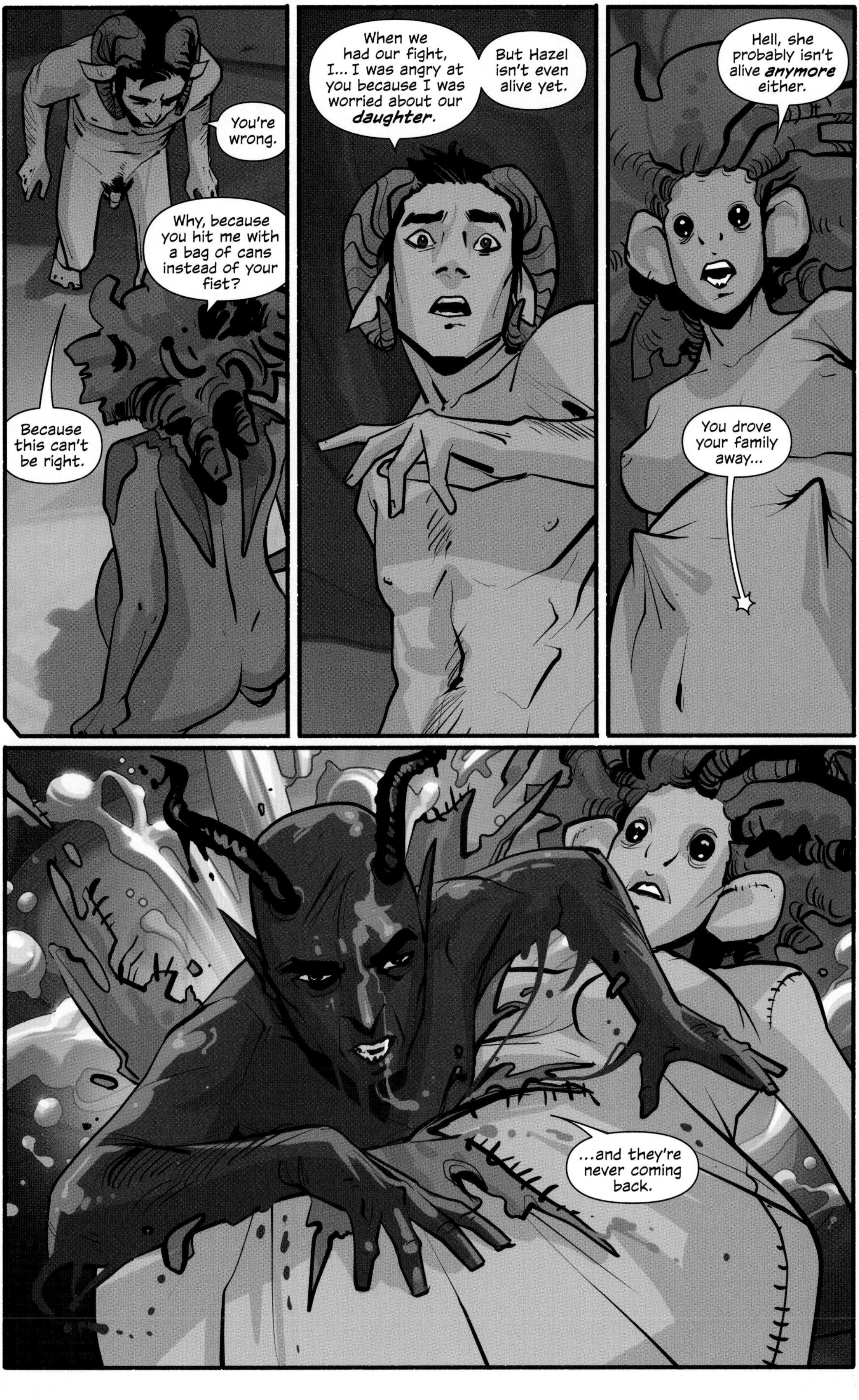
You're wrong.
Why, because you hit me with a bag of cans instead of your fist?
Because this can't be right.
When we had our fight, I... I was angry at you because I was worried about our *daughter*.
But Hazel isn't even alive yet.
Hell, she probably isn't alive *anymore* either.
You drove your family away...
...and they're never coming back.

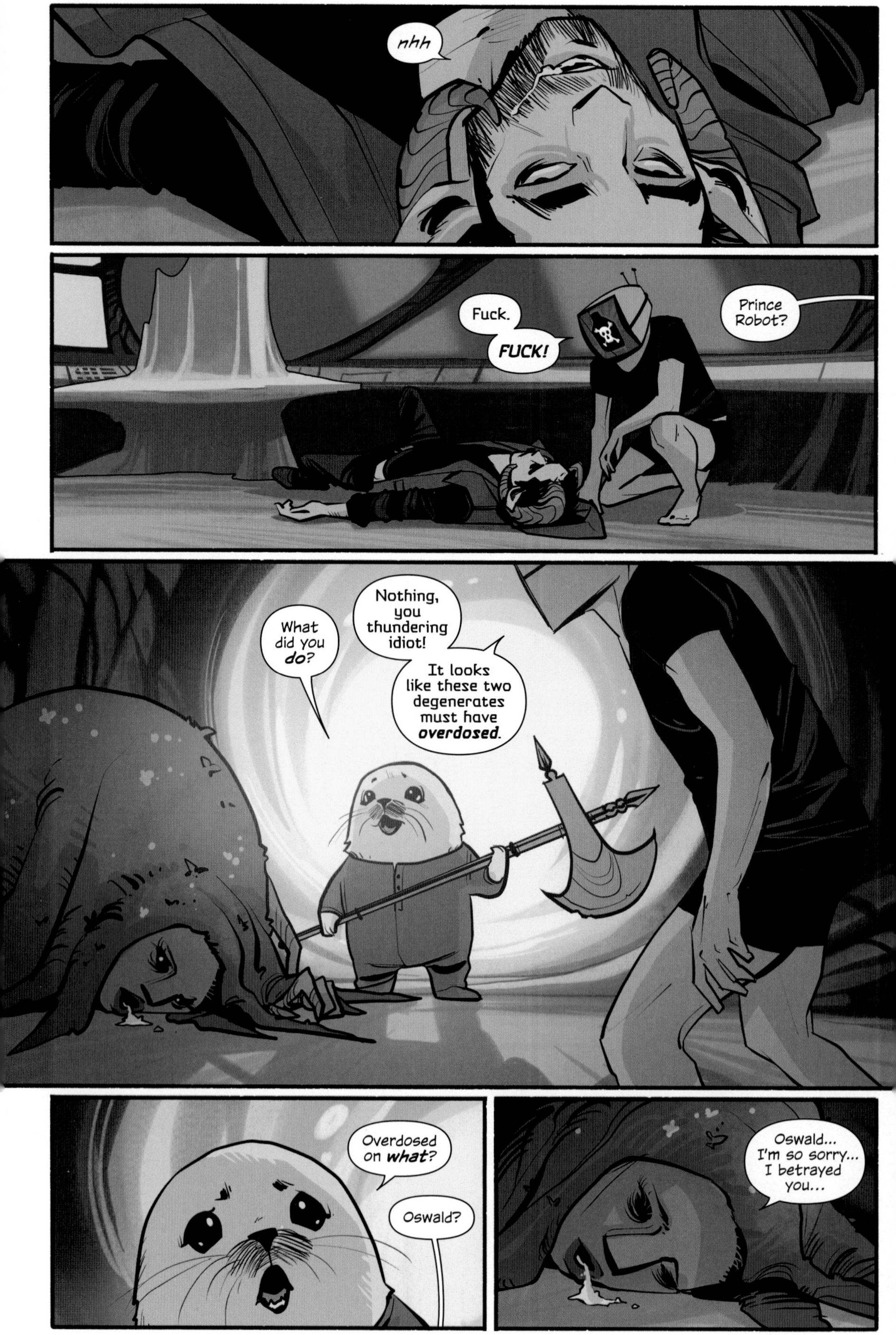
nhh
Fuck.
FUCK!
Prince Robot?
What did you do?
Nothing, you thundering idiot!
It looks like these two degenerates must have overdosed.
Overdosed on what?
Oswald?
Oswald... I'm so sorry... I betrayed you...

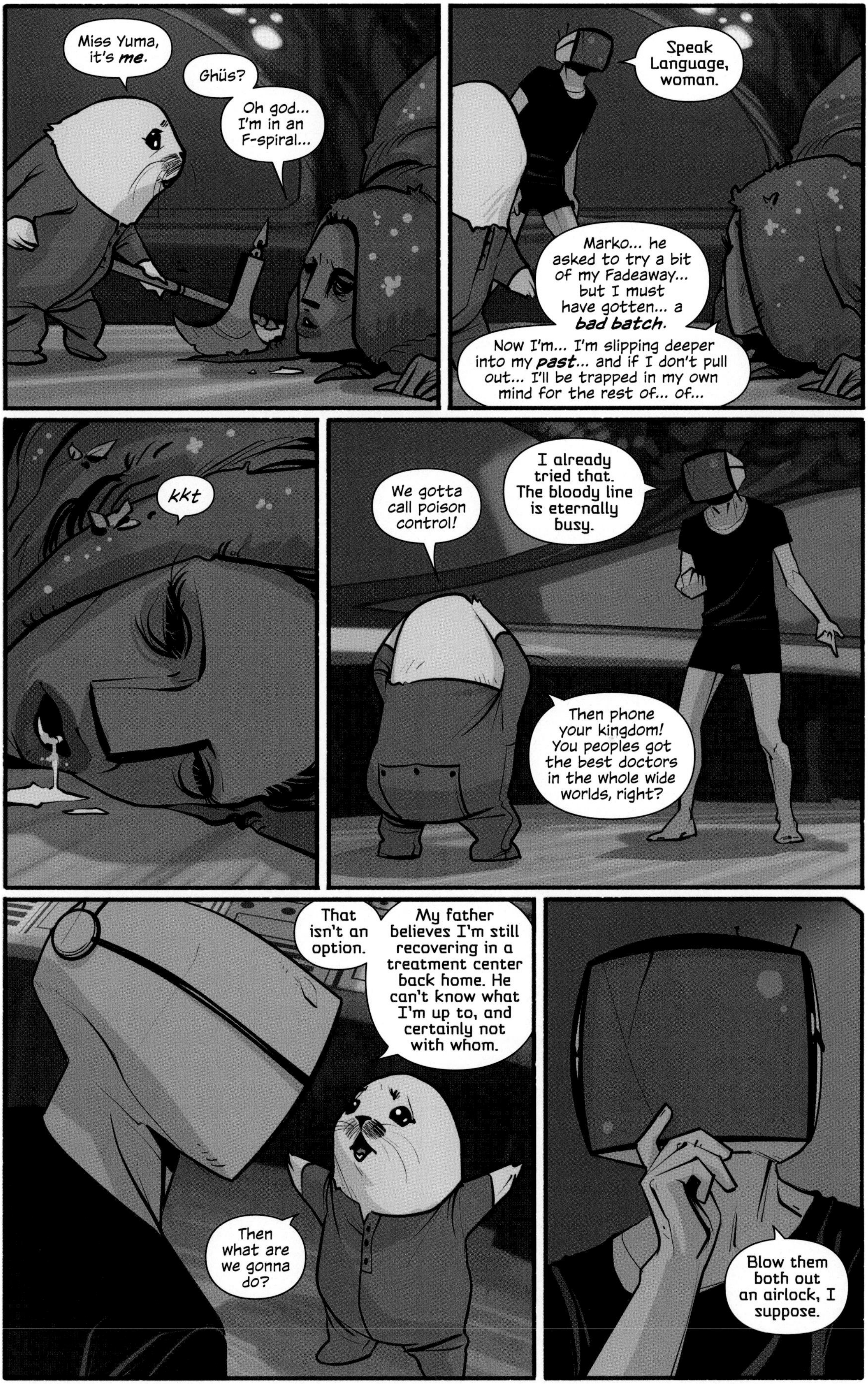
Miss Yuma, it's *me*.
Ghüs?
Oh god... I'm in an F-spiral...
Speak Language, woman.
Marko... he asked to try a bit of my Fadeaway... but I must have gotten... a ***bad batch***.
Now I'm... I'm slipping deeper into my ***past***... and if I don't pull out... I'll be trapped in my own mind for the rest of... of...
kkt
We gotta call poison control!
I already tried that. The bloody line is eternally busy.
Then phone your kingdom! You peoples got the best doctors in the whole wide worlds, right?
That isn't an option.
My father believes I'm still recovering in a treatment center back home. He can't know what I'm up to, and certainly not with whom.
Then what are we gonna do?
Blow them both out an airlock, I suppose.

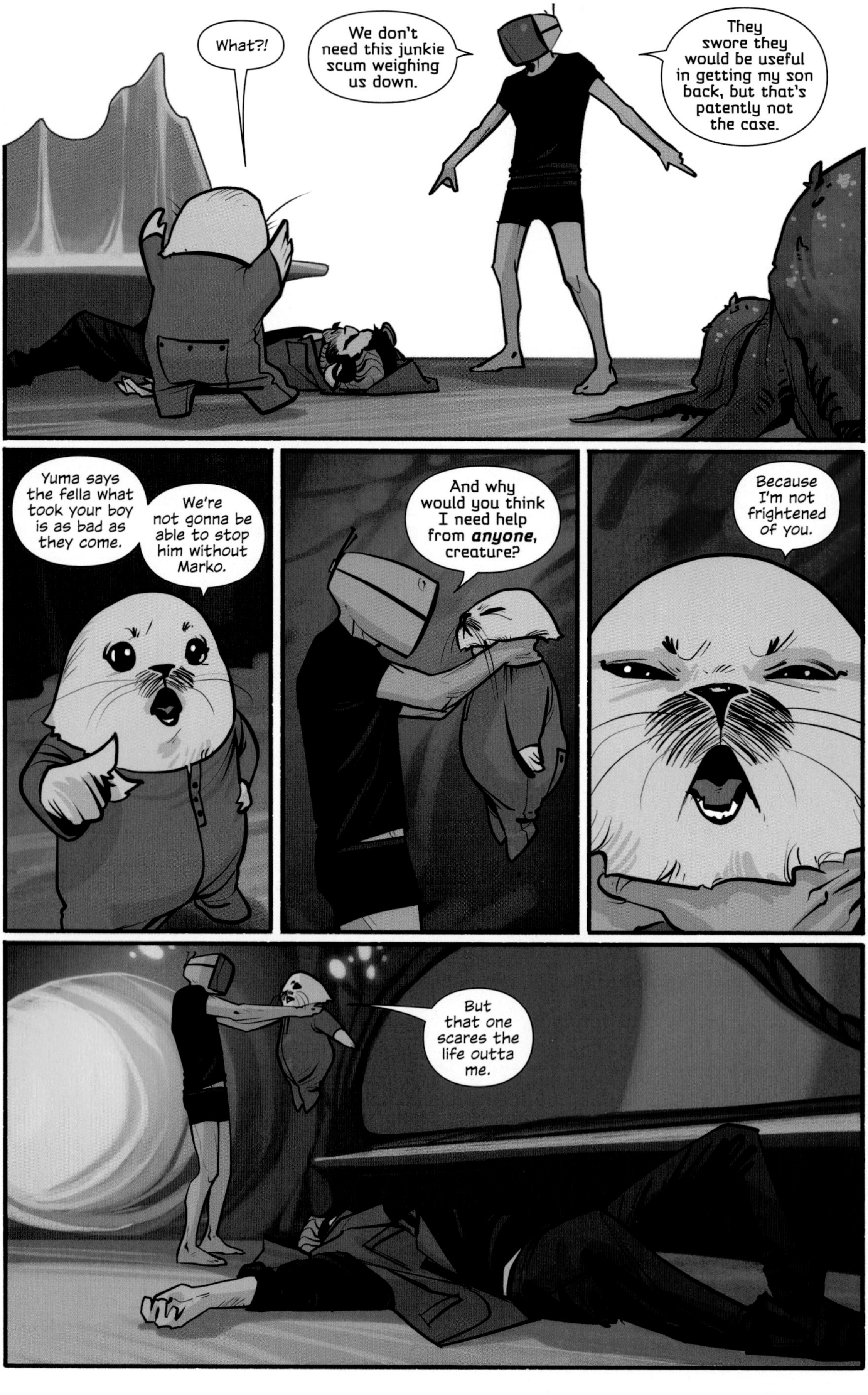
What?!
We don't need this junkie scum weighing us down.
They swore they would be useful in getting my son back, but that's patently not the case.
Yuma says the fella what took your boy is as bad as they come.
We're not gonna be able to stop him without Marko.
And why would you think I need help from **anyone**, creature?
Because I'm not frightened of you.
But that one scares the life outta me.

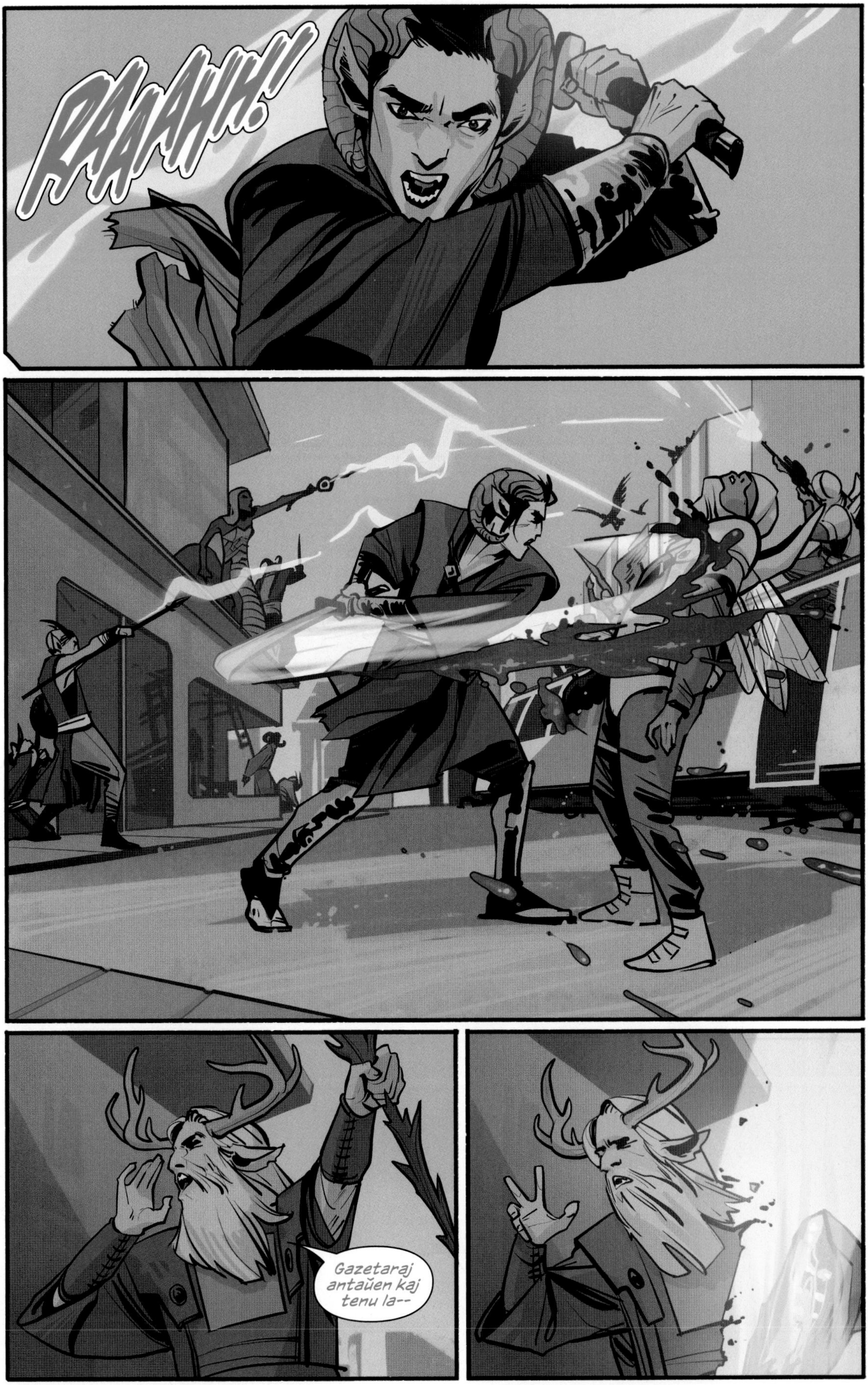
RAAAHH!!
Gazetaraj antaŭen kaj tenu la--

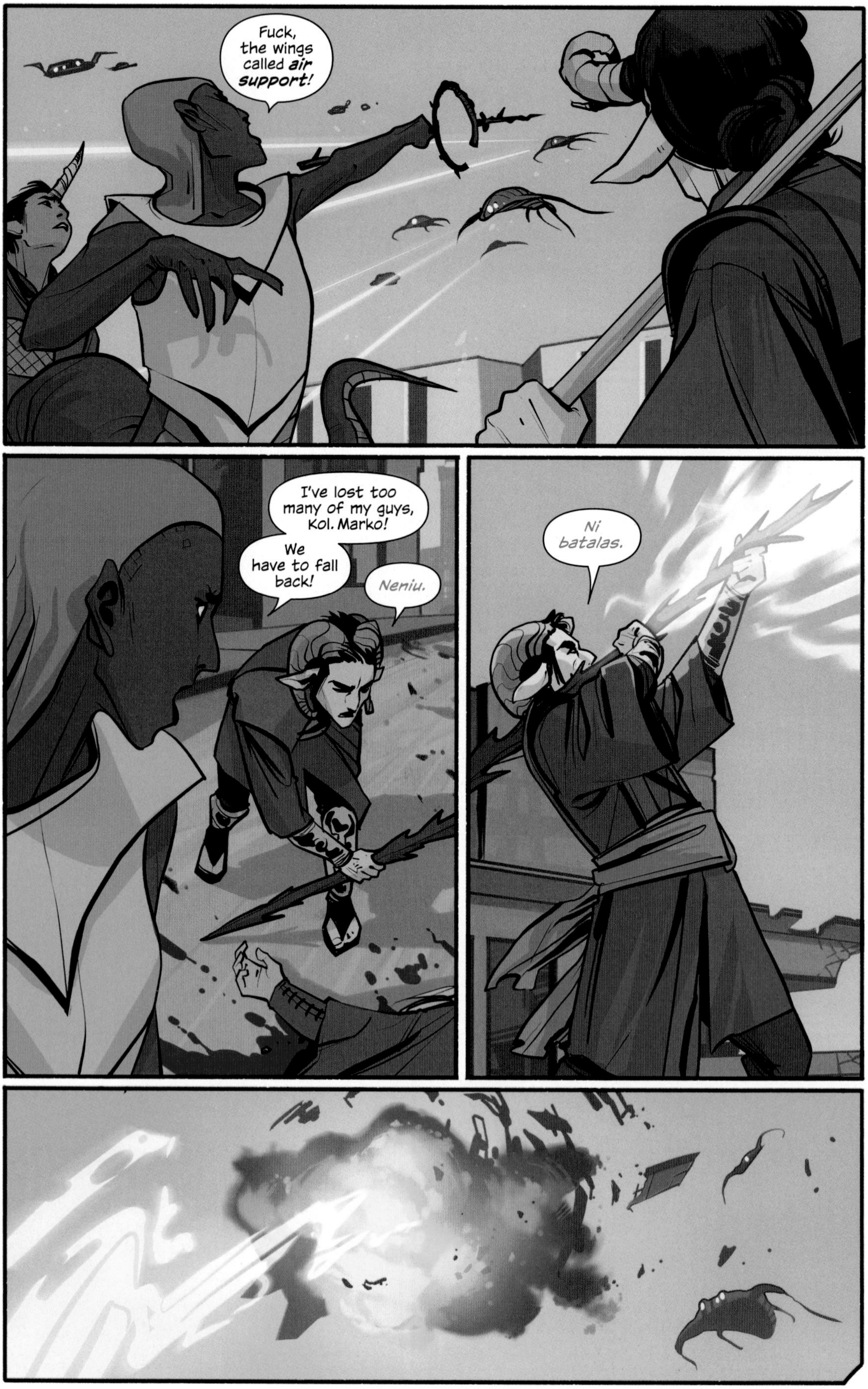

Fuck, the wings called *air support!*
I've lost too many of my guys, Kol. Marko!
We have to fall back!
Neniu.
Ni batalas.

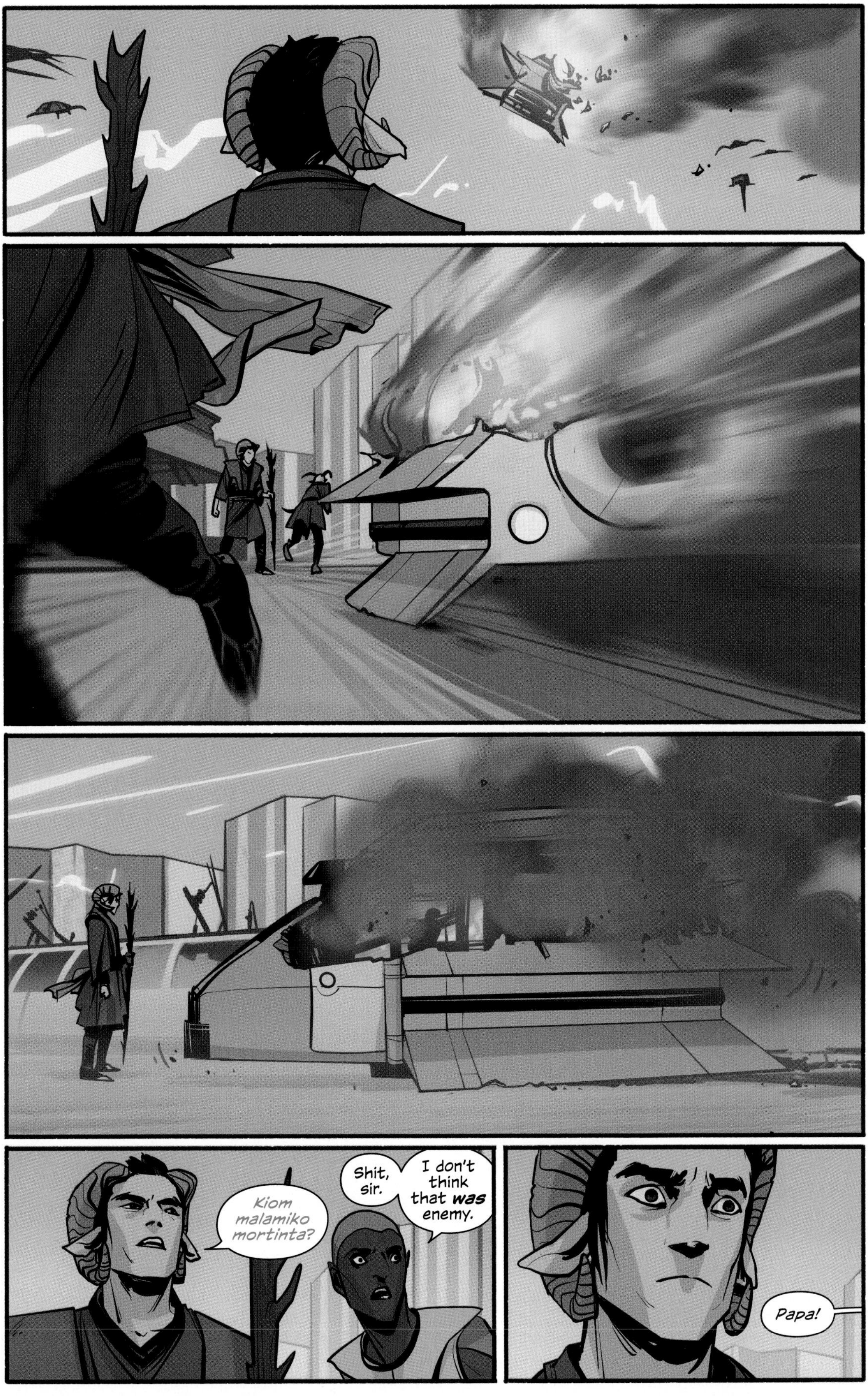
Kiom malamiko mortinta?
Shit, sir.
I don't think that **was** enemy.
Papa!

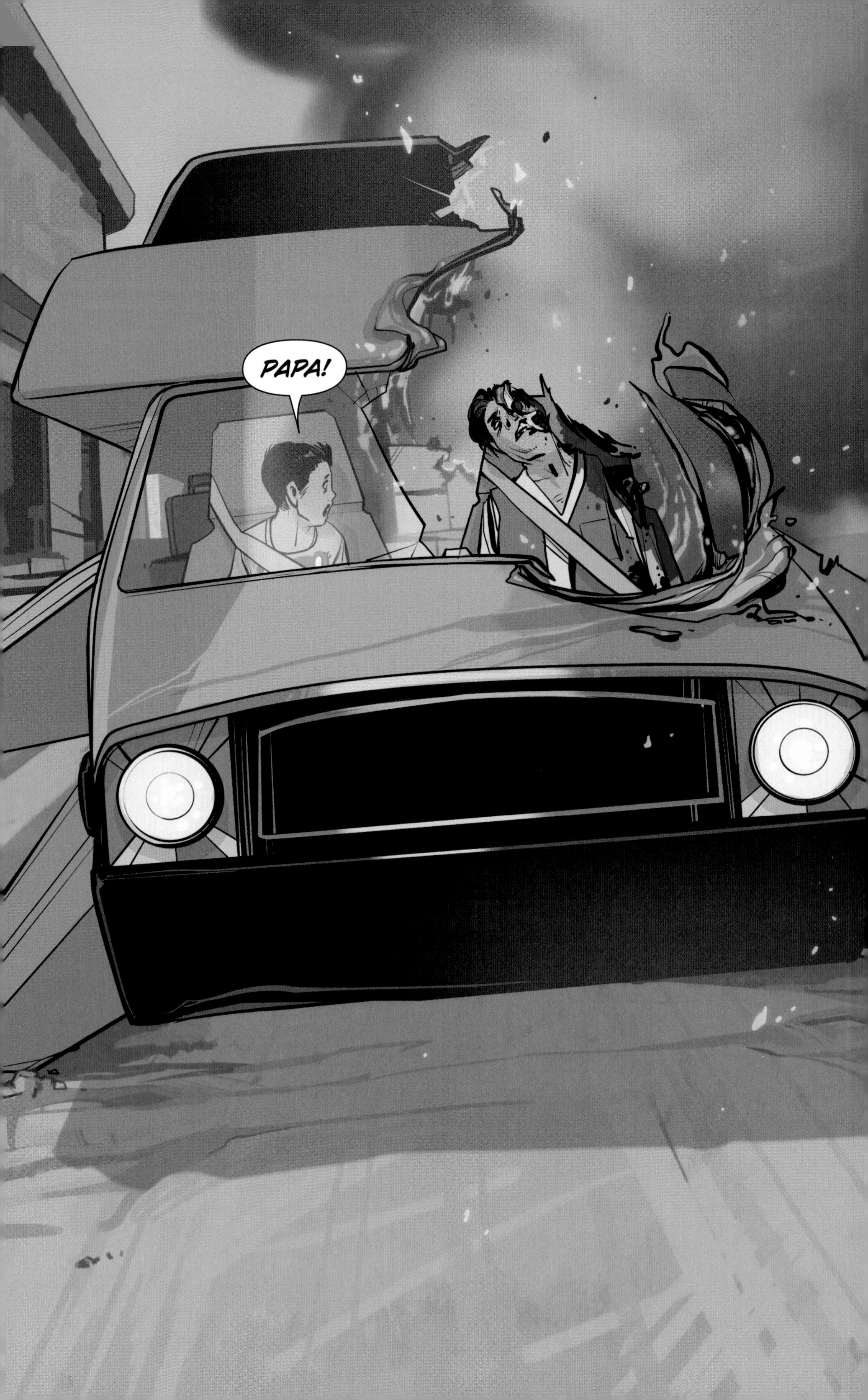
PAPA!

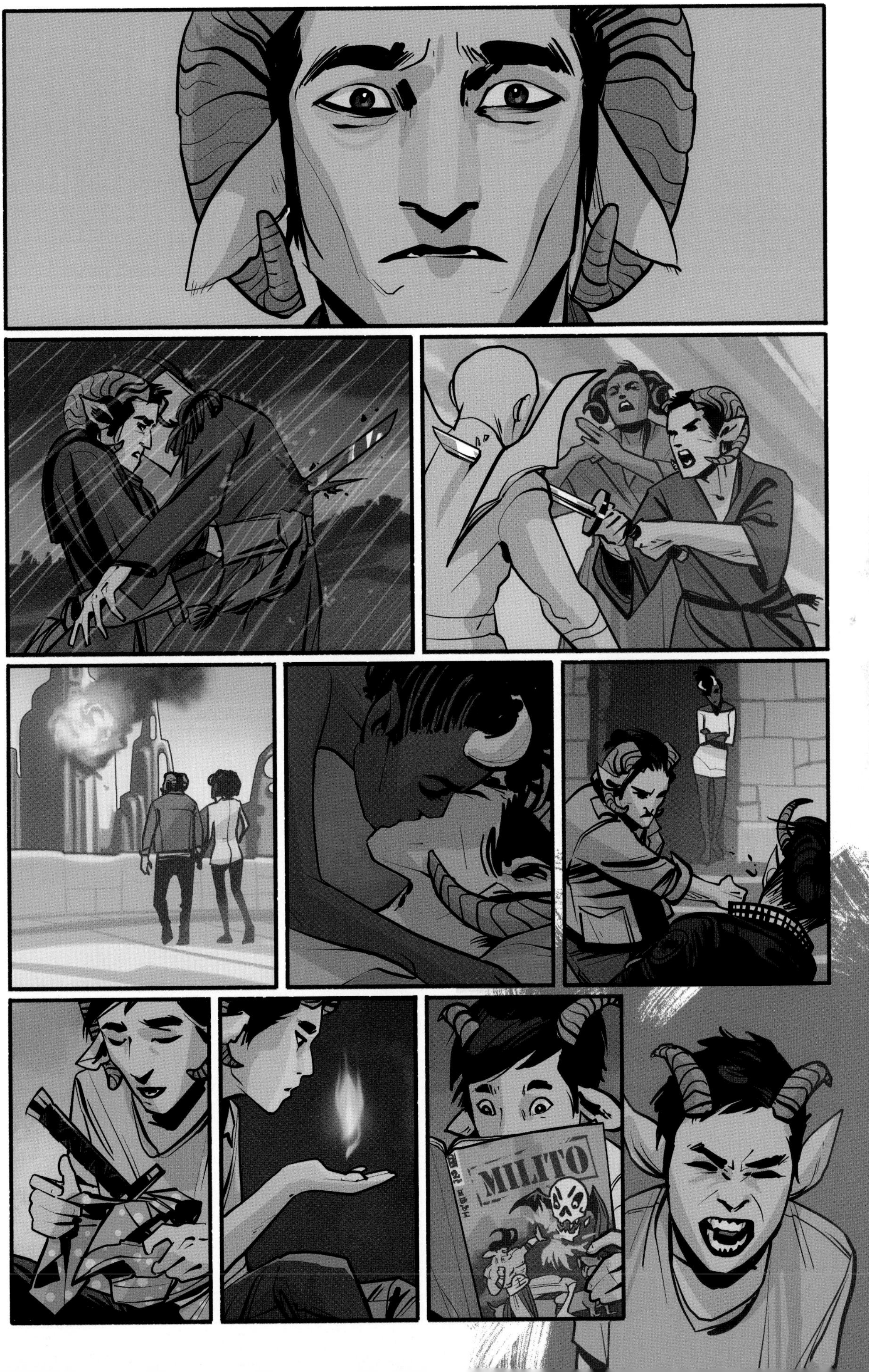
MILITO

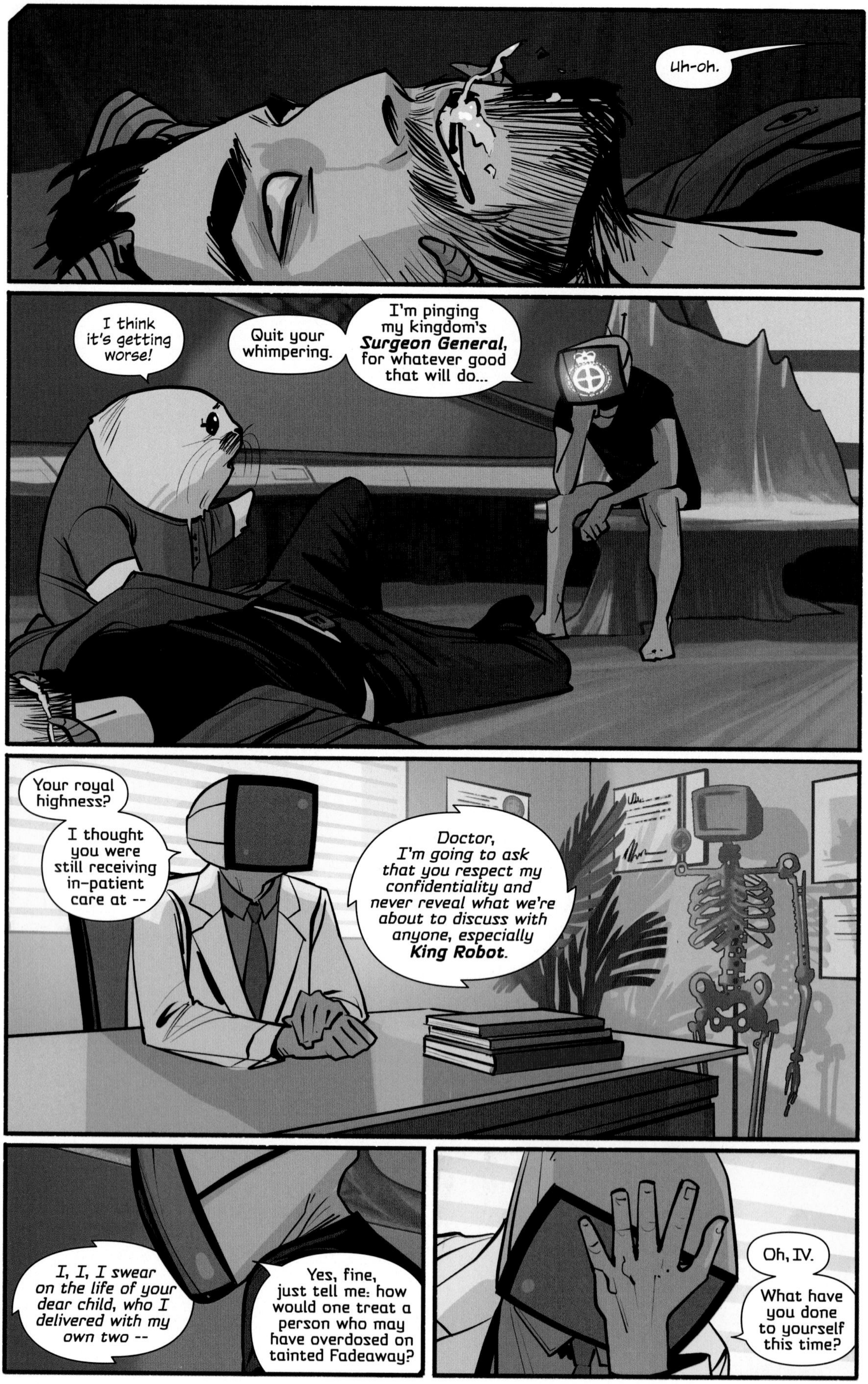
Uh-oh.
I think it's getting worse!
Quit your whimpering.
I'm pinging my kingdom's **Surgeon General**, for whatever good that will do...
Your royal highness?
I thought you were still receiving in-patient care at --
*Doctor, I'm going to ask that you respect my confidentiality and never reveal what we're about to discuss with anyone, especially **King Robot**.*
I, I, I swear on the life of your dear child, who I delivered with my own two --
Yes, fine, just tell me: how would one treat a person who may have overdosed on tainted Fadeaway?
Oh, IV.
What have you done to yourself this time?

This isn't about me, it's for two... acquaintances.

Fellow robots?

Quite the opposite, I would say.

You're not back on **Sextillion**, are you?

Son, I've seen men come back from that place with some of the most virulent anal warts in the --

Doctor, for the love of fuck, just tell me what I'm supposed to do.

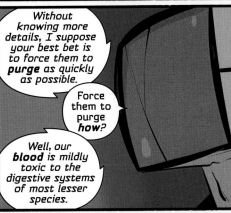

Without knowing more details, I suppose your best bet is to force them to **purge** as quickly as possible.

Force them to purge **how**?

Well, our **blood** is mildly toxic to the digestive systems of most lesser species.

Huh.

You don't say.

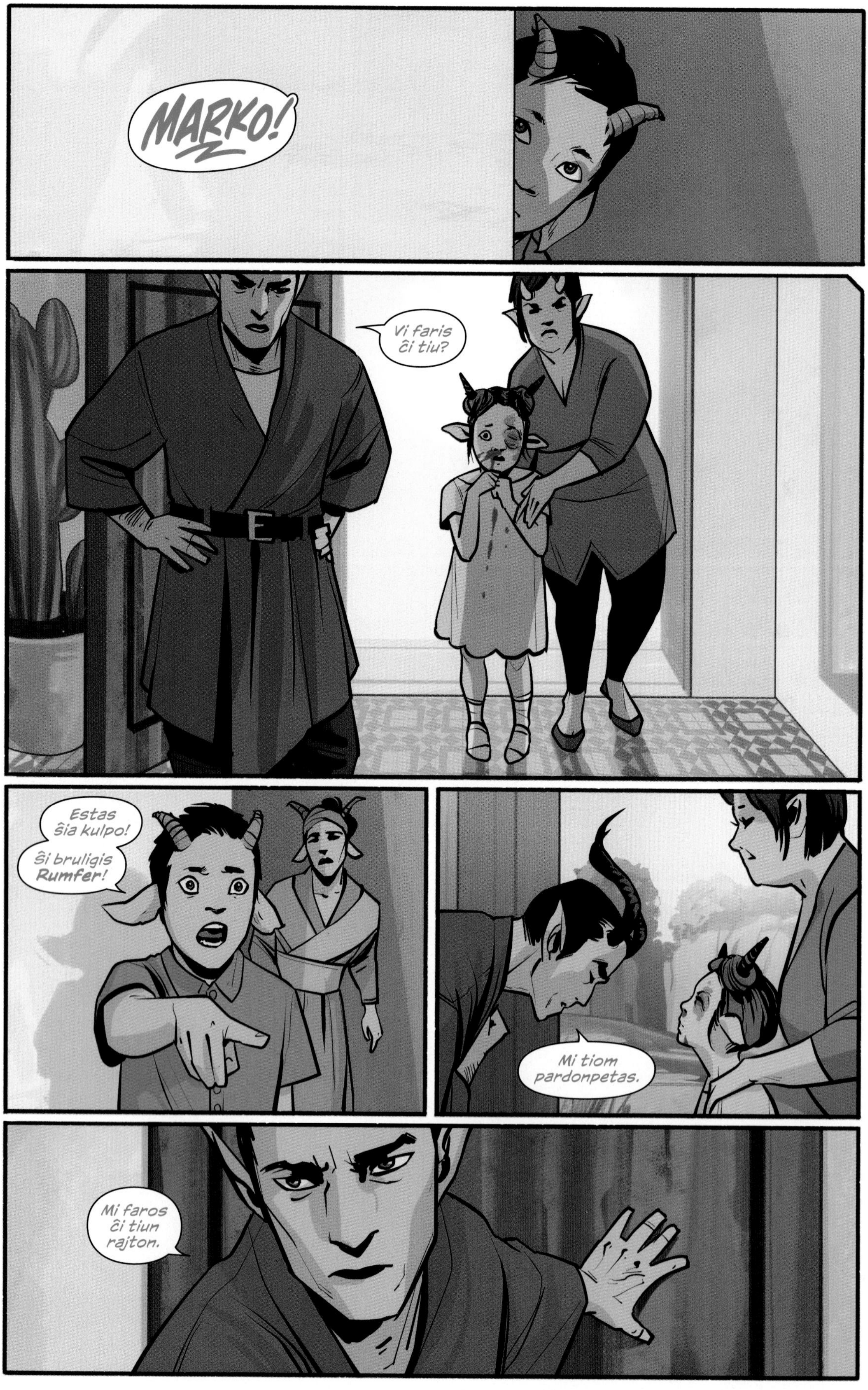
MARKO!
Vi faris ĉi tiu?
Estas ŝia kulpo!
Ŝi bruligis Rumfer!
Mi tiom pardonpetas.
Mi faros ĉi tiun rajton.

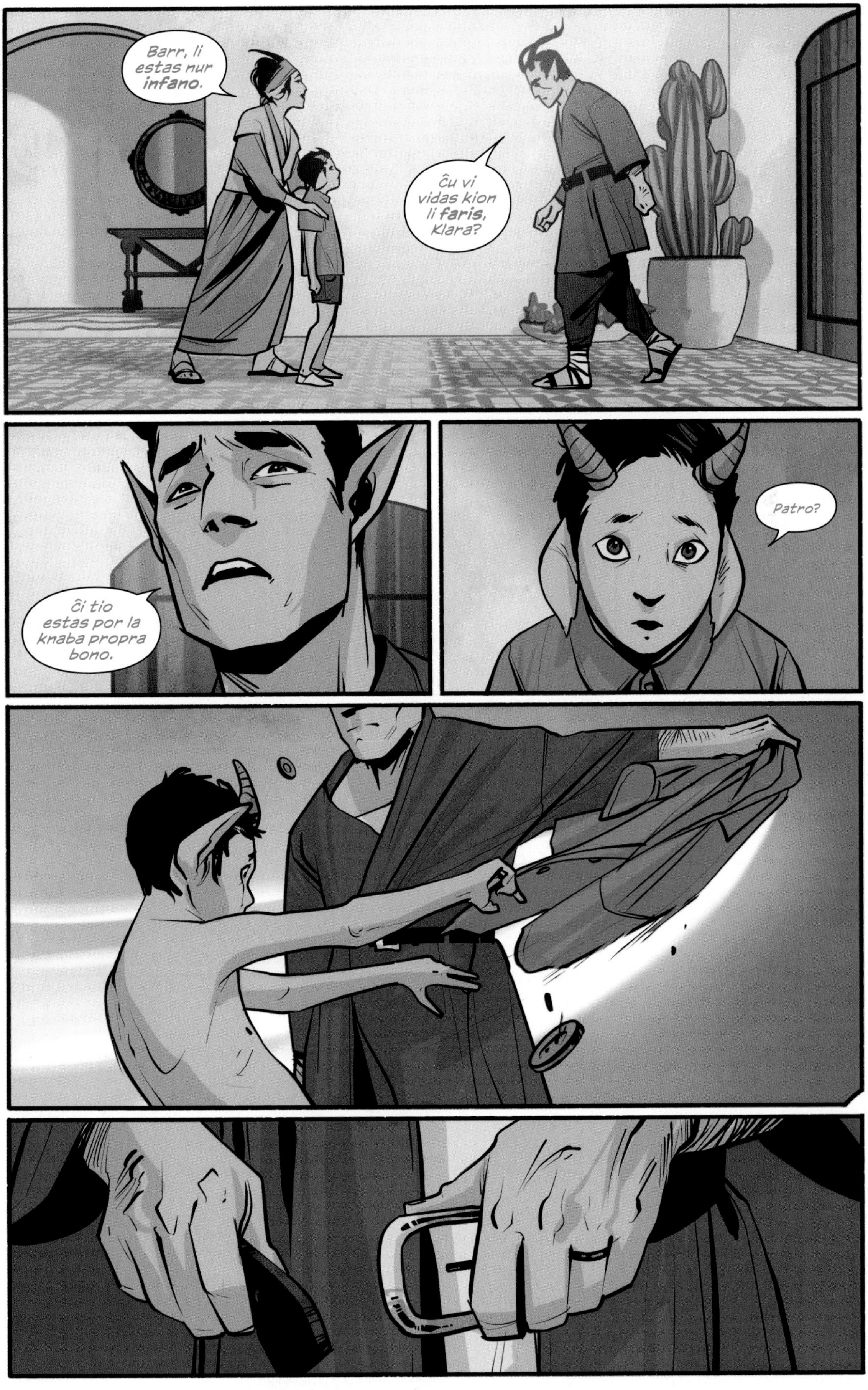
Barr, li estas nur **infano**.
Ĉu vi vidas kion li **faris**, Klara?
Ĉi tio estas por la knaba propra bono.
Patro?

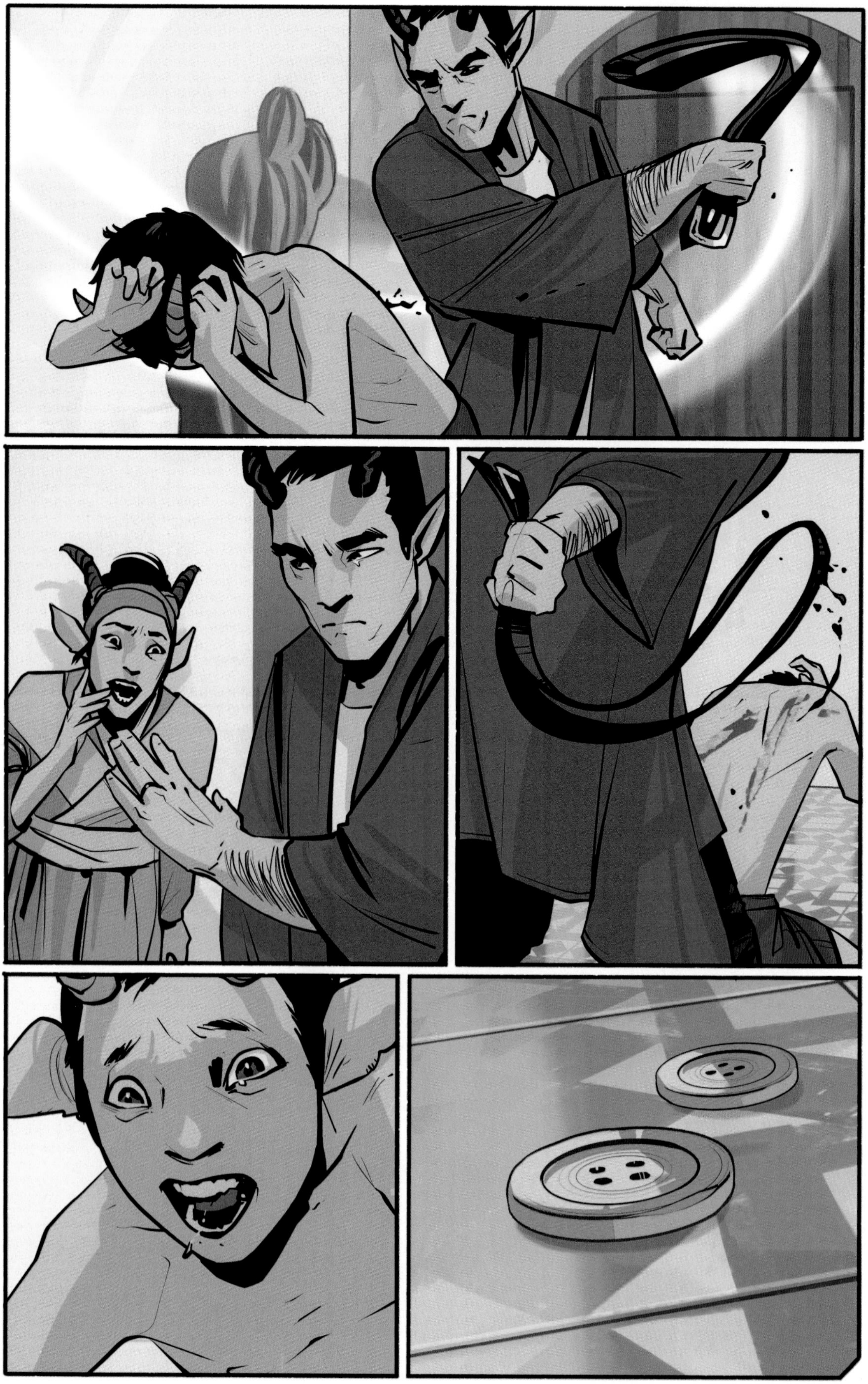

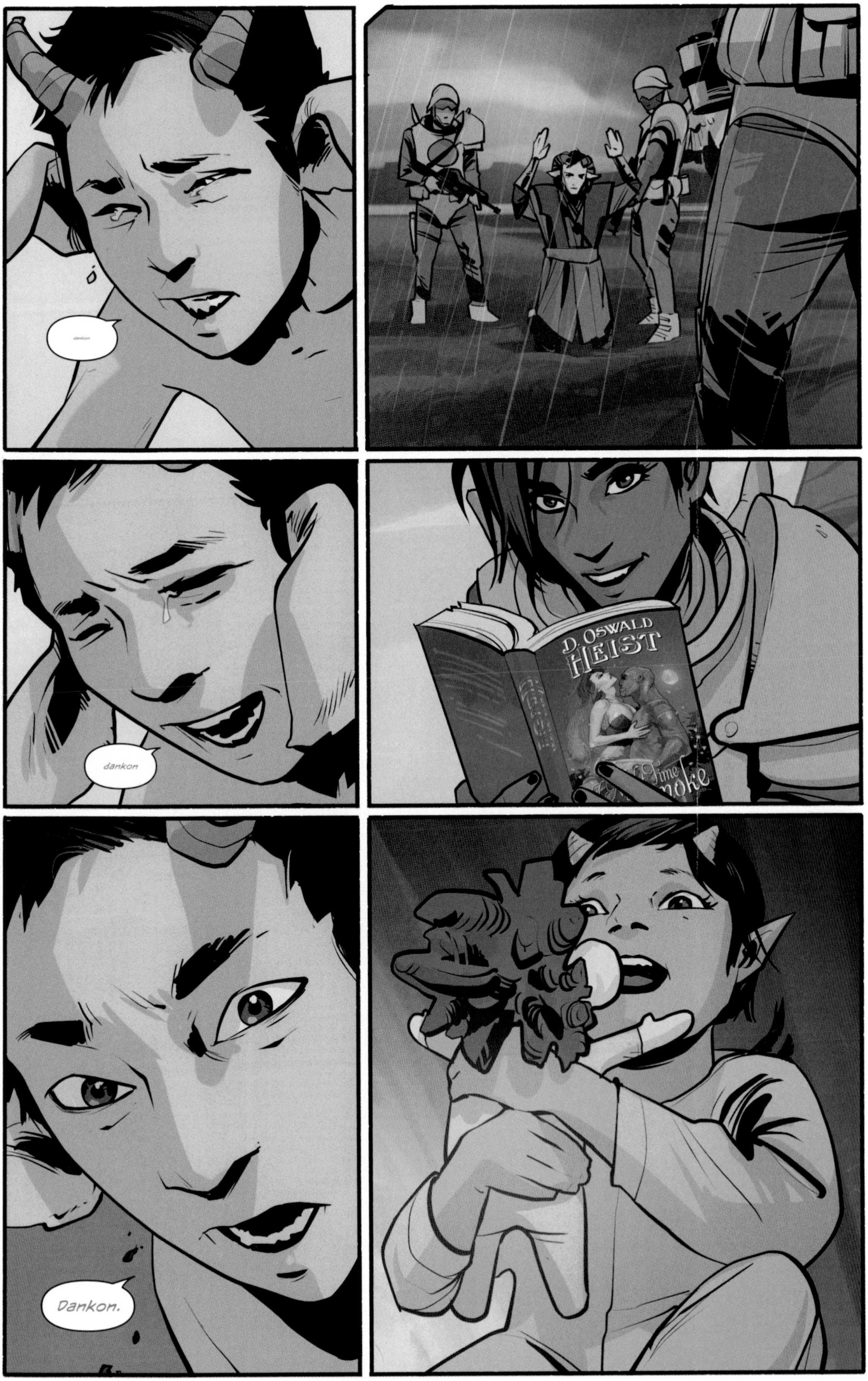
dankon
dankon
D. OSWALD
HEIST
Dankon.

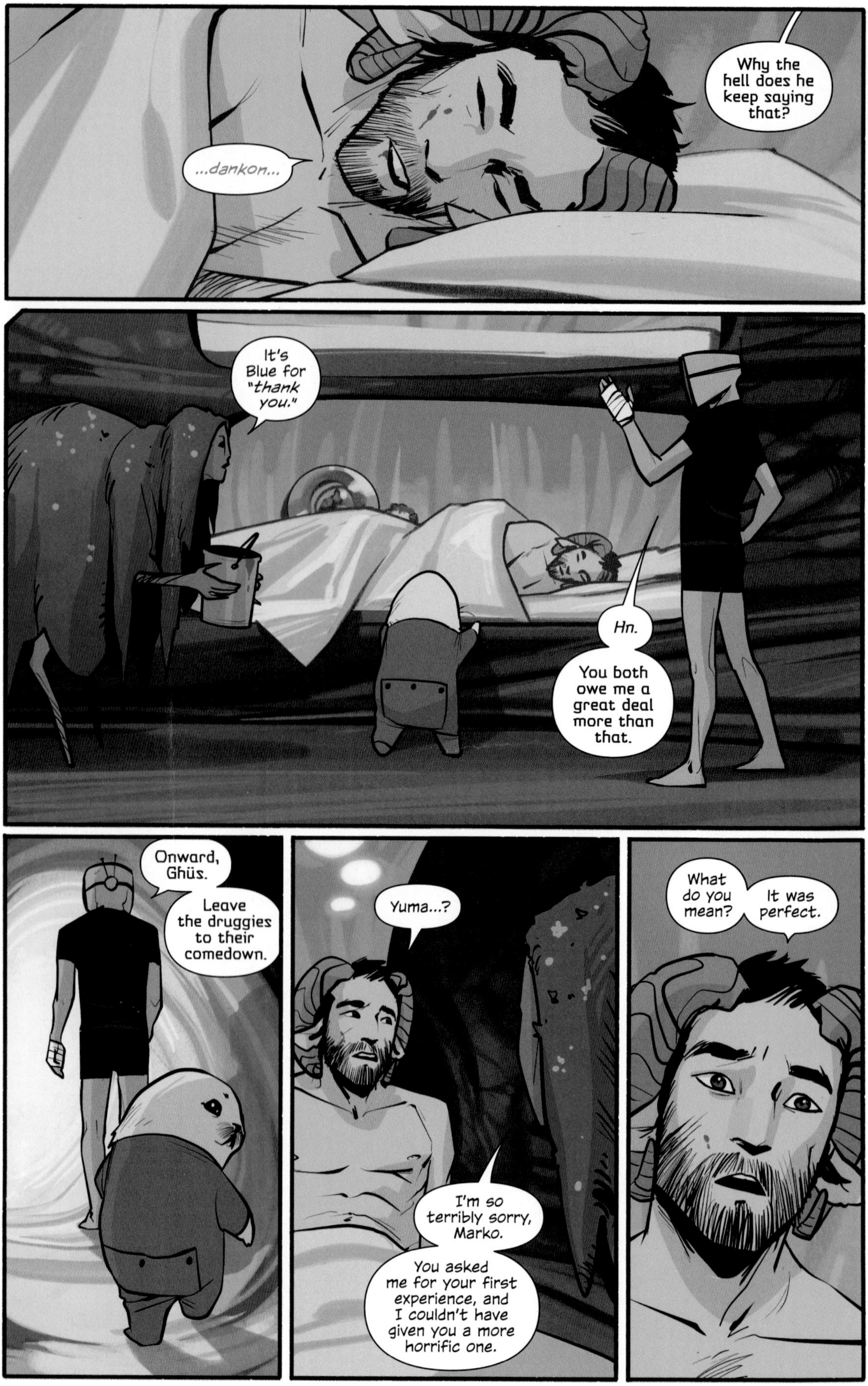
...dankon...
Why the hell does he keep saying that?
It's Blue for "thank you."
Hn.
You both owe me a great deal more than that.
Onward, Ghüs.
Leave the druggies to their comedown.
Yuma...?
I'm so terribly sorry, Marko.
You asked me for your first experience, and I couldn't have given you a more horrific one.
What do you mean?
It was perfect.

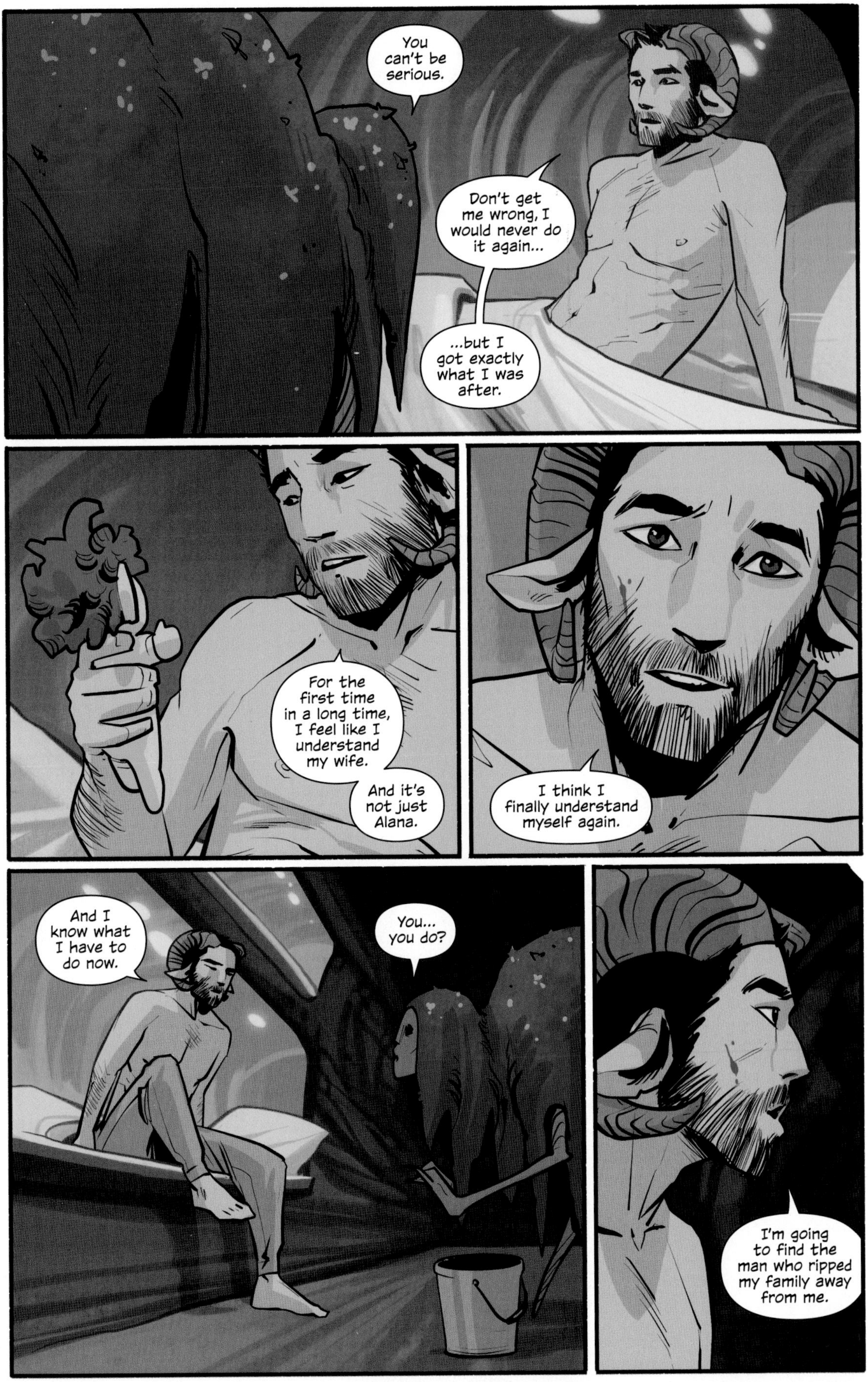
You can't be serious.
Don't get me wrong, I would never do it again...
...but I got exactly what I was after.
For the first time in a long time, I feel like I understand my wife.
And it's not just Alana.
I think I finally understand myself again.
And I know what I have to do now.
You... you do?
I'm going to find the man who ripped my family away from me.

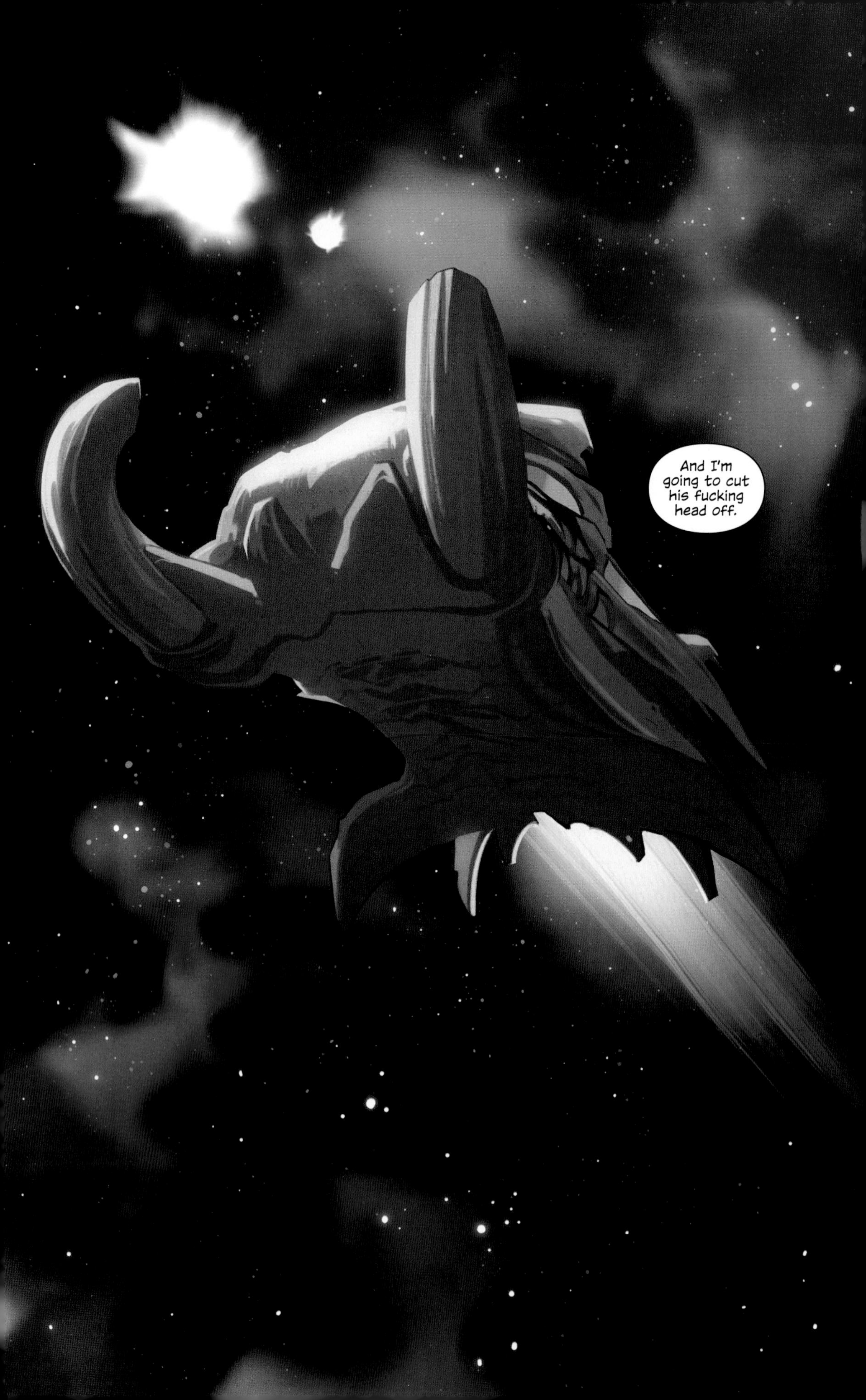
And I'm going to cut his fucking head off.

end chapter twenty-seven

CHAPTER
TWENTY-EIGHT

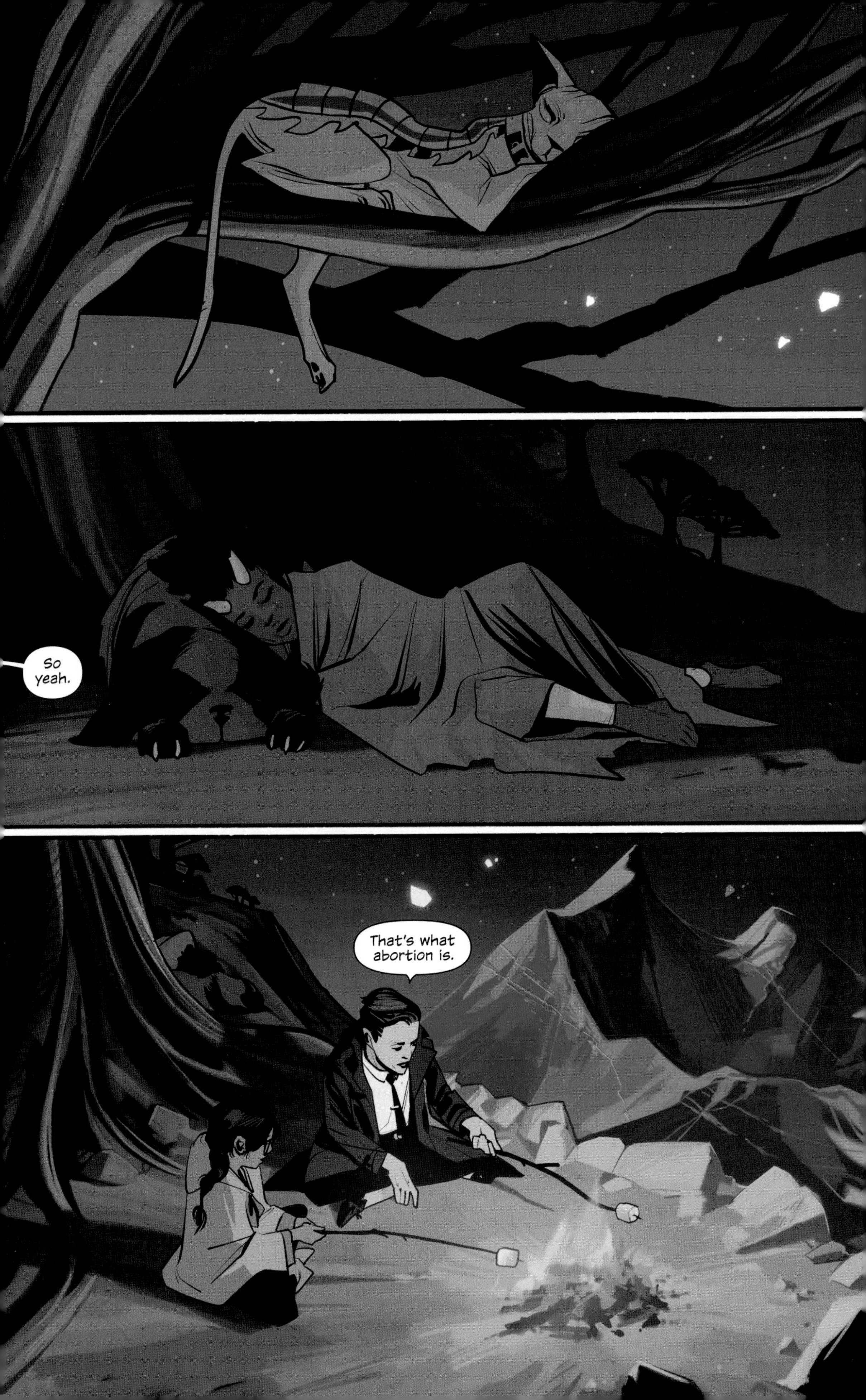
So yeah.
That's what abortion is.

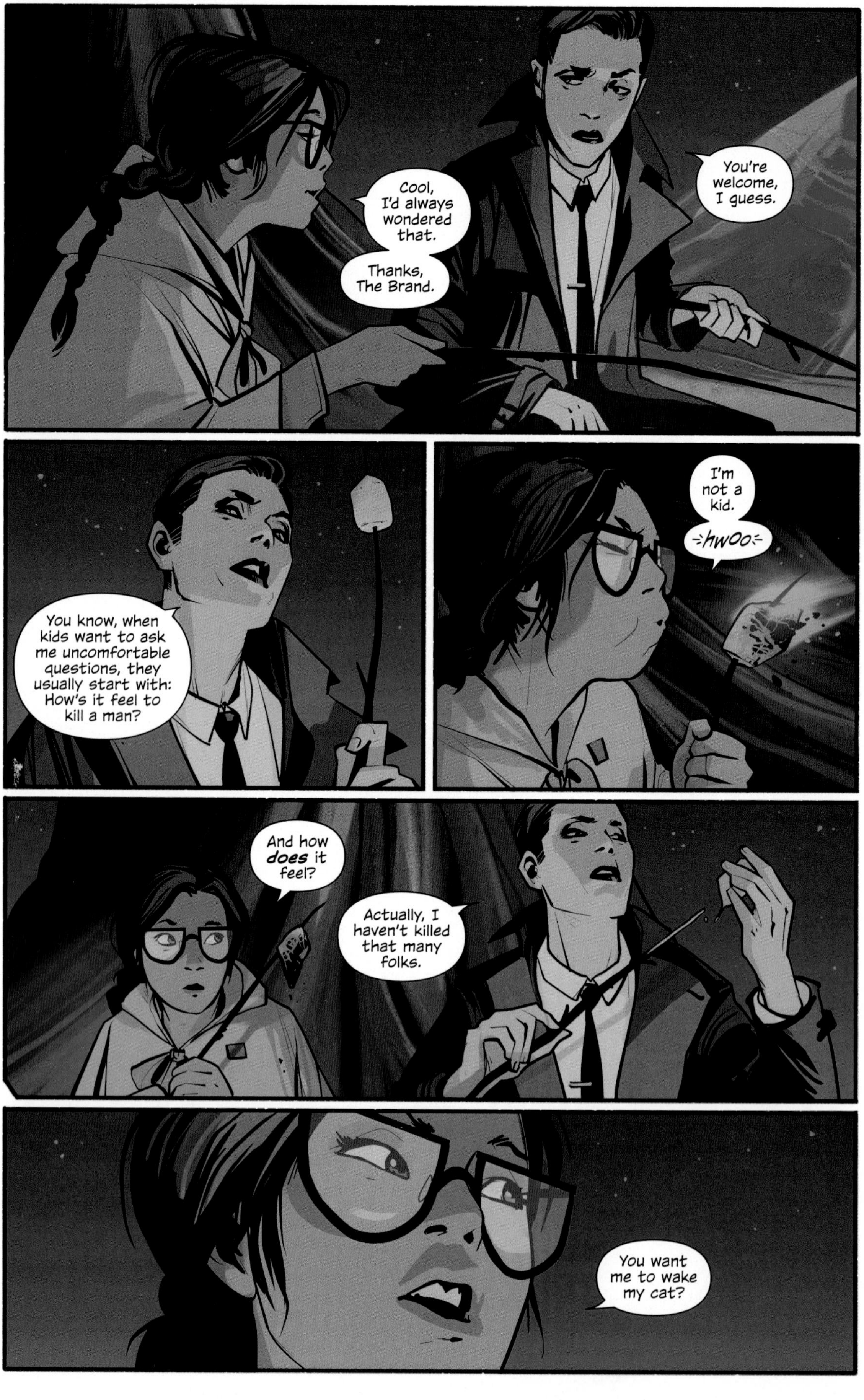
Cool, I'd always wondered that.
Thanks, The Brand.
You're welcome, I guess.
You know, when kids want to ask me uncomfortable questions, they usually start with: How's it feel to kill a man?
I'm not a kid.
hwoo
And how **does** it feel?
Actually, I haven't killed that many folks.
You want me to wake my cat?

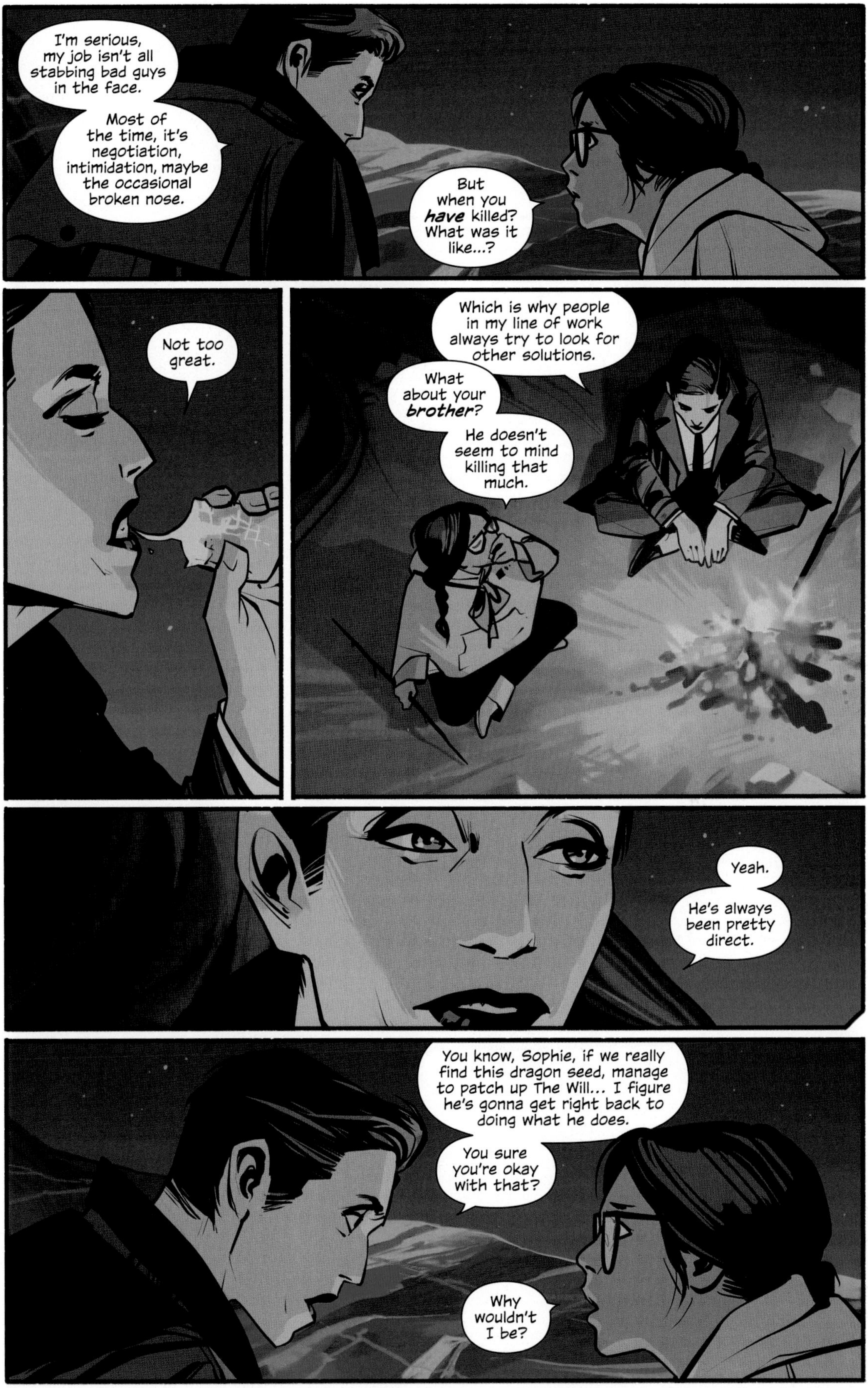
I'm serious, my job isn't all stabbing bad guys in the face.
Most of the time, it's negotiation, intimidation, maybe the occasional broken nose.
But when you *have* killed? What was it like...?
Not too great.
Which is why people in my line of work always try to look for other solutions.
What about your *brother*?
He doesn't seem to mind killing that much.
Yeah.
He's always been pretty direct.
You know, Sophie, if we really find this dragon seed, manage to patch up The Will... I figure he's gonna get right back to doing what he does.
You sure you're okay with that?
Why wouldn't I be?

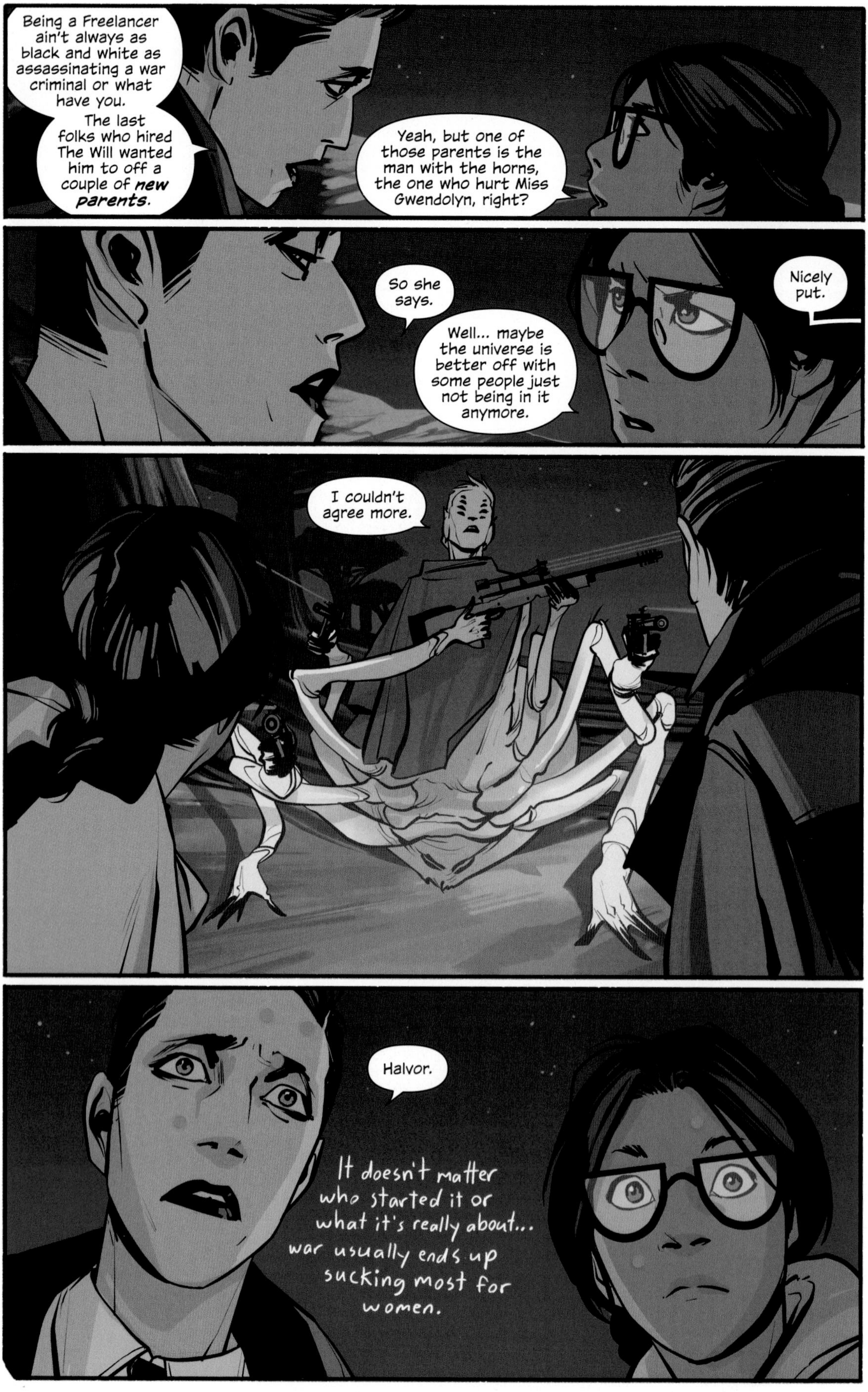

Being a Freelancer ain't always as black and white as assassinating a war criminal or what have you.
The last folks who hired The Will wanted him to off a couple of **new parents**.
Yeah, but one of those parents is the man with the horns, the one who hurt Miss Gwendolyn, right?
So she says.
Well... maybe the universe is better off with some people just not being in it anymore.
Nicely put.
I couldn't agree more.
Halvor.
It doesn't matter who started it or what it's really about... war usually ends up sucking most for women.

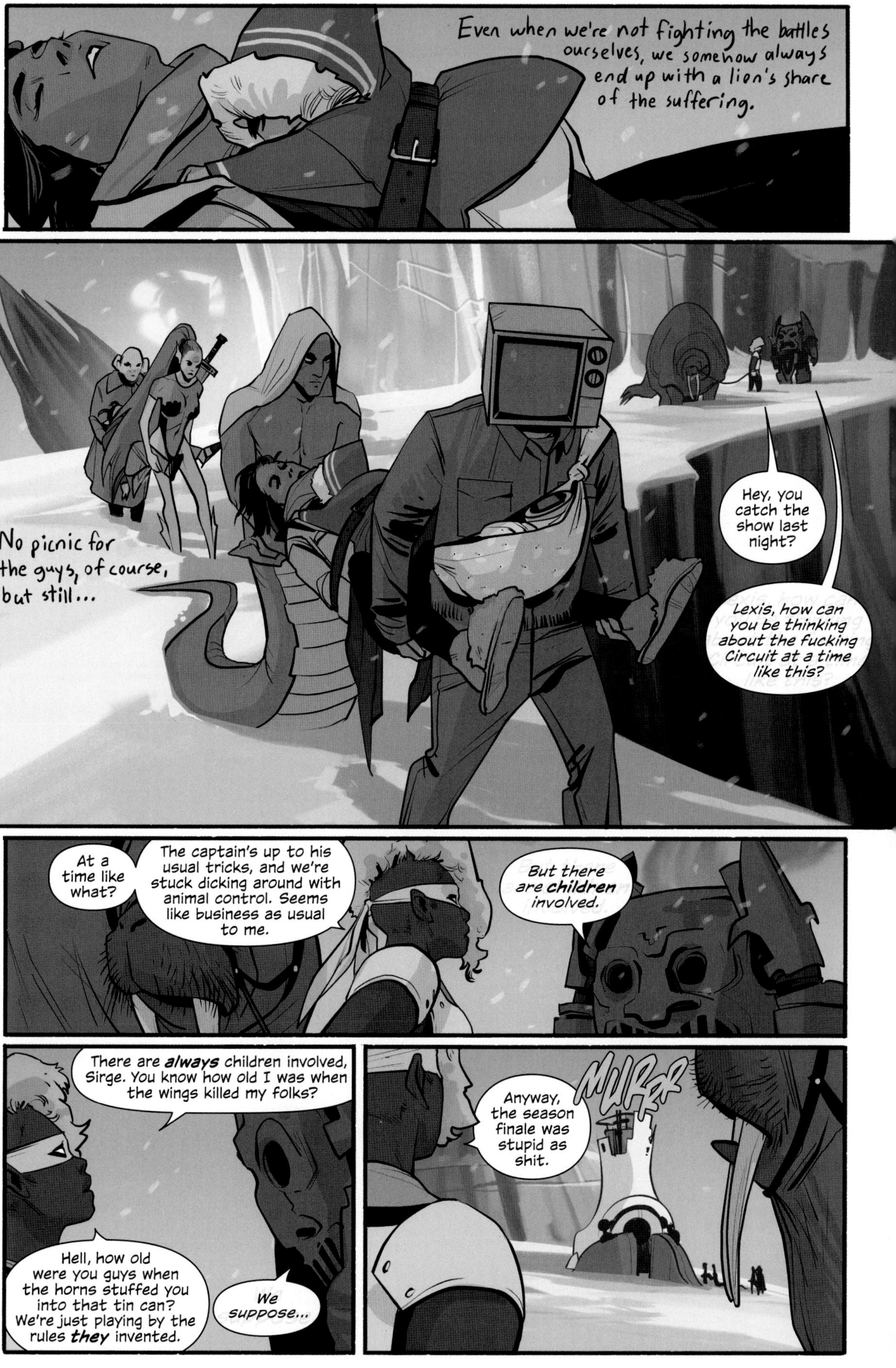
Even when we're not fighting the battles ourselves, we somehow always end up with a lion's share of the suffering.
No picnic for the guys, of course, but still...
Hey, you catch the show last night?
Lexis, how can you be thinking about the fucking Circuit at a time like this?
At a time like what?
The captain's up to his usual tricks, and we're stuck dicking around with animal control. Seems like business as usual to me.
But there are **children** involved.
There are ***always*** children involved, Sirge. You know how old I was when the wings killed my folks?
Hell, how old were you guys when the horns stuffed you into that tin can? We're just playing by the rules ***they*** invented.
We suppose...
MURR
Anyway, the season finale was stupid as shit.

hhhase

HAZEL!

She's fine, Alana.

We're safely aboard the Last Revolution's transport. Your daughter and her grandmother were merely --

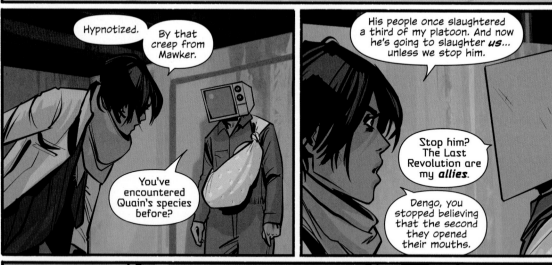

Hypnotized.

By that creep from Mawker.

You've encountered Quain's species before?

His people once slaughtered a third of my platoon. And now he's going to slaughter *us*... unless we stop him.

Stop him? The Last Revolution are my *allies*.

Dengo, you stopped believing that the second they opened their mouths.

It's written all over your face.

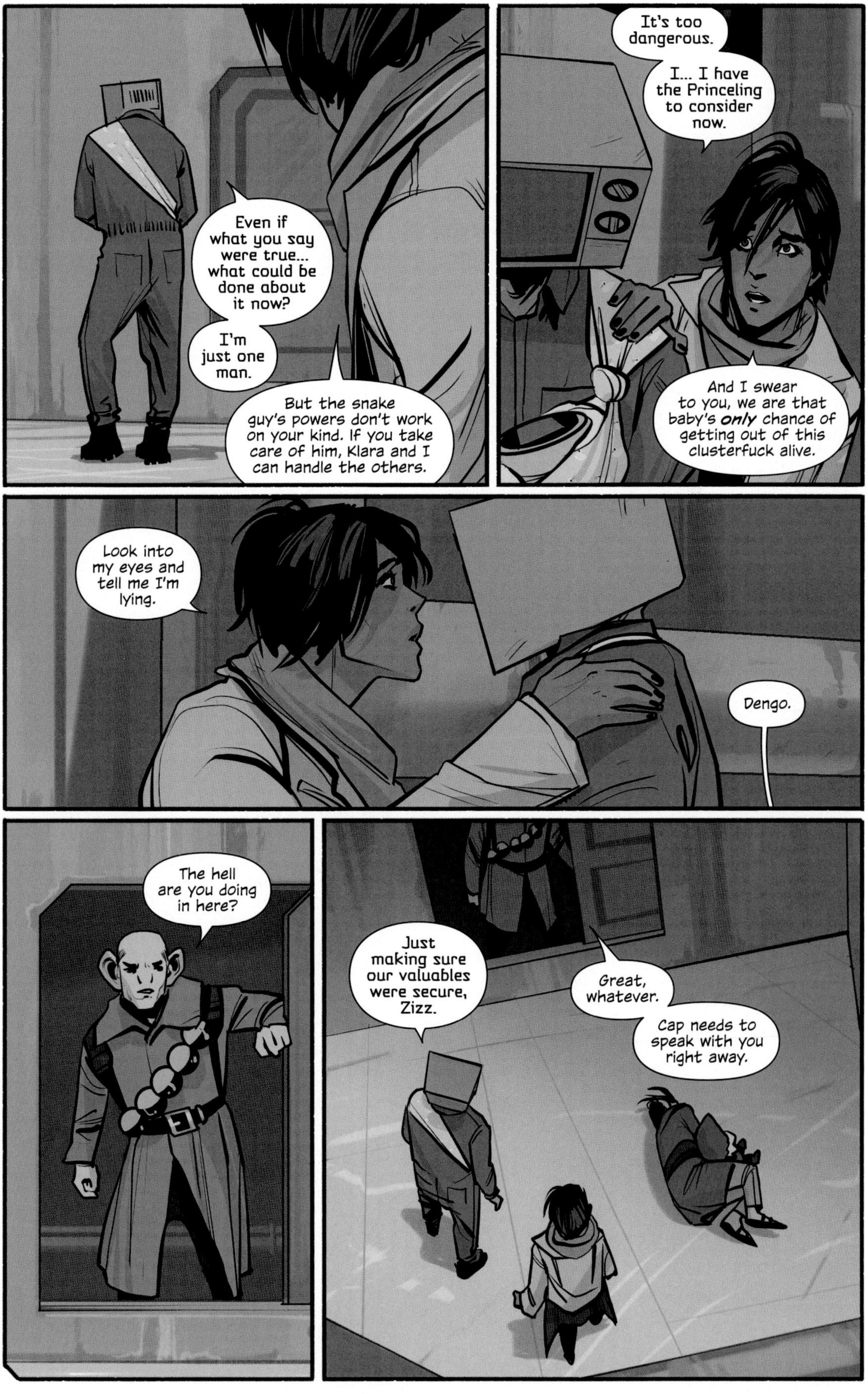
Even if what you say were true... what could be done about it now?
I'm just one man.
But the snake guy's powers don't work on your kind. If you take care of him, Klara and I can handle the others.
It's too dangerous.
I... I have the Princeling to consider now.
And I swear to you, we are that baby's ***only*** chance of getting out of this clusterfuck alive.
Look into my eyes and tell me I'm lying.
Dengo.
The hell are you doing in here?
Just making sure our valuables were secure, Zizz.
Great, whatever.
Cap needs to speak with you right away.

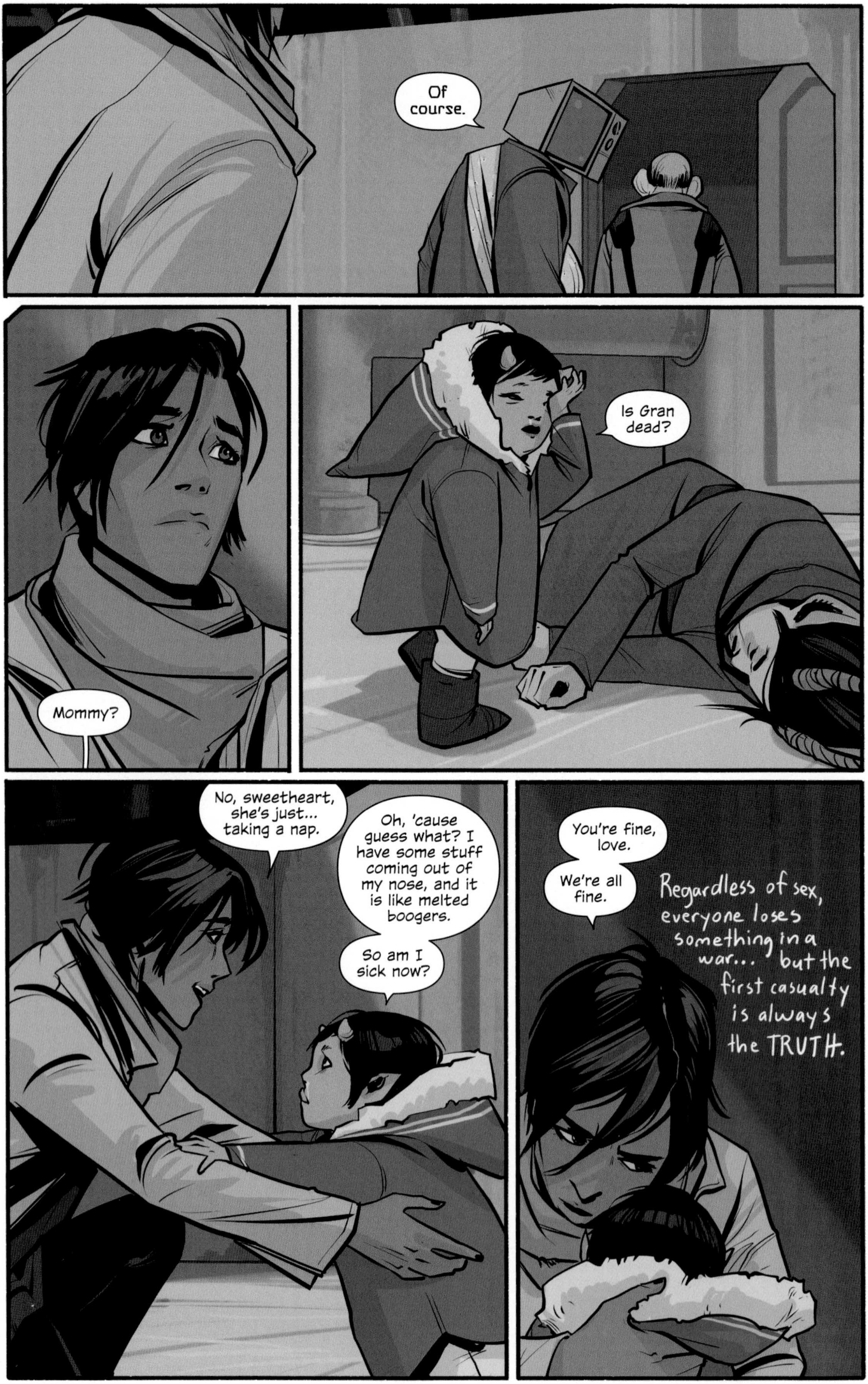

Of course.
Is Gran dead?
Mommy?
No, sweetheart, she's just... taking a nap.
Oh, 'cause guess what? I have some stuff coming out of my nose, and it is like melted boogers.
So am I sick now?
You're fine, love.
We're all fine.
Regardless of sex, everyone loses something in a war... but the first casualty is always the TRUTH.

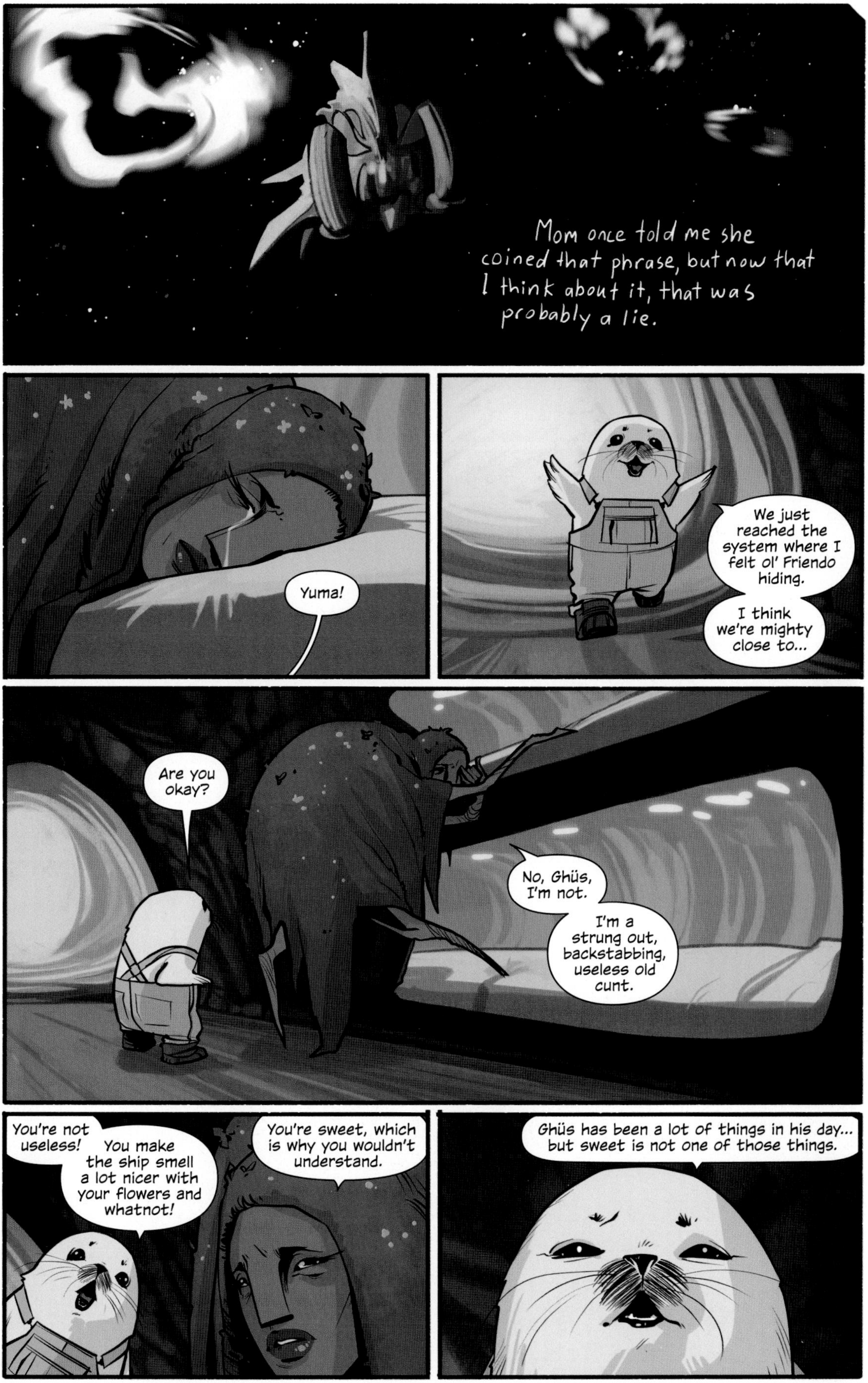
Mom once told me she coined that phrase, but now that I think about it, that was probably a lie.
Yuma!
We just reached the system where I felt ol' Friendo hiding.
I think we're mighty close to...
Are you okay?
No, Ghüs, I'm not.
I'm a strung out, backstabbing, useless old cunt.
You're not useless!
You make the ship smell a lot nicer with your flowers and whatnot!
You're sweet, which is why you wouldn't understand.
Ghüs has been a lot of things in his day... but sweet is not one of those things.

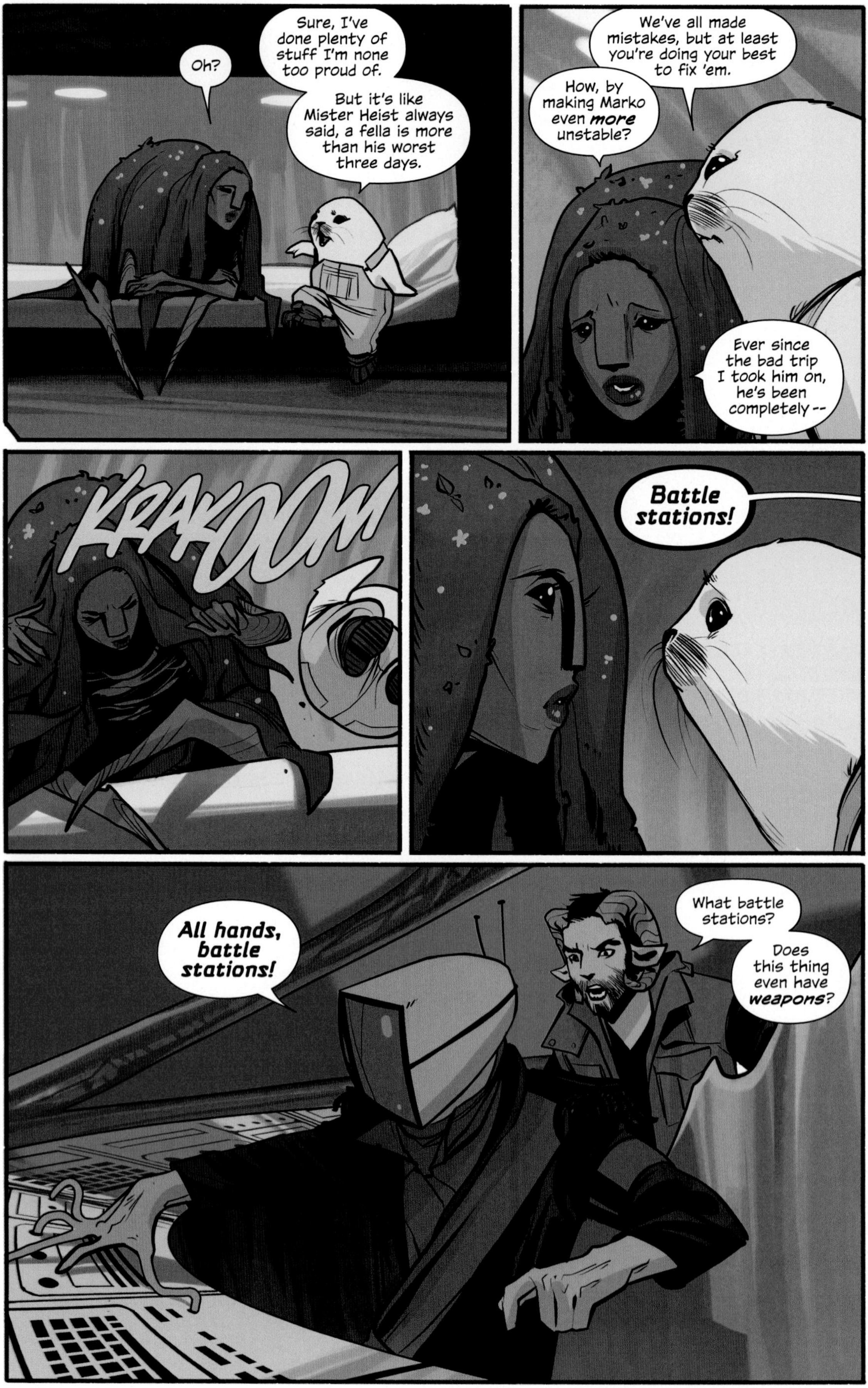
Oh?
Sure, I've done plenty of stuff I'm none too proud of.
But it's like Mister Heist always said, a fella is more than his worst three days.
We've all made mistakes, but at least you're doing your best to fix 'em.
How, by making Marko even *more* unstable?
Ever since the bad trip I took him on, he's been completely --
KRAKOOOM
Battle stations!
All hands, battle stations!
What battle stations?
Does this thing even have ***weapons***?

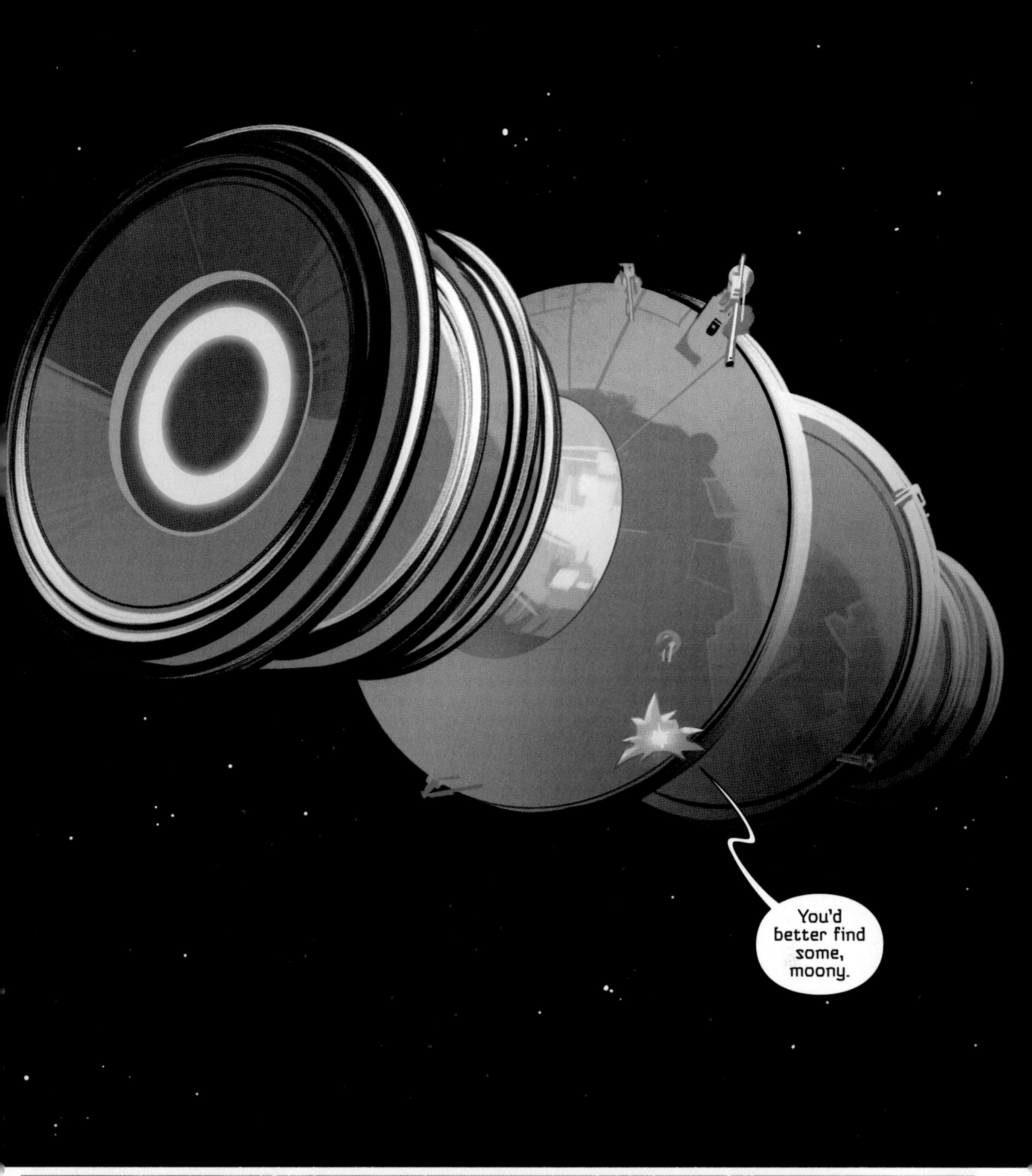
You'd better find some, moony.

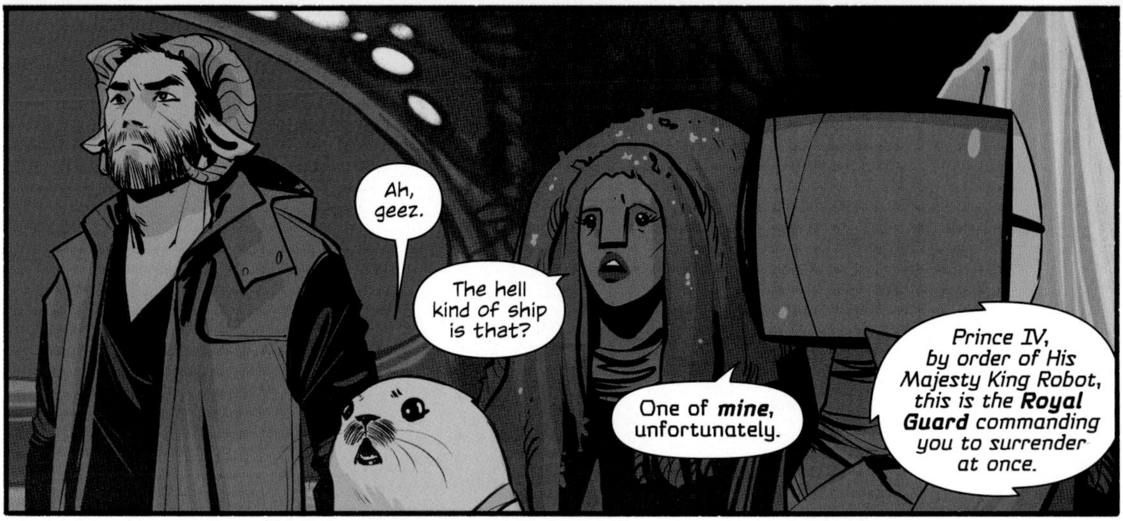
Ah, geez.
The hell kind of ship is that?
One of ***mine***, unfortunately.
*Prince IV, by order of His Majesty King Robot, this is the **Royal Guard** commanding you to surrender at once.*

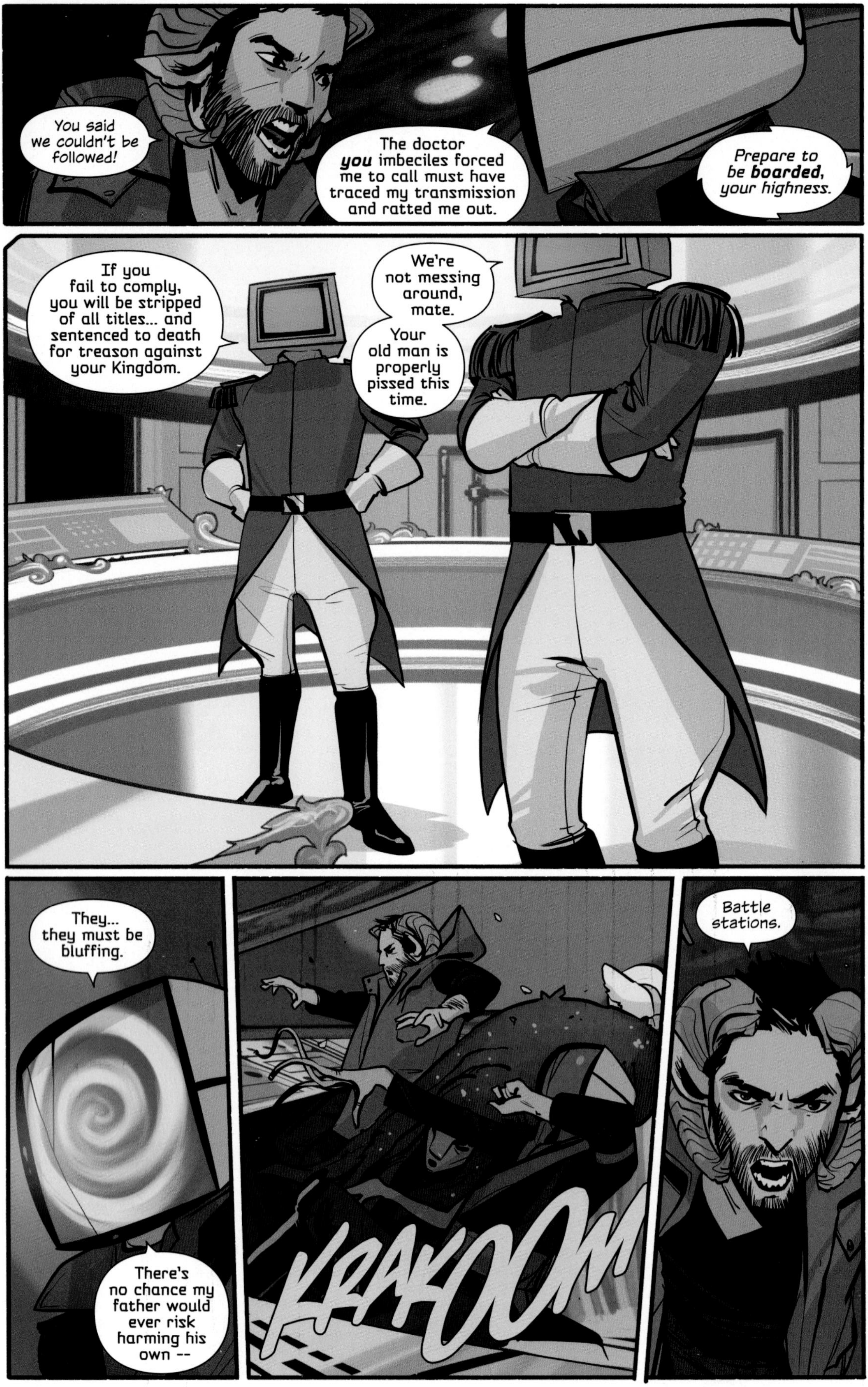
You said we couldn't be followed!
The doctor *you* imbeciles forced me to call must have traced my transmission and ratted me out.
*Prepare to be **boarded**, your highness.*
If you fail to comply, you will be stripped of all titles... and sentenced to death for treason against your Kingdom.
We're not messing around, mate.
Your old man is properly pissed this time.
They... they must be bluffing.
There's no chance my father would ever risk harming his own --
KRAKOOM
Battle stations.

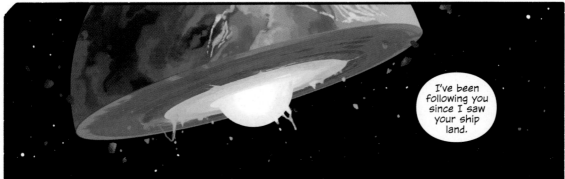

I've been following you since I saw your ship land.

Or your idiot **brother's** ship, I should say.

Where is the dullard anyway?

You shut your ugly mouth about him!

He's why we're here, Halvor.

The Will is... indisposed at present. We're looking for something that might be able to help him.

To help **him**?

What about what you owe my **family**?

Drop the lightshow, chief.

Or I lance you like a boil.

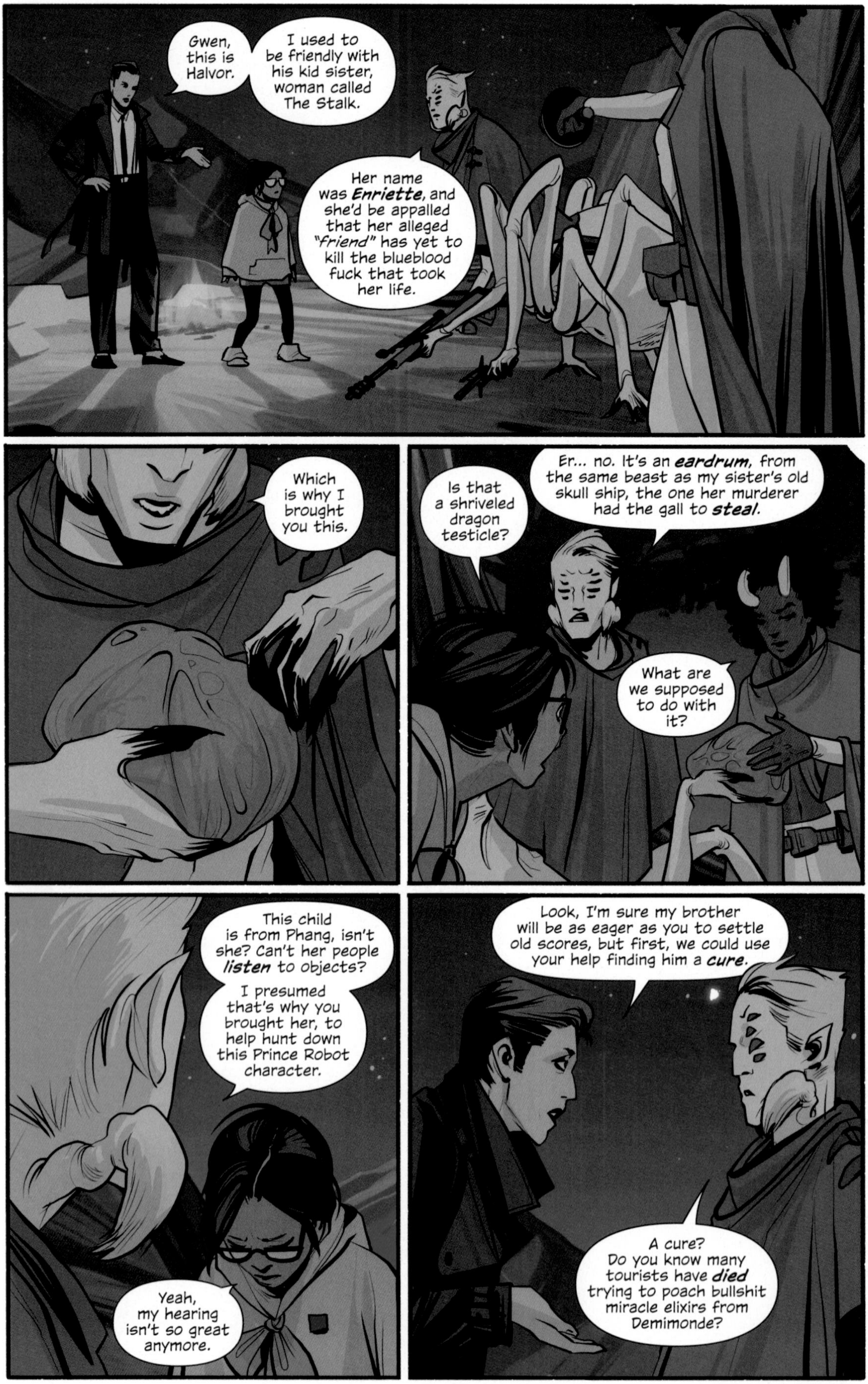
Gwen, this is Halvor.
I used to be friendly with his kid sister, woman called The Stalk.
Her name was *Enriette*, and she'd be appalled that her alleged *"friend"* has yet to kill the blueblood fuck that took her life.
Which is why I brought you this.
Is that a shriveled dragon testicle?
Er... no. It's an *eardrum*, from the same beast as my sister's old skull ship, the one her murderer had the gall to *steal*.
What are we supposed to do with it?
This child is from Phang, isn't she? Can't her people *listen* to objects?
I presumed that's why you brought her, to help hunt down this Prince Robot character.
Yeah, my hearing isn't so great anymore.
Look, I'm sure my brother will be as eager as you to settle old scores, but first, we could use your help finding him a *cure*.
A cure? Do you know many tourists have *died* trying to poach bullshit miracle elixirs from Demimonde?

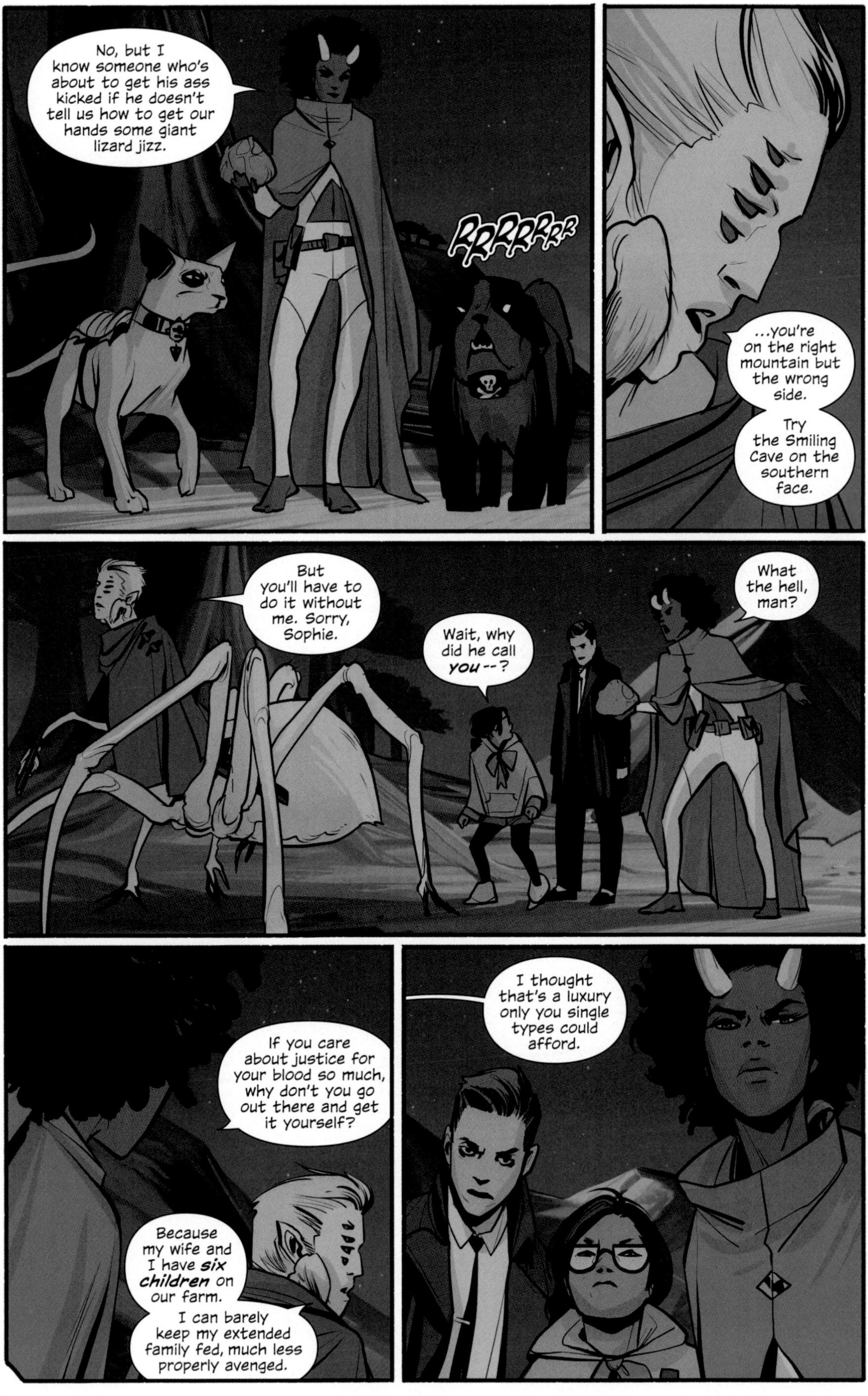
No, but I know someone who's about to get his ass kicked if he doesn't tell us how to get our hands some giant lizard jizz.
RRRRRRR
...you're on the right mountain but the wrong side.
Try the Smiling Cave on the southern face.
But you'll have to do it without me. Sorry, Sophie.
What the hell, man?
Wait, why did he call *you*--?
If you care about justice for your blood so much, why don't you go out there and get it yourself?
Because my wife and I have ***six children*** on our farm.
I can barely keep my extended family fed, much less properly avenged.
I thought that's a luxury only you single types could afford.

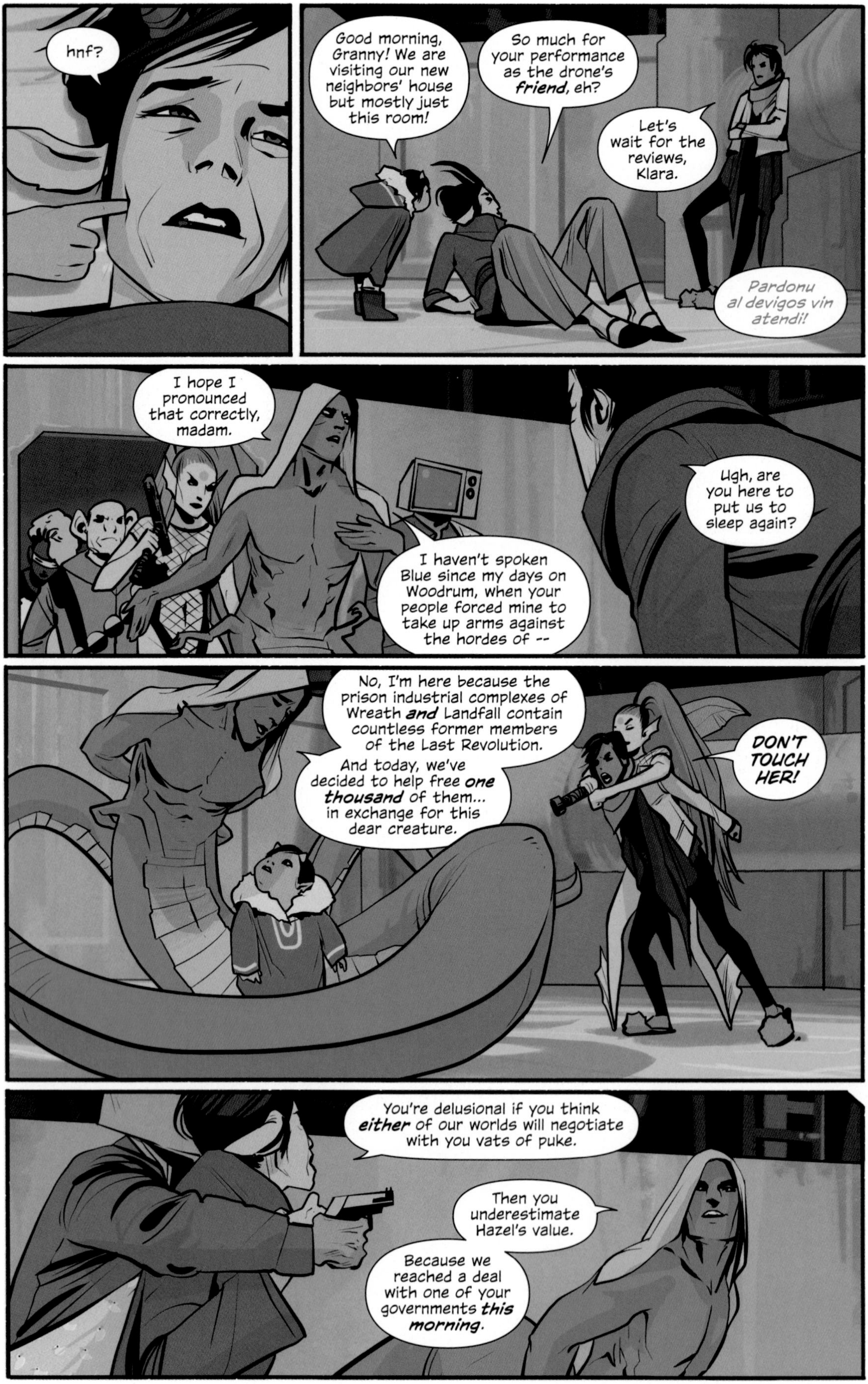
hnf?
Good morning, Granny! We are visiting our new neighbors' house but mostly just this room!
So much for your performance as the drone's *friend*, eh?
Let's wait for the reviews, Klara.
Pardonu al devigos vin atendi!
I hope I pronounced that correctly, madam.
I haven't spoken Blue since my days on Woodrum, when your people forced mine to take up arms against the hordes of --
Ugh, are you here to put us to sleep again?
No, I'm here because the prison industrial complexes of Wreath *and* Landfall contain countless former members of the Last Revolution.
And today, we've decided to help free *one thousand* of them... in exchange for this dear creature.
DON'T TOUCH HER!
You're delusional if you think *either* of our worlds will negotiate with you vats of puke.
Then you underestimate Hazel's value.
Because we reached a deal with one of your governments *this morning*.

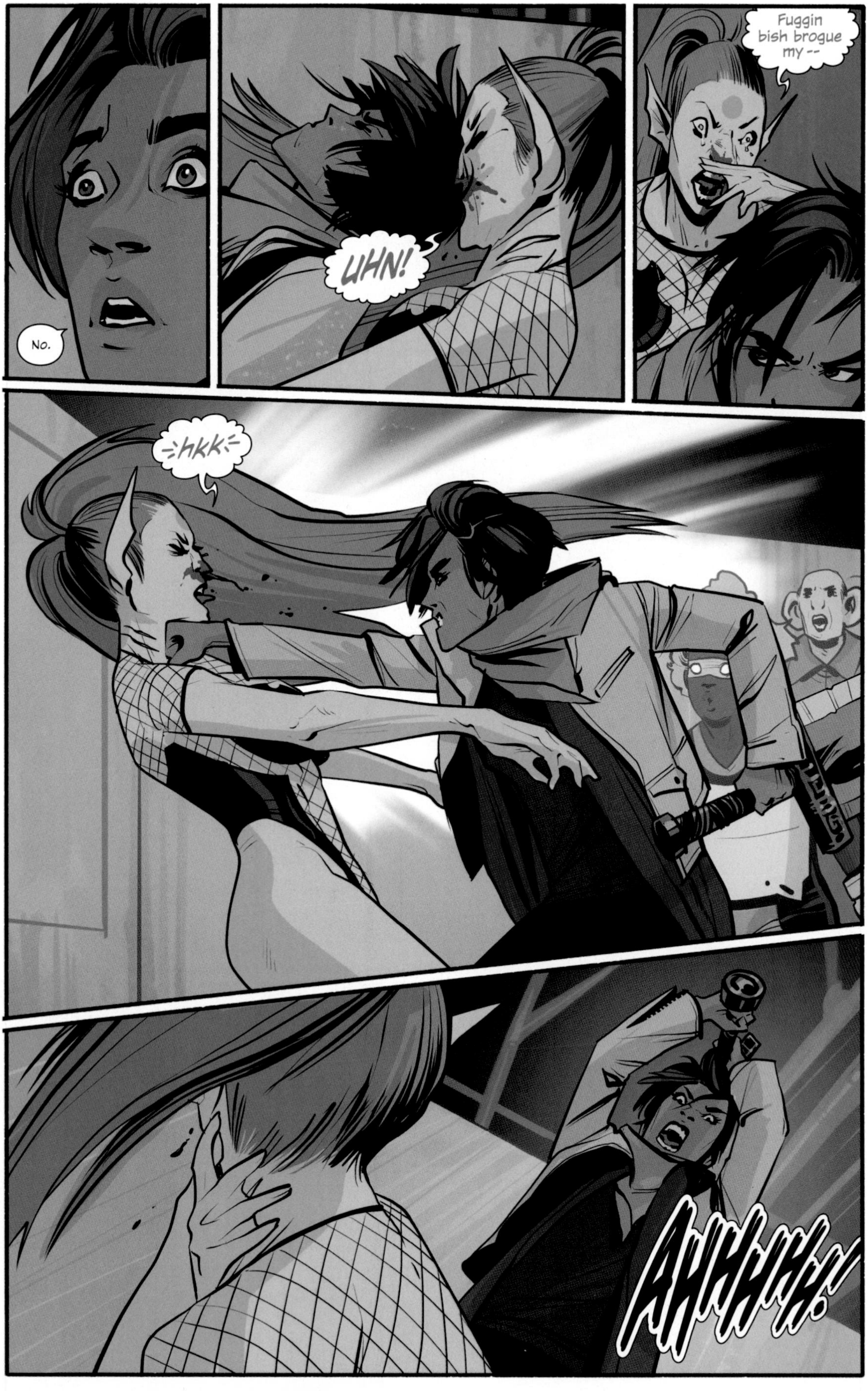
No.
UHN!
Fuggin bish brogue my --
hkk
AHHHHH!

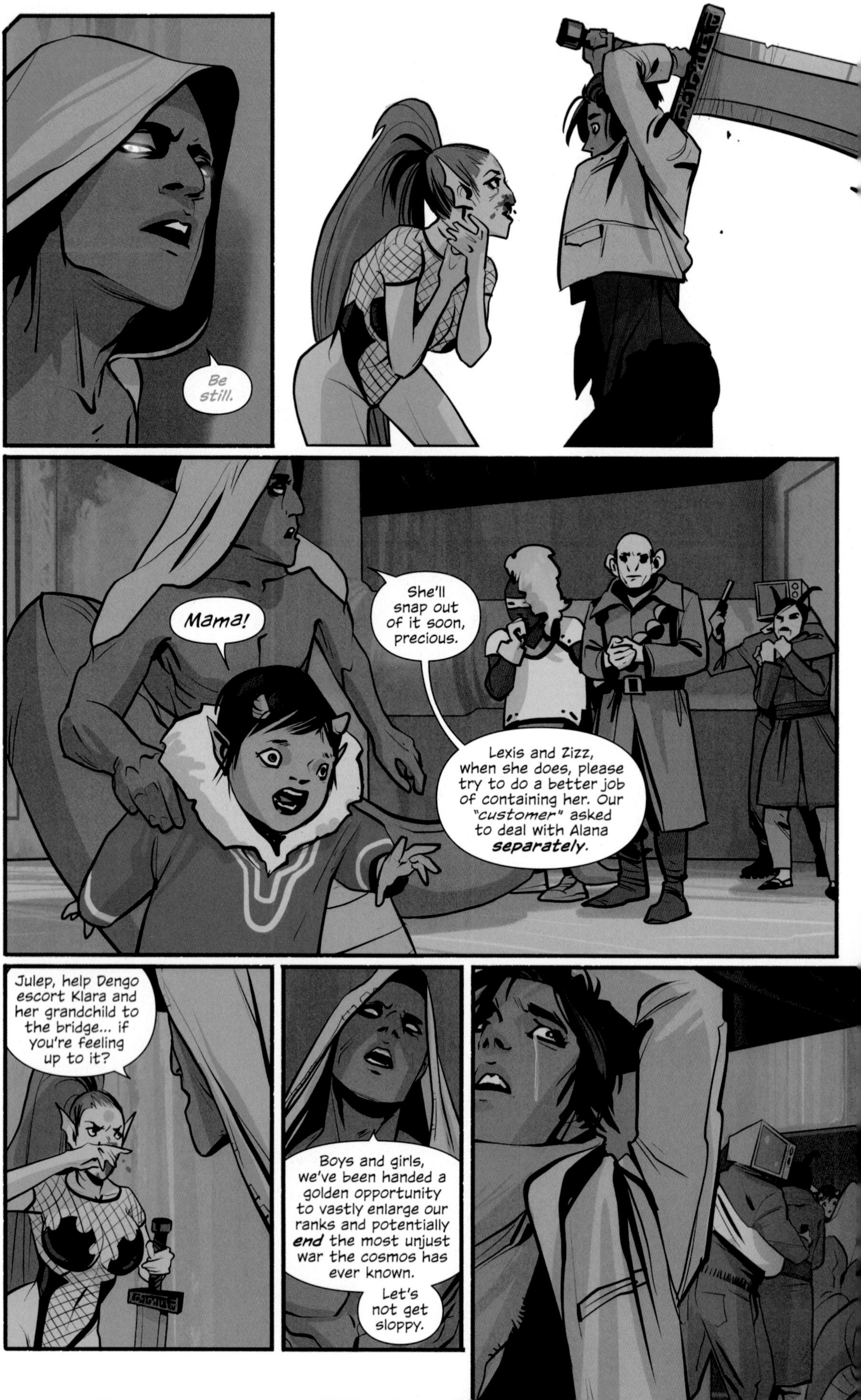

Be still.
Mama!
She'll snap out of it soon, precious.
Lexis and Zizz, when she does, please try to do a better job of containing her. Our "customer" asked to deal with Alana **separately**.
Julep, help Dengo escort Klara and her grandchild to the bridge... if you're feeling up to it?
Boys and girls, we've been handed a golden opportunity to vastly enlarge our ranks and potentially **end** the most unjust war the cosmos has ever known.
Let's not get sloppy.

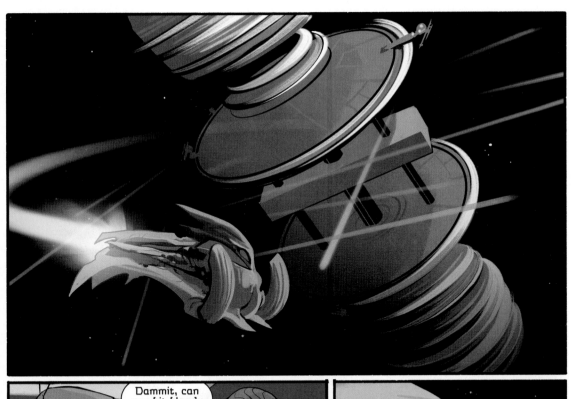

Dammit, can you hit bloody *anything?*

When I'm being piloted by someone who actually knows how to --

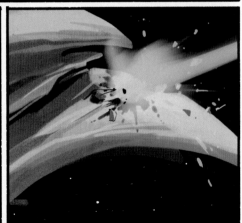

We've got some kind of *warning light* flashing for the engine room!

Freeloaders, get down there and *fix it!*

This isn't a fight we can win! We should try to *run* before --

Just *go*, Yuma!

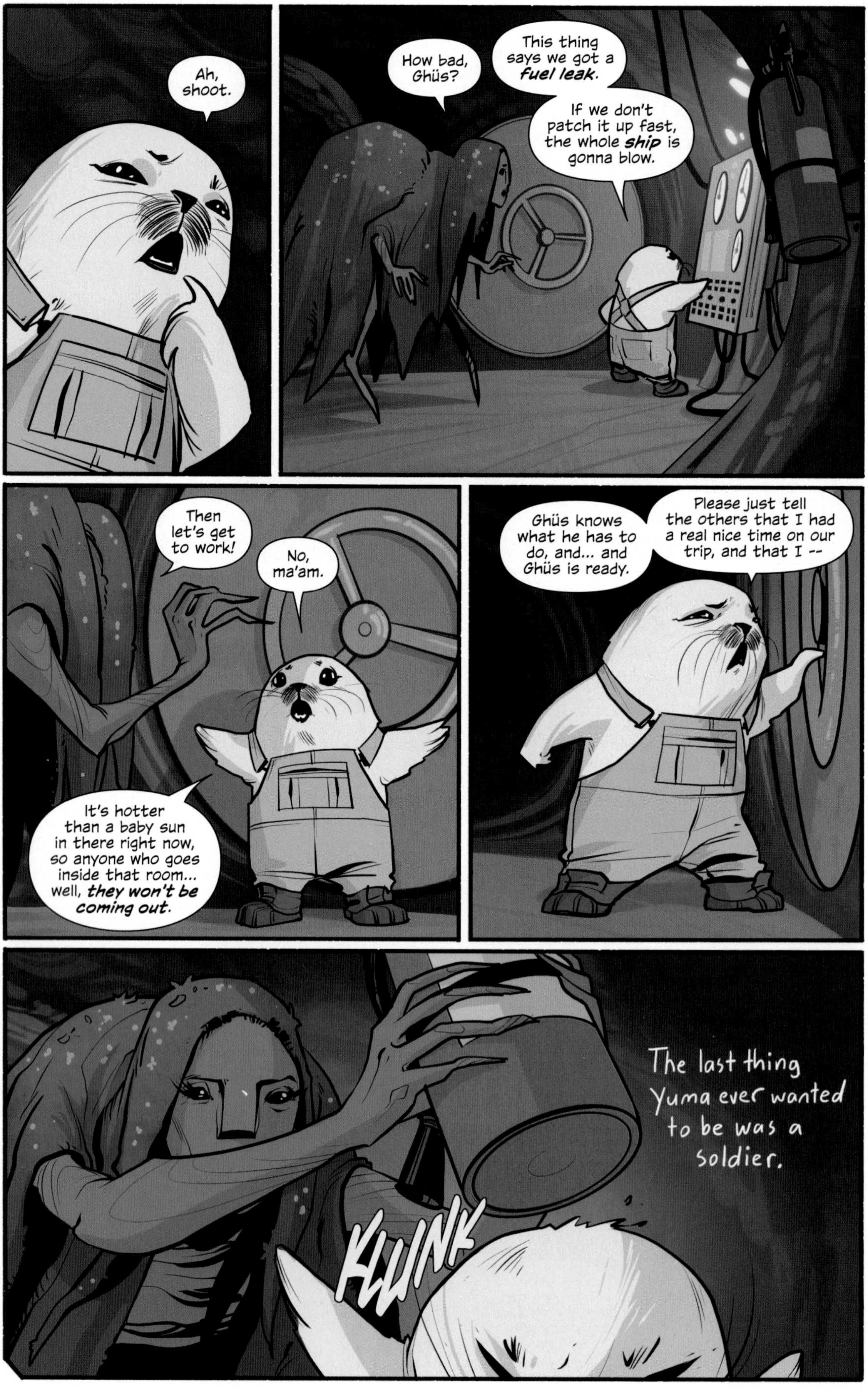
Ah, shoot.
How bad, Ghüs?
This thing says we got a ***fuel leak***.
If we don't patch it up fast, the whole ***ship*** is gonna blow.
Then let's get to work!
No, ma'am.
It's hotter than a baby sun in there right now, so anyone who goes inside that room... well, ***they won't be coming out***.
Ghüs knows what he has to do, and... and Ghüs is ready.
Please just tell the others that I had a real nice time on our trip, and that I --
The last thing Yuma ever wanted to be was a soldier.
KLUNK

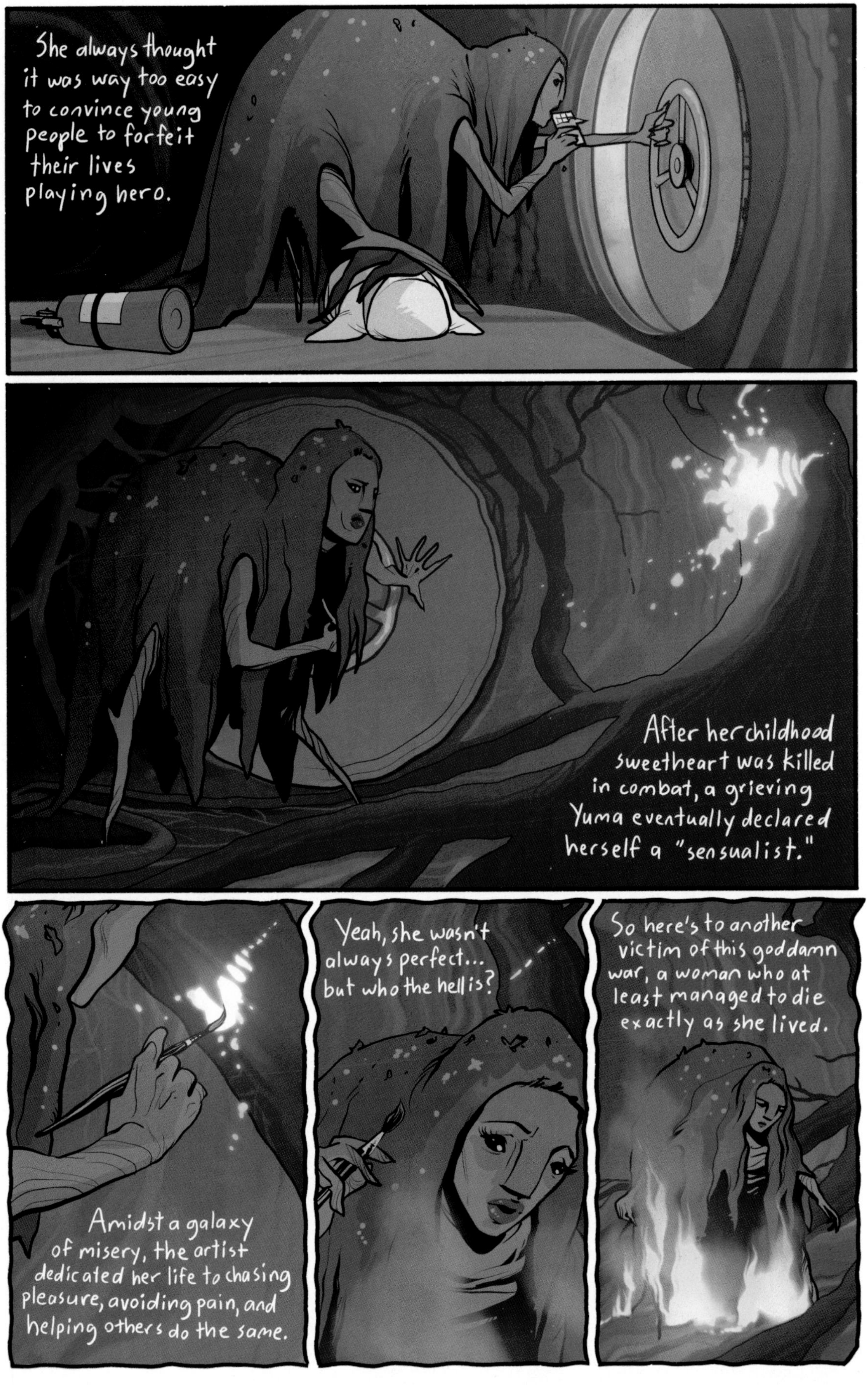
She always thought it was way too easy to convince young people to forfeit their lives playing hero.
After her childhood sweetheart was killed in combat, a grieving Yuma eventually declared herself a "sensualist."
Amidst a galaxy of misery, the artist dedicated her life to chasing pleasure, avoiding pain, and helping others do the same.
Yeah, she wasn't always perfect... but who the hell is?
So here's to another victim of this goddamn war, a woman who at least managed to die exactly as she lived.

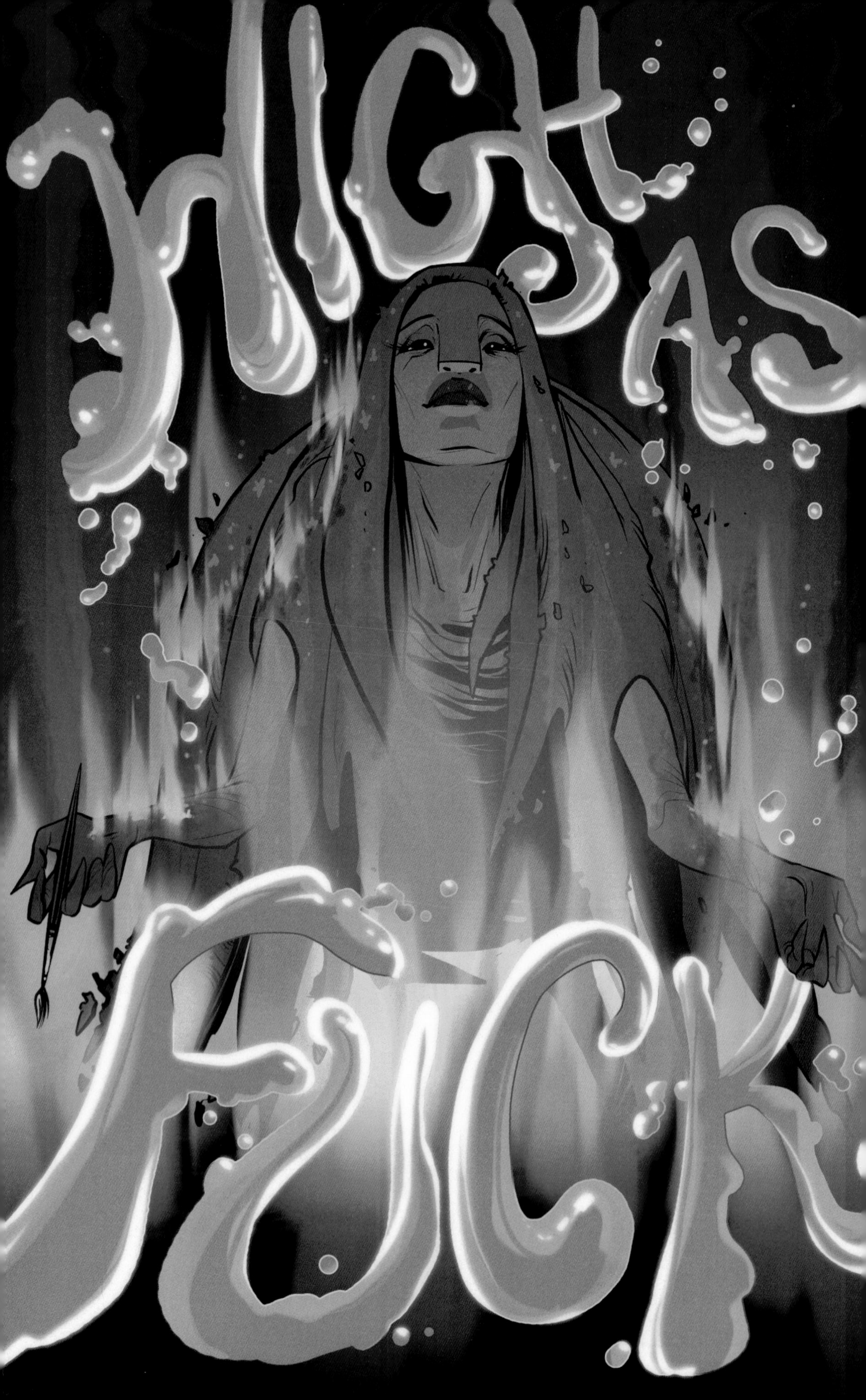
HIGH AS
FUCK

end chapter twenty-eight

CHAPTER

TWENTY-NINE

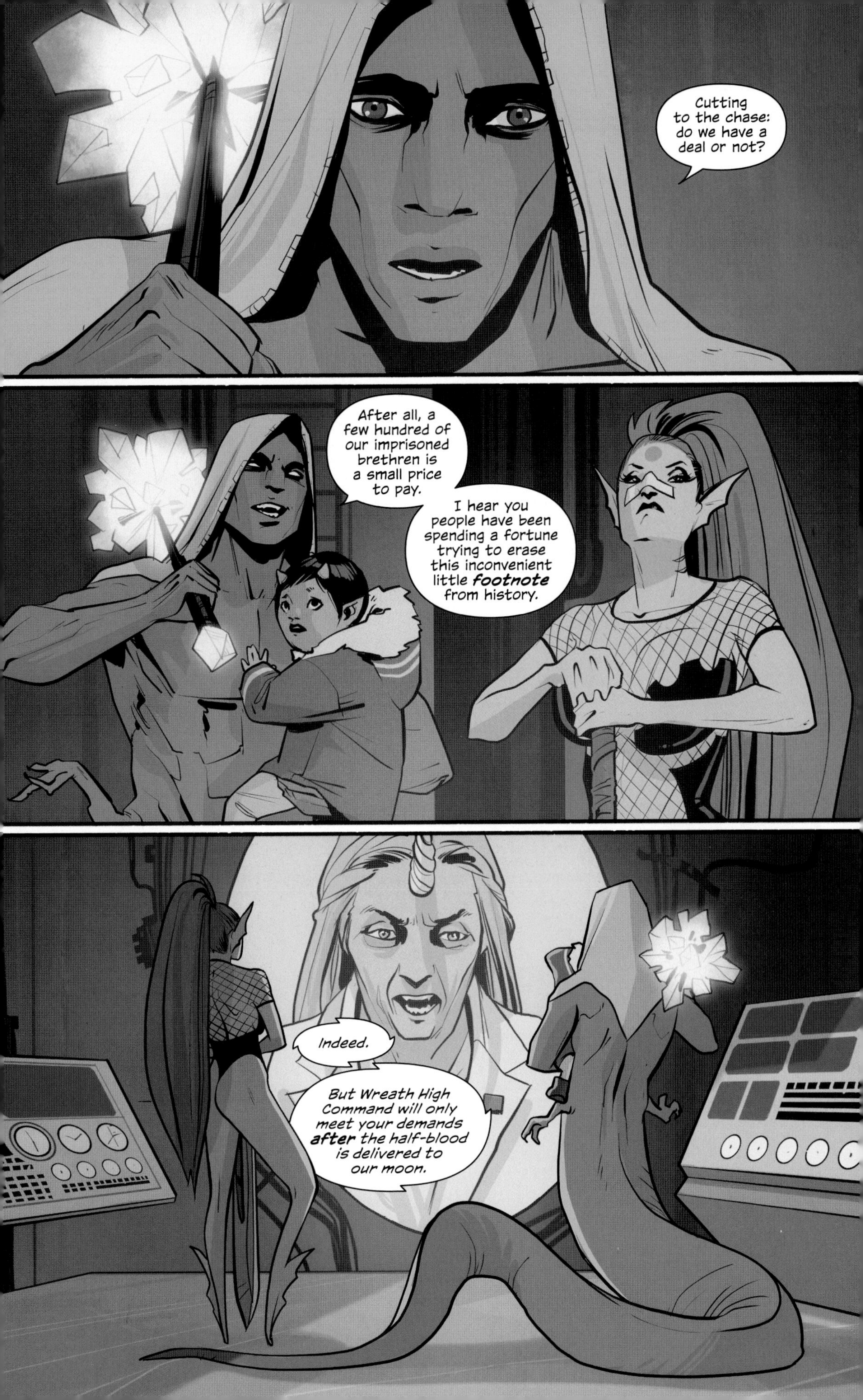
Cutting to the chase: do we have a deal or not?
After all, a few hundred of our imprisoned brethren is a small price to pay.
I hear you people have been spending a fortune trying to erase this inconvenient little *footnote* from history.
Indeed.
But Wreath High Command will only meet your demands **after** the half-blood is delivered to our moon.

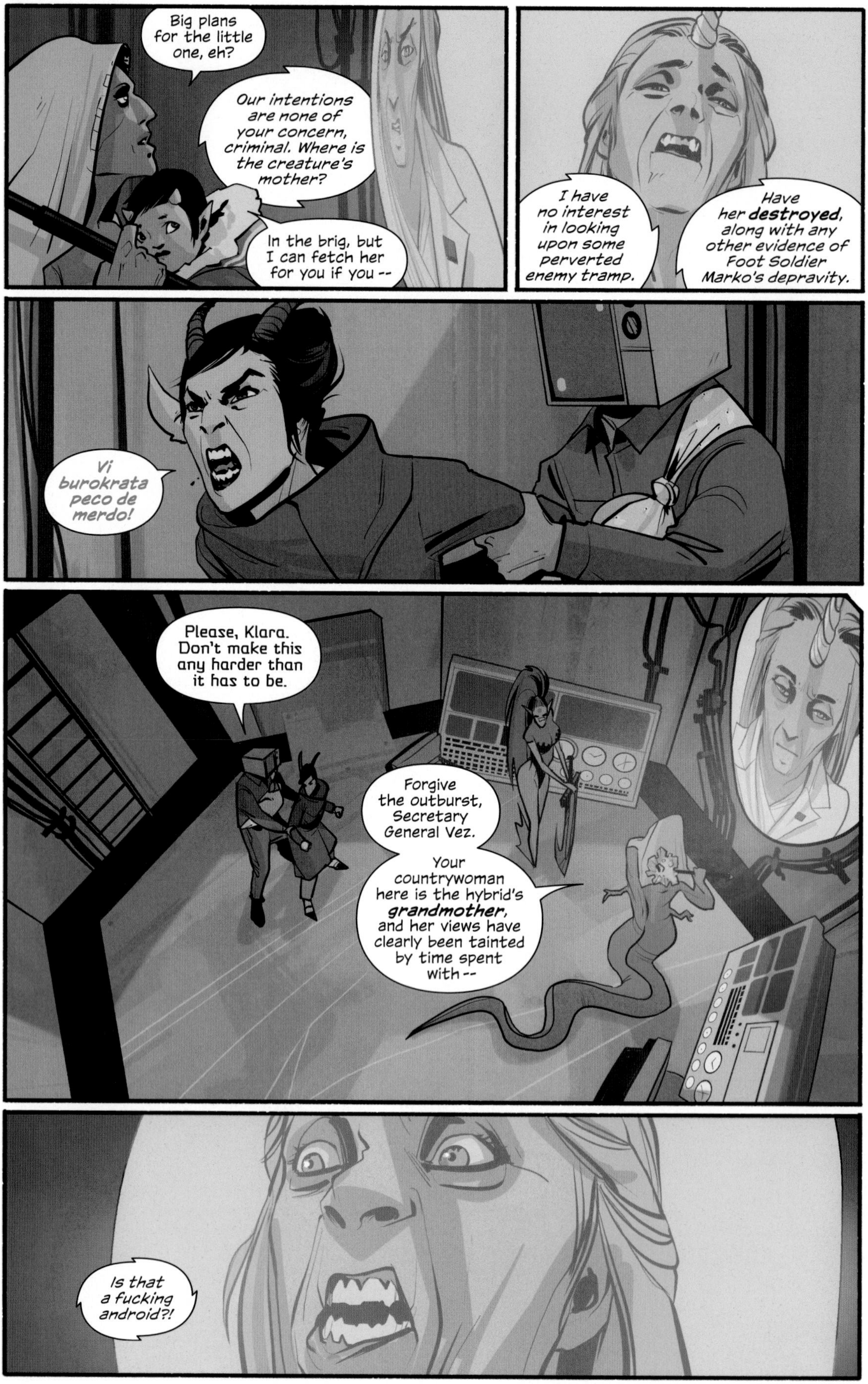
Big plans for the little one, eh?
Our intentions are none of your concern, criminal. Where is the creature's mother?
In the brig, but I can fetch her for you if you --
I have no interest in looking upon some perverted enemy tramp.
Have her **destroyed**, along with any other evidence of Foot Soldier Marko's depravity.
Vi burokrata peco de merdo!
Please, Klara. Don't make this any harder than it has to be.
Forgive the outburst, Secretary General Vez.
Your countrywoman here is the hybrid's ***grandmother***, and her views have clearly been tainted by time spent with --
Is that a fucking android?!

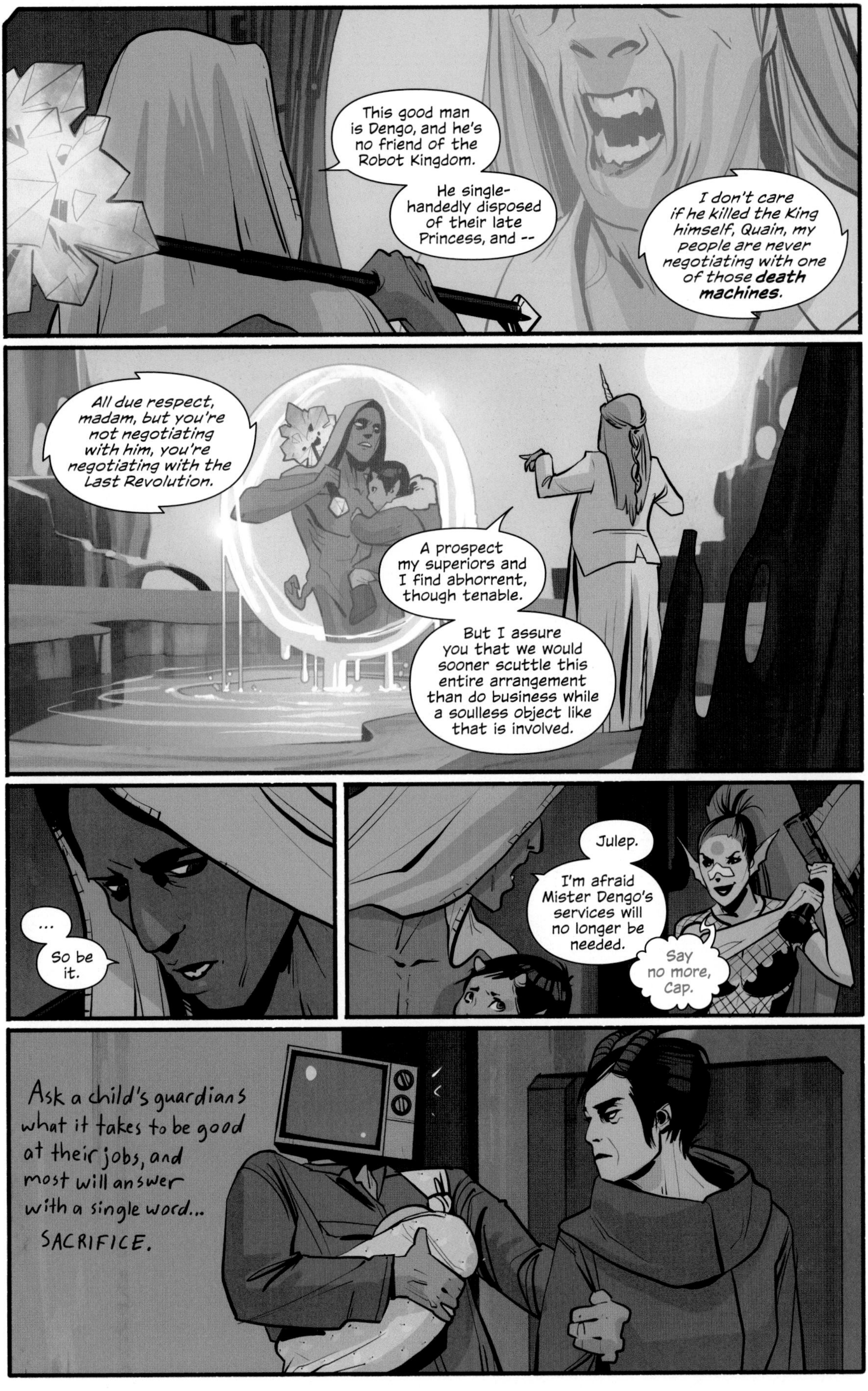
This good man is Dengo, and he's no friend of the Robot Kingdom.
He single-handedly disposed of their late Princess, and --
I don't care if he killed the King himself, Quain, my people are never negotiating with one of those death machines.
All due respect, madam, but you're not negotiating with him, you're negotiating with the Last Revolution.
A prospect my superiors and I find abhorrent, though tenable.
But I assure you that we would sooner scuttle this entire arrangement than do business while a soulless object like that is involved.
...
So be it.
Julep.
I'm afraid Mister Dengo's services will no longer be needed.
Say no more, Cap.
Ask a child's guardians what it takes to be good at their jobs, and most will answer with a single word... SACRIFICE.

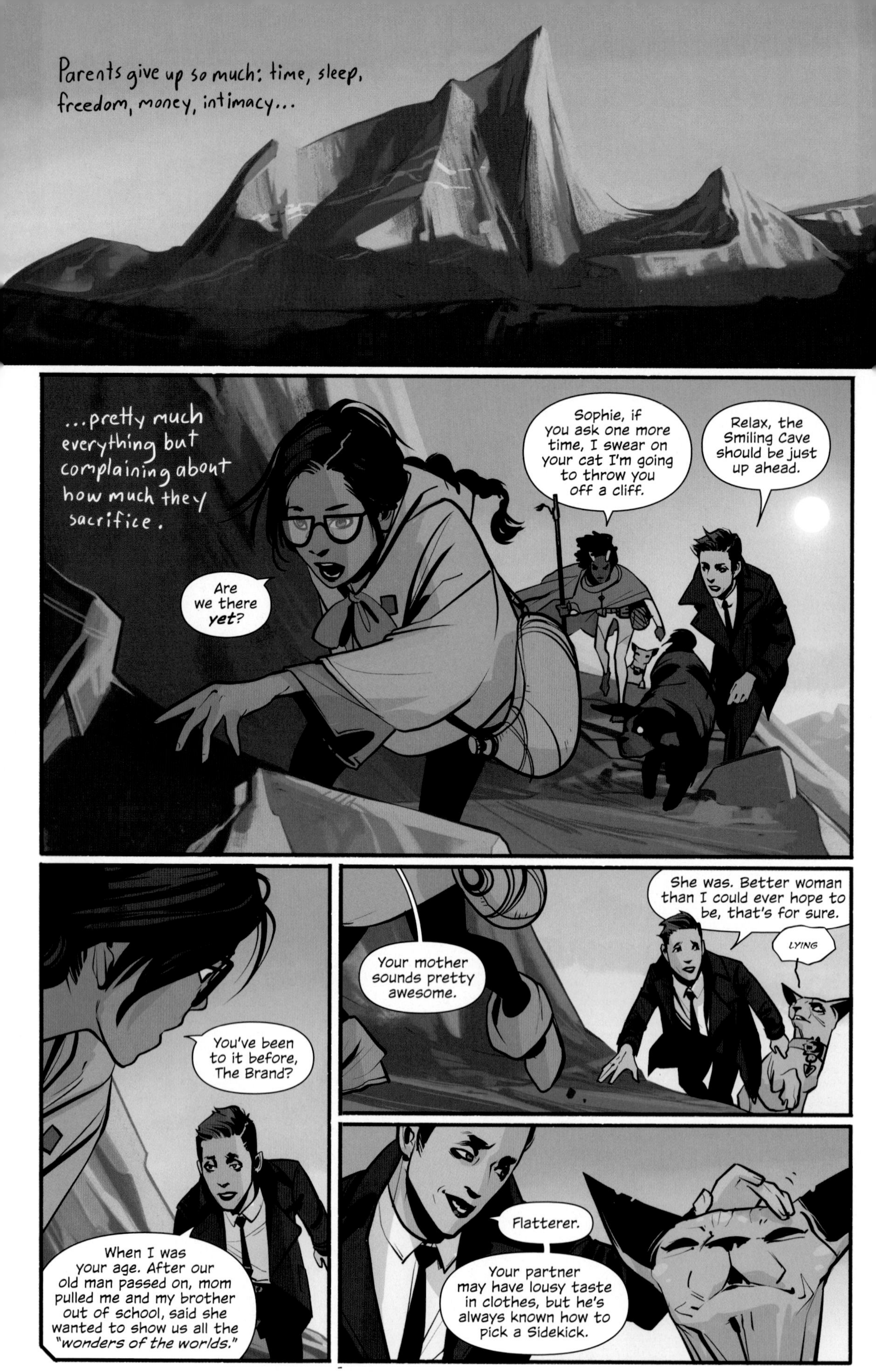
Parents give up so much: time, sleep, freedom, money, intimacy...
...pretty much everything but complaining about how much they sacrifice.
Sophie, if you ask one more time, I swear on your cat I'm going to throw you off a cliff.
Relax, the Smiling Cave should be just up ahead.
Are we there *yet*?
You've been to it before, The Brand?
When I was your age. After our old man passed on, mom pulled me and my brother out of school, said she wanted to show us all the "*wonders of the worlds.*"
Your mother sounds pretty awesome.
She was. Better woman than I could ever hope to be, that's for sure.
LYING
Flatterer.
Your partner may have lousy taste in clothes, but he's always known how to pick a Sidekick.

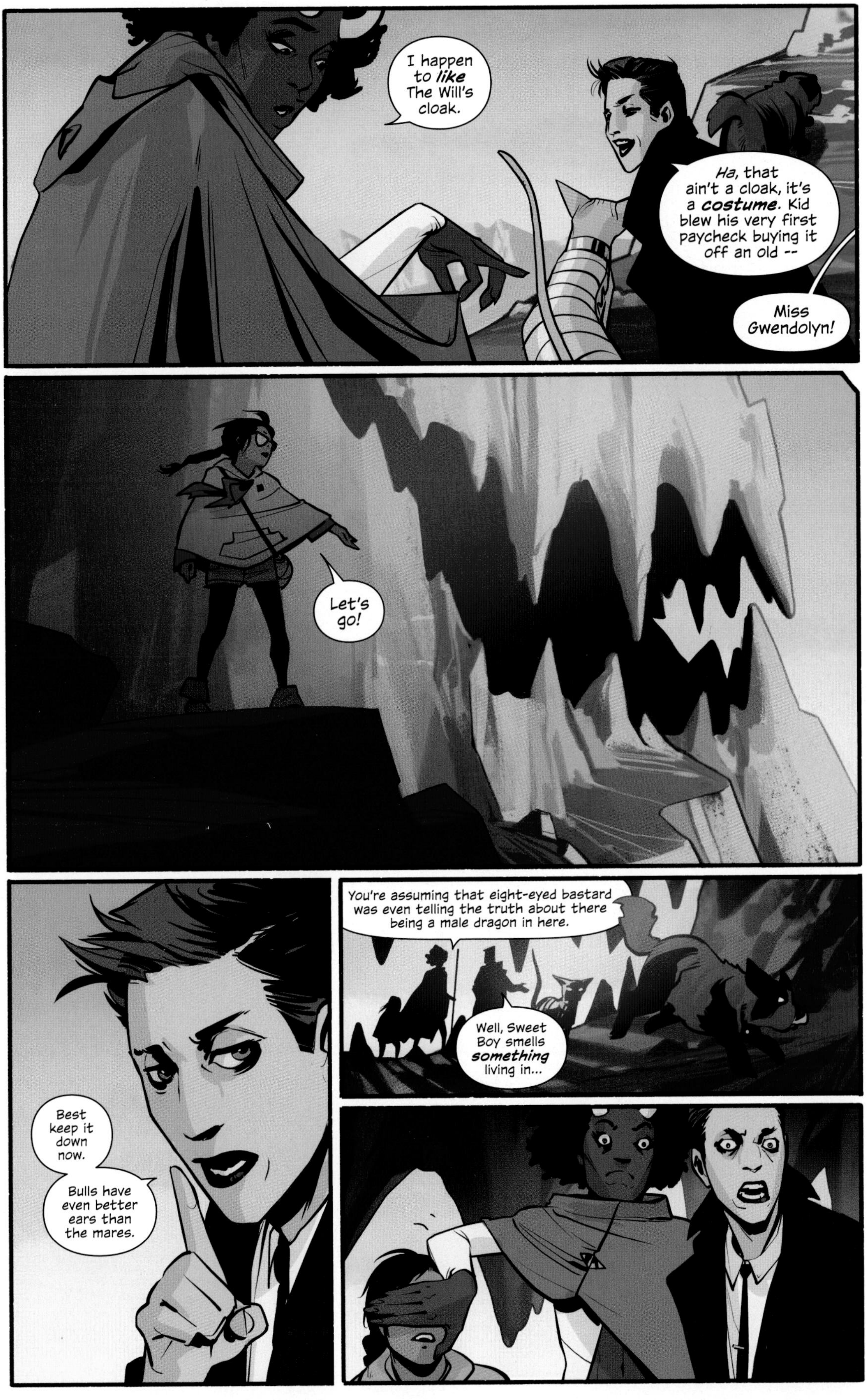
I happen to *like* The Will's cloak.
Ha, that ain't a cloak, it's a ***costume***. Kid blew his very first paycheck buying it off an old --
Miss Gwendolyn!
Let's go!
Best keep it down now.
Bulls have even better ears than the mares.
You're assuming that eight-eyed bastard was even telling the truth about there being a male dragon in here.
Well, Sweet Boy smells ***something*** living in...

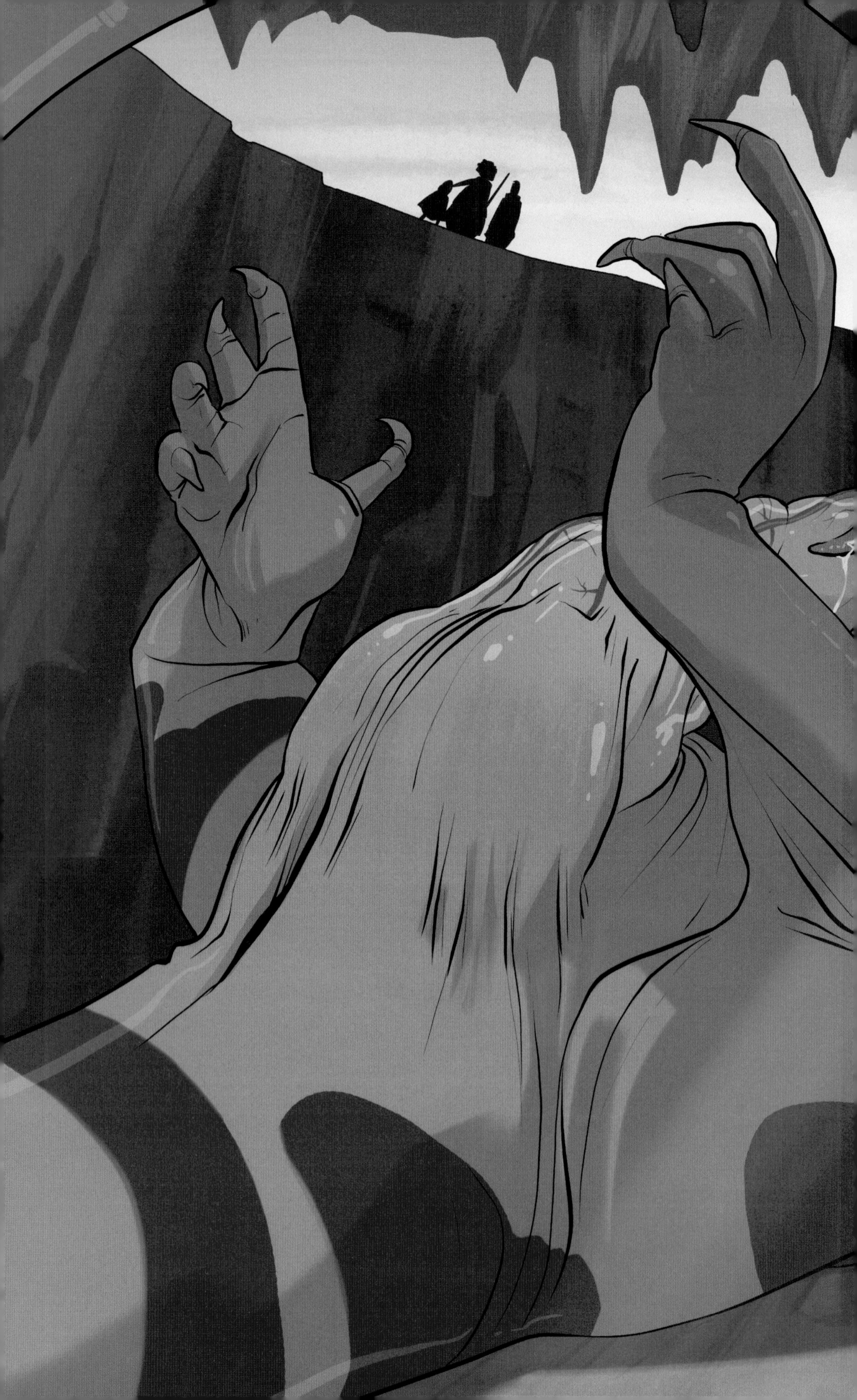

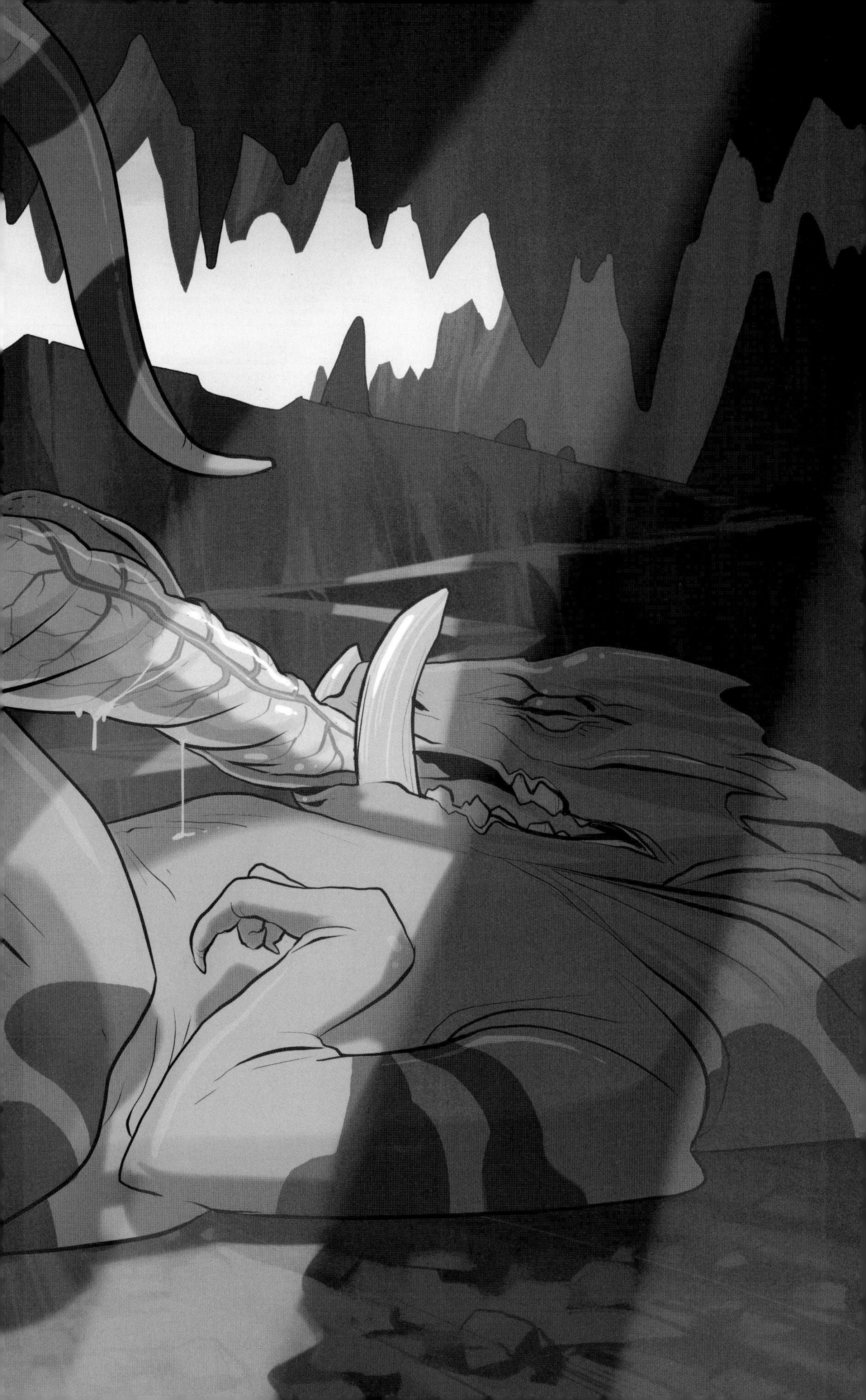

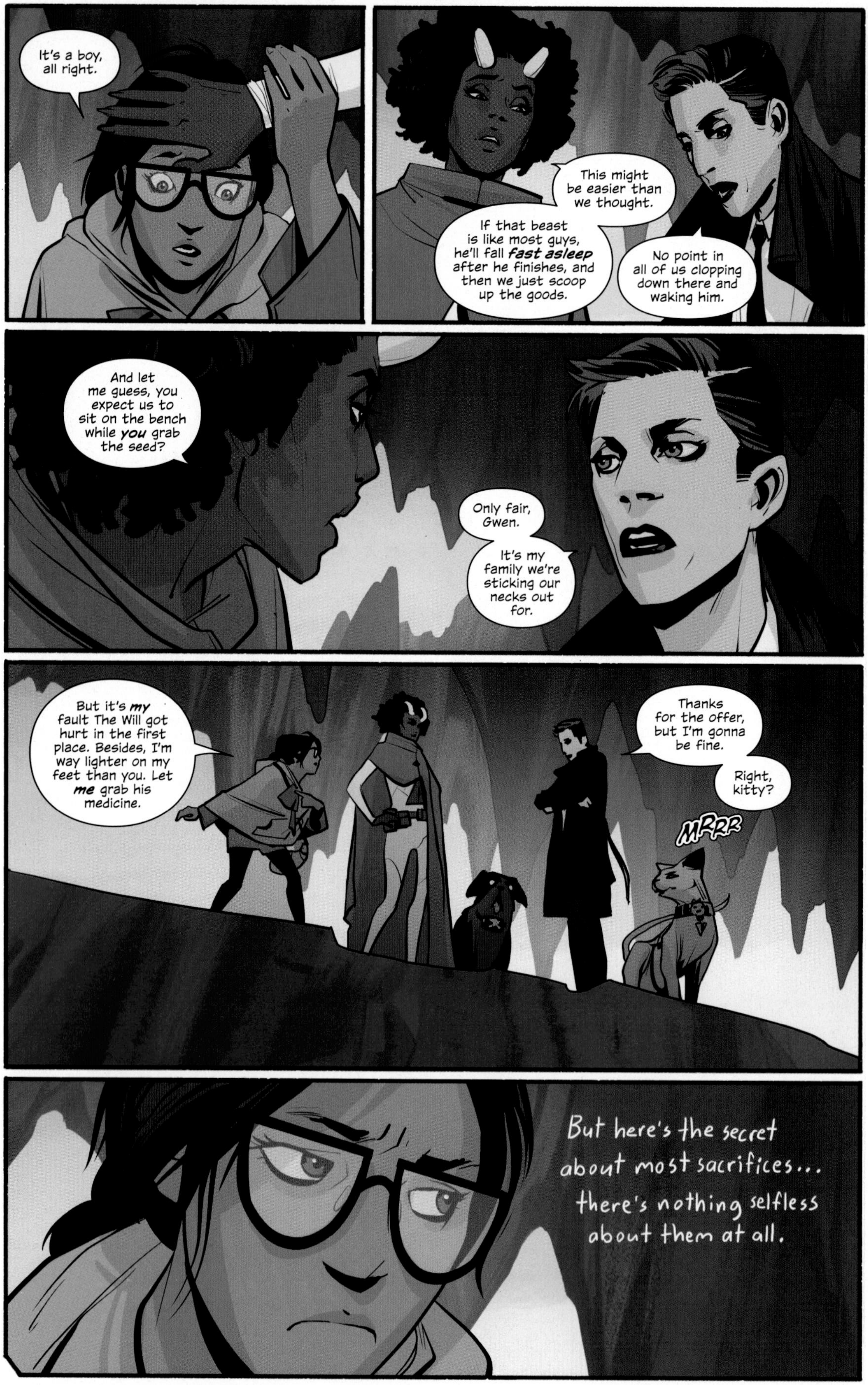
It's a boy, all right.
This might be easier than we thought.
If that beast is like most guys, he'll fall fast asleep after he finishes, and then we just scoop up the goods.
No point in all of us clopping down there and waking him.
And let me guess, you expect us to sit on the bench while you grab the seed?
Only fair, Gwen.
It's my family we're sticking our necks out for.
But it's my fault The Will got hurt in the first place. Besides, I'm way lighter on my feet than you. Let me grab his medicine.
Thanks for the offer, but I'm gonna be fine.
Right, kitty?
MRRR
But here's the secret about most sacrifices... there's nothing selfless about them at all.

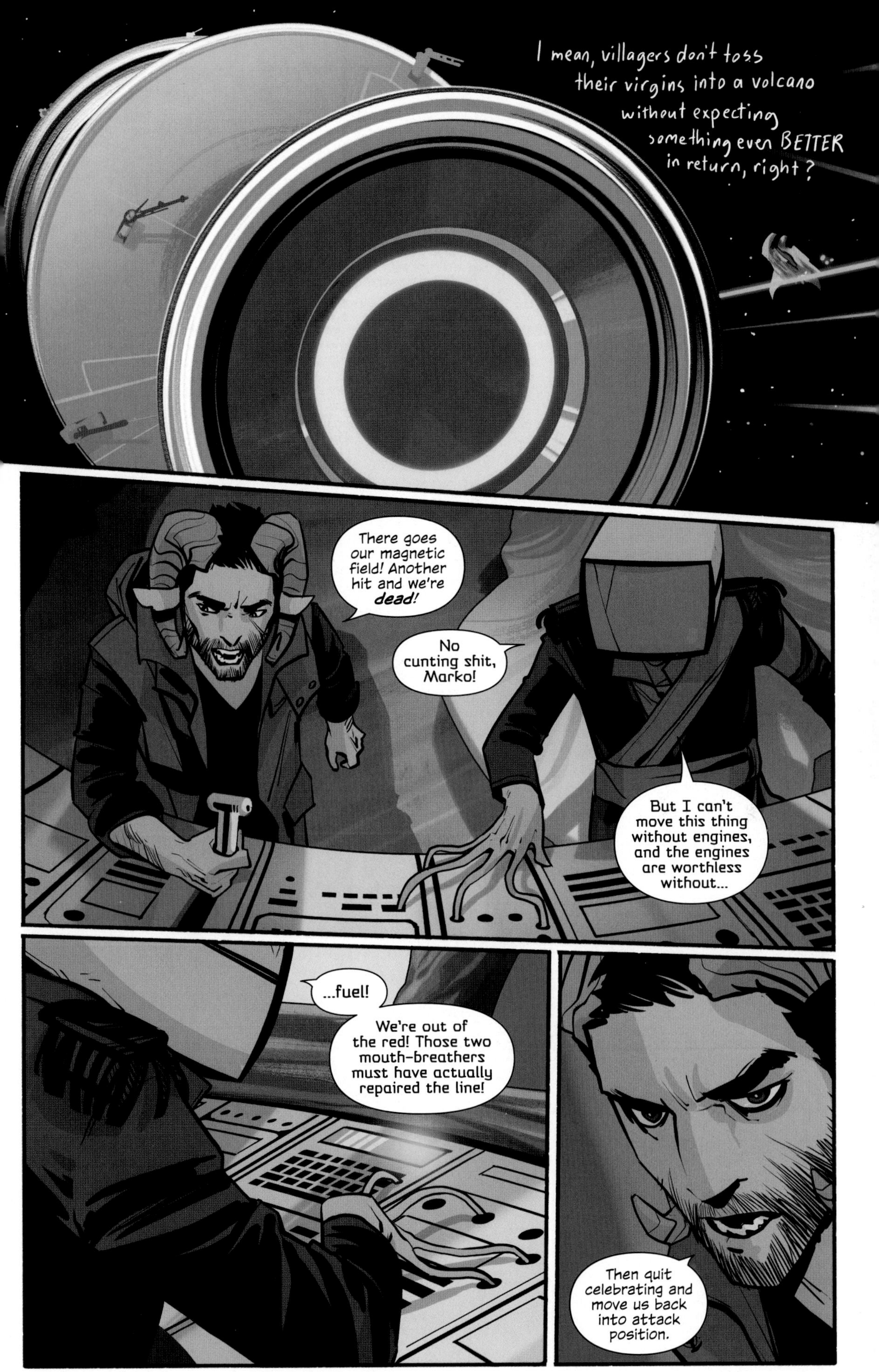
I mean, villagers don't toss their virgins into a volcano without expecting something even BETTER in return, right?
There goes our magnetic field! Another hit and we're *dead*!
No cunting shit, Marko!
But I can't move this thing without engines, and the engines are worthless without...
...fuel!
We're out of the red! Those two mouth-breathers must have actually repaired the line!
Then quit celebrating and move us back into attack position.

Belay that fuckery.

We're getting the hell out of here, like we should have done when Yuma suggested it.

We can still take these assholes!

These *assholes* are my own people.

Who just tried to *assassinate* you!

And while I admire your sudden evolution from pansy to warlord, maybe there's something to be said for retreating to fight another day.

We couldn't outrun that thing if we wanted to!

Not with thrusters, but we have just enough power for one last *hopscotch*.

Teleporting without mag fields is *suicide*!

Or homicide, if I can take you insufferable losers out with me...

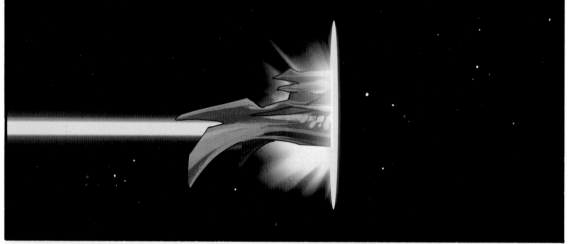

Did the Prince just...?

He ain't a prince anymore.

And we ain't gonna have *heads* once his father gets word.

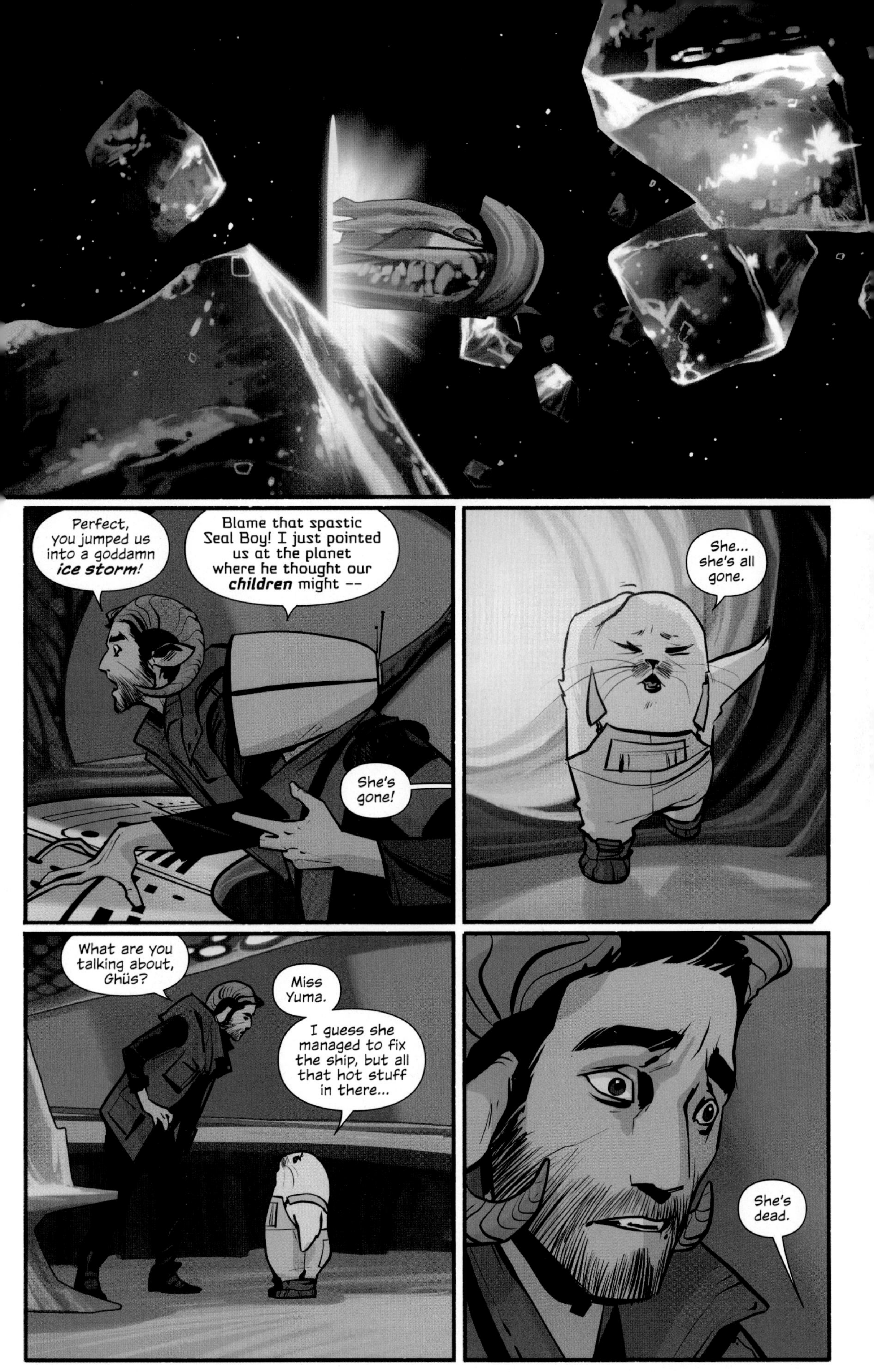
Perfect, you jumped us into a goddamn *ice storm!*
Blame that spastic Seal Boy! I just pointed us at the planet where he thought our **children** might --
She's gone!
She... she's all gone.
What are you talking about, Ghüs?
Miss Yuma.
I guess she managed to fix the ship, but all that hot stuff in there...
She's dead.

I... I don't know what to say.

She wasn't a saint, but the old girl deserved better than --

IV!

Oh.

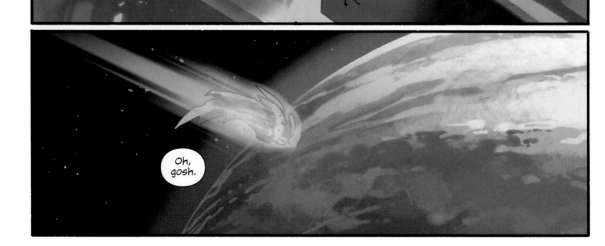

Oh, gosh.

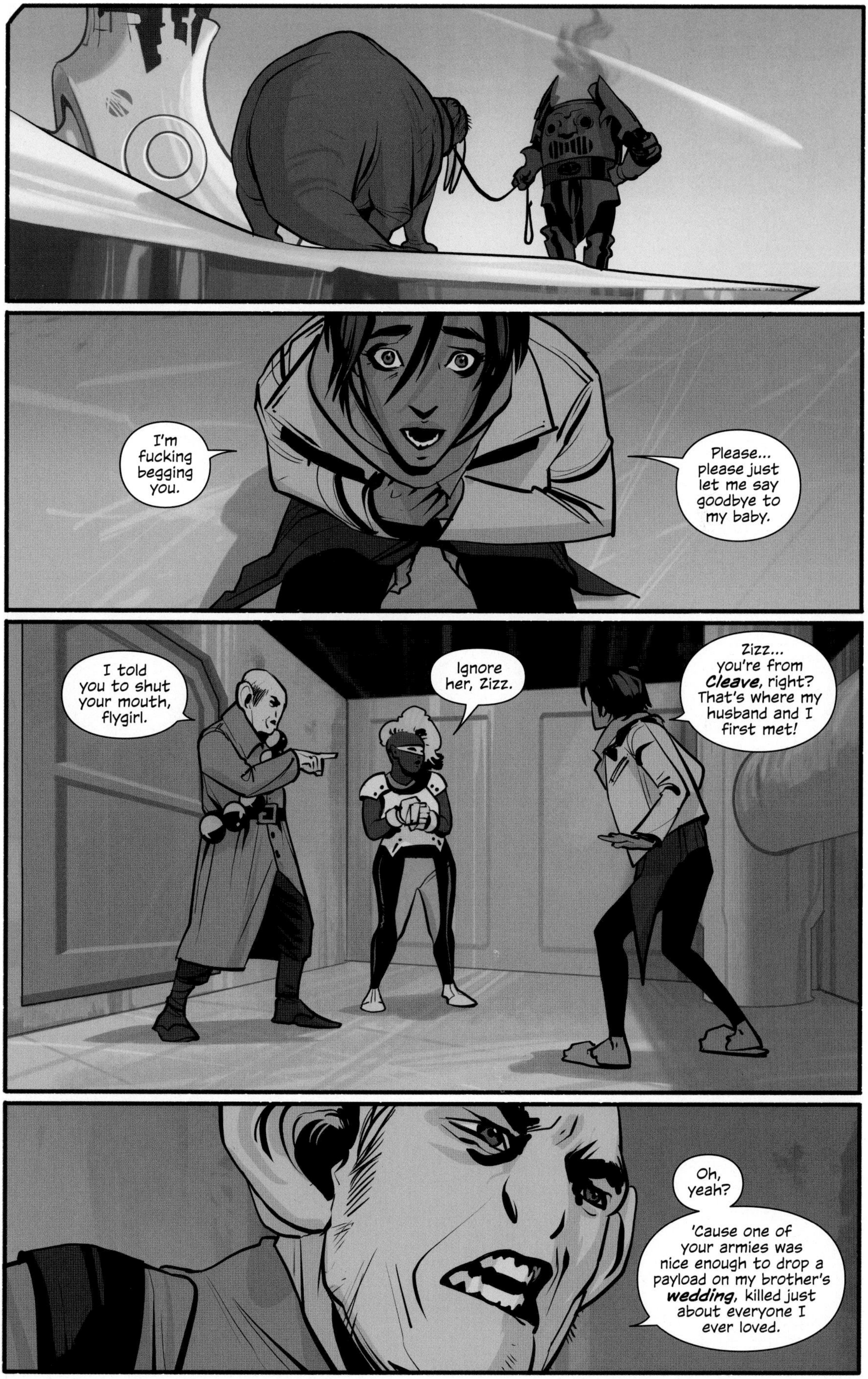

I'm fucking begging you.
Please... please just let me say goodbye to my baby.
I told you to shut your mouth, flygirl.
Ignore her, Zizz.
Zizz... you're from **Cleave**, right? That's where my husband and I first met!
Oh, yeah?
'Cause one of your armies was nice enough to drop a payload on my brother's **wedding**, killed just about everyone I ever loved.

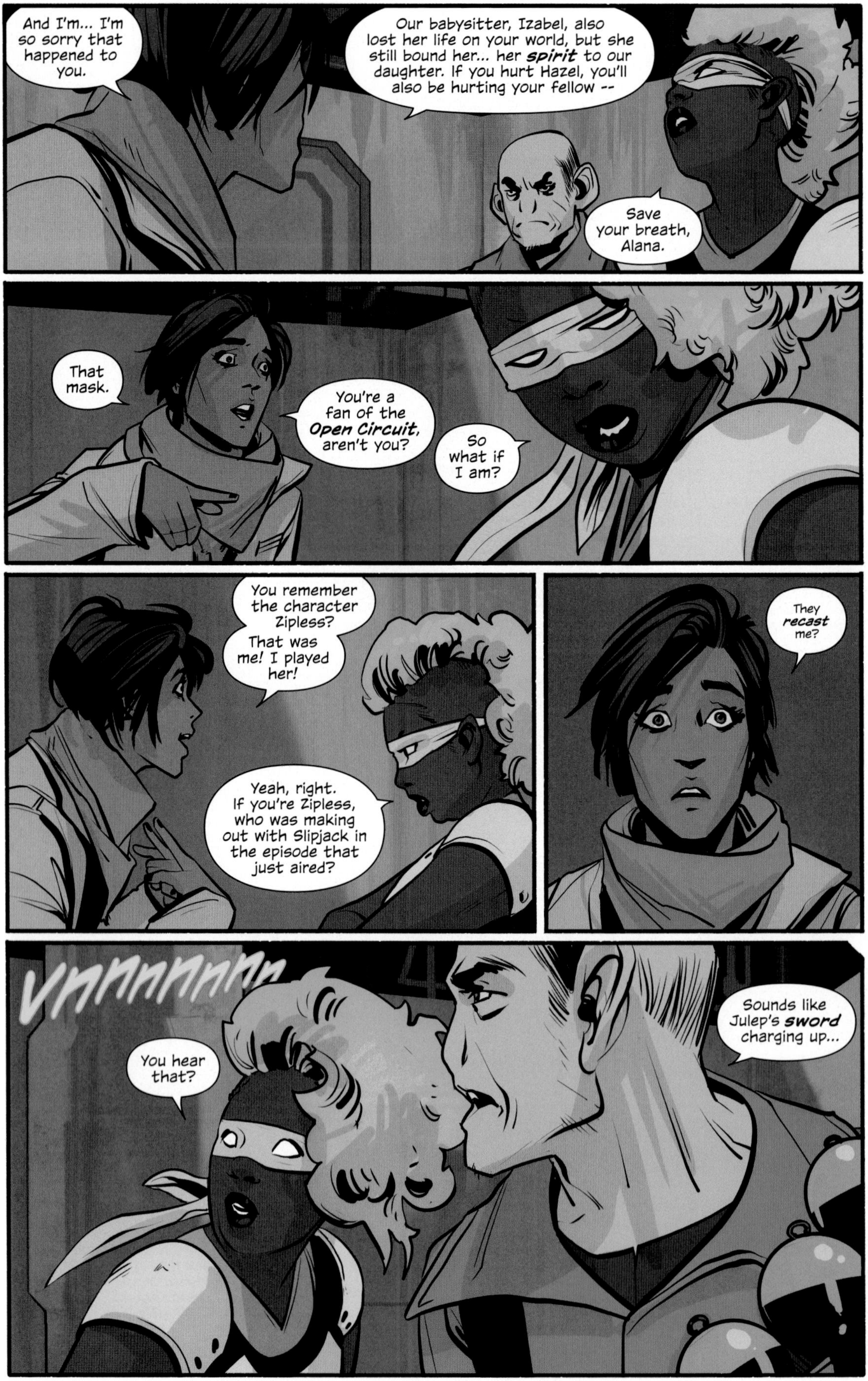
And I'm... I'm so sorry that happened to you.
Our babysitter, Izabel, also lost her life on your world, but she still bound her... her *spirit* to our daughter. If you hurt Hazel, you'll also be hurting your fellow --
Save your breath, Alana.
That mask.
You're a fan of the *Open Circuit*, aren't you?
So what if I am?
You remember the character Zipless?
That was me! I played her!
Yeah, right. If you're Zipless, who was making out with Slipjack in the episode that just aired?
They *recast* me?
VNNNNNNN
You hear that?
Sounds like Julep's *sword* charging up...

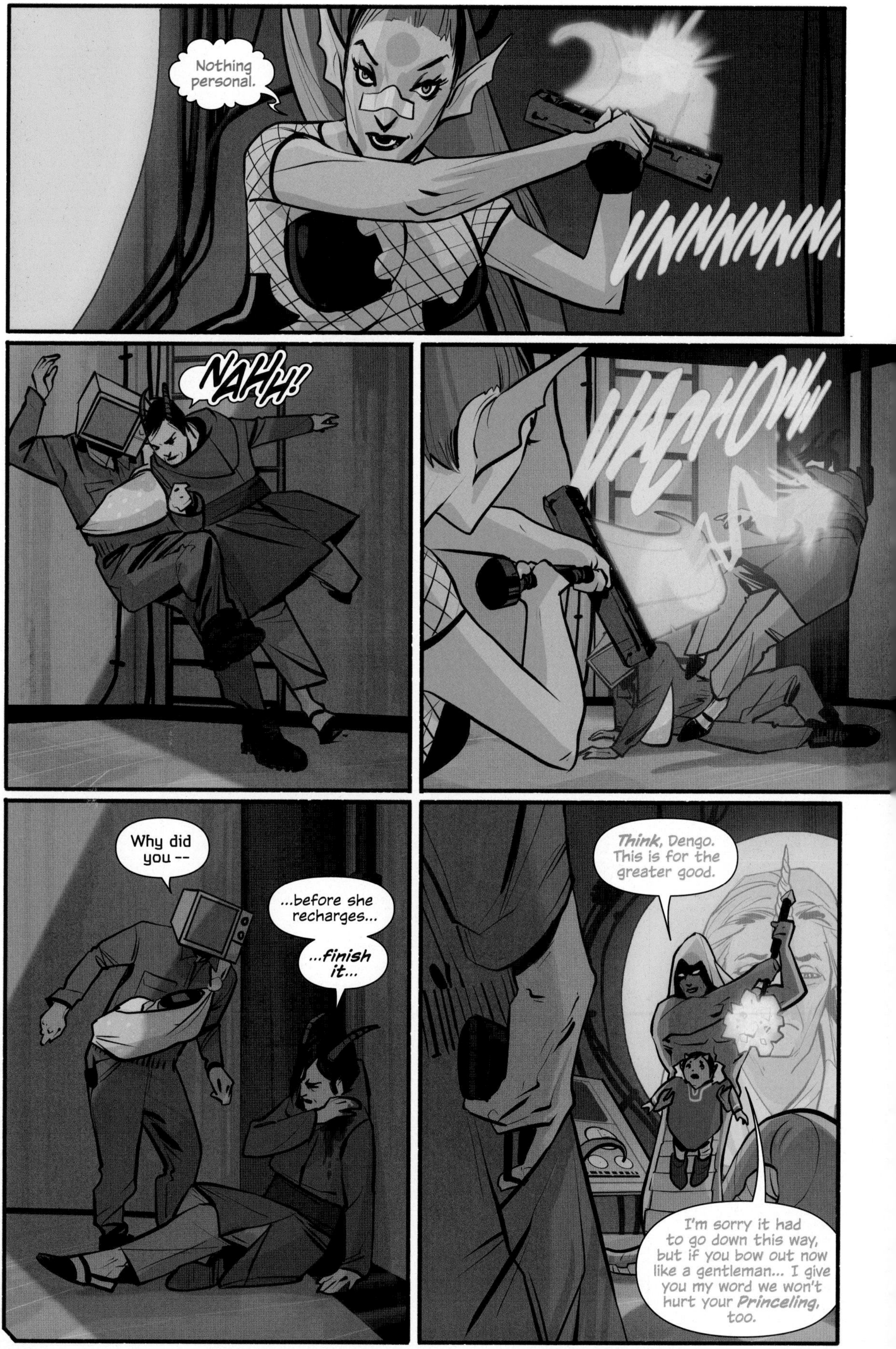
Nothing personal.
VNNNNNNN
NAHH!
VACHOWW
Why did you --
...before she recharges...
...finish it...
Think, Dengo. This is for the greater good.
I'm sorry it had to go down this way, but if you bow out now like a gentleman... I give you my word we won't hurt your Princeling, too.

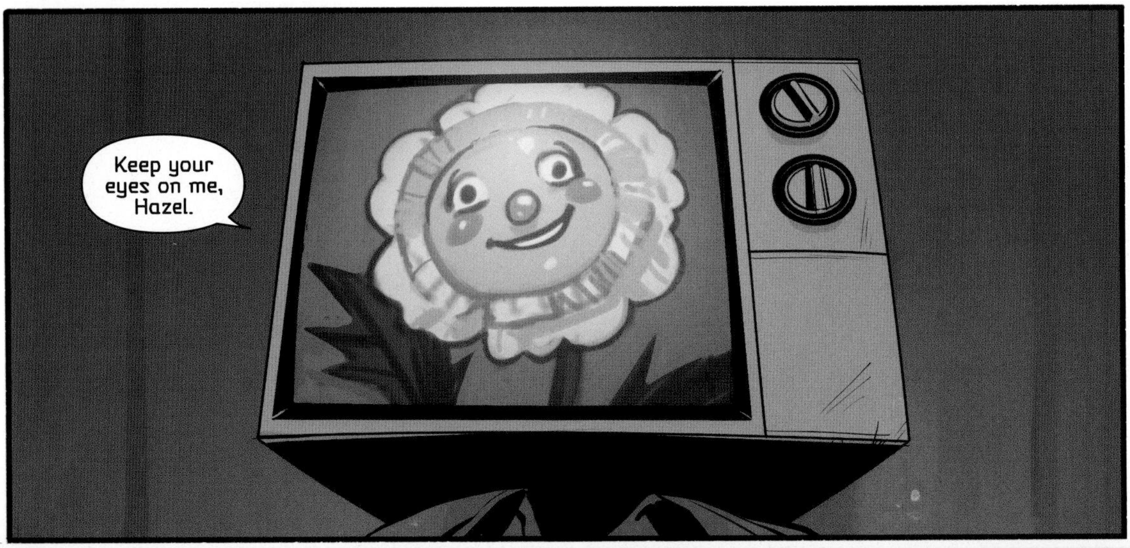
Keep your eyes on me, Hazel.

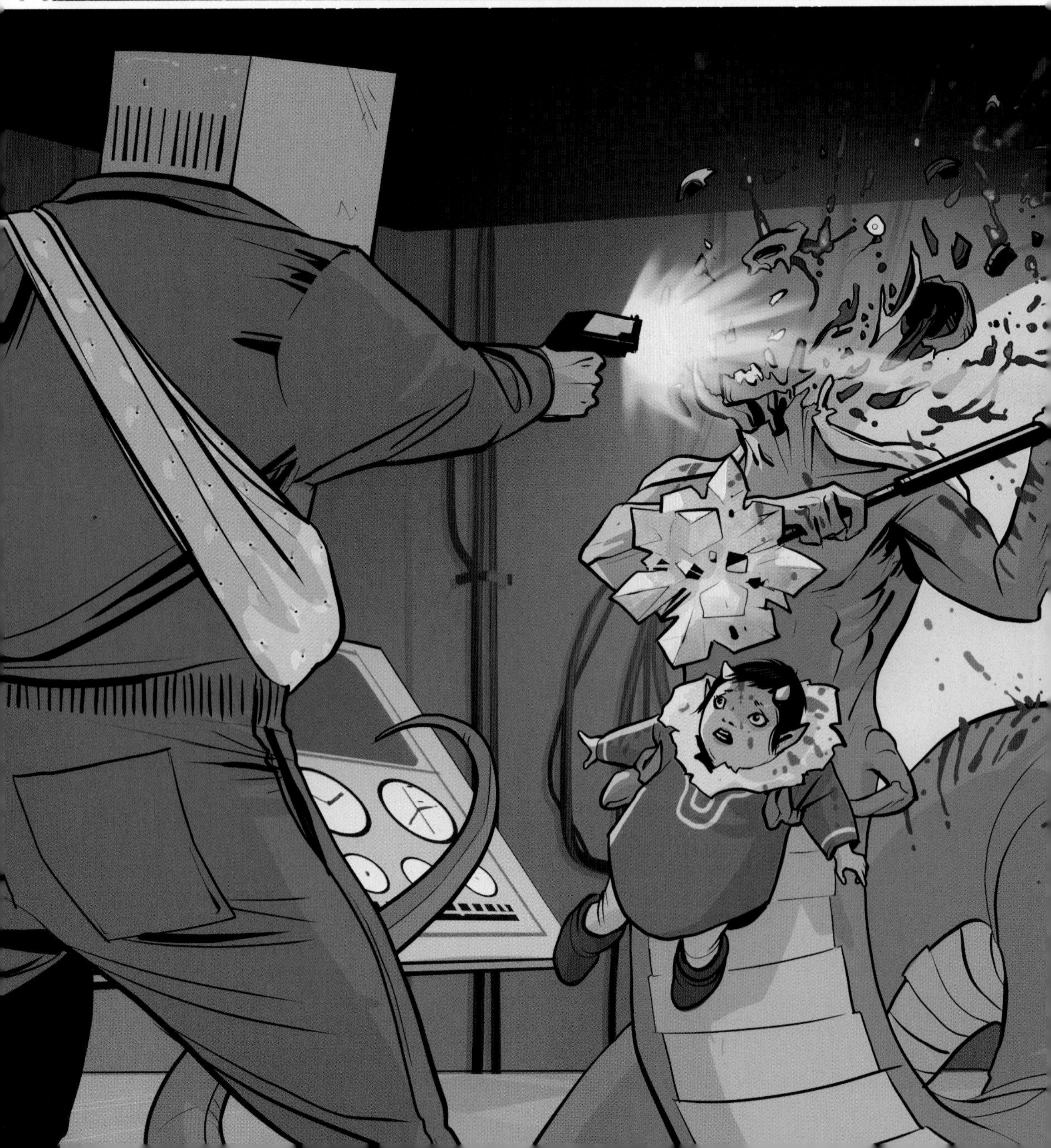

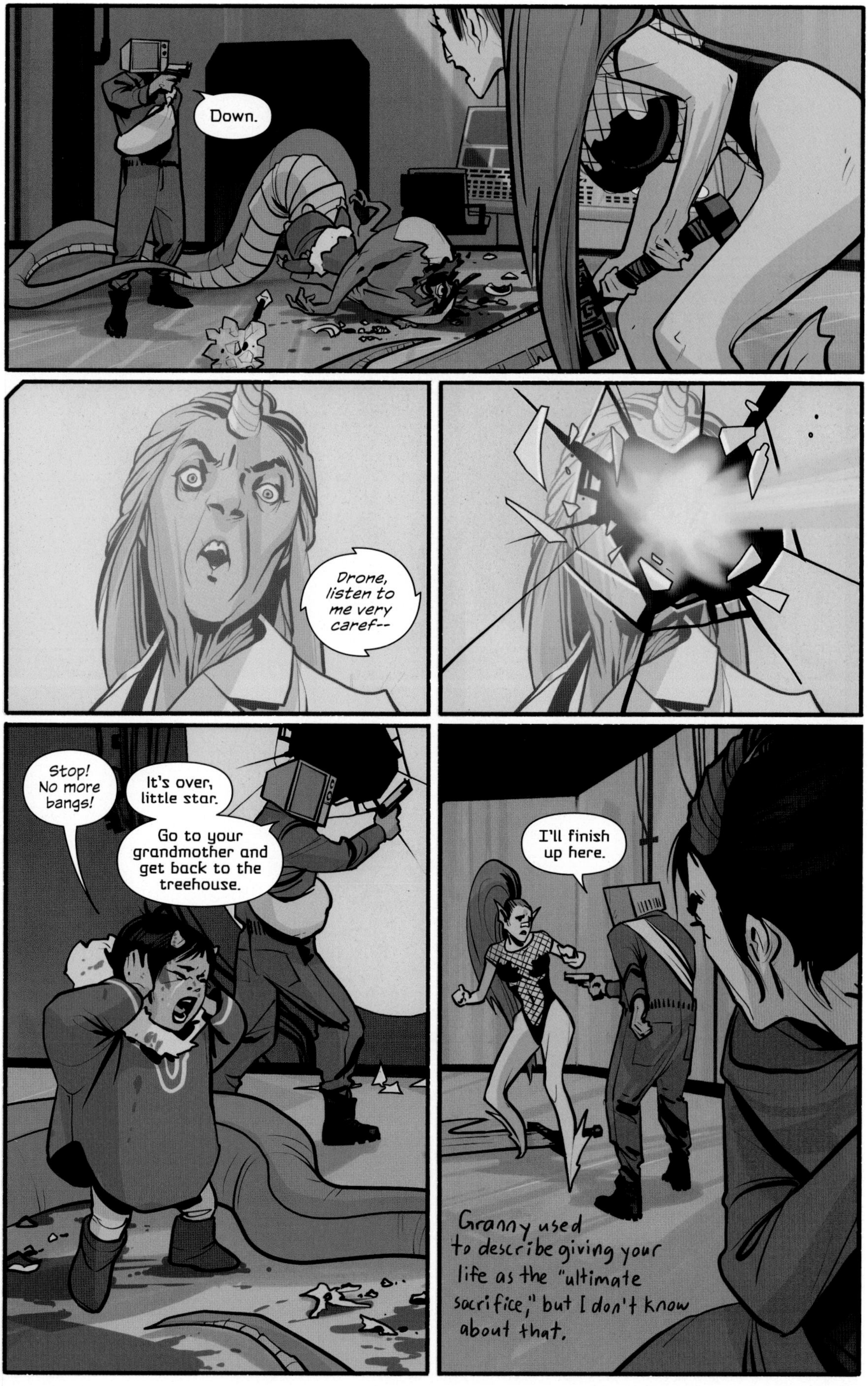
Down.
Drone, listen to me very caref--
Stop! No more bangs!
It's over, little star.
Go to your grandmother and get back to the treehouse.
I'll finish up here.
Granny used to describe giving your life as the "ultimate sacrifice," but I don't know about that.

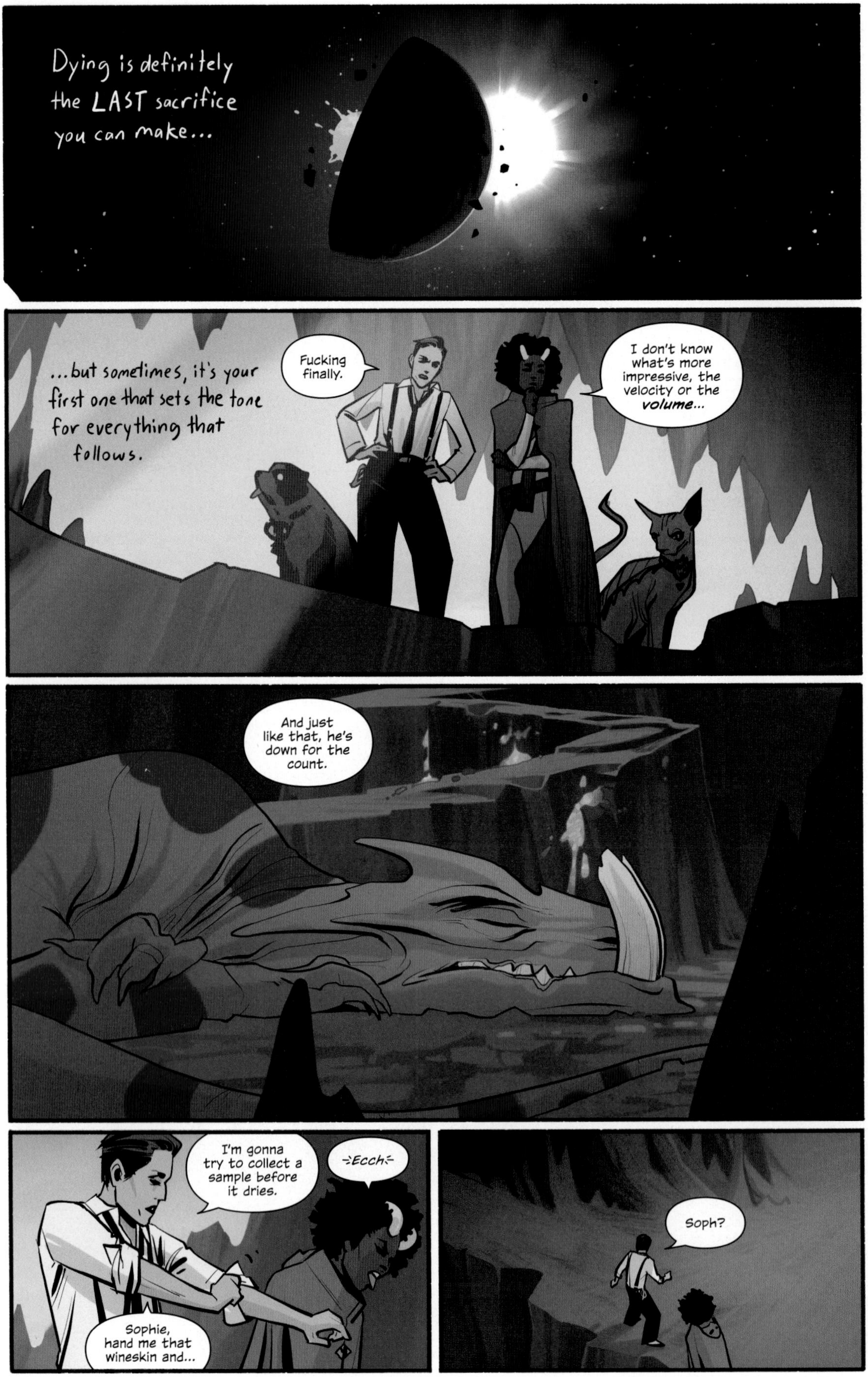
Dying is definitely the LAST sacrifice you can make...
...but sometimes, it's your first one that sets the tone for everything that follows.
Fucking finally.
I don't know what's more impressive, the velocity or the *volume*...
And just like that, he's down for the count.
I'm gonna try to collect a sample before it dries.
Sophie, hand me that wineskin and...
Ecch
Soph?

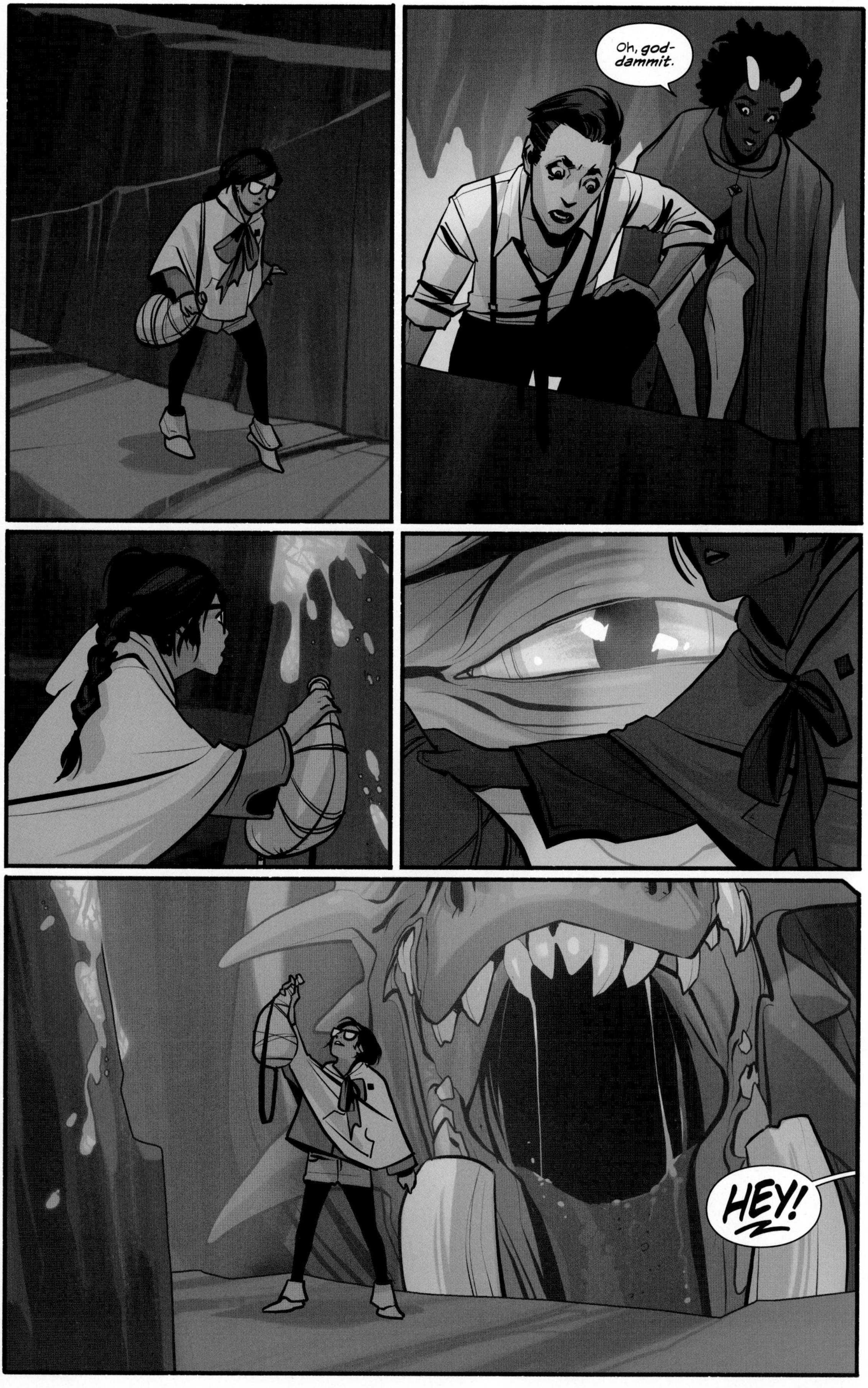
Oh, god-dammit.
HEY!

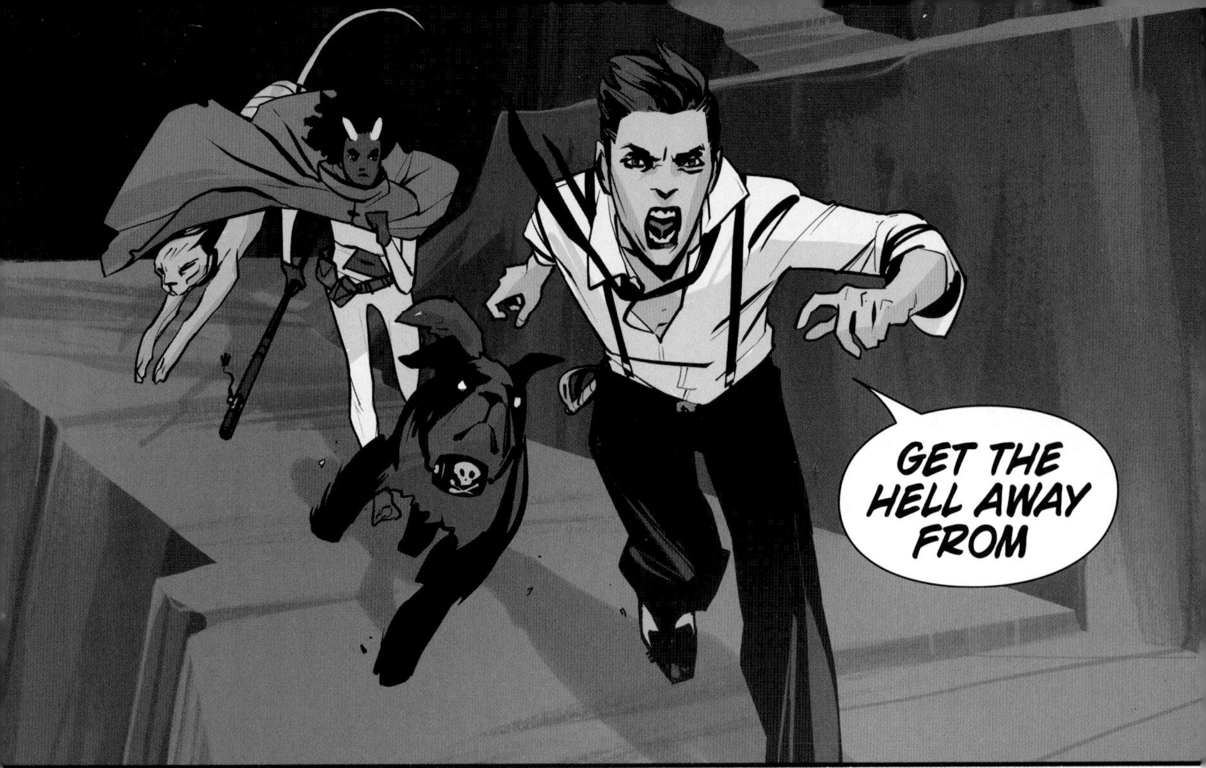
GET THE HELL AWAY FROM

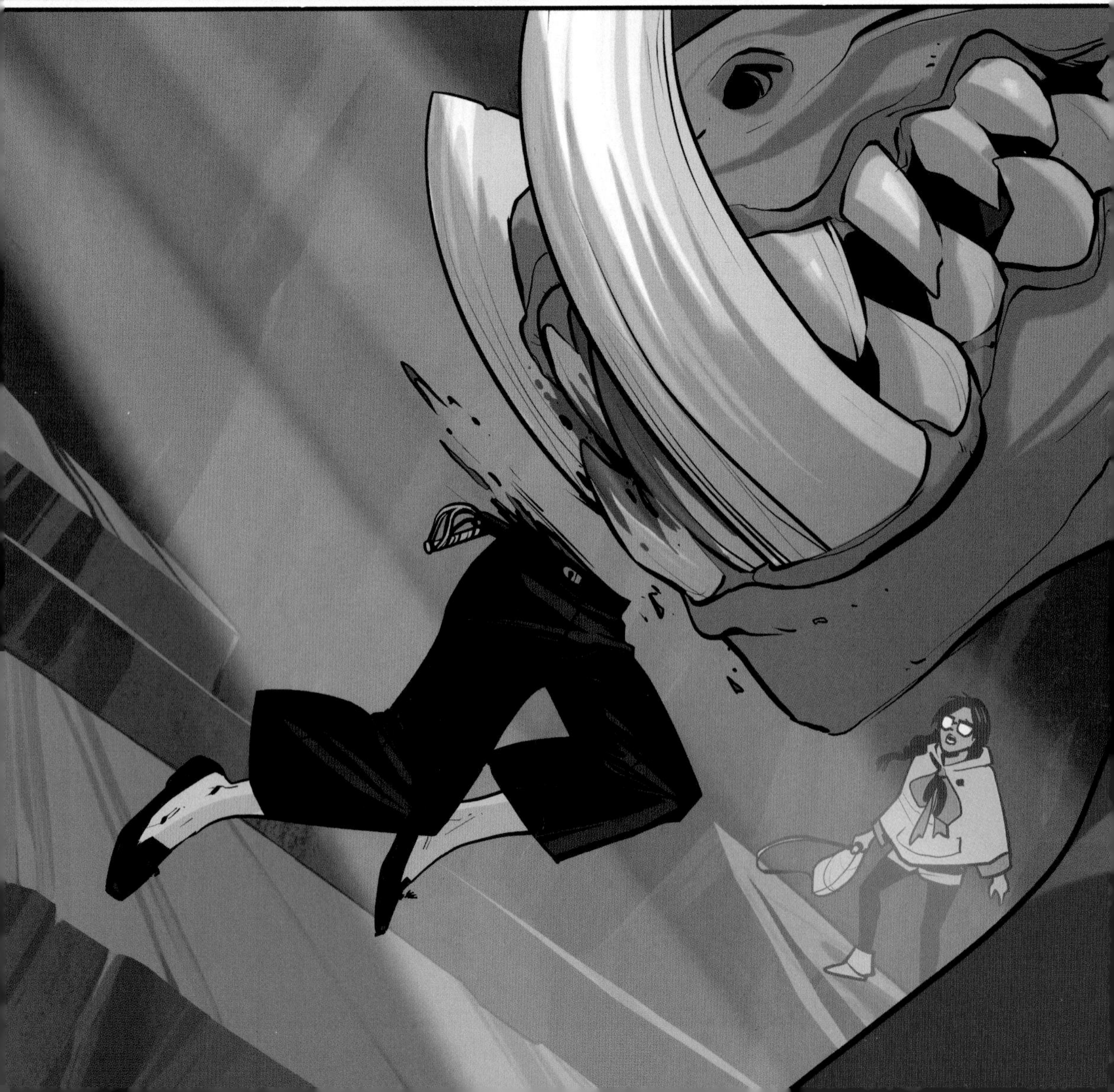

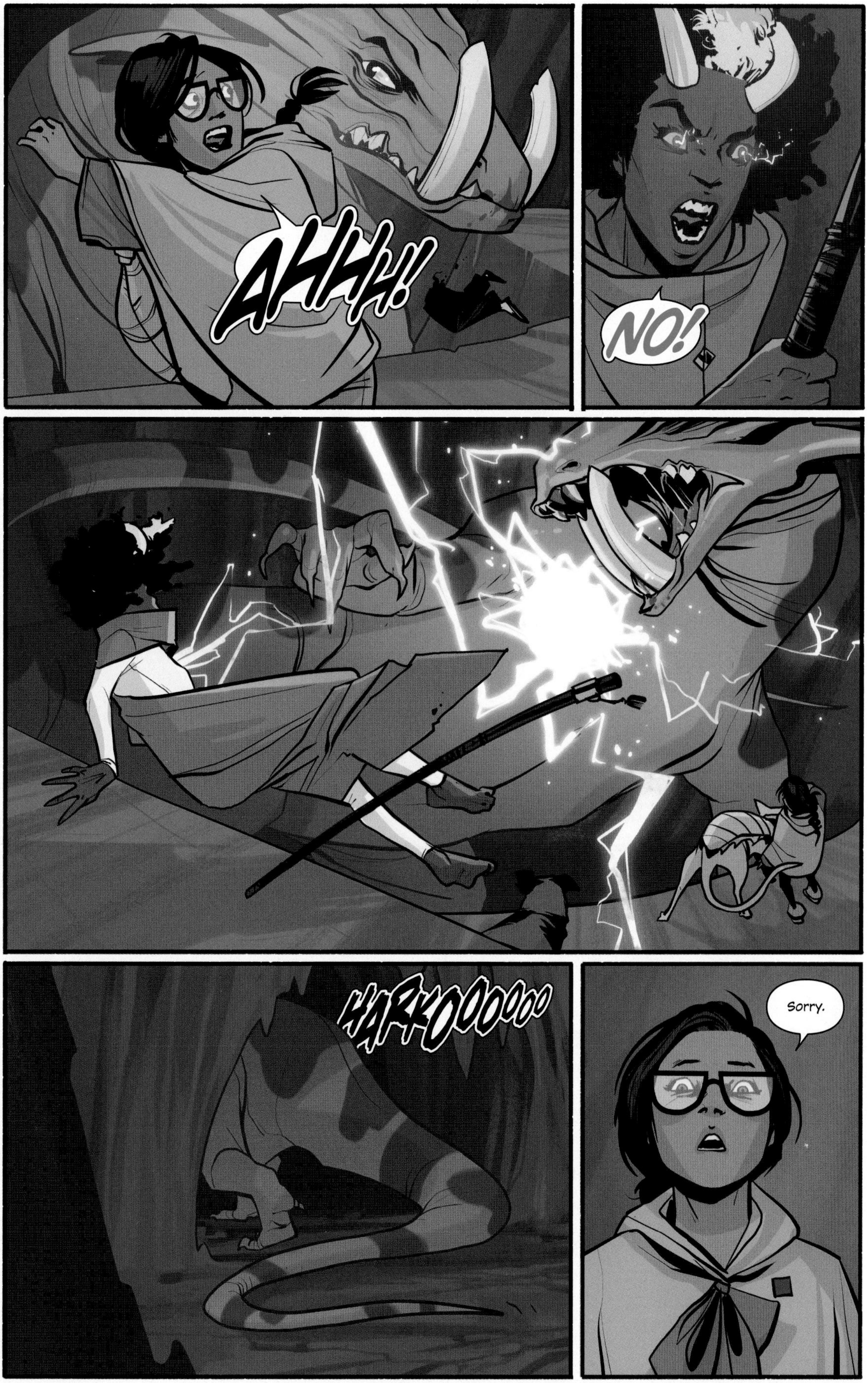
AHHH!
NO!
HARKOOOOOO
Sorry.

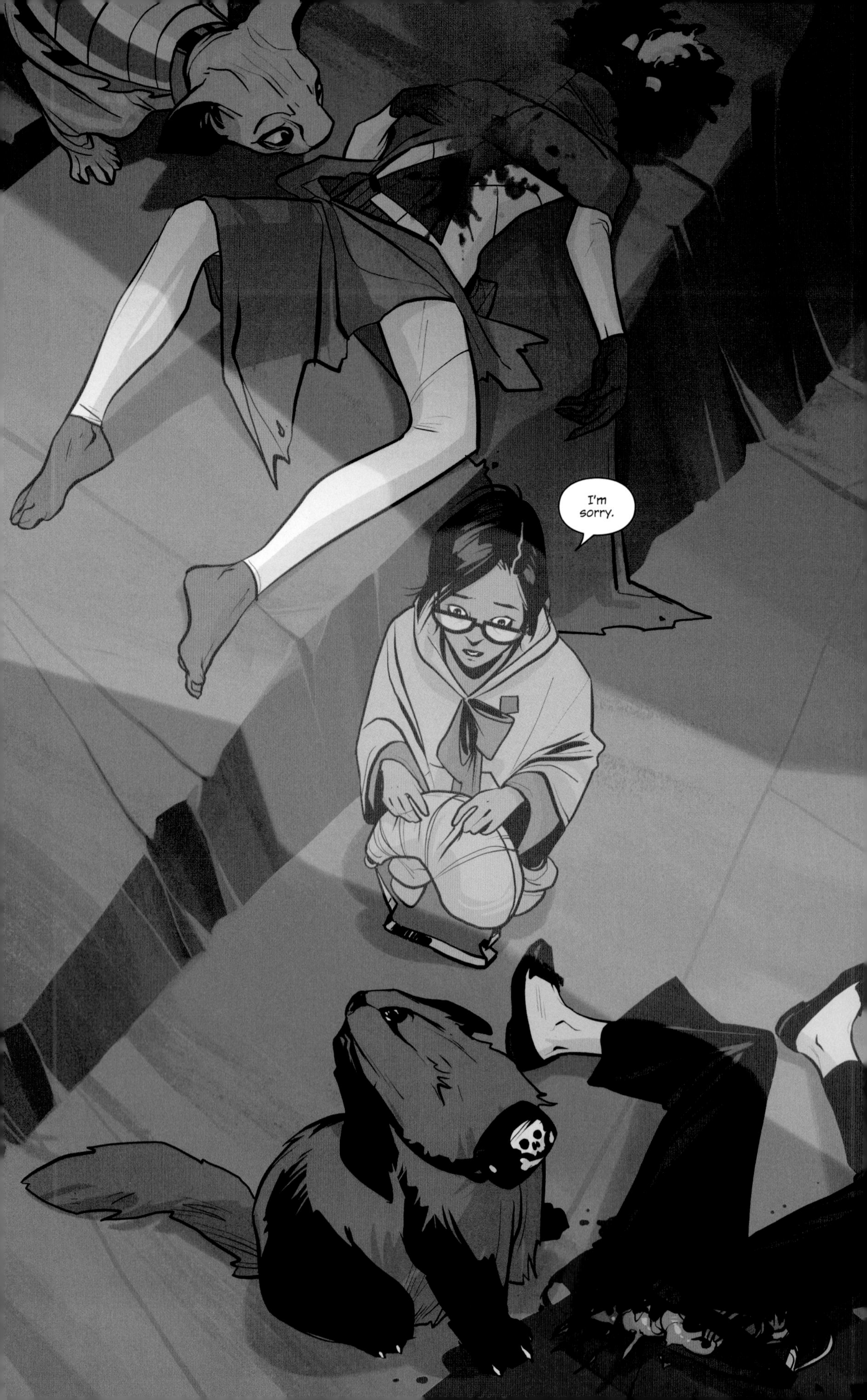
I'm sorry.

end chapter twenty-nine

CHAPTER
THIRTY

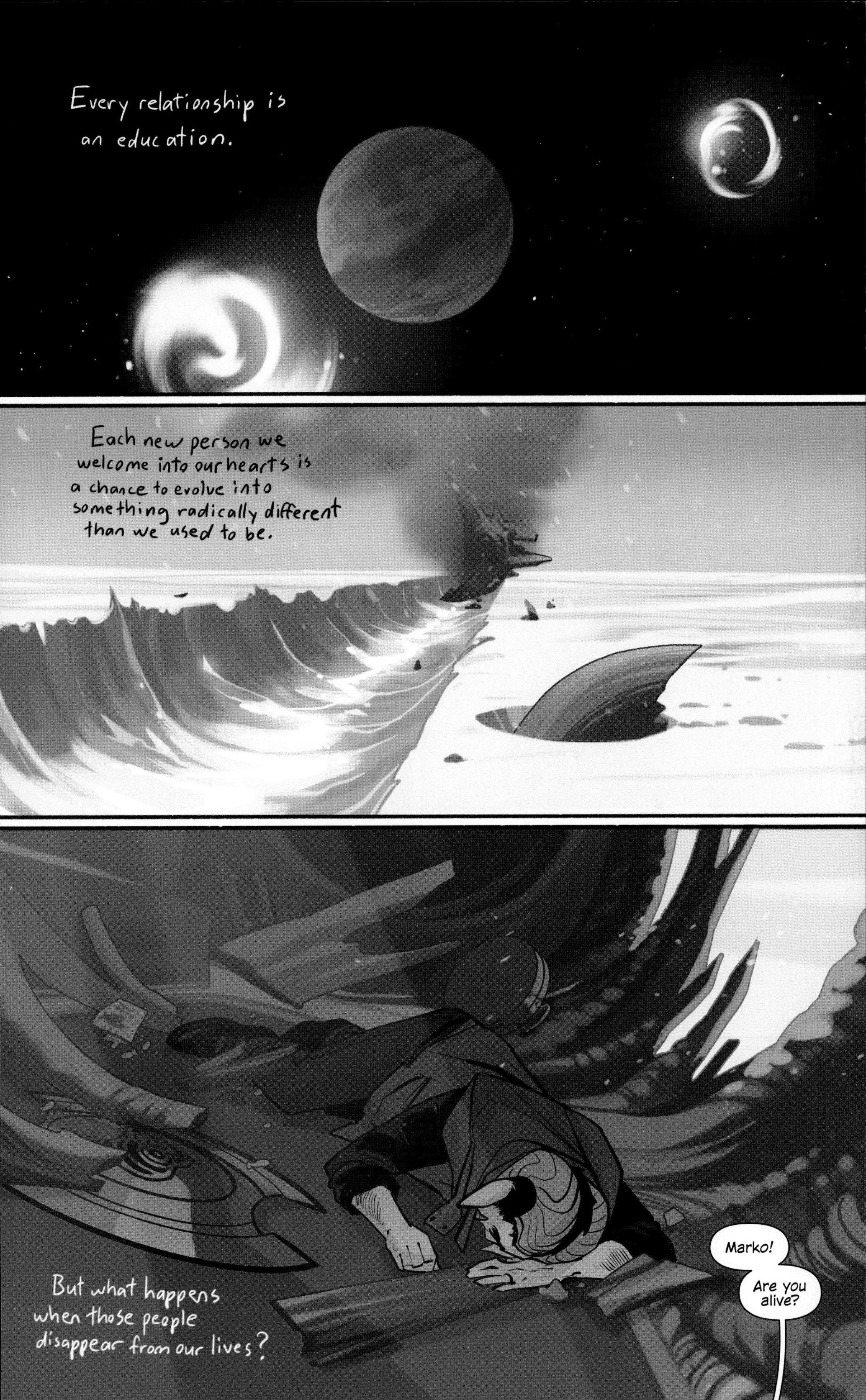
Every relationship is an education.
Each new person we welcome into our hearts is a chance to evolve into something radically different than we used to be.
But what happens when those people disappear from our lives?
Marko!
Are you alive?

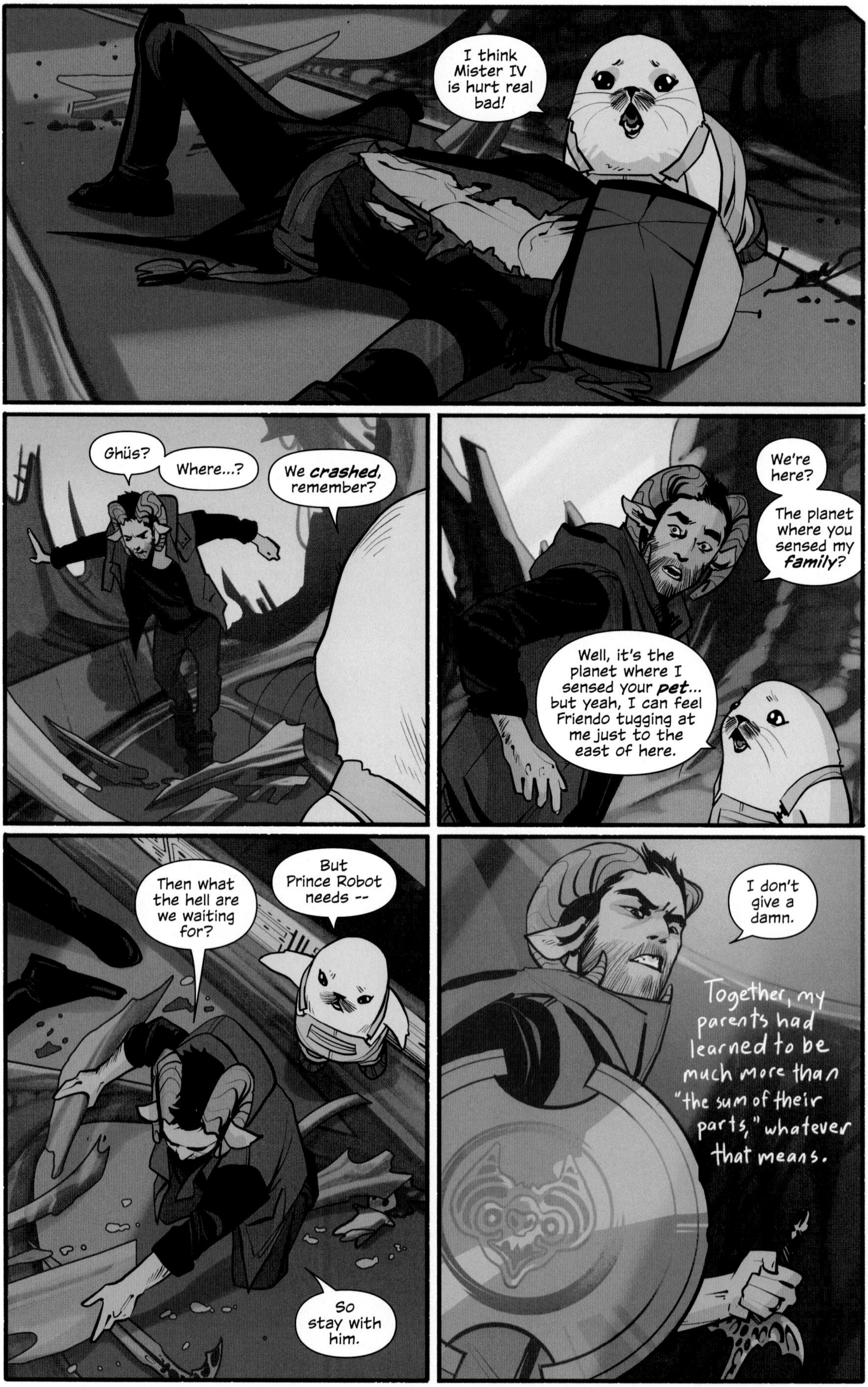
I think Mister IV is hurt real bad!
Ghüs?
Where...?
We *crashed*, remember?
We're here?
The planet where you sensed my *family*?
Well, it's the planet where I sensed your *pet*... but yeah, I can feel Friendo tugging at me just to the east of here.
Then what the hell are we waiting for?
But Prince Robot needs --
So stay with him.
I don't give a damn.
Together, my parents had learned to be much more than "the sum of their parts," whatever that means.

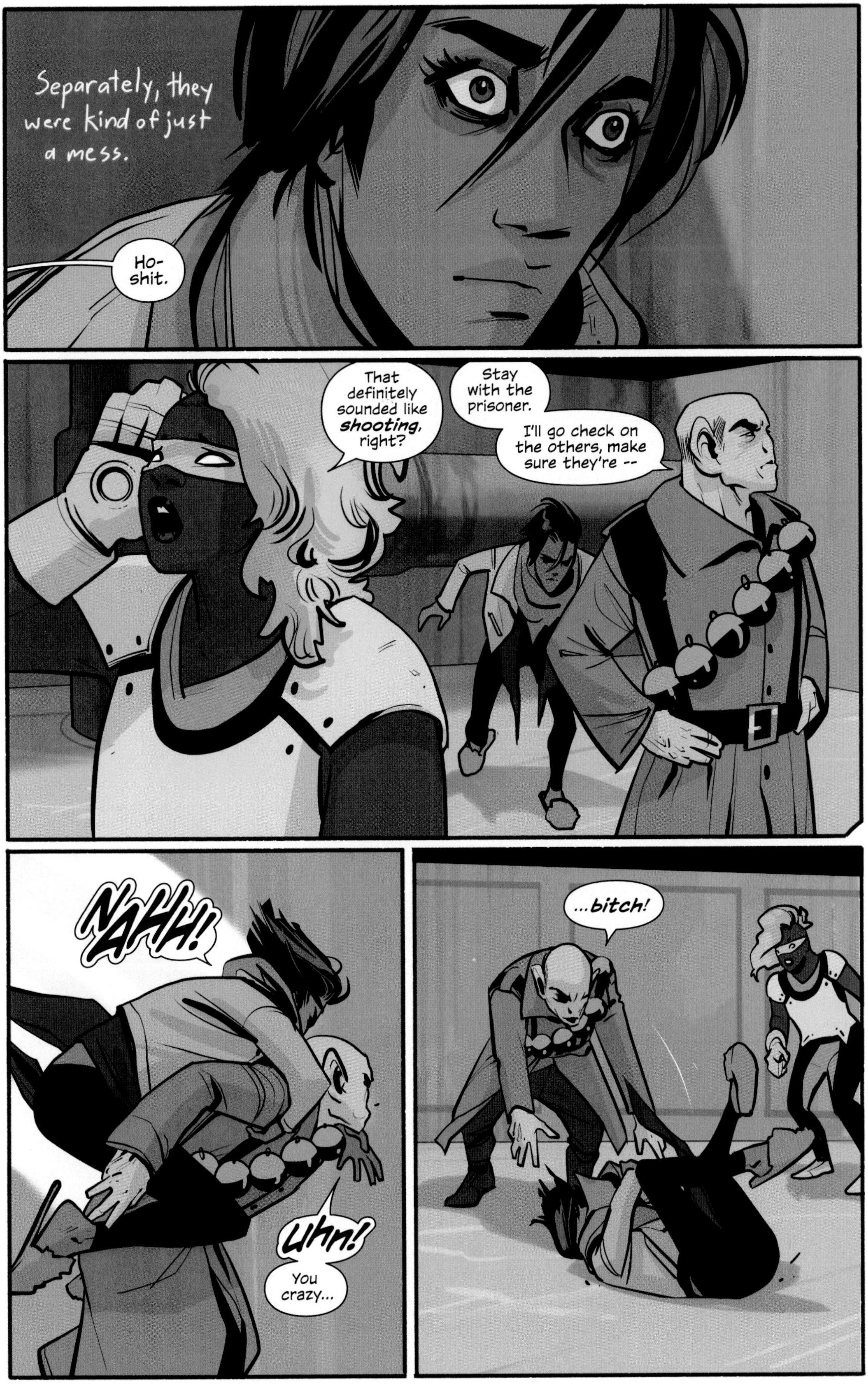
Separately, they were kind of just a mess.
Ho-shit.
That definitely sounded like **shooting,** right?
Stay with the prisoner.
I'll go check on the others, make sure they're --
NAHH!
Uhn!
You crazy...
...**bitch!**

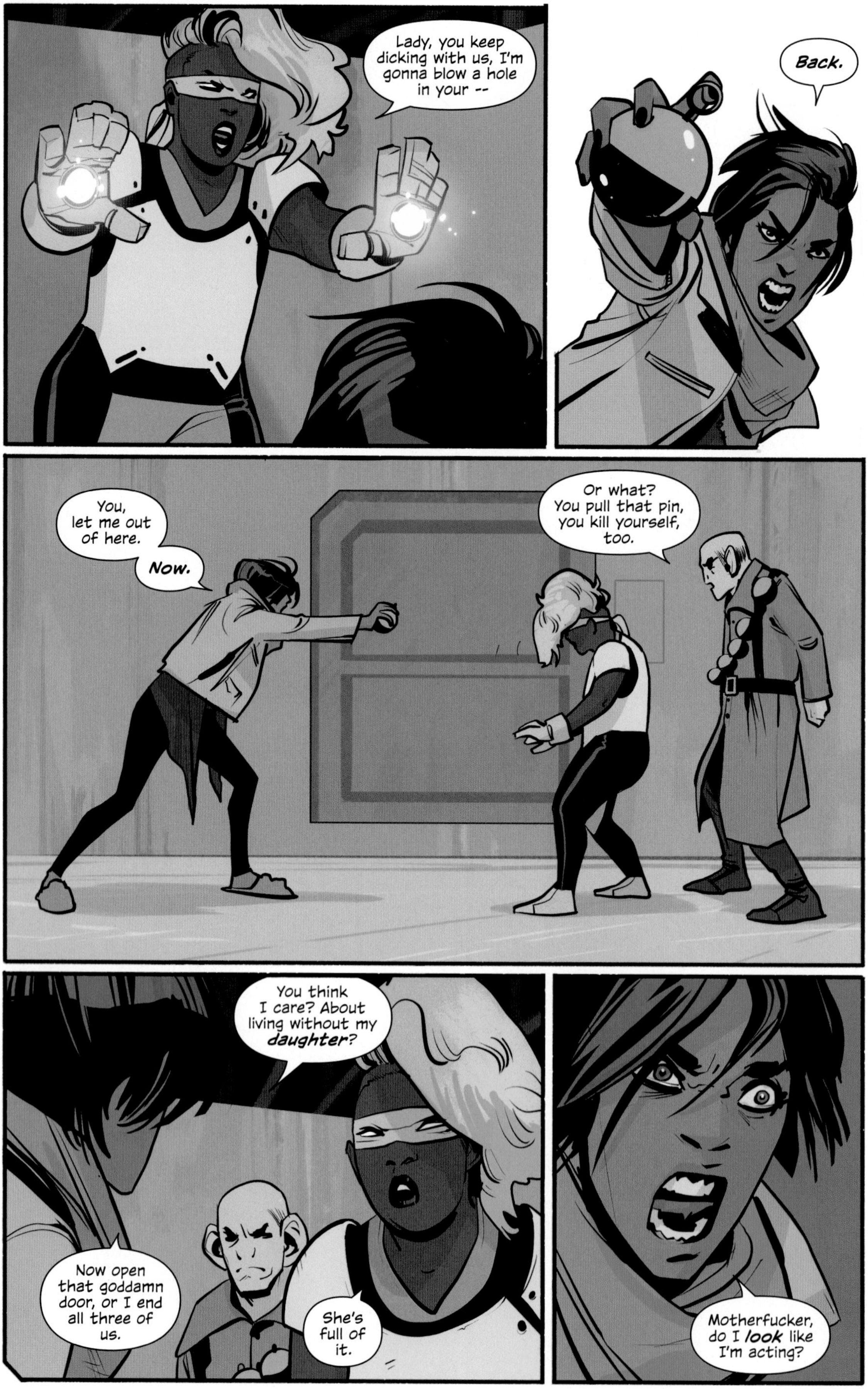
Lady, you keep dicking with us, I'm gonna blow a hole in your --
Back.
You, let me out of here.
Now.
Or what? You pull that pin, you kill yourself, too.
You think I care? About living without my daughter?
Now open that goddamn door, or I end all three of us.
She's full of it.
Motherfucker, do I look like I'm acting?

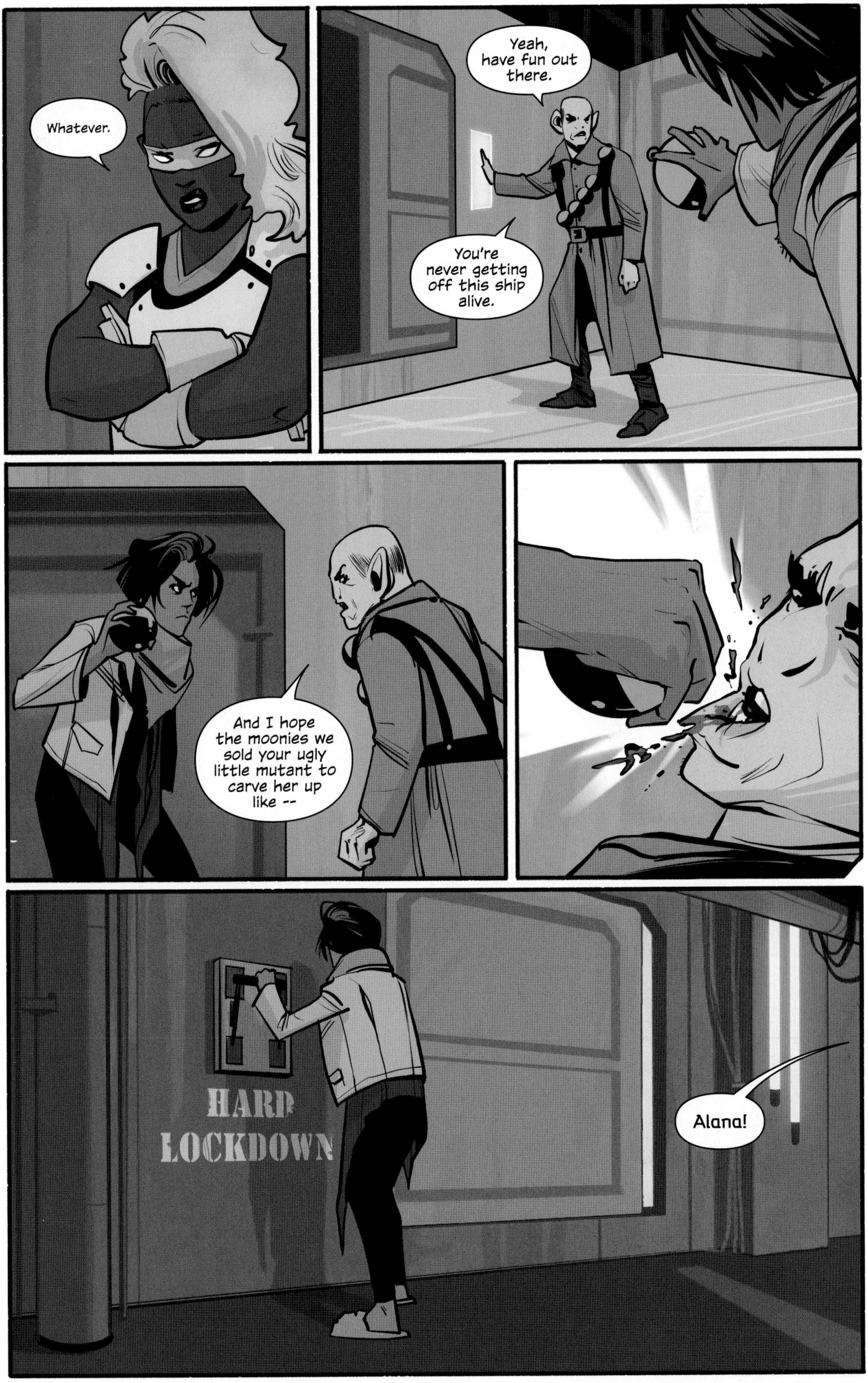
Whatever.
Yeah, have fun out there.
You're never getting off this ship alive.
And I hope the moonies we sold your ugly little mutant to carve her up like --
HARD LOCKDOWN
Alana!

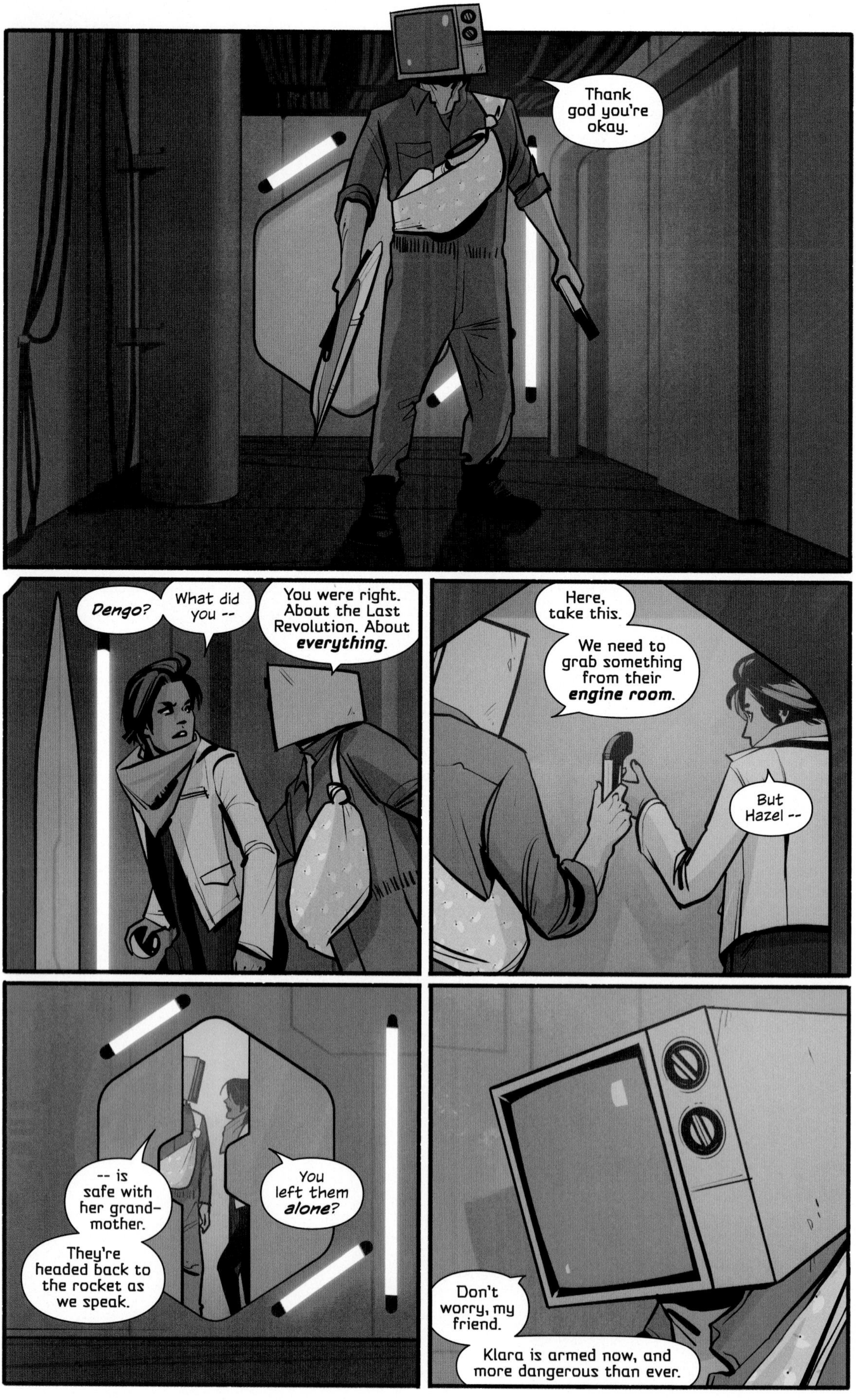
Thank god you're okay.
Dengo?
What did you --
You were right. About the Last Revolution. About everything.
Here, take this.
We need to grab something from their engine room.
But Hazel --
-- is safe with her grand-mother.
They're headed back to the rocket as we speak.
You left them alone?
Don't worry, my friend.
Klara is armed now, and more dangerous than ever.

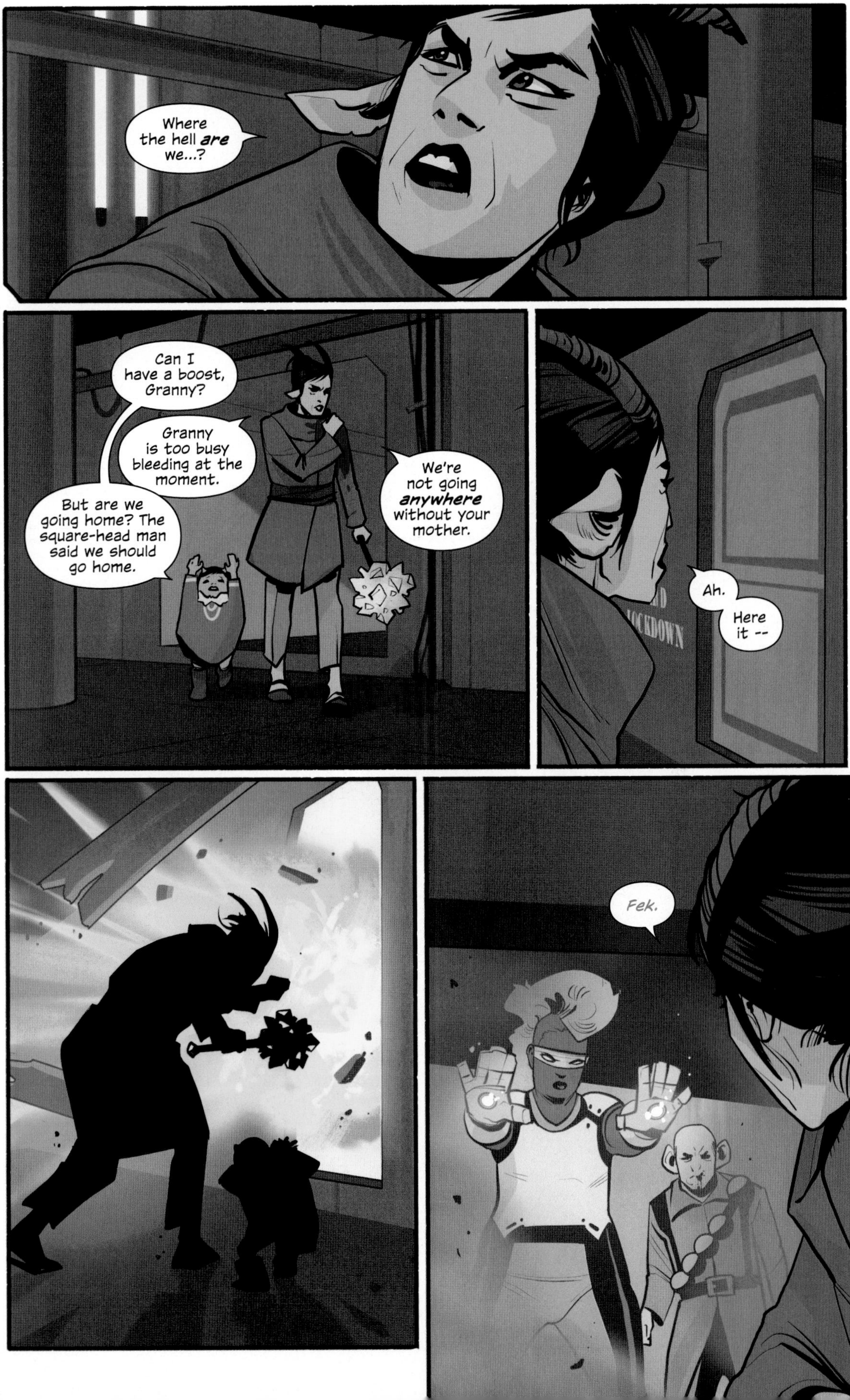
Where the hell *are* we...?
Can I have a boost, Granny?
Granny is too busy bleeding at the moment.
But are we going home? The square-head man said we should go home.
We're not going ***anywhere*** without your mother.
Ah.
Here it --
Fek.

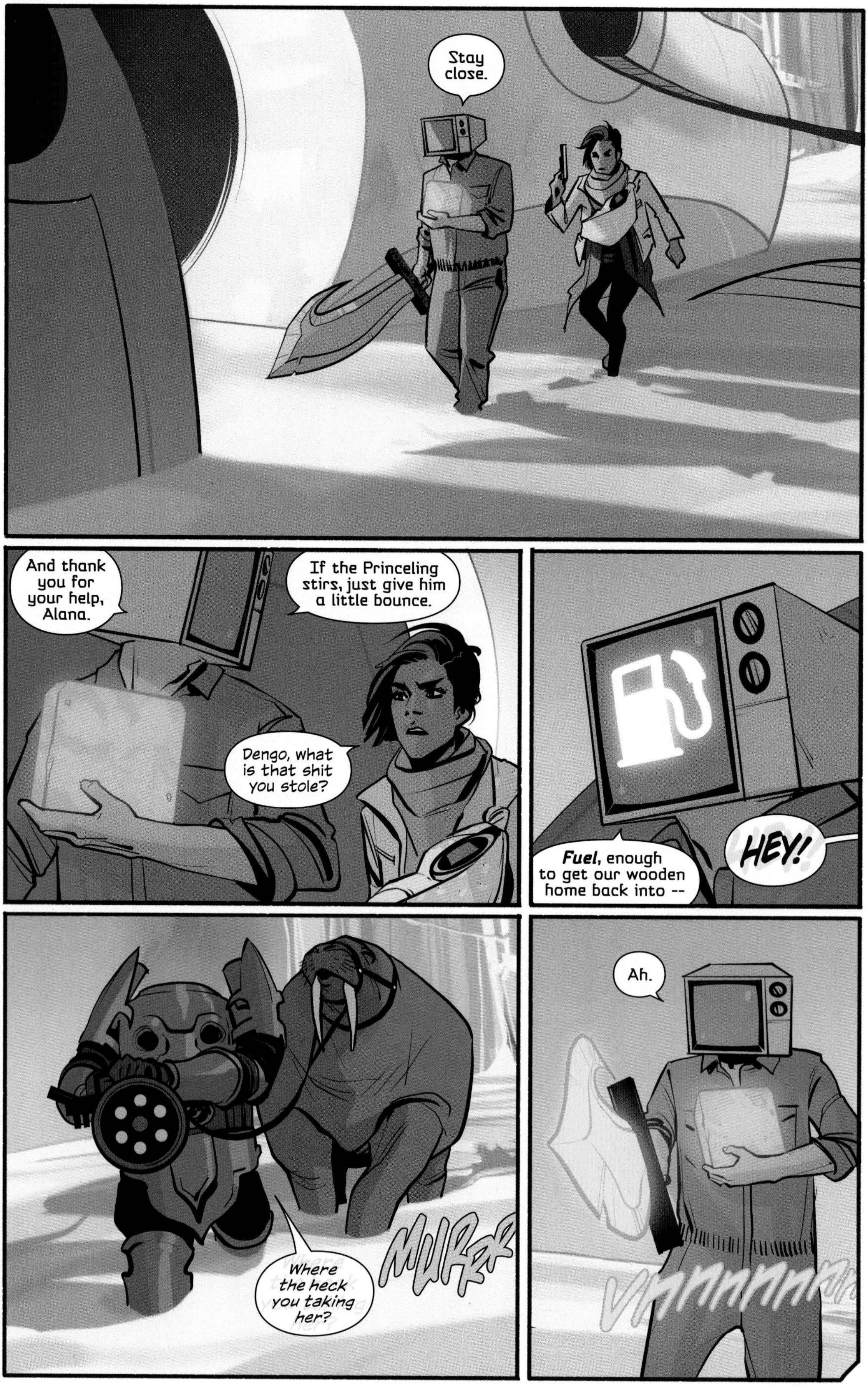
Stay close.
And thank you for your help, Alana.
If the Princeling stirs, just give him a little bounce.
Dengo, what is that shit you stole?
Fuel, enough to get our wooden home back into --
HEY!
Where the heck you taking her?
MURRR
Ah.

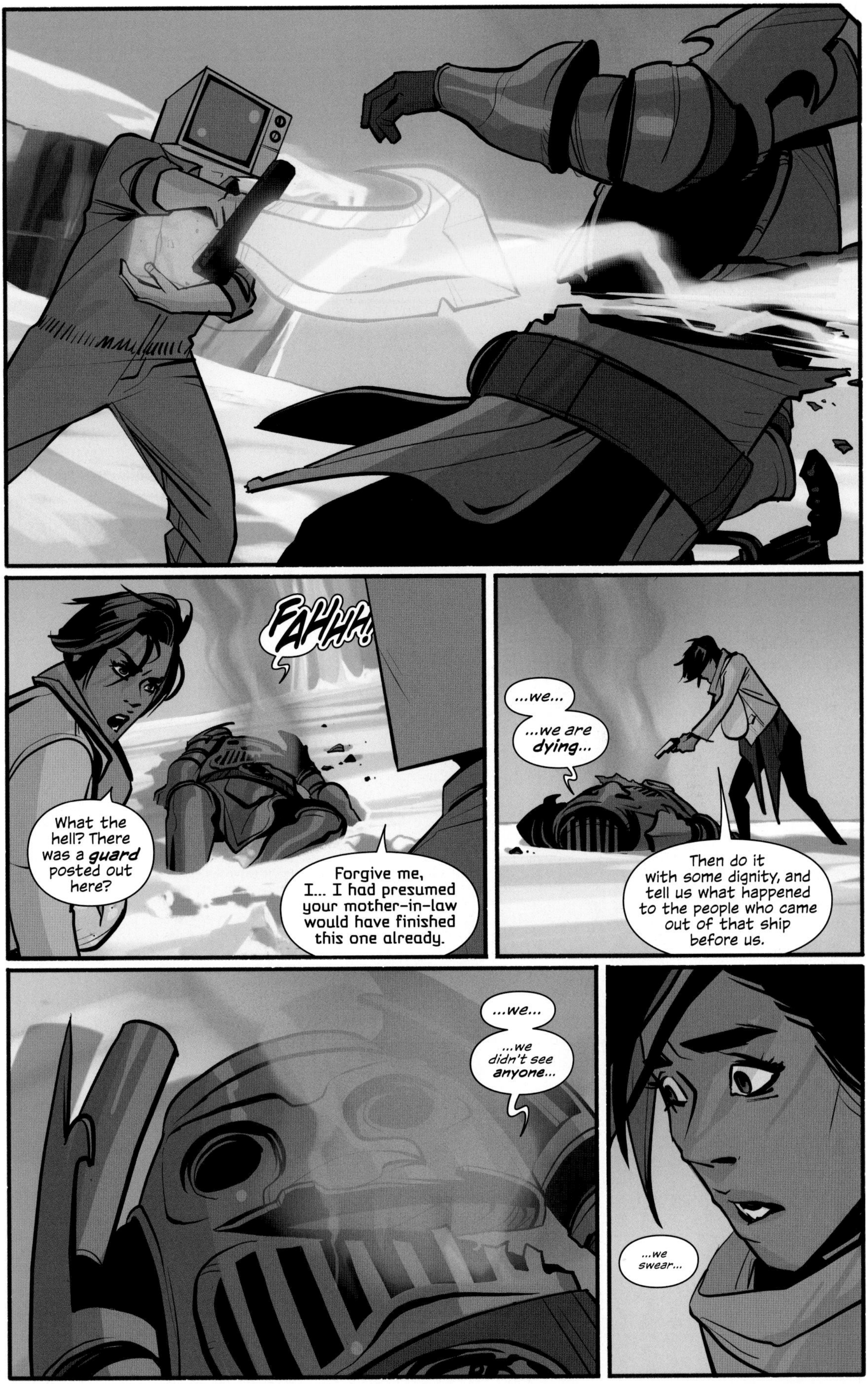
FAHHH!
What the hell? There was a guard posted out here?
Forgive me, I... I had presumed your mother-in-law would have finished this one already.
...we...
...we are dying...
Then do it with some dignity, and tell us what happened to the people who came out of that ship before us.
...we...
...we didn't see anyone...
...we swear...

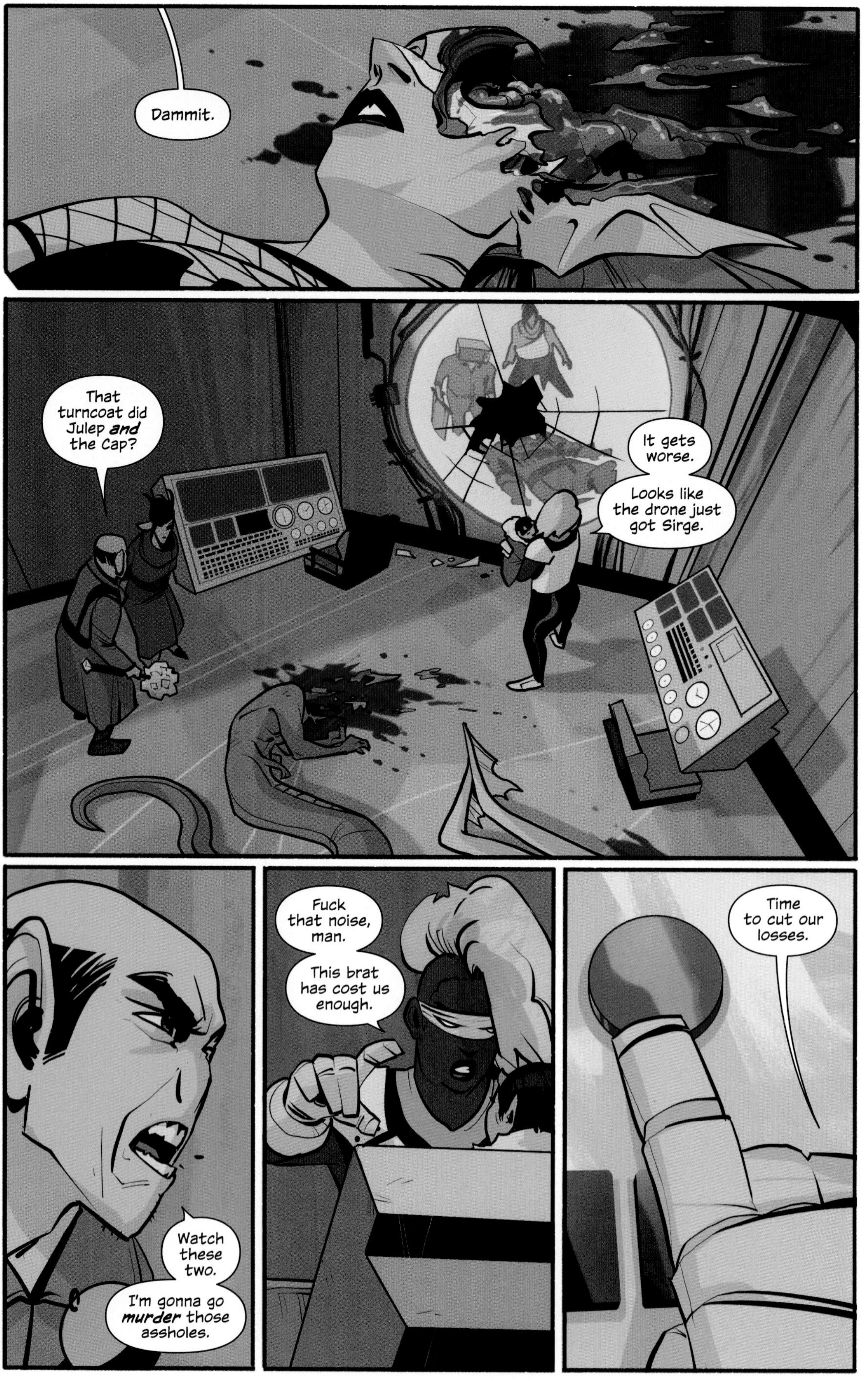
Dammit.
That turncoat did Julep *and* the Cap?
It gets worse.
Looks like the drone just got Sirge.
Watch these two.
I'm gonna go *murder* those assholes.
Fuck that noise, man.
This brat has cost us enough.
Time to cut our losses.

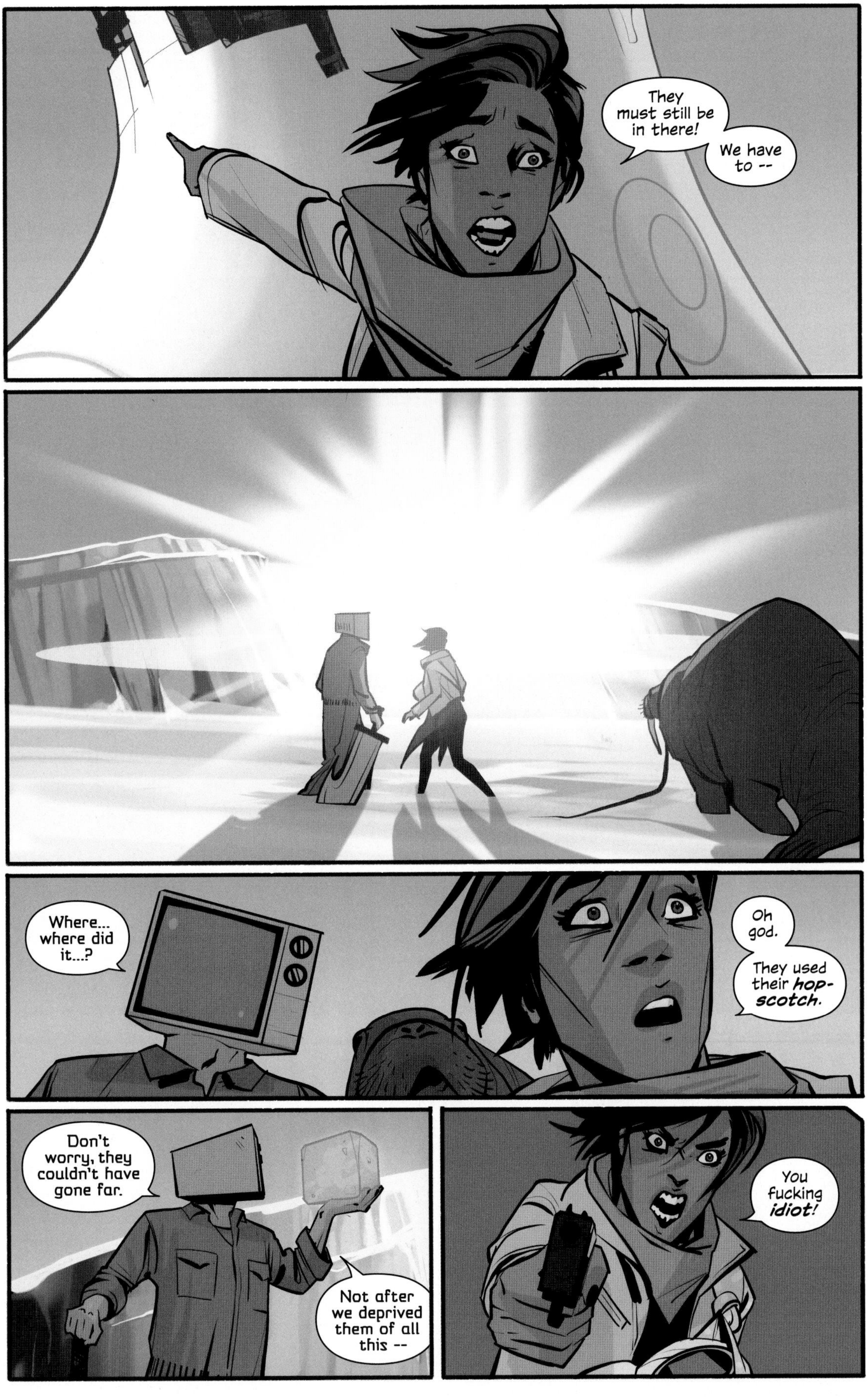
They must still be in there!
We have to --
Where... where did it...?
Oh god.
They used their *hop-scotch*.
Don't worry, they couldn't have gone far.
Not after we deprived them of all this --
You fucking *idiot!*

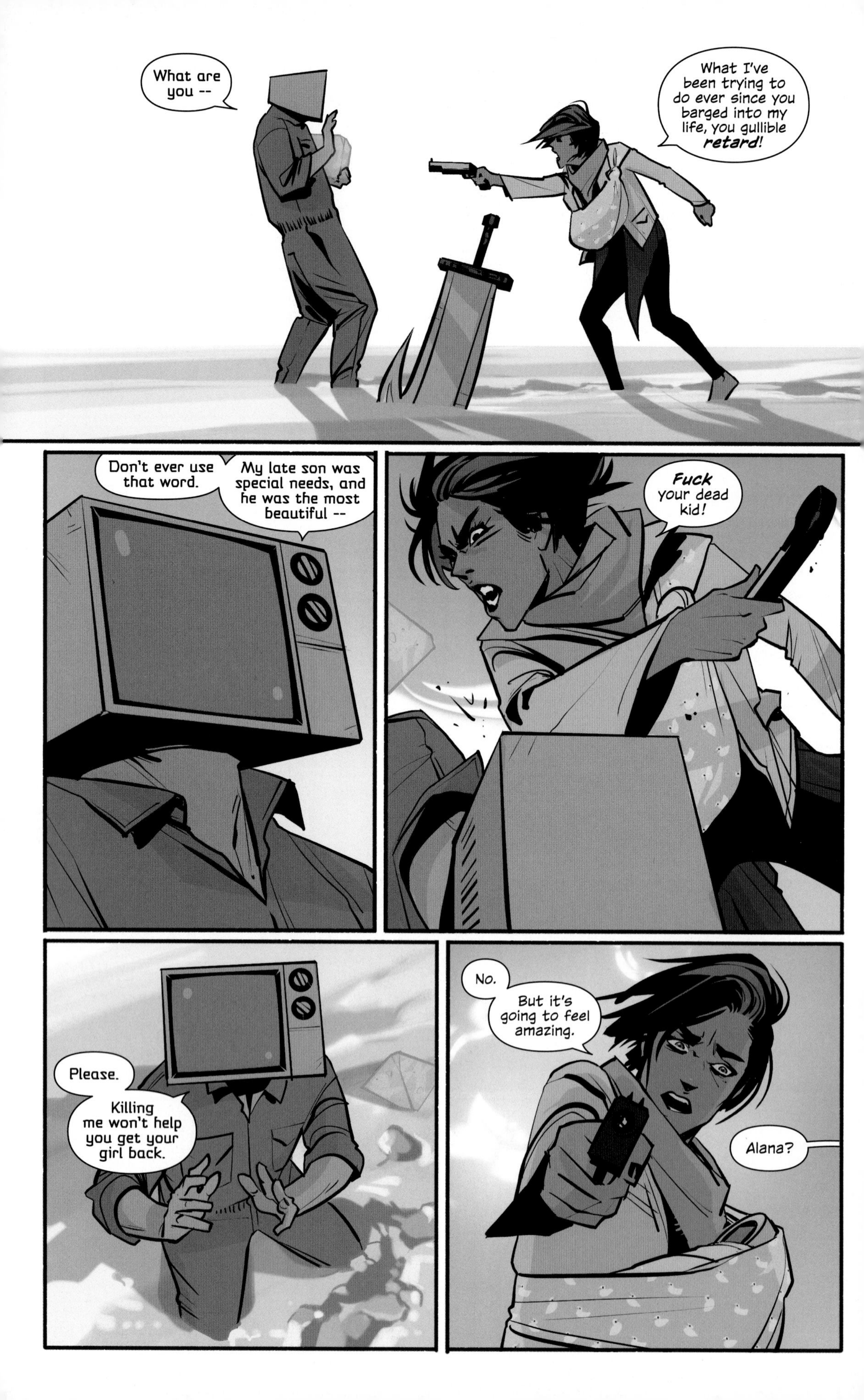
What are you --
What I've been trying to do ever since you barged into my life, you gullible **retard**!
Don't ever use that word.
My late son was special needs, and he was the most beautiful --
Fuck your dead kid!
Please.
Killing me won't help you get your girl back.
No.
But it's going to feel amazing.
Alana?

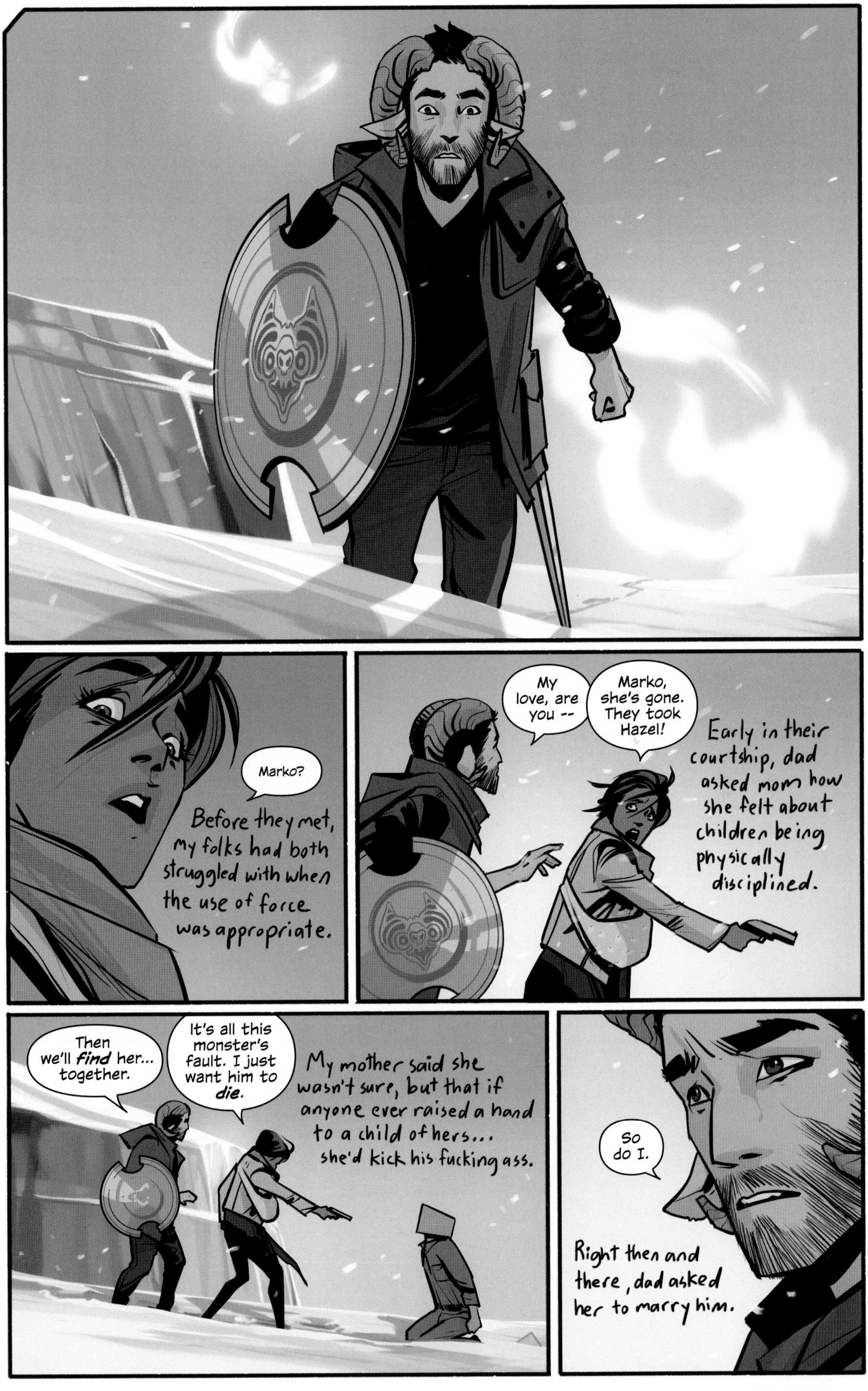
Marko?
Before they met, my folks had both struggled with when the use of force was appropriate.
My love, are you --
Marko, she's gone. They took Hazel!
Early in their courtship, dad asked mom how she felt about children being physically disciplined.
Then we'll *find* her... together.
It's all this monster's fault. I just want him to *die*.
My mother said she wasn't sure, but that if anyone ever raised a hand to a child of hers... she'd kick his fucking ass.
So do I.
Right then and there, dad asked her to marry him.

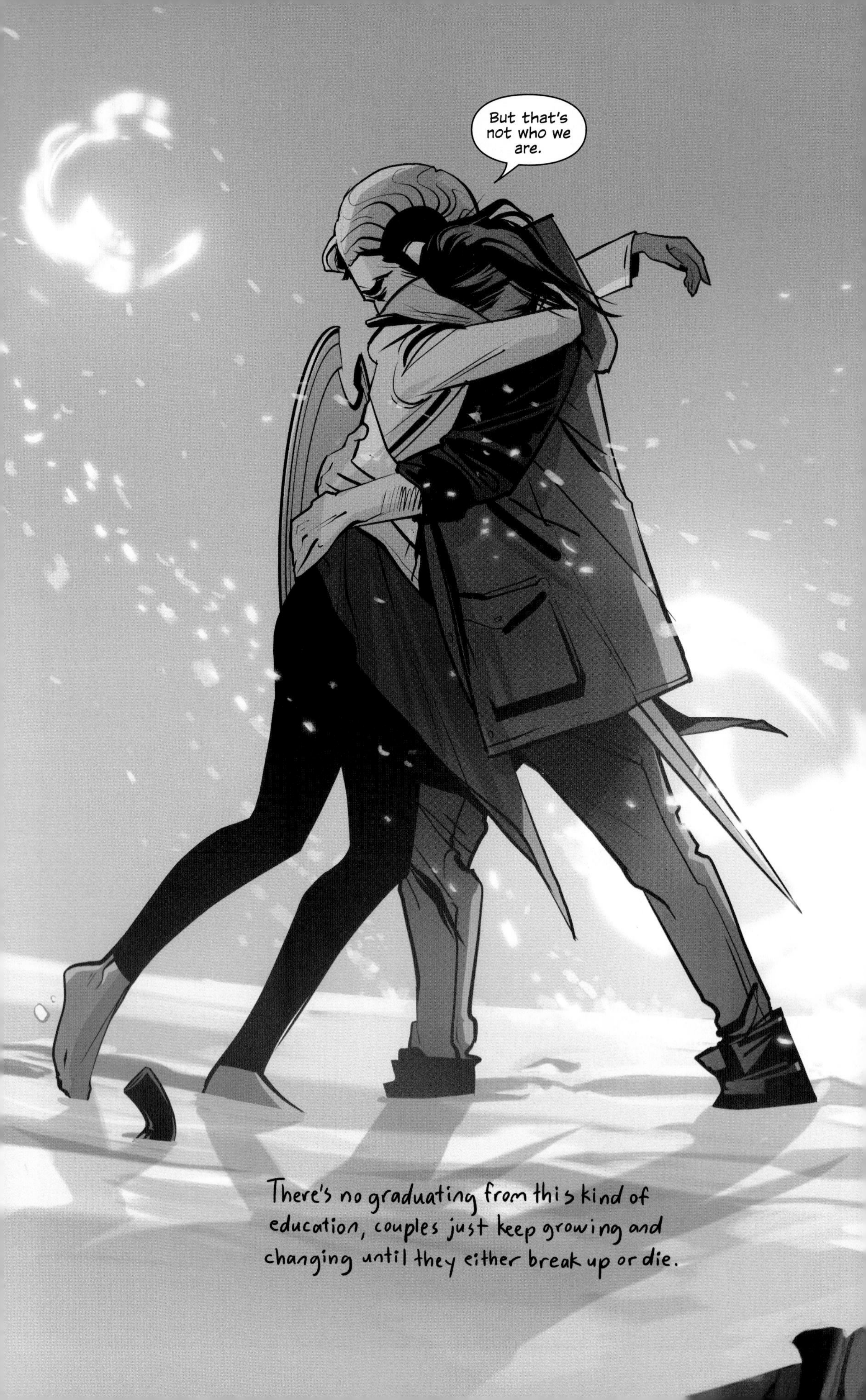
But that's not who we are.
There's no graduating from this kind of education, couples just keep growing and changing until they either break up or die.

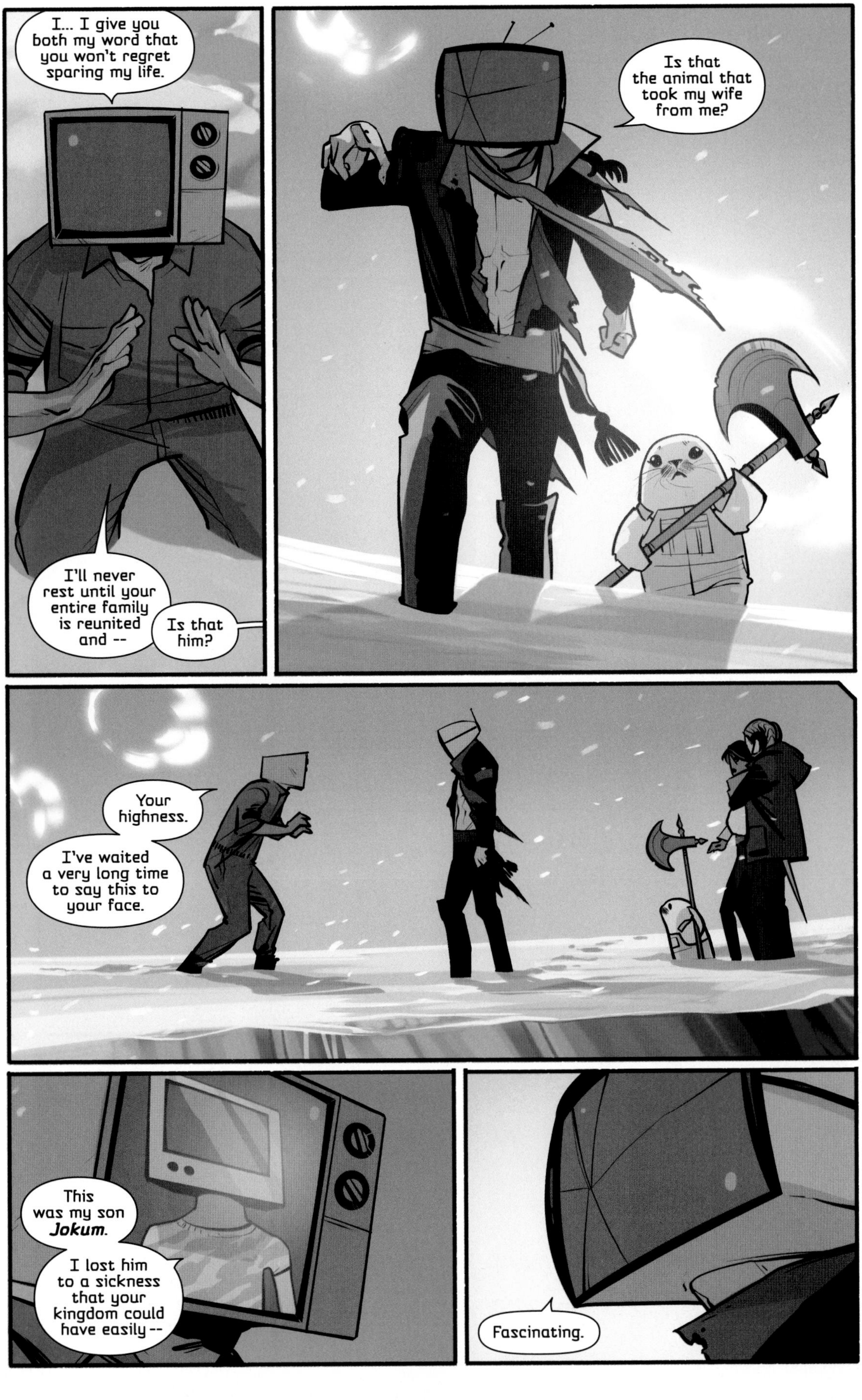

I... I give you both my word that you won't regret sparing my life.
Is that the animal that took my wife from me?
I'll never rest until your entire family is reunited and --
Is that him?
Your highness.
I've waited a very long time to say this to your face.
This was my son *Jokum*.
I lost him to a sickness that your kingdom could have easily --
Fascinating.

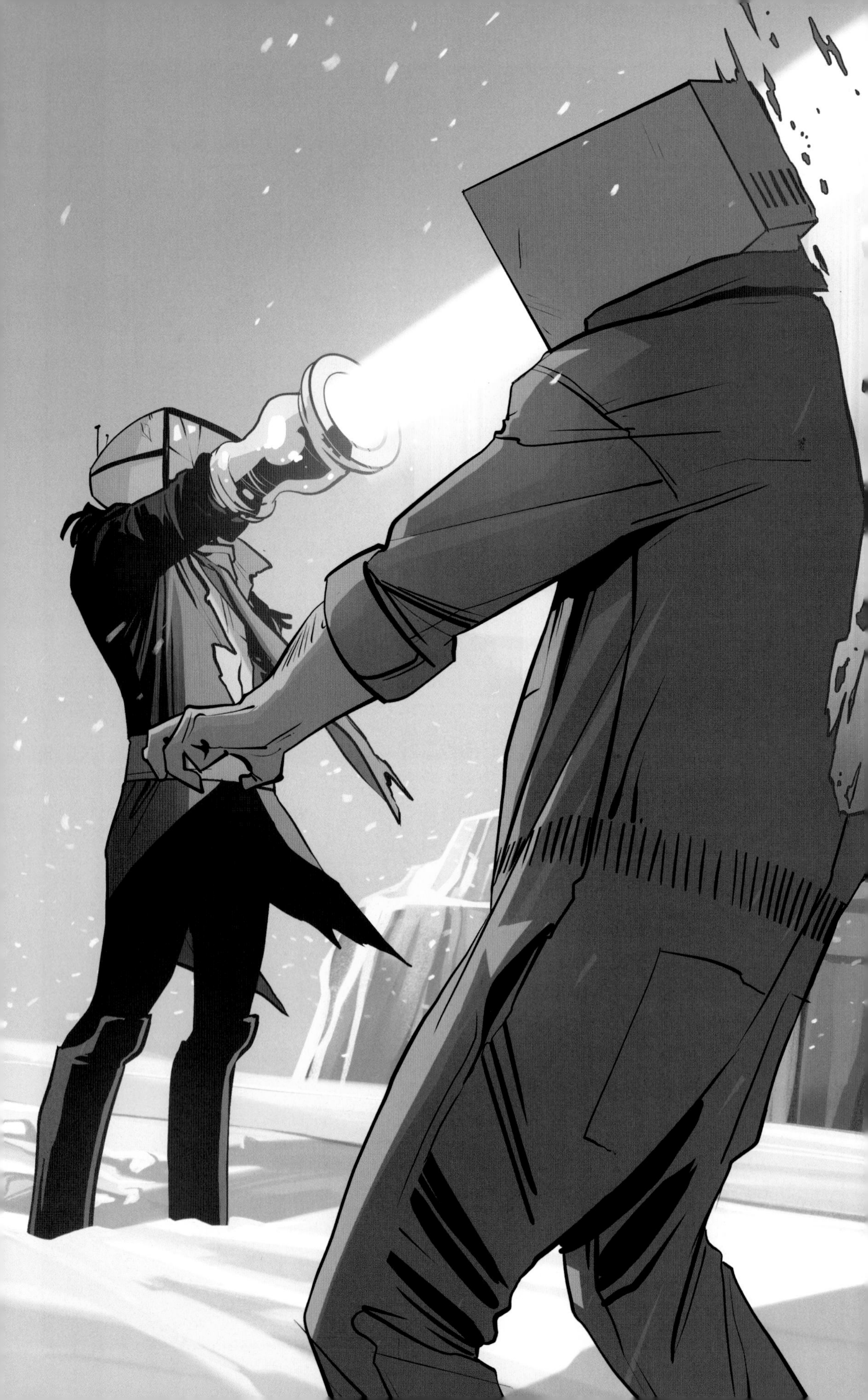

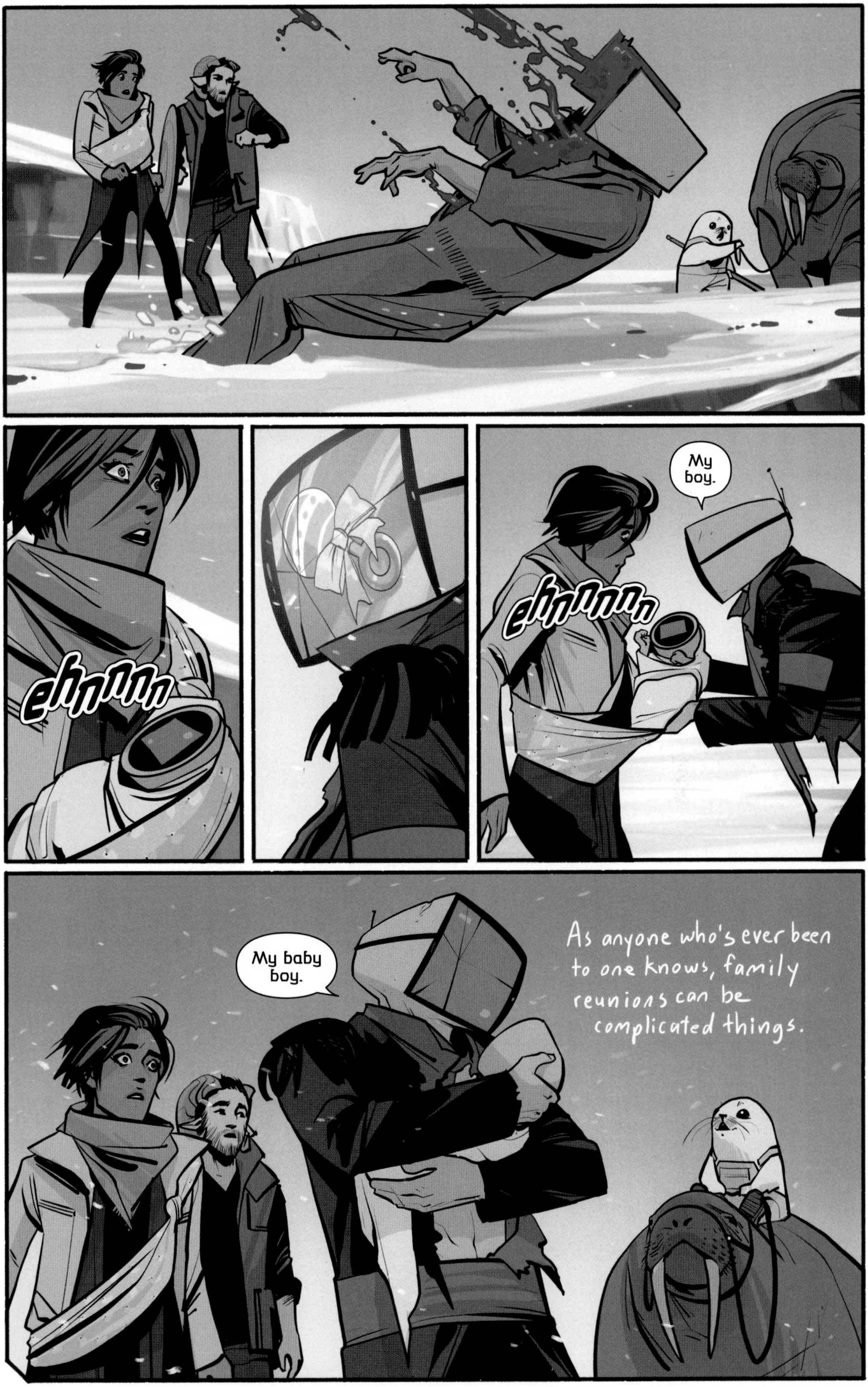
ehnnnn
My boy.
ehnnnnn
My baby boy.
As anyone who's ever been to one knows, family reunions can be complicated things.

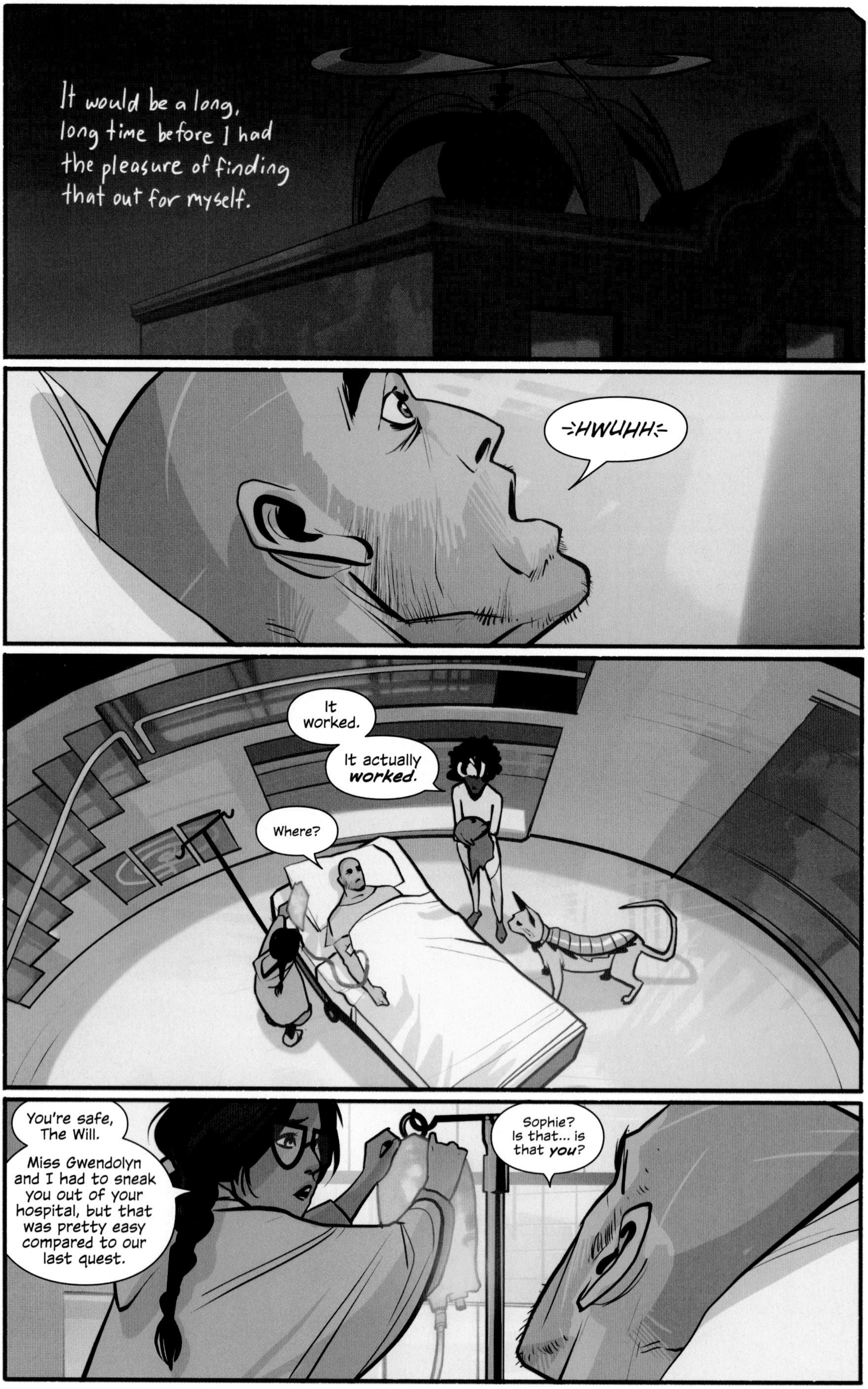
It would be a long, long time before I had the pleasure of finding that out for myself.
HWUHH
It worked.
It actually worked.
Where?
You're safe, The Will.
Miss Gwendolyn and I had to sneak you out of your hospital, but that was pretty easy compared to our last quest.
Sophie? Is that... is that you?

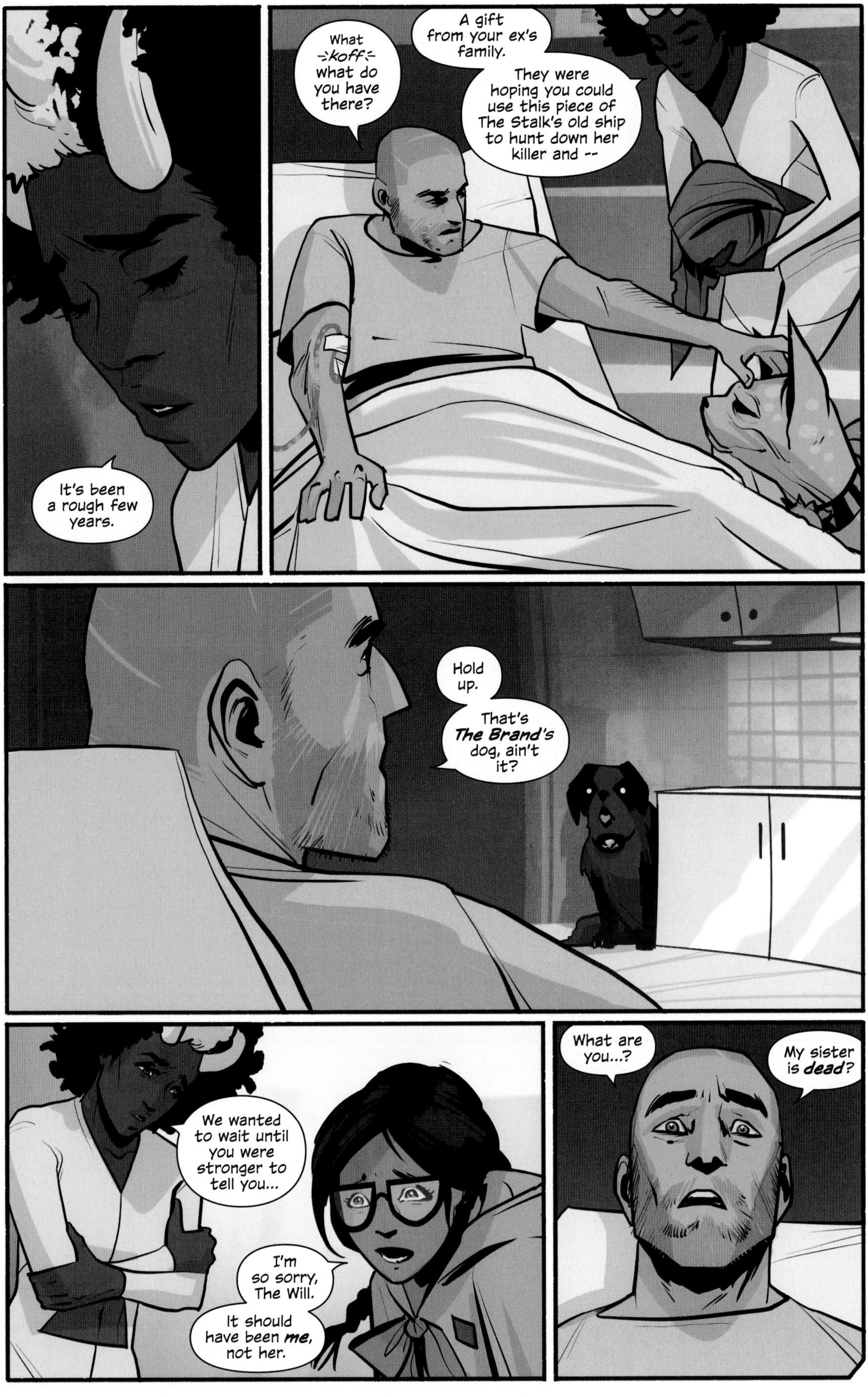

It's been a rough few years.
What -koff- what do you have there?
A gift from your ex's family.
They were hoping you could use this piece of The Stalk's old ship to hunt down her killer and --
Hold up.
That's *The Brand's* dog, ain't it?
We wanted to wait until you were stronger to tell you...
I'm so sorry, The Will.
It should have been *me*, not her.
What are you...?
My sister is *dead*?

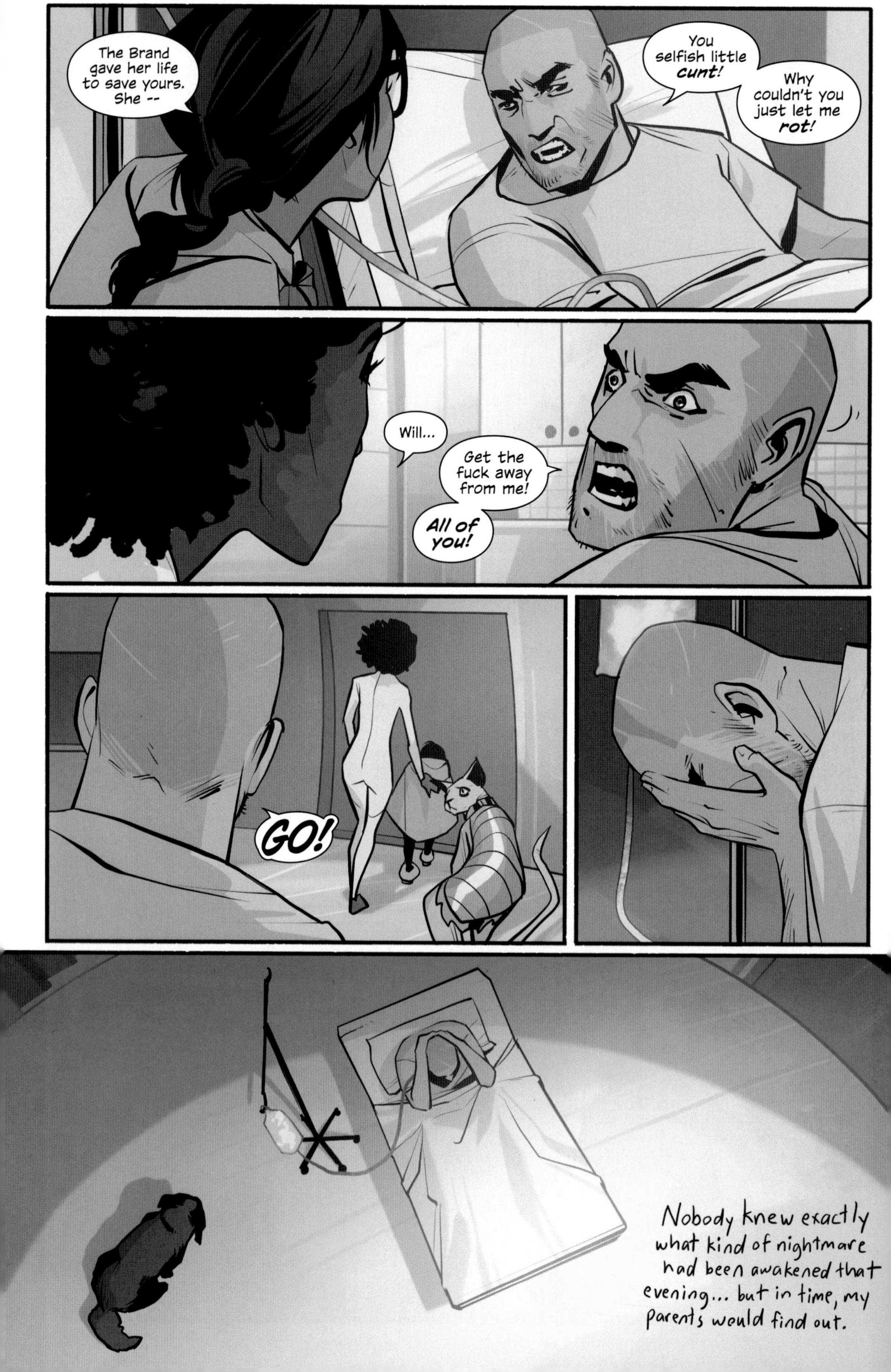

The Brand gave her life to save yours. She --
You selfish little *cunt!*
Why couldn't you just let me *rot!*
Will...
Get the fuck away from me!
All of you!
GO!
Nobody knew exactly what kind of nightmare had been awakened that evening... but in time, my parents would find out.

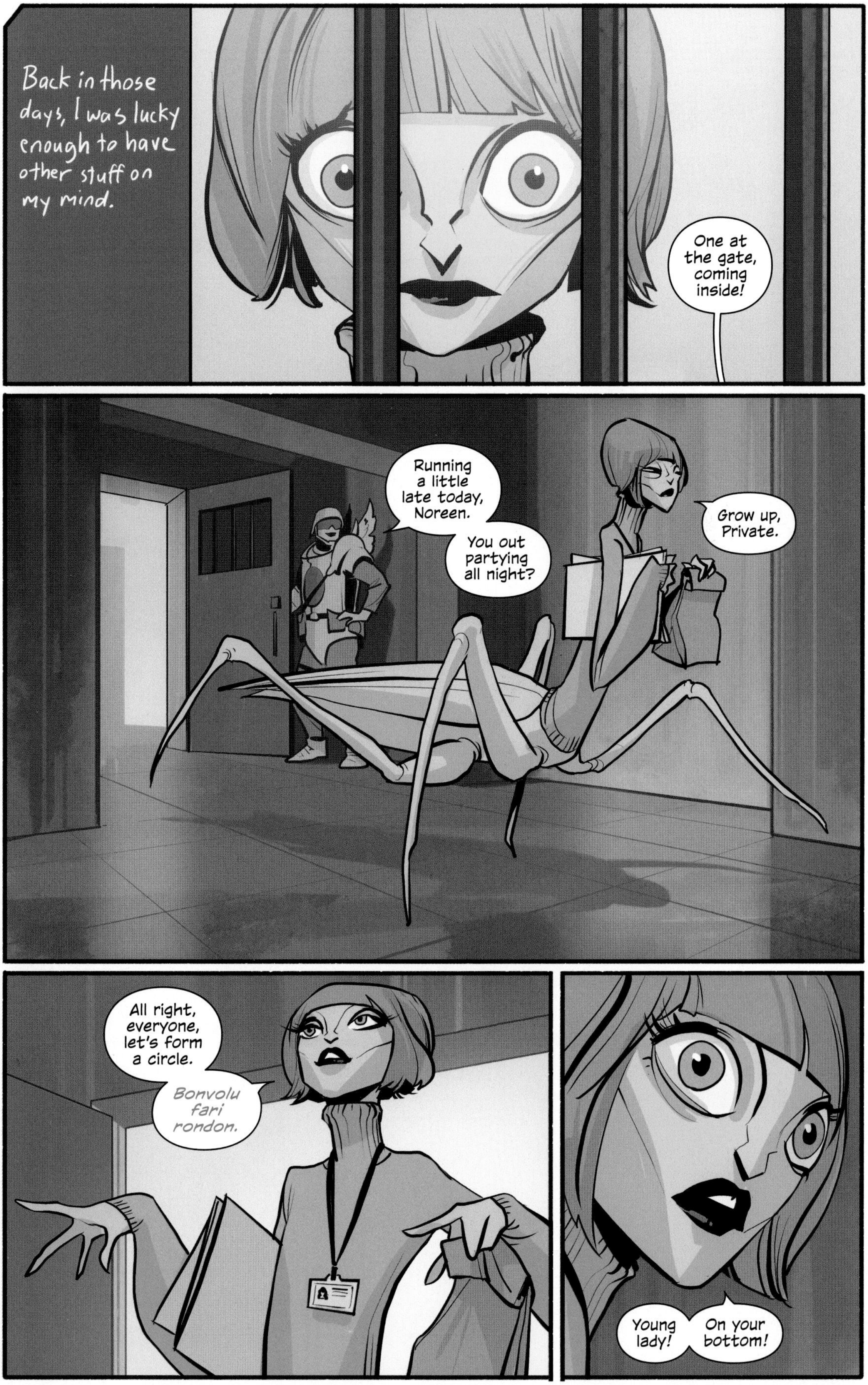
Back in those days, I was lucky enough to have other stuff on my mind.
One at the gate, coming inside!
Running a little late today, Noreen.
You out partying all night?
Grow up, Private.
All right, everyone, let's form a circle.
Bonvolu fari rondon.
Young lady!
On your bottom!

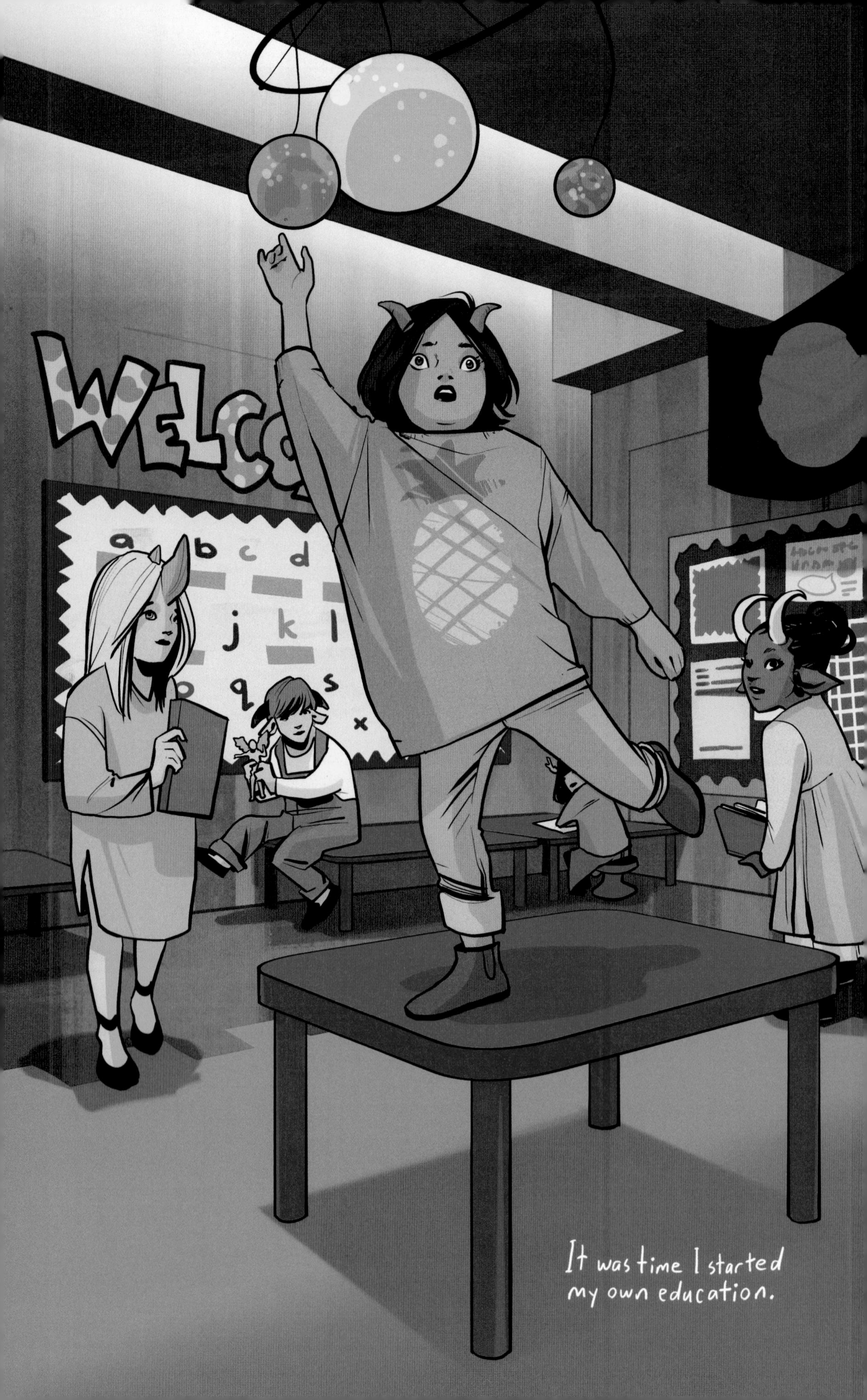

WELCO
a b c d
j k l
q s
x
It was time I started my own education.

to be continued

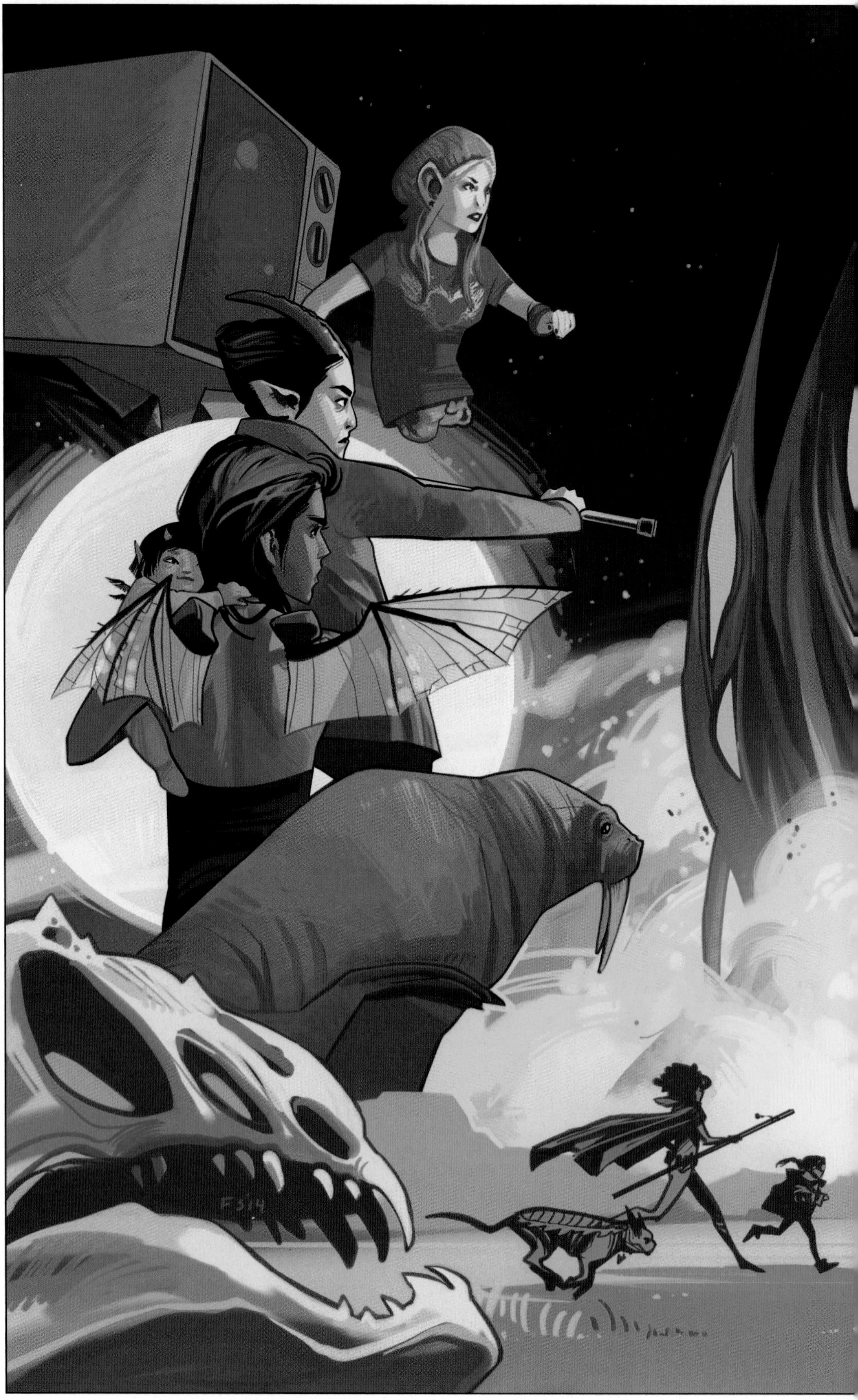
FS14

Fiona's full wraparound cover art…

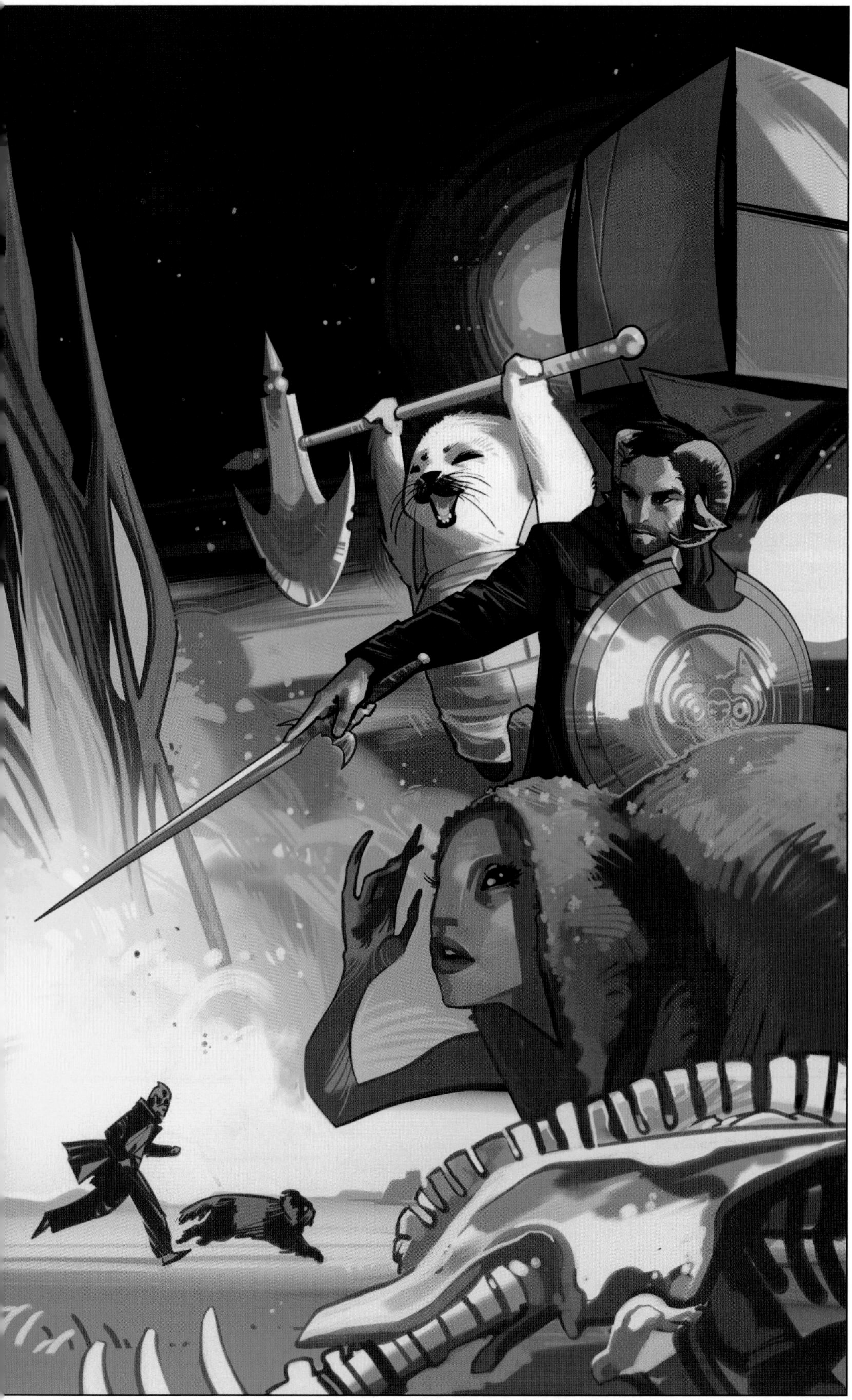

…for the milestone Chapter Twenty-five.

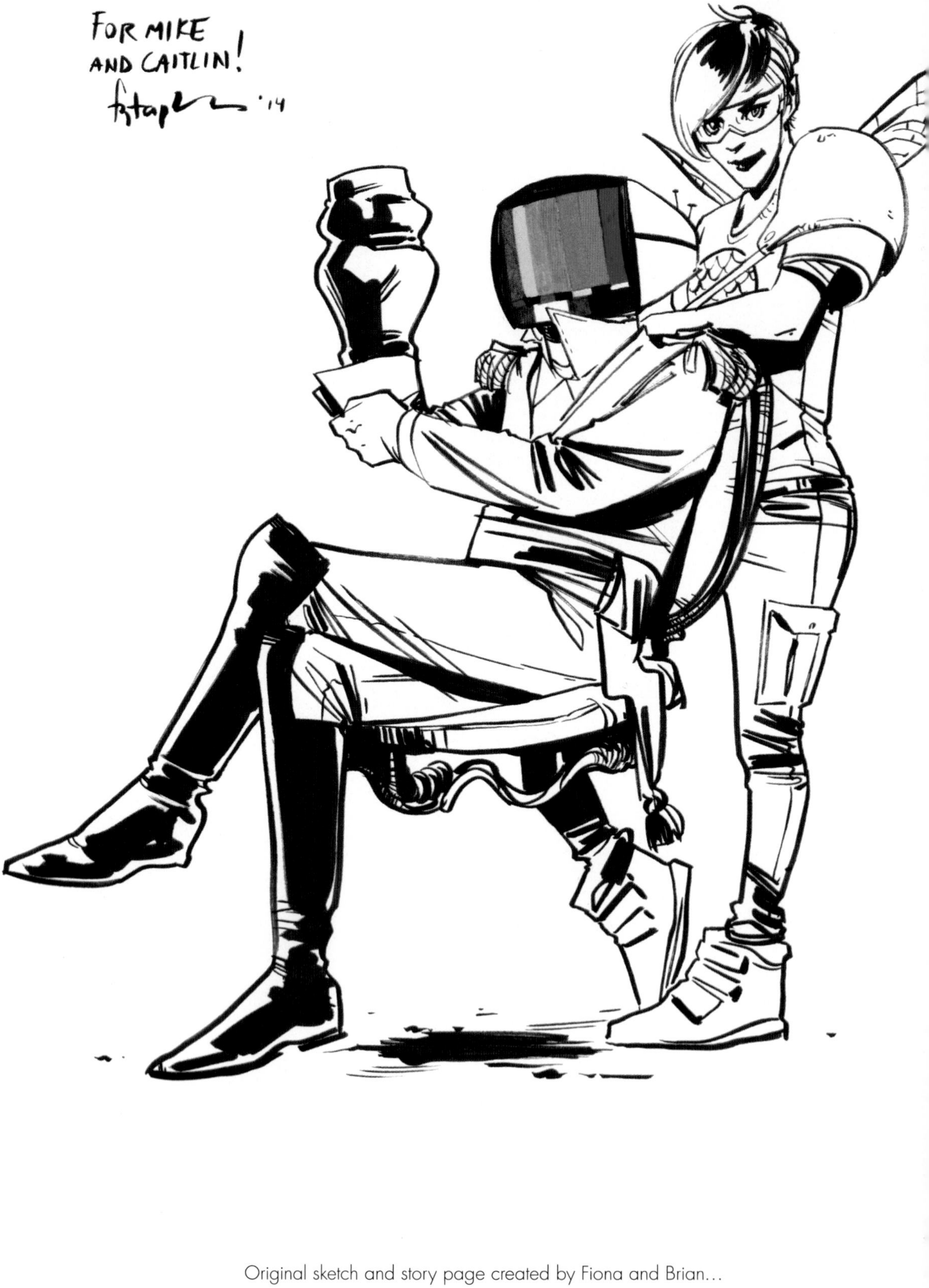
FOR MIKE
AND CAITLIN!
'14

Original sketch and story page created by Fiona and Brian...

SAGA - Story for Costume Contest Winner - November 14, 2014

PAGE ONE

Page One, Panel One
A Landfallian PLATOON LEADER with majestic parrot wings shouts right in our fucking face.

1) Platoon Leader: SOLDIERS, FORM UP FOR INSPECTION!

Page Twenty-one, Panel Two
Pull out to the largest panel of the page to reveal that we're in MILITARY BARRACKS, where a DOZEN LANDFALLIAN SOLDIERS snap to attention in front of their modest bunks, as PRINCE ROBOT IV makes a dramatic entrance. This is obviously a flashback to IV's past.

No Text

Page Twenty-one, Panel Three
Push in on an impressed Prince Robot, as he starts walking down this long row of male and female troopers.

2) Prince Robot IV: Excellent work, Lieutenant.
3) Prince Robot IV: I commend you on running such a tight…

Page Twenty-one, Panel Four
But now Robot STOPS in front of a nervous REDHEADED FEMALE SOLDIER. He points at a small spot of RED on her armor.

4) Prince Robot IV: Private, what the hell is that?

5) Private: Um, blood, sir. Moony blood. From our battle on Whipp?
6) Private: I… I haven't had a chance to clean my costume yet.

Page Twenty-one, Panel Five
Push in on the Prince, as the image of a BILLOWING SMOKESTACK flashes across his face-screen.

7) Prince Robot IV: These are not fucking "costumes," these are **uniforms**, and they're what separate us from the **savages** that we're fighting.

8) Prince Robot IV: **Am I understood?**

Page 1/1

…for Mike Dickens, winner of the Second Saga Costume Contest

ALSO AVAILABLE

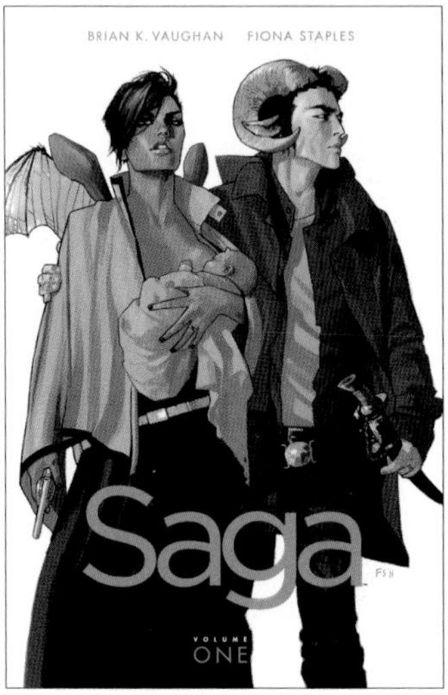
BRIAN K. VAUGHAN
FIONA STAPLES
Saga
ONE

VOLUME ONE
collects chapters 1–6
160-page softcover
ISBN 978-1-60706-601-9
$9.99

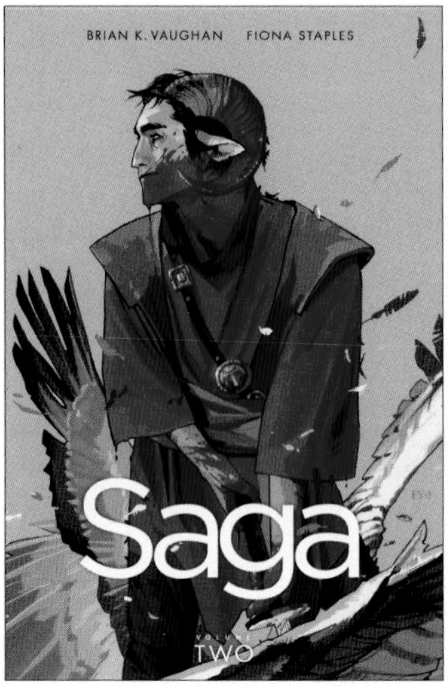
BRIAN K. VAUGHAN
FIONA STAPLES
Saga
TWO

VOLUME TWO
collects chapters 7–12
152-page softcover
ISBN 978-1-60706-692-7
$14.99

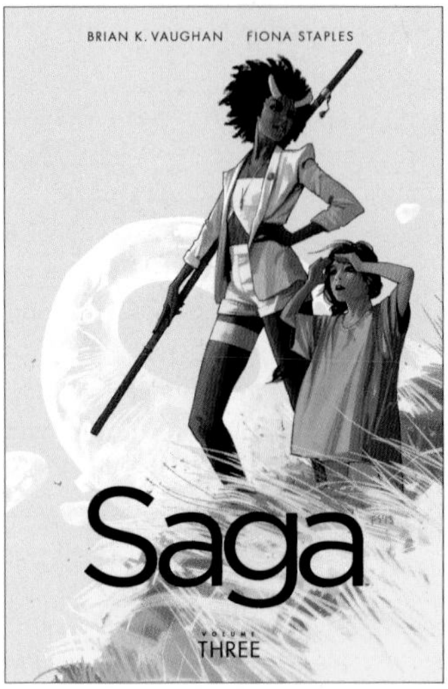
BRIAN K. VAUGHAN
FIONA STAPLES
Saga
THREE

VOLUME THREE
collects chapters 13–18
152-page softcover
ISBN 978-1-60706-931-7
$14.99

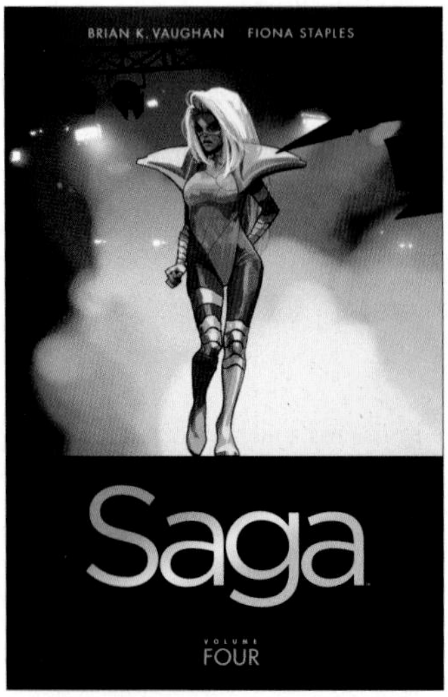
BRIAN K. VAUGHAN
FIONA STAPLES
Saga
FOUR

VOLUME FOUR
collects chapters 19–24
152-page softcover
ISBN 978-1-63215-077-6
$14.99

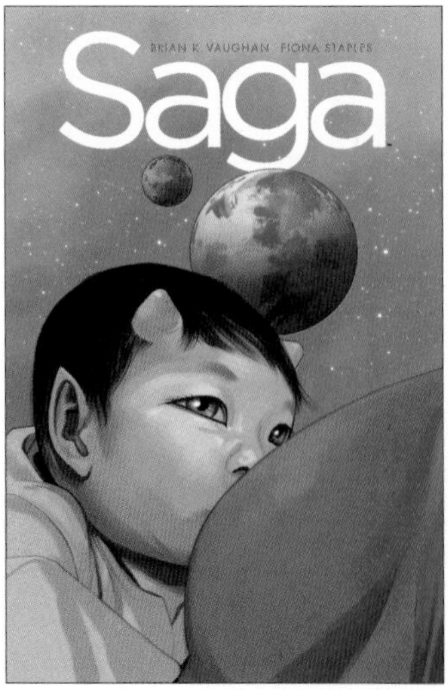
Saga

BOOK ONE
collects chapters 1–18
plus exclusive bonus material
504-page oversized hardcover
ISBN 978-1-63215-078-3
$49.99

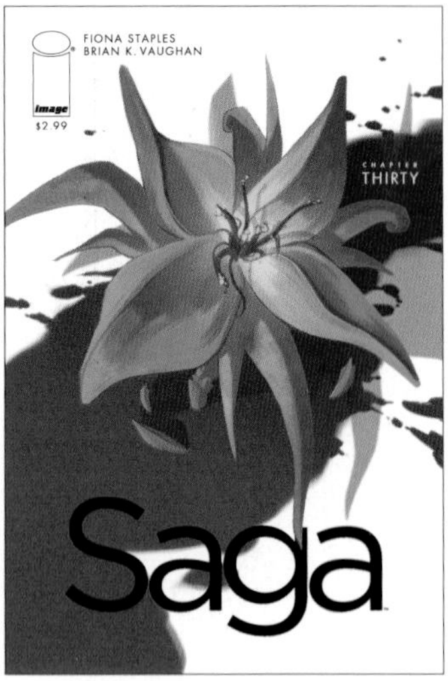
FIONA STAPLES
BRIAN K. VAUGHAN
$2.99
THIRTY
Saga

ONGOING SERIES
monthly from Image Comics
$2.99
Call 1-800-COMIC-BOOK or
visit *comicshoplocator.com* to find
your nearest comic book retailer.

imagecomics.com